I0614125

Life in the Limelight

by

DeDe Ramey

Dalton Skies, Book 3

This is a work of fiction. Names, characters, places, and incidents are either the product of the author's imagination or are used fictitiously, and any resemblance to actual persons living or dead, business establishments, events, or locales, is entirely coincidental.

Life in the Limelight

COPYRIGHT © 2022 by Deanna Saplin (Zebu Enterprises LLC)

All rights reserved. No part of this book may be used or reproduced in any manner whatsoever without written permission of the author or The Wild Rose Press, Inc. except in the case of brief quotations embodied in critical articles or reviews.
Contact Information: info@thewildrosepress.com

Cover Art by *Kristian Norris*

The Wild Rose Press, Inc.
PO Box 708
Adams Basin, NY 14410-0708
Visit us at www.thewildrosepress.com

Publishing History
First Edition, 2022
Trade Paperback ISBN 978-1-5092-4207-8
Digital ISBN 978-1-5092-4208-5

Dalton Skies, Book 3
Published in the United States of America

"You have to know how it seems and what is going through my head. I told you in the hospital, with everything I've been through, the lies and manipulation, I just can't—"

"I know," Brant barked, and regret immediately filled his expression. His fingers dug into his hair as a rush of air escaped his lungs. Bekah swallowed back the knot in her throat seeing a tear sliding down his cheek. He walked over to the sink and stared outside. "I don't want to lose you, Bekah. You are the best thing that has ever happened to me. But you need to do what is best for you and Maizy, and I'm not naïve. I know right now, that isn't me." He turned back to her. "Regardless of what happened, Sarge is right, it's going to take time to fix." His hands reached out letting his fingers graze her arm. She watched his hand slide down to her hand but didn't pull away. "I promise, I will fix it. I just don't know how long it will take. I need you to know though, I love you, and I love Maizy."

Praise for DeDe Ramey

Author of the Dalton Skies series novels, 24 to Life and A Life Unknown. Each of which have received many five star reviews.

"These stories from Dalton Skies get better and better."

~ Tierney James-Author

Dedication

To all the First Responders and military heroes that risk
their lives every day to keep us safe.

Chapter One

Brant pulled up in his black SUV and stared at the white wood-framed house in front of him. There was nothing ominous about it. In fact, it appeared rather charming with its ruby red door and white wicker rocking chairs on the expansive front porch. He could imagine people sitting there drinking tea on a warm day. Yet his heart raced as he sat and stared at it like it might come alive and tear him apart. He was a soldier. Nothing should scare him. So why did it take him weeks to get up enough nerve to make the call? *She's a little unconventional,* his friends said.

Pressing the button on the seatbelt, he slid it to the side and turned off the car. He leaned his head against the headrest as his eyes landed on the front of the house again. It reminded him of someone's grandma's house. Why was he so nervous; so hesitant?

With a deep breath he pushed open the door, stepped out of the car, and headed for the red brick stairs. The air was crisp, with the smell of winter still lingering. For February, it was a mild day. That was all about to change though. Snow was in the forecast.

His foot hit the first step, and he halted, contemplating turning around. Pausing for a second, he took another deep breath then continued. Bells jingled as he pushed open the door. There was no turning back now.

Ivy plants hung in macramé baskets on either side of the large double windows. Crystals dangled in a cluster, spraying prisms across the room. On one wall was a large fireplace flanked by narrow windows topped with etched glass. The adjoining wall contained a set of well-lit bookshelves separated by a large vibrant piece of abstract art. A gold velvet sofa sat facing a fireplace with a distressed wooden coffee table in front of it. To the side sat a round, glass-topped table displaying several succulent plants and a couple of old magazines.

Brant stood, taking in his surroundings, then had a seat in a well-worn leather chair next to the fireplace. Everything looked like it came from a thrift store, though it somehow fit together.

A sweet, lemony smell filled the room like someone had dusted. The thought crossed his mind that he might be in the wrong place, but he recalled seeing a small sign out front. His forearms rested on his jean-covered thighs as he wondered what he was in for.

When Brant left rehab, his mentor encouraged him to find a counselor. He put it off until his friend April, and his buddy Cody, gave him the same counselor's name.

Brant and Cody were training to become paramedics, and both worked out at the gym Cody owned. Cody had said the counselor, although a little unconventional, had helped him through his recent trauma. That word. Unconventional. Brant had a hard time getting past it. What exactly did Cody mean?

Continuing to look around, he felt a vibration and reached in his pocket for his phone. An unknown number popped up on his screen.

—I miss you—

What the hell? An uneasy flutter skated through his chest. After deciding it had to be a wrong number, he did a quick check of the time, then heard a voice from the hallway off the corner of the room. "I will be right out." The quietness of her voice made it barely detectible over the peaceful music playing.

A couple of minutes passed before a young woman appeared. Dressed in a floor length, navy and pink, flower-printed dress with a flowy, long-sleeved, fuzzy cover, the woman looked like she stepped right out of Woodstock. Her wavy caramel hair was pulled into a messy loose ponytail. A folded denim bandana wrapped her head and had a neat bow at the crown.

Brant stood and let out a long breath. Like the waiting area, her outfit seemed mismatched, yet somehow it worked. She had a softness to her, and her smile was captivating, but it didn't quite look natural. He sensed he was interrupting her.

"Can I help you?" Her voice was deep and rich with a slight rasp. She glanced at her chest then smoothed the front of her dress before returning her focus to him.

"I'm here to see Dr. Adkins?" Rubbing his hands in front of him, he added, "I'm Brant Ellington."

The smile she had earlier returned. "Nice to meet you." She lifted her hand, and Brant noticed her fingers were covered in chunky silver rings, and two tattoos wrapped her wrist. A powdery scent caught his nose as he leaned in closer. Vanilla maybe, mixed with something. "Sorry, I've been running a little behind." Her cheeks turned a deep rosy shade. "I'm Dr. Bekah Adkins."

The silver bracelets layered on her wrist jingled as they moved over leather bands when Brant shook her hand. A bit bizarre, he had to admit, but intriguing. She was his best bet, unless he wanted to drive to Fayetteville, which he didn't.

"Come on back," she said on a breath and turned. He rubbed the back of his neck, trying to calm his nerves that had kicked up even more meeting her, and followed her down a hallway, then through a doorway into another room.

A large bookshelf lined one wall, with two wingback striped chairs in front of it, sharing a floor lamp and small wooden table. Under a large picture window adorned with ivy and crystals sat a small scraped-up wooden desk with folders scattered across it and a small lamp on the corner. The only things that didn't look like they'd come from an estate sale were the beige microfiber sofa that sat up against the dusty paneled wall, and the glider chair with ottoman that sat across from it. Another floor lamp sat next to it overlooking a dark stained wooden table that held a gray box, which appeared to be a small speaker, emitting a soft white noise. Brant studied it. *Probably some device to calm the patient. Or maybe it just notifies her when someone comes in the door.* Overall, the room seemed inviting and...normal. His chest loosened a bit.

The doctor pushed the door closed before speaking. "Have a seat wherever you feel comfortable." Brant removed his jacket and laid it on the corner of the sofa then sat down leaning his elbows on his knees. "Would you like some water?" When her focus landed on him, a shiver ran down his spine. The color of her eyes was hypnotic. Light green, to the point they were almost translucent, like the crest of a wave.

"Yes, if you don't mind." His mouth had become pasty, and he had hoped the water would at least alleviate the issue enough to where he could talk. Even though he wasn't necessarily up for a lengthy conversation. Or any for that matter.

Dr. Adkins pushed open a door in the corner of the room and disappeared. When she reappeared, she had a glass of water in each hand. Passing one off to Brant, she set hers on the side table, picked up a folder and small writing tablet from her desk, and sat down in the glider. After slipping off her shoes, she tucked her feet up underneath her. *Yeah, unconventional was a good description of her*. Silence took over as she skimmed the papers in the folder. The way she studied him when she glanced up through her long lashes caused heat to suddenly creep up his neck. It was like she had some supernatural ability that stripped him bare. His breath escaped, and he sat back into the sofa and averted his attention hoping it would break the spell. Unfortunately, just as he was gaining control, she spoke, and the rasp of her voice echoed through the room and sent a hum through his body.

"Since this is a consult, let's get to know each other."

No, let's not. He shifted his weight trying to get comfortable. *Is it getting hot in here?*

"I read the paperwork you e-mailed me. You stated you have recently been in rehab?"

Shifting in his seat again, he wrestled with answering, or not, then decided since he was there, he might as well try to power through it so he could report back to his mentor at the rehab center. "No." He winced. "I mean, yes." *Geez. Her voice. I can't think. This was a bad idea, and it's getting worse by the minute. I wonder how rude it would be to get up and walk out.* "I got out around the first of November."

"You checked yourself in? Or was it mandatory due to an arrest?"

Wow, she gets right to the point. "I checked myself in."

"Why did you feel like you needed to go to rehab?"

How the hell can she be so direct and make me feel so off balance? He rubbed his hands together and swallowed hard. "I lost my wife and baby in a car accident in March, and I wasn't handling it so well. I started drinking and self-medicating."

Concern brushed across her face, her lips pursed, and she paused. *Oh, for Pete's sake. First it was her eyes, then her voice, now her mouth.* "And it was your choice to go to rehab?"

"Well, not exactly. My grams…grandma kind of tricked me into going. But I am glad she did."

"Grandparents can be very wise." She smirked as she let out a breath, and Brant knew she could relate. "How have you been doing since you got out?"

He shrugged. "Pretty well. I've tried to avoid places that might trip me up."

"What made you decide to make this appointment?"

Taking a deep breath, he let it out, puffing his cheeks with his release. "Honestly? My counselor at rehab encouraged me to continue with counseling, and my friends April Westerman and Cody Spencer both suggested you."

He crossed his ankle over his knee, now wondering why they made the suggestion. He really had been handling things fine. *Right?*

"And why do you think they made the suggestion?"

Geez, add mind reading to her superpowers. Brant wrapped his hand around his mouth and glanced around the room. "I really don't know." Feeling all his muscles tighten, he stood. She was making him uncomfortable, but it wasn't the questions as much as it was…her. He couldn't put his finger on it but was now sure it was a bad idea to come. The door was right there. He could walk out. He had his counselor at rehab. He could call him if he needed to talk to someone, not some hippie chick that probably had no idea what she was doing and accidentally stumbled on a golden opportunity to spread her hippie voodoo in this tiny town. Brant scanned the walls for a diploma. *Is she even legal? Does she really have a degree?* His mind raced trying to come up with a polite way to get out of the consultation. He cleared his throat and applied his most genuinely sorrowful expression. "Maybe this was a mistake. I'm sorry to have wasted your time."

His attention drifted back to her, and he hoped he sounded sincere. She tipped her head, and her mouth drew into a thin line. "Oh, I don't think it was a mistake at all. I think you know that. Your friends may have suggested it; however, there had to have been a reason you finally chose to come." She stared at him and propped her feet up on the edge of the ottoman. Her tanned toes, with the nails painted hot pink, pushed against the cushion, and she started to rock. "Tell me a little about yourself."

7

Dammit. She wasn't going to let him go that easily. He forced himself to sit back down on the sofa, leaned forward and laced his fingers, then stared out the large window. Did he really want to let this woman delve into his life?

He glanced back at her. She had a natural beauty, a softness. Her skin looked fresh with a hint of rose to her olive cheeks and no sign of makeup other than maybe mascara. Something about her made his body tingle like someone flipping an electric switch. "You don't want to know about me."

She peered up with a bit of mischief in her expression. "Uh, yeah, I do. That's why I went to school and get paid the big bucks...well not so big bucks, but yeah, lay it on me." She grinned and winked, and superpower number...*was it five or six...* was revealed; making him laugh. Not much did lately.

Still chuckling, he took a breath, going to war with his thoughts, and stood again. Something made him want to let her in. There weren't many in the small community who knew him, and his privacy was important. "What school did you go to?"

Her head tilted and she sucked in one cheek appearing a little perturbed. "University of Missouri for undergrad and master's degree, and—" She pointed to a framed diploma on the wall. "—I have a doctorate of Forensic Psychology from Pepperdine." Raising a brow, she scolded, "Now that you have my credentials, stop deflecting and tell me about you."

He glanced back at her to see her smile of satisfaction and bit down on his bottom lip, holding back another chuckle. *Okay. Maybe she isn't that bad.*

"Oh, and before you ask why I chose Dalton

instead of somewhere bigger, my grandpa is here. I wanted to live near him."

He sat back down on the sofa and leaned his head back wondering where to start. Dragging his hands down his face, he finally asked, "Do you go to the movies much?"

"I used to. I haven't in a while though."

Leaning forward, his elbows landed on his knees again. "Do you know who Sandra Gerard is?"

"Yeah," she said, drawing the word out. "Wasn't she in all of those Elizabeth Scott spy movies?"

"Yes." He rubbed his palms together. "She…is my mom." His eyes lifted to hers studying her reaction. She nodded and tipped her head which was less of a reaction than he expected.

"Okay." She scribbled on her pad. "So, tell me why you started with her."

"What do you mean?" he questioned, scooting back on the sofa and crossing his ankle over his knee.

"Did you have a reason why you started with her? Or did you think I would be impressed?"

What the hell? "No. I wasn't trying to impress you. Although, I have to say, most people have a different reaction than you did."

"People are people. I lived in California for most of my life. I've met different people in the film industry. They just happen to have jobs that make them more well known. So, why did you start with her?"

I have no idea. Can we move on? "You grew up in California? What part?"

The doctor glimpsed up at him again and gave him a lopsided smile. "Outside of San Francisco, and you are deflecting again."

Damn. Brant rolled his eyes and smirked. Nothing was getting past her and God if that didn't add to the superpowers she had stacked up that got under his skin.

"I left California when Abbie and the baby died. Until then, we frequented the industry parties and dinners. They all provided anything you could ever want, to make you feel good. I never really was a drinker growing up though. The drinking ramped up a little when I went into the military, but nothing serious. When Abbie died, I went in search of anything that would silence the voices, and alcohol was readily available, no prescription needed. I thought moving here, putting some miles between me and the craziness of the industry, would get me back on track and give me a fresh start."

"Why did you think that?"

He rubbed his hands together nervously and let the memories slowly form. "When I was a kid, my parents sent me to stay with my grandparents, who live here, for the summer. Or basically whenever they needed to get rid of me. Arkansas always gave me good memories. My grandpa let me work with him on his cars or he'd take me hunting and fishing. My grandma…well, Grams, she's feisty and hilarious and doesn't know how old she is. She was the disciplinarian. I got in trouble with her quite a bit as a kid. Still, I knew it was because she loved me. I moved here because of the memories, thinking I would get a job and start over. I couldn't get away from the voices though. And even though Grams was here, I became lonely. I spiraled out of control and wound up in rehab." He glanced out the window. "Things have been going well since I got out. That's why I haven't been in a hurry to find a counselor. But I got a call from my mom a couple of weeks ago. They are planning to shoot a film here, in the old Farington hotel and around town. They want me to be in it."

"And how do you feel about that?"

"I don't know." He leaned back on the sofa and rested his head on the cushion for a moment, then tipped forward. "Isn't this where you come in and tell me what is best for me in this situation?"

"What situation might that be?"

Brant closed his eyes and leaned his head back again trying to calm his temper. *Dear God, this woman asks too many damn questions.* He sat up letting out an exasperated breath. "I have made appearances in a few of my mom's movies. Most were cameo appearances. Still, enough to know there is alcohol and other substances readily available on most of the sets. I just wonder if I should decline, to protect myself from temptation. Or do I accept and realize this is real life and I need to learn how to be around it?"

"Do you want to be in the movie?"

A growl resonated in his chest. "I don't know. Initially when I got the call from my mom I was excited and filled out all the paperwork they sent me. But after thinking about it, I'm not sure." He stood and paced so he could avoid her gaze. Her sultry voice and her magical eyes almost had him crawling out of his skin. "I mean, it's a decent part. I'd be in several scenes, but it's not going to make me a star."

"Is that what you want…to be a star like your mom?"

Turning toward her, he grimaced. "Oh hell no. I hated my childhood. Paparazzi popped out of nowhere trying to get a picture of us. I was sent to boarding school for months on end. If I have a family, I don't want that for my kids." His mind wandered back to Abbie as his hand grazed one of the books on the shelf. "The reason I'm even considering it, is it sounds like it would be fun, and right now I am finishing up my certification to be a paramedic so I'm not terribly busy."

"It sounds to me like you want to do it."

Of course, I would like to do it. "But is it a good idea?"

"Have you been around anyone who has been drinking since you have been out of rehab?"

He wiped his finger across his lip. "Yeah, on a few occasions."

"Did they offer you any?"

"A few times."

"And what did you do?"

He suddenly felt like he was on some rapid-fire round of a gameshow. "I declined."

"So, what makes you think you won't be able to do the same on a set or at a party?"

"Well, there will be a whole lot more there. What if I don't have the willpower?"

"You think because there would be more available, it would make a difference? Whether it's one beer or fifteen, if you have the willpower to decline one, don't you think you could decline them all?"

"I don't know. Can I?"

"I can't answer that for you." Brant rolled his eyes. *This isn't helping.* "Some people can kick the habit and not have another drink. Some can handle a drink or two and not have a problem, and some can't stop themselves once they've started the flow. Think about where you were in your life when you drank, and why. Then consider where you are now." She leaned forward in her chair. "Do you feel differently?" Her focus was squarely on him again, and heat creeped up his spine. *Geez, that look is dangerous.* "Do you think you have the tools you need to resist?"

"I think I do."

She sat back in her chair and began to rock again. "Then, I think if this is something that makes you excited, it might be something to think about. It will keep you busy until your next adventure, and that is probably better than having a lot of free time on your hands."

Well, that's probably true. It will keep my mind busy. "Okay."

"I'm not sure what tools you learned in rehab, but I have a few things that I normally use, like yoga, mindful breathing, and grounding techniques."

Brant squeezed his eyes shut. *Unconventional is an understatement.* "I think I'm good," he said, hoping it would end there. Dr. Adkins looked up, her light green magical orbs leveled with his, telling him it wouldn't. But before she could speak, the small gray box on the table made a raspy noise. Dr. Adkins quickly turned her attention to it, and Brant noticed an almost panicked expression cross her face. The noise continued, and then came a muffled whimper. Brant stared at the box, then his focus jerked up to Dr. Adkins who met his gaze and she mumbled, "I'll be right back," before disappearing through the door.

His attention was glued on the gray box where he heard more raspy noises followed by a baby's cry. Pain filled his chest. *What the hell?* His throat thickened hearing the tiny cry, and he swallowed hard trying to hold back the tears as his thoughts turned to his own child's life that was taken away. Dr. Adkins' gentle soothing whispers came through the box. "Shhh…it's okay, sweet girl."

Brant stood, wondering if he should go ahead and leave. Obviously, the appointment was over. The door opened, and Dr. Adkins reappeared carrying a tiny baby with a pink bow wrapped around her thick dark brown hair. "I am so sorry," she said, humiliation filling her tone. Her eyes darted around searching for something. "She fell asleep when I tried to feed her right before you came. Now, I think she is hungry." The baby's cry ramped up, and Dr. Adkin's search turned frantic. She left again through the door, and Brant stood with his hands in his pockets wondering what he should do. Reappearing with a blanket, she sat down in the glider, and pulling the thin blanket up, she covered the baby and her shoulder. Brant realized what was about to happen, and his nerves started to unravel. She stared down at the tiny infant as her hand went to work beneath the blanket.

His gaze drifted to the hallway. "I probably should leave."

Distress seized her expression as her eyes connected with his. "You've only been here twenty minutes."

"That's okay, you kind of addressed my issue already."

She remained silent as she returned her focus to the baby and left Brant hanging, not knowing whether to leave, sit and watch, or turn away. She sure didn't seem to care. As bad as he wanted to find something to distract him, he couldn't seem to tear his attention away from her. There was something in her expression. She was completely enraptured by the infant under the blanket. Her eyes shimmered, and a smile pulled at her lips. *My God she is breathtaking.* "Can you come the same time next week? I will let you have a full hour."

Her voice brought him out of his stupor, and he hoped she didn't catch him staring at her as her eyes finally lifted to his. He was growing more uncomfortable by the second, and she moved her hand under the blanket once again. He could feel the warmth fill his cheeks. "Sure."

"Okay." She leaned forward and picked up the pen. Brant averted his gaze in case the blanket decided to fall. "Tuesday at one then?"

Something in her voice didn't sound right, and he paused. Was it anger? Was she mad he was leaving? "Sounds good," he said with a nod and walked toward the door. But somehow, in those few short steps, it felt like the air was sucked out of the room. His hand reached for the knob, and he was two seconds from escaping when he heard a sniffle. Letting out a long sigh, he peeked back at her, just as she leaned her head back against the glider chair. His chest tightened when her hand flew over her eyes, and she sniffed again. Releasing the knob, his hand dropped to his side. "Are, are you okay?" he questioned, his back still to her. In his peripheral he caught her swiping her face, and he slowly turned. She was clearly crying. "What's wrong?"

"I'm sorry. I'll be fine," she responded softly, with a thickness to her voice. "My daughter isn't doing so well on her schedule, and I haven't had much sleep."

He slowly approached her, and her face lifted when he came into her line of sight. Tears now wet her cheeks. "Can't your husband help, so you can get some sleep?"

"Boyfriend. And he works during the week in Oklahoma. He's only home on the weekends when he doesn't have to work those too."

Brant sat back down on the sofa. Something about her was drawing him in. He tried desperately to keep his gaze focused on anything other than the woman in front of him with the blanket draped across her shoulder. His mind raced. *What the hell am I doing? I was so close to being free of this place. Unconventional my ass. This is crazy. Who breastfeeds their baby in front of a client?* He glanced at her. Her foot was propped up on the ottoman, gently rocking with her eyes closed. Exhaustion was written all over her face.

"Why don't I watch her while you take a nap?" *Where the hell did that come from? I don't know her, and I damn sure don't know anything about babies. I guess I do need a counselor because I have obviously lost my damn mind.*

"No. I can't ask you to do that."

"You didn't. I offered. Do you have any other appointments?" Her brows drew together. "I mean, if you are okay with it."

"It's not that I'm not okay with you watching her. I know April and Joe and Cody and Jenna, and if you are friends with them, then you must be okay. It's just..." She glanced off, and tears flowed again. Brant's eyes met hers, widening as he waited for her to continue, but she stayed silent putting the back of her hand to her mouth as she cried.

Damn. "Am I your last appointment?" he asked again.

"Yes," she said in a whisper, nodding her head.

"Then let me watch her. I was a Medic in the Air Force. I've got some training. You can sack out on the sofa in here or out there, whichever is more comfortable. She will be fine."

She dropped her chin and stared at him with glistening unshed tears. "Are you sure?"

Not at all, but for some reason I feel like being a damn hero today. "Yeah. However, the offer expires in one minute—" He lifted his arm and checked his watch. "—So you better be making a decision quick."

"Oh, I've decided. Let me get her into a good milk coma, and I will gladly take you up on your offer."

Silence hung in the air except for the occasional noise coming from under the blanket, and Brant couldn't help feeling like he was invading her privacy. "Maybe I should wait out there until you are done."

"Only if it bothers you. I don't care if you are in here."

He rubbed his hand up the back of his head and took a deep breath. *I've been here this long. Might as well stay.* But with every tiny grunt from under the blanket, it sent his brain to thoughts he knew he shouldn't have, so he broke the silence. "How old is she?"

"She will be six weeks tomorrow. The first couple of weeks she did great sleeping. This week has been brutal though. She hasn't slept longer than about an hour at a time." She shifted her attention under the blanket and Brant quickly focused on the ceiling and rubbed his hands together nervously. "Can you take her for a minute? I will get you set up in here."

He stood and walked slowly to Dr. Adkins. Glimpsing at the tiny infant, he hesitated, wondering what he had committed to. Then leaning down, he gently gathered her in his arms. The doctor's scent surrounded him, followed by the soft lavender scent of the sweet sleeping baby, and his breath stalled as he saw her up close. "What is her name?"

"Maizy."

Adjusting her position in his arms, he watched as her rosebud lips pressed together and a smile snuck onto his face.

Dr. Adkins continued to move her hands beneath the blanket, and then stood, pulling the blanket from her shoulder and draping it over Brant's. "Prop her up on your shoulder and pat her back. Try to get her to burp."

"Won't that wake her up?"

"It shouldn't." She watched as he shifted the baby to his shoulder and started patting her. "You can rub your hand up her back too. Sometimes that works." She studied him then dropped her gaze to the baby. "Are you sure about this? I mean I appreciate the offer—"

"I'm good. Go. Do what you need to do to get us set up. My afternoon is wide open."

Dr. Adkins disappeared behind the door and returned with what looked to be a portable crib. "Diapers are here on the side. Baby wipes are next to them. Since she ate well, she shouldn't get hungry for a few hours. If she gets fussy, you might try this." She pulled out a pacifier tucked in a side pocket and held it up. "When you put her down, lay her on her back."

Brant tried to keep track of all the instructions.

"Got it."

Reaching out, she stroked Maizy's soft hair with the back of her fingers. "If you need anything don't hesitate to come and get me."

"Oh, don't worry. I will." His hand continued to pat Maizy, and he was blessed with a loud burp.

Dr Adkins grinned. "She burps like her momma." Brant's brow lifted, and he chuckled as she turned and grabbed a tan throw blanket draped across one of the wingback chairs and disappeared up the hall.

"Well, Maizy, you are stuck with me for a while, little girl." He laid her down and covered her with the thin blanket from his shoulder, then kicked his shoes off. After removing the button-down that covered his T-shirt, he draped it on top of his jacket and stretched out on the sofa. Tucking a tan chenille pillow under his head, he closed his eyes and the white noise from the baby monitor lulled him into oblivion. He was awakened by a soft, high-pitched whine.

Searching the room, Brant tried to remember where he was. He sat up and sucked in a deep breath. Little grunts mingled with whimpers came from the small fabric crib in front of him. He checked his watch. Two hours had passed. He stood and gazed into the crib. Maizy stared up at him and for a moment, he thought he saw a smile, then her face wrinkled, and she let out another whine.

He gently scooped her up, grabbed the blanket, tossed it over his shoulder, then pressed her against it, rubbing softly up and down her back as she fussed. He swayed back and forth making shushing noises hoping to soothe her back to sleep. Still, she continued to grunt and whimper. Laying her in his arms, he rocked her, but her whimpers only became longer, louder cries.

"You do not like that. Okay." Carefully shifting her to his shoulder again, he gently patted her bottom as he continued to sway. A distinct smell reached his nose and he winced, suddenly realizing what might be the issue. "Oh. Great. Okay." Glancing in the crib, he tried to remember Dr. Adkins' instructions. "This should be fun," he said aloud sarcastically, then sighed. "What the hell was I thinking."

Laying Maizy in the crib, he reached into the diaper holder hanging from the end and grabbed a diaper and the baby wipes. He stared down at the tiny dark-haired girl and smiled. Her eyes locked on him, and he suddenly had an unexplained need to make whatever was bothering her right. It was like she spoke real words to him to help her. He unsnapped her sleeper and tenderly pulled it up out of the way.

As he pulled on the adhesive tabs and lowered the front of the diaper, the disgusting sight and the full brunt of the smell hit him. His stomach lurched, and his gag reflex immediately took hold. Coughing, he turned away quickly, putting his fist to his mouth, hoping the roast beef sandwich he had for lunch stayed put. Quickly pushing the front of the diaper back up, he breathed out a heavy breath and gagged again as he frantically searched for a garbage can. After locating one by the desk, he set it next to the crib and stood, with one hand on his hip, the other wiping his watery eyes as he peered down at the baby and chuckled. "I can't do this." *How can something so small make something so nasty? I gotta wake the doc. She can deal with this.*

He reattached the adhesive tabs and picked up

Maizy, wrapping her up with the blanket without snapping her sleeper. Frustration coursed through him, knowing he didn't take care of her problem. She whimpered a couple of times, and his lips pecked her soft hair as he patted her back. The realization hit him of what he did, and a thick knot formed in his throat. Heading up the hallway, he stopped abruptly as the sleeping woman came into view. The sunlight filtered through the crystals hanging in the window, dropping shards of prisms across her face. Her thick lashes lay softly against her cheeks and her plump pink lips parted slightly. *Damn.*

Air escaped in a hiss from his lips. His eyes darted from the baby resting on his shoulder to the beautiful woman as he wrestled with the decision he needed to make. Then he turned slowly and walked back up the hallway to the crib. "Okay baby girl," he said as he gently laid Maizy down and pulled her sleeper up. "We're doing this."

He pressed his hands to the edge of the crib and stared down at her. Sliding the second diaper under her, he filled his lungs with air, preparing for what came next. His fingers pulled at the adhesive tabs, and he leaned away. Yanking a couple of wipes from the box with one hand, he covered his nose with the other before pulling down the front. His stomach lurched, and his eyes watered as he coughed and turned away. Keeping his hand over his nose, he reached out and folded the dirty diaper, then quickly cleaned Maizy.

After securing the diaper and snapping her back into her sleeper, he propped her back on his shoulder and grabbed the dirty diaper, hunting for a faraway place to dispose of it. "My goodness, sweetheart, those things should be considered toxic waste," he said in a sweet voice. He found a small kitchen down the hall and disposed of the diaper in a trashcan under the sink.

When he made it back to the room, he noticed Maizy had gotten quiet. Peering down at her, she blinked back at him. A smile spread across his face, and he kissed her on her forehead. "I'm thinking you feel better now, and I guess you are good and awake. So, what do you want to do?"

He sat down in the glider, propped his socked feet up on the ottoman, and laid her on his lap. His heart thudded as the tiny baby stared up at him moving her mouth like she wanted to tell him something. He held out his fingers and let her wrap her hands around them. His thumbs gently skimmed her delicate skin, and his mind drifted. This could have been his life if it hadn't taken such a horrible turn. He would have had a baby boy or baby girl by now, about Maizy's age.

Lifting her, he placed soft kisses on her cheek. Her face flexed beneath his lips, and he kissed the other cheek, then pulled her away and stared at her as he laid her back in his lap. His heart filled, and a smile crossed his face. Her thick dark hair stood up in the back and swept to the side in the front under the pink velvet band. Obviously, her mom had tried to tame the unruly mop.

With her legs curled to her chest, he pressed his hand to her feet, and she stuck her tongue out as she pushed against him. A smile filled his face and he picked her up again, bringing her close to his face. "Hey baby girl," he said popping his lips and making noises.

She gave him a toothless grin, and he grinned back

at her. "You like my silly noises?" He stood her up on his legs and bounced her up and down. She huffed a couple of times then whined. "Uh oh, you don't like that."

Lifting her to his shoulder, he pressed his hand firmly against her back and patted her on the diaper, then stood and swayed slowly back and forth, continuing to pat her. Minutes went by, and she settled. He leaned his head down and noticed her eyes shut, mouth open. "She sleeps like her momma." He slowly lay down on the sofa and adjusted her in the middle of his chest.

Chapter Two

Bekah stood in the corner of the room with her fingers to her mouth, staring at the massive man sacked out on the sofa, with her tiny baby sprawled in the middle of his chest. One large hand covered Maizy, and his other arm draped across his eyes. She had heard nothing while she slept. Four glorious hours of uninterrupted sleep. Probably more than she had gotten the entire week.

She was so exhausted she gladly allowed this stranger to take care of her six-week-old baby. What was she thinking? When she passed Maizy off to him, it was obvious he had very little experience with babies, if any. But for some reason, she trusted him. What was it that made her trust him? She had already made up her mind before he offered up that he had medical training. Why in the world would anyone in their right mind make such an offer?

He had a presence. She noticed it the minute she met him. Military, she figured, by the way he carried himself, and his clean-cut appearance. His hair was perfectly styled, longer on top and short on the sides, with a neatly trimmed five o'clock shadow. A navy T-shirt peeked out from under his jacket and white pressed button-down that sat perfectly untucked on his dark washed denim jeans, which gave him an air of sophistication. But beyond that, he was a paradox, a bit intense but vulnerable.

Somewhere along the way, he had removed the button-down and now slept with Maizy perched on his T-shirt that appeared to be painted on his impressive torso. Regardless of how well-groomed he was though, that still shouldn't have been enough to place the care and safety of her precious child in his hands. Not that the vision she had right now was anything less than adorable. It had her heart doing double time. Brant moved and brought his arm down but didn't open his eyes. *I really shouldn't want to take a photo.* She chewed on her lip. *What am I thinking? He's a client.* She stood silently staring. *Screw it.* Quietly, she snuck away to grab her phone and snapped a couple of quick pictures. Her heart pinched. For a split second she imagined him as Maizy's daddy, but quickly wiped the thought away with a shake of her head.

She wished Maizy's dad was that attentive. Bobby was uncomfortable around Maizy and hadn't bonded with her. He said she was too small, too fragile, and it made him nervous to hold her. She didn't fault him for that, but wished he wasn't gone so much. She missed him, and she figured if he were home more, he would be more comfortable around Maizy. One more day and he would be home. It took a little bit for him to get used to there being a baby, but he was starting to come around a little.

He was there for her the first week, then he said he needed to get back to work. Since then, he'd had a couple of weeks he wound up staying in Oklahoma for the weekend which wasn't uncommon for him to do before the baby was born. The last two weeks were hell though, trying to adjust her work schedule with a baby that refused to sleep.

Her mind traveled back to the fight they had months ago when she found out she was pregnant. He wasn't happy. No, it wasn't planned, though after five years of dating there was bound to be a time when there was a slip up, especially when alcohol was involved. It only takes once though, and always involves two. He refused to accept that.

After meeting Bobby at Pepperdine while they were both studying for their PhDs, Bekah thought she had found *the one*. Sparks flew when he swept her off her feet with flowers and gifts and sweet words, and it didn't take long for her to envision a life with him. It finally felt like her life was coming together, especially when she found a job after graduation as a counselor in Dalton, where her grandpa Dale lived.

And then Bobby followed her. He got a small apartment, then found an oil and gas job in Oklahoma. He wasn't excited about the drive at first. However, after seeing the apartment the company provided, he was all in, and they focused on making it work. Two years into their new location, things were going well she thought, then…bam!

He wasn't happy about the news, saying he wasn't ready. He felt trapped. After Maizy was born though, it seemed he was starting to warm up to the idea of being her daddy, even though he wavered at times from hot to cold. This week was cold. He had left Sunday without saying goodbye after Bekah had lost it when he wouldn't even take the baby while she took a shower. They were both exhausted. That's all it was. Right?

The stress of a newborn had taken a toll on their relationship. Her head was swimming. It took everything within her to hold it together. And today, obviously, she hadn't. In a big way.

God, she couldn't take her eyes off the vision in front of her. Who was this guy who stumbled into her office and saved her from a complete meltdown? He moved again, this time just to pat Maizy and rub her back. Bekah bit her lip watching the sweet scene playing out in front of her.

She quietly strolled into the kitchen and grabbed a soda out of the fridge and popped the top. When she walked back through, she debated whether to go back into the waiting area then heard a soft deep rumble from the sofa.

"Can I have one of whatever you just opened?"

"Oh, crap, I'm sorry. I didn't mean to wake you," she said just above a whisper.

"Not asleep, just resting. What are you drinking?"

"Ginger spritzer?"

"Perfect."

She went back through the door and returned with the can and set it on the coffee table. Brant sat up with his hands pressing Maizy against him. He glanced down at her and rubbed her tiny head, then hoisted her up to his shoulder like an expert. Popping the top of the soda with one hand, he took a long swig, then twisted the can to see the label and tipped his gaze up to Bekah.

"This is really good."

Bekah stood at the corner of the sofa. "Do you want me to take her?"

"No. She's fine." He sat back on the sofa and let Maizy snuggle.

"How did she do?" Bekah spoke quietly as she sat down in the glider.

"She slept for about two hours and then started fussing." He paused then pointed to the kitchen door. "Don't let me forget to take the kitchen garbage out before I leave."

Her face immediately heated. "Oh, geez. Was it bad?

"I only puked twice."

"Oh God. Are you serious? I am so sorry. I know they can be—"

He grinned putting his hand up. "I'm kidding… mostly."

"Why didn't you come and get me?"

"I thought about it and even made it to the end of the hallway, but you were sleeping so peacefully I couldn't bring myself to disturb you."

She narrowed her eyes. *Is he for real? What is his game?* He seemed so standoffish a few hours ago.

"After I got her diaper changed, she was ready to play for a little bit. I think I got a couple of smiles out of her." A smile tugged at his lips as he peeked at the infant. "She's been asleep for"—he switched hands on her bottom to look at his watch— "maybe an hour?"

She swallowed, fighting back tears. "I don't know how to thank you."

Slowly, he sat forward on the sofa and slipped his shoes back on. "No need. I'm glad I could help. Although, I'm not promising the diaper will hold whatever comes out of her next. I am not trained in diaper duty."

She found herself mesmerized watching him gently rubbing Maizy's back. "Well obviously you are well trained in sleep duty." The corner of her mouth tipped.

Brant finished his ginger spritzer, then, still holding

Maizy, he carefully stood just as Maizy stirred. Rubbing her back, he leaned his face close to her ear softly shushing her. "She probably is getting hungry." His hands pulled her away from his shoulder, and he stared at her one last time before he gently passed her off to Bekah. The smell of his cologne filled her nose with a scent of warm leather and nutmeg. Their hands met, and prickles of electricity shot through her like an arrow. His fingers grazed the back of Maizy's head to say goodbye. "I guess I should go." He picked up his jacket and slid it on, then tossed his shirt over his shoulder.

She cleared her throat. "So, Tuesday then?" Her eyes followed him as he walked away.

He hesitated, then answered, "Sure," adding a nod. Then with a jerk of his head, he cocked his thumb and asked, "Is the dumpster out back?"

"It's around on the side. It's best to go out the front."

Brant nodded and disappeared behind the door. When he returned, he held the garbage bag away from his body with his head turned away. Bekah tried not to laugh but failed miserably.

"Thank you."

"No problem," he responded, his voice strained.

She turned her head and heard the bells jingle when he opened the front door.

Her focus turned back to Maizy. "Well, that was an interesting afternoon. What did you think of Mr. Ellington?" She propped her feet up on the ottoman, sat Maizy on her lap, and rocked. Her phone chimed, and she shifted to reach into her sweater pocket and pull it out. "Oh, it's Daddy," she whispered to the baby.

"Hi, sweetie."

"Hey. How are things going?"

"Better. I actually got some sleep today." She wasn't about to tell him how though.

"Great. I know it's been hard, and I'm sorry I haven't been more help. I shouldn't have been so short this weekend. I guess I was just tired too."

"It's okay. I know it hasn't been easy for you either."

"I'll admit, I've been stressed. There have been some big changes going on at work that had me on edge. I didn't want to bring it up to you with the baby, although today I got some news that was pretty cool."

"Awesome. You sound excited. What is it?"

"I got a promotion."

"Seriously? Oh my gosh, babe, that's fantastic."

"It gets better. My whole team has been pegged for a new project. It's a three-year pilot program and if it goes well, it will be huge. I will be heading it up."

A smile spread across her face. "I am so proud of you."

"There is something else. I'm serious, this is like the best day ever."

"What's that?" Anticipation had her heart racing. She scolded herself for the negative thoughts she had earlier. Bobby sounded so excited.

"It's in Houston. We will be able to live near the coast, just like we had dreamed about. And we will be less than an hour from my folks."

Bekah's excitement evaporated. Yes, she had talked about wanting to live near the coast at one time. However, it was more to appease Bobby. And when her grandma died, those dreams didn't seem important anymore. Her grandpa played such a huge role in her life as a kid. Though her parents loved her, they didn't give her any direction like her grandparents did. She loved her parents' carefree life, and many of the things they instilled in her she still held dear. They lived on the west coast, so it wasn't like she couldn't visit the beach when she needed her salt air fix.

Her grandparents, on the other hand, taught her how to think for herself. They always saw the potential in her and taught her the value of a good education. The thought of packing up and moving away from her grandpa was unimaginable since she had been living in his backyard for the past two years. She had talked about living near her grandpa hundreds of times with Bobby and how important it was to her. Now that she had made it a reality, it felt like home. Especially now with Maizy. He loved Maizy. *How can I take her so far away from him? But maybe this is what it will take for Bobby to commit...*

"Bekah?" His voice brought her back to the conversation.

"That's...that's great. When are they expecting you to be down there?"

"They want us up and running by the end of April, so basically, I need to be down there now. I will be heading down next week to talk to the execs and get a little more information on the full project. They are going to put the team up in apartments until we can find places to live. I will have a little time to check out the area, then later we can go down together."

"Sounds great. We can kind of get a game plan together when you get home tomorrow."

"Um...about that. I am going to have to stay here

this weekend. There is too much that needs to be done with my team before we head down next week."

She closed her eyes. Even though they parted last weekend on kind of a bad note, she was counting down the hours before he got home. Regardless of how much he helped with Maizy, she still felt she could breathe when he was there. "What about your birthday?" she asked, trying not to sound too disappointed.

"Don't worry about that, babe. You have enough to deal with, taking care of Maizy. It's not a big deal. I will probably go out and have a beer with the others, and that will be it."

"I was looking forward to celebrating with you and Maizy."

"I know, and I'm sorry. It can't be avoided. It's too important. I want to make sure everything is perfect. This is huge for me."

"I understand. I'm just a little disappointed."

"I know. I would love to spend my birthday with you and Maizy. When I get back, I promise we are going to go out and celebrate everything."

She didn't know what to say. Bekah was happy for him, but disappointment hung in her throat. "Okay."

"What is it?" Bobby questioned suddenly sounding annoyed.

"It's nothing."

"No, it isn't. You're upset. I can tell."

"It's just, of all the times for you to be gone, I wasn't expecting it to be your birthday. I was really looking forward to having you here so we could spend it together. I am proud of you and happy for you, but it sucks. I know I'm whining but with Maizy not sleeping, I'm exhausted and overwhelmed. I'm having to juggle appointments, and trying to organize everything around her schedule isn't working and—"

"That's why I said I wasn't ready for a baby, Bekah. We are still trying to get our feet under us and, don't get me wrong, I love Maizy to death, but she has put a huge wrench in everything, and now, with this transition, it's going to be complicated because of her."

She could feel the anger crawling up her throat. Words she knew she shouldn't say were scraping the tip of her tongue. Even though he acted like he was excited to be a daddy when she was born, he obviously wasn't. How in the world could he think of Maizy as a complication? *My client today showed Maizy more love than you ever did.*

"Bekah, we will make it work. Don't worry, babe." His voice softened.

The gentleness of his voice suddenly made her feel guilty for what she was thinking. Bobby loved Maizy. She knew that. "I know. I'm sorry. It's just a lot to take in. This is a wonderful opportunity for you."

"I'm really excited. This is exactly what I had hoped for." He paused and she stayed silent. "Okay, so I will keep you posted with how things are coming together. You might want to start searching for a place to live. I am going to send you a list of neighborhoods and suburbs of Houston that Marissa has already compiled."

Marissa. Bobby had hired her initially as an intern a little over a year ago, then pulled her onto his team fulltime a few months later. Bekah liked her when they met shortly after being hired. Marissa was sweet, very open and had a real enthusiasm about her. However, Bekah noticed early on, how closely Bobby had been working with her, and how often he talked about her. Marissa was young and strikingly beautiful. Blonde bombshell fit her to a T. Bekah couldn't help but feel like a beached whale at the end of her pregnancy and Bobby was working with Marissa, the beautiful platinum-blonde babe, with a flat belly and perfect ass, and Bobby was an ass man. Jealousy had taken hold, and Bekah had wondered a couple of times if Bobby had strayed, since he had become so distant recently.

"Marissa is familiar with that area?" She fought to keep the edge out of her voice.

"Yes, her family has a beach house."

"Oh, well that's going to be great for her then," she said sharply, then paused. "Yes, send me the list and I will start looking."

"What's that supposed to mean?"

"What?"

"It's good for her."

"I mean it's good that she gets to live close to her family."

"It's a vacation house, and the way you said it sounded rude."

She let out a huff. "I'm just worried about Grandpa Dale."

"You know, if I didn't know better, I kind of get the feeling you aren't that happy about my news." The annoyance returned to his voice.

"I'm sorry if I sound less than enthusiastic. I'm working off very little sleep, and I am stressed trying to juggle a baby and my clients."

"Your grandfather is going to be fine. I don't understand why you are so worried about him. He is healthy and happy. He is constantly working, or going somewhere, or doing something with friends. He is living his life. Heck, if you are that worried about him, maybe we can talk him into moving down to Houston so you can still be close to him."

He didn't understand. His family had a whole different dynamic. They weren't that close. Although she heard Bobby talking about his parents off and on, he never talked about his grandparents.

Bekah had seen her grandpa when her grandma died. Grandma Dottie was his world. He treated her like a queen. When she died, she took a part of his heart with her. She had seen how he'd shut down on several of her visits before she moved to Arkansas. It was only after she moved into the cottage behind him that he started to get past his grief and go out with friends. She enjoyed living close to him. They had shared many meals together and had lots of long talks sitting on his porch watching the fireflies. Bekah loved watching his eyes twinkle anytime he was around Maizy. She couldn't imagine what it would do to him if she took her away.

A knot grew in her stomach. Her heart pounded. She could not deal with all this right now. Maizy whined. Propping her up on her shoulder, she bounced her hoping it would settle her until she finished the phone call. Instead it only made her whine turn into a wail.

"Bobby, let's talk about this—"

"Yeah, I hear her. I will talk to you later." His voice was thick with irritation, and the phone went dead.

Inhaling a deep breath, she let out a growl as she chucked the phone on the sofa. Her heart squeezed. He sounded so frustrated with her, and she couldn't blame him. She had been on edge ever since Maizy was born. Navigating a newborn was much harder than she had anticipated. She had been so excited about the pregnancy, and when she found out it was going to be a girl she daydreamed about the cute nursery and cute outfits. She'd decorated a small area in her bedroom with peach and white paper flowers to match the peach-colored fabric rocker she'd found. Somehow the reality of the sleepless nights and incessant crying never factored in.

Plus, her love life was put on hold for the time being. Not that she really cared that much; she didn't particularly feel attractive at the moment. She hadn't had a decent shower since who knows when, her hair always seemed to resemble a bird's nest, and she had a baby belly, stretch marks included. Good thing she had a closet full of long dresses. Bobby didn't seem to appreciate her appearance either. He hadn't really touched her since she told him she was pregnant, saying he was worried he would hurt her or the baby. Still, in the worst of times, she wouldn't trade that beautiful baby girl for the world.

Now though, with the promotion and move thrown into the mix, she really needed to get her life back on track. The move would be hard, but she couldn't put her grandpa above Bobby. He was her future. Geez, she had been a real bitch to Bobby. He was so excited, and she crapped all over his good news. She needed to make it up to him and in a big way. But how?

She rocked Maizy as she nursed and pulled together a plan she thought would surely make Bobby see her in a new light.

Chapter Three

The cold bite of the winter air hit Brant's nose and burned as he opened the door of his SUV. It was early morning, and daylight had barely brightened the sky. The sound of gravel crunching beneath his sneakers broke through the eerie silence around him. He pulled open the door on the 24 to Life gym and heard the familiar chime. As he strolled toward the counter, "Sweet Home Alabama" could be heard through the speakers. Joe sat at the welcome desk and nodded his head to greet him. They both smiled.

It hadn't been that long ago that a smile would have been the last thing they would have exchanged. Nearly a year had passed since that night at the bar in Cimarron. Brant had sucker punched Joe in a fit of drunken rage after thinking he was hitting on his wife. Cody, Joe's best friend, retaliated. As a result, Brant and Cody both had assault charges filed against them.

After completing rehab, Brant realized how his life had gone off the rails. He dropped the charges against Cody and apologized, and asked Joe to drop the charges against him.

His phone buzzed in his pocket and when he retrieved it, it was another message from the unknown number.

—*Can't wait to see you*—

A cold chill skated through him briefly, and he

again wondered who it was. He didn't respond to the first one, thinking someone simply sent the text to the wrong number. *Could this be the same? I miss you, and now I can't wait to see you? Or is someone playing a cruel prank?* He wracked his brain thinking about who knew what he had gone through this past year, and wondering who it might be, but came up empty. He finally figured whoever it was had the wrong number.

Returning his phone to his shorts, Brant stepped up to the counter. "Where have you been?" He held out his hand, and Joe clasped it like they were about to arm wrestle.

"April and I took a little trip to celebrate."

"Celebrate?"

Joe's face filled with a sheepish grin. "Yeah, I proposed."

Brant's brows lifted as a smirk crawled across his face. "Oh, don't tell me she agreed to marry your sorry ass."

"Hey, for the record, she thinks I have a very nice ass."

"Whatever." He chuckled although a twinge pierced his heart thinking about the day he proposed to Abbie. It wasn't anything elaborate. He had gone to the BX and arranged to have the ring placed at the bottom of an ice cream cone when he arrived with Abbie later. It worked out perfectly. They got their cones and went for a stroll in the nearby park and ate their ice cream. When she found the ring, she immediately began crying and couldn't even answer when he got down on one knee. She simply nodded her head.

"Seriously though, I'm happy for you. Where did you go?"

"We headed to the Maldives for a couple of weeks. April has always wanted to go. It was paradise. The weather was nothing less than perfect, and the place was amazing. We stayed in a little villa on the water. The floor was solid plexiglass. You could watch the fish swim beneath you while you were eating dinner."

"I think I've heard about that place."

"Oh, and they have rooms that are completely underwater too. I couldn't handle that."

"Yeah, that would be a hard no for me. One crack—"

"Yeah, my thoughts exactly. The Maldives was definitely amazing though. April is talking about wanting to have a destination wedding there."

"Is that the place with the glowing algae or something?"

"Yes. They call it 'The Sea of Stars.' We were lucky it appeared while we were there. We took a few evening walks along the beach. The plankton is really cool to look at, although it doesn't smell that great."

Brant walked around the edge of the counter into the gym. "Well congratulations. I am happy for you."

"Thanks."

He headed for one of the lockers, stopping abruptly when he saw Cody coming out of his office holding a couple of rolls of paper towels. "I have a good mind to knock you in the head with one of these weights." Cody stopped, stunned at Brant's comment. "Unconventional? Lord, try batshit crazy." Cody smiled at Brant's comment.

"So, you went to see Doc Adkins, huh?"

"You could say that. I nearly saw more than I needed to. Let's just say, that's a one and done son. She said something about yoga and mindfulness and grounding, and I'm really surprised she didn't start chanting something over me."

"Hey, don't knock it until you try it. I wasn't a fan either. I promised Jenna I would try it for six weeks, but I didn't expect to get anything out of it. I'll admit though, I use some of the stress relieving methods now. Especially with the baby coming. Jenna is about to drive me insane with all her planning. I am seriously thinking about burning those damn baby books she bought. They have her freaking out."

Brant opened a locker. "Speaking of babies, did you know doc had a baby?"

Cody's eyes opened wide. "What? No. When?"

"Like six weeks ago. Baby girl named Maizy. I was awkwardly introduced to her Tuesday."

"What happened?"

He loaded his small bag into the locker and wrapped earbuds around his neck. "She started crying during my consultation, and doc went and got her and started feeding her right in front of me."

"Feeding her like—" Cody motioned to his chest.

"Yeah. Again, I nearly saw more of her than I needed to. I mean, she was at least discrete about it and threw a blanket over her shoulder. But then when I got up to leave, the doc started crying. She said she hadn't slept in days and her boyfriend was out of town, so I stayed and watched Maizy while she slept.

"You did what?" Brant nodded. "Seriously?"

He slammed the locker and started walking. "Changed a godawful diaper too." His face soured, and Cody busted out laughing.

"You did not." Brant nodded.

"Don't laugh buddy, your day is coming sooner than you think. I'm going to point and laugh when you realize those suckers will instantly make you wanna puke."

"Diapers will have to be Jenna's job then. I gag at the smell of our garbage. I *will* puke. Trust me on that."

"Oh, I know. I seriously wondered if I was going to make it without losing my lunch. I quickly found the garbage can just in case."

"I can't believe you changed a diaper," Cody said continuing to chuckle. "Will wonders never cease."

Brant grabbed two weights and loaded them on a bar sitting in a rack. "Hey, I'm not all bad."

"That remains to be seen." Cody smirked. "So, when are you seeing her again? And let me say, now that I know you babysit, I *will* be calling once baby Spencer arrives."

"She has me down for next Tuesday for my first session. But like I said, I think I'm one and done. I don't know that I will keep that appointment."

"Why?"

Brant tipped his mouth to the side. "I don't know if I agreed to a counseling session or babysitting." Cody laughed. "Seriously though, she is a little out there for me, and that is coming from someone who spent most of their life in one of the most 'out there' places in America."

Cody nodded to the bench. "Trust me on this. Go. I know her methods seem odd, but they work."

Brant sat down and dropped his head beneath the bar. After setting the paper towels on the floor, Cody stepped behind the bench ready to spot Brant as he lifted. "I'll think about it." He pushed the bar up from its stand and lowered it slowly to his chest.

****

Stepping inside Arnie's deli, Brant removed his beanie and scarf and searched the area. A short, portly man with black curly hair and rectangular plastic-framed glasses waved him over to a booth in the corner. Although he'd aged since Brant had seen him last, and his suit looked a bit wrinkled, he still carried a bit of an elitist air about him. Approaching the booth, Brant shook the man's hand. "Hi, Skip." He slid in and immediately locked eyes with the chic woman in the booth across from him. Skip pulled up a chair at the end of the table.

Brant smiled politely, but there was very little warmth. "Hi, Mom." She grabbed his hand across the table and squeezed. It wasn't that he didn't love her. He did. And he knew she loved him and his brother Greg. She had been in the industry for nearly thirty-five years, and it had afforded him and his brother a life of luxury, something she didn't have as a child. However, for most of his life, he felt like they were more acquaintances than family.

She had accidentally stumbled into the business when a director, scouting out a location for his new horror movie, had engine trouble and took his car to Brant's granddad's shop. She had worked in the shop from the time she was little. His grandpa always fostered her desire to learn, and when she showed an interest in his work, he taught her everything he knew. His shop made decent money, but it didn't make them rich.

Covered in grease and grime, his mom was perfect for one of the parts in the movie, the director said when he arrived with his car and saw her.

His dad, on the other hand, came from a film industry family that had won awards for special effects. Brant never had the opportunity to get close to his dad's side of the family because they were hardly ever home and the older Brant got, the same went for his dad. He was always doing projects far away from home, and Brant felt like he never got to know him. His brother didn't mind it so much. He joined in the family business and started writing screenplays. A few had already been turned into movies.

But Brant didn't want that life for his family. He wanted something normal where he came home to a wife and kids every day. For now, though, it didn't hurt to have some fun wallowing in the muck with the stars.

Brant turned to Skip. "So, what do you have for me?"

"Some paperwork for you to sign and the full script with a tentative schedule. You are already set up in the system, since your mom sent us your contact information in the e-mail. This is the contractual agreement." He pulled a pile of papers from the bag and slid them across the table. "We plan to start shooting, if all goes well, in a few weeks. I will have the call sheet sent to you as soon as it is set up. Be sure to let us know if you have any class or other conflicts as soon as possible." He dug a pen from his bag and handed it to Brant. "Shooting should take about six weeks, and as of right now, it appears it will all be shot in this area, so you won't need to fly out anywhere."

"That works for me."

"The Farington hotel has opened the top two floors for the cast and crew to stay, to make shooting more convenient."

"Wait, I thought the place was shut down."

"It was. They are in negotiations with a company to turn it into senior housing. Finalization is several months out though, so we were able to contract with them to open it up for the shoot and let us stay there for the entire time. It worked out perfectly because there wasn't anywhere else to put the cast and crew all together locally."

"I don't need a room. I can drive in."

"Well, we aren't going to make you stay at the hotel, but we have a room reserved for you regardless. There will be meetings there, and since we will be shooting primarily in and around the area at different hours, it might be easier to stay at the hotel."

"True." He picked up the pen and stared down at the papers in front of him. His mom had yet to say a word. His gaze met hers for a second then returned to the paperwork.

"How have you been?" Her voice was warm. She had written him letters while he was in rehab, and it meant a lot to him. Still, no one from his family visited other than his grandma Betty. She came like clockwork every Sunday afternoon.

He glanced back up to see her staring at him. It was a bit unsettling. "I'm doing well. Thanks for asking, and thanks for giving me this opportunity. It seems like a fun project," he said, before returning his attention to the papers.

"It will be. The script is very well written."

Skip interrupted. "Your character's part has been expanded, by the way."

"It has?" Caught a little off guard by the new

information, he gave Skip a side glance. "It was already pretty significant to the storyline." His eyes tipped up to his mom again. "Did you have something to do with this? I mean, I know I have the part because of you—"

"No. Not in the least bit. And as far as getting you the part, Chauncy asked me if you might be interested, not the other way around. All I did was tell him I would see what you thought and gave him your e-mail address."

She had his full attention now. "Really? You didn't pull strings?"

"No. He said you had the exact look he was going for and since you already proved yourself with speaking rolls in other movies, he thought you would be perfect for the part."

"I had no idea."

Skip gathered up all the papers as Brant signed them and continued to chat. "If this movie goes over like we hope, it might get your foot in the door for other major projects."

"Oh, I'm not wanting to become famous. I'm just having fun."

"Watch out. Sometimes it has a way of happening anyway." Skip turned around and motioned to the server who brought over menus and glasses of water.

"What is good here?" His mom asked perusing the menu.

"Everything. There is no way you could go wrong."

She laid the menu down. "I love the atmosphere. It's really nice and airy."

"Did you see the sign outside?"

"No?"

"They are famous for their funny sidewalk signs. Today it said 'It's too cold to be funny, come inside and get warm. We'll feed you.'"

The server returned with her pad in hand. "What can I get you guys?"

Brant's mom glanced up. "This will all be on one ticket. I'll have the Something Fishy with a side salad and a sweet tea."

Brant glared at her. "You don't have to do that."

"Please let me. I don't get to see you that often now that you are on the other side of the country."

He rolled his eyes. "Whatever," then turned to the server. "I'll have the Bottomless Bleu with unsweetened tea."

The server then focused on Skip. "I'll have the Spicy fingers with a White Top IPA."

The server shoved her pen and pad in her apron then held up a sign that was similar to the sidewalk sign out front. "If you need me my name is Amber." She scribbled her name in chalk on the sign. "Hang this at the end of the table, and I will come right over." She handed the sign to Brant with a grin. "You know the drill," and walked away. Brant's mom peered up at him.

"Grams and I eat here some."

"Are you okay with Skip drinking a beer?"

"Pssh. Yeah. I promise I won't tackle him for it. Anyway, I better be stronger than that, if I am going to be on a movie set."

Skip nodded. "That's true."

Brant glimpsed back at his mom. "Did you see her shirt?"

"Yeah. I didn't catch what it said though."

"It said 'you are one sign away from a good day.'"

"Aww, that's cute. I love this place."

"You should see if they can shoot a scene here."

"I don't have that much pull." Brant lifted one brow.

"Are you kidding me?"

His attention was captured when he heard the ding of the door and saw Dr. Adkins standing in the doorway with the glow of the sunlight casting perfectly into her chestnut waves. It caused a shimmer across her rosy cheeks. She wore wide legged, navy pants with a white blouse and a long, red sweater, and cradled the baby carrier at her elbow. Scanning the area, she donned a delicate smile when she saw April waving her to the table, and she headed toward a booth in the corner of the restaurant. He hadn't seen that look Tuesday. It made his chest warm, and a smile crept across his face. When he returned his focus to his mom, she was staring at him curiously. "Who is she?"

Brant sat for a moment, suddenly feeling a sting of embarrassment. "She is my new counselor, Dr. Adkins," he confessed and then corrected. "Well, I had a consult with her. I don't know if I'm going back."

"Oh, I didn't know you were continuing with your counseling."

"I wasn't sure if I was going to. However, she came highly recommended." The server returned with their food.

"Are you having issues again?" His mom smiled at the server when she set the food in front of her, then returned her focus to Brant.

"No. I thought it would be a good idea, since I will be on a movie set, to have some tools in place before I started. You know what it can be like."

His mom nodded in agreement. "That's smart. So, why aren't you going back to her?"

"I don't know that I am comfortable with her methods." He subtly shifted his attention, scanning the restaurant, searching for her, and felt a surge of electricity the moment he caught sight of her running her fingers through her hair. *Geez, what am I doing?* His mind flashed to Abbie, and a blanket of guilt wrapped around him when he realized the anniversary of her, and their baby's death was approaching.

The conversation ended as they began to eat their lunch. The sounds of tinkling utensils and murmurs of conversation filled the small diner, and Brant mindlessly let his attention wander until he stopped to linger in one spot a little longer. Stealing a glimpse of her, Brant pinched his lips together trying to stifle a smile as he watched her throw her head back in laughter at something someone said. Her laugh. Although it wasn't loud, it was deep and rich, and he could hear it clear across the restaurant. It made him chuckle. Out of the corner of his eye, he caught his mom glance at him and smile.

Knowing he'd been caught, he tried to avoid the questions that would be coming, by asking, "When is Dad coming in?"

She chuckled, and the look she gave him told him she knew exactly what he was doing. "He won't be here until the week of filming. He is in Jamaica right now working on a documentary."

"Why didn't you go with him?"

She waved her hand. "I never get as much done when I am traveling with him, and I needed to work on this script. I've been there before, so I opted to stay home this time." He gazed at her a minute longer. "And I wanted to see you and Grandma."

"When do you have to head back?"

"Tomorrow evening." Brant lifted a brow, but he wasn't totally surprised. "I know it's short. I will be back in a few weeks."

He grabbed a fry and dredged it through some ketchup. "Why don't you just stay?"

"Too many loose ends to tie up."

He knew that comment meant she wanted to be in familiar surroundings, which unfortunately was not here. Though he knew she loved him and his grams, her life was somewhere else. So, he let it go.

With their plates empty and the contract signed, Brant grabbed the script and stood to leave, but quickly turned when he heard someone call his name. April was waving from across the restaurant. She was never known for being discreet. As she approached, her face lit up. "Sandra! What are you doing here?" Brant's mom, confused at first from someone calling her by name, quickly smiled when April wrapped her in a hug. The two families had known each other for years, from the countless charitable gatherings they had attended together.

Pulling out of the hug, Sandra said, "I'm getting ready to start a project here." Her hands rubbed April's arms. "It's so good to see you. You look wonderful."

"Thank you. You are too sweet. So, what's this about a project?"

"We will be shooting a feature in and around Dalton and the Farington Hotel."

"Isn't that place shut down?"

"They are letting us use it for the project."

"Oh, how fun."

"They will be needing extras," Sandra added in a persuasive tone.

Brant's attention turned to Jenna and Dr. Adkins who were approaching behind April. He fought to return his focus to April, to avoid staring at the doctor, then commented, "I hear congratulations is in order." April held out her hand and flitted her fingers in front of him. He grabbed her hand and stared at the pink diamond surrounded by smaller white diamonds, and a smile pulled at his lips. "I have to say, Joe did good."

"Yeah he did. We just got back from celebrating."

"I heard."

"I hope he didn't give you all the details."

Brant chuckled. "Well, you never know what the topic of conversation at the gym will be." He looked up at Jenna who was staring past him, and a rush of embarrassment suddenly sent heat up his neck. "Oh, I'm so sorry. Jenna and Dr. Adkins, this is my mom, Sandra Gerard, and our lawyer, Skip Ferguson. Mom, Skip, this is Jenna Spencer and Dr. Bekah Adkins. April, you've met Skip before. Am I right?"

"I believe so."

"It's nice to meet you both," Sandra said, while Skip just waved.

Bekah set the carrier down and glared at Brant playfully then turned to Sandra. "Just Bekah please."

"Oh, and this"—Brant pointed at the covered carrier— "is Maizy." Bekah pulled the blanket to reveal the baby girl who was in a hooded white fuzzy sleeper that had fuzzy pink ears on top. Her rosebud lips pursed. A smile filled Brant's face as Maizy's eyes opened and her gaze settled on him for a long moment as they shared a silent hello.

Sandra cooed. "She's beautiful. She has a lot of hair."

"She does and if I pulled the hood off you would see, it stands straight up."

Brant's gaze finally lifted to Bekah. "So, what are you girls doing here?"

Jenna piped up pulling April to her. Both wore hot pink scrubs, although Jenna had an obvious baby belly. "We escaped from the craziness at the vet.

"And I called Bekah to join us since her man is out of town." Brant tensed at April's comment. The memories of Tuesday flooded back. Bekah's tears from complete exhaustion, and the realization that she had no relief coming, had him revisiting the ache in his chest that had appeared when he nearly abandoned her too. Her eyes met his, and the way she studied him had him wondering if she was revisiting their encounter also.

"The fun is over though. We are going to have to head back." Brant refocused, hearing Jenna's voice. She smiled at Sandra. "It was very nice meeting you," then glanced at Skip. "You too, Mr. Ferguson." Her focus then turned to Brant. "Hey, if you aren't busy, Cody is going to be making his debut with his band next Friday at TopHops. I know he would like for you to come."

"Like, this coming Friday?"

"No. Next Friday." Jenna made a sweeping motion with her hand to emphasize her meaning.

He crossed his arms across his chest. "Got it."

"I have been kind of putting out the word. He is a little nervous, so he's not promoting it. It's the first time for a band to play at the brewery and first time for his band to play in public. I think it would make him happy if he had his friends there."

"Thanks for letting me know. Send me a text with the information, and I'll be there."

"Great."

Brant glimpsed at Maizy, then his attention settled on Bekah, wondering if she would be there. His pulse kicked up. *I have got to get ahold of myself.* She leaned down to cover Maizy up and glanced up at him. Her green eyes held him captive, and he couldn't keep the smile from flitting across his face. *Dammit. She is your counselor...sort of. She has a baby. She's in a relationship. She's so...different. This has to stop.* He let out a deep breath hoping his little pep talk to himself had worked. But after hugging his mom bye, he suddenly found himself following Bekah to her car, a bright yellow Bolt with crystals hanging from her rearview mirror. She opened the door, locked Maizy's carrier into the holder, then shut the door and turned to face him. Her forehead wrinkled obviously questioning him, and he searched his brain for the reason he followed her and found nothing.

A sheepish smile filled his face. He twitched his head motioning to the car. "Electric?"

"I'm doing my part to be environmentally conscious."

"That's great until all those lithium batteries wind up in the landfills," he said snidely.

"They're recyclable," she countered sarcastically.

Damn she's good. His lips formed into a smirk as he ran his hand along the car. "Were you scared people couldn't see you on the highway?"

Her hands flew to her hips. "Did you follow me just to bust my chops? Anyway, I think it fits my sunshiny personality." She crossed her arms and bobbed her head.

"I wouldn't call it sunshiny."

"Tuesday didn't count. I was trying to be professional while not falling asleep."

"Are you saying I'm boring?"

She laughed then took a step back and quieted. "I really do appreciate what you did."

"Eh, it was nothing."

"Oh, and just so you know, you underestimated your diapering skills. It held up well."

He peeked at her wondering if she was telling the truth or lying to increase her chances of grabbing a nap at his next appointment. His emotions were all over the place remembering the day before. He leaned against the fender of the car and crossed his arms. "So, are you doing okay?"

She pulled open the driver's side door. "Yes," she said, hitching her thumb over her shoulder. "She actually decided to sleep longer than an hour last night. I got a solid six hours of sleep, which was glorious. They weren't back-to-back of course but, hey, I'll take it."

"Great. You look better today." She lifted her brow and smirked. "Not that you looked terrible yesterday, I mean…" Her arms crossed in front of her as her tongue slowly made its way over her teeth obviously trying to make him sweat. And it was working. "I was meaning you look happy today." With a tilt of her head, he tried again to clarify. "Not that you seemed angry…" Her mouth pursed. Breathing deep, he gave up. "I think it would be a good idea for me to stop talking now."

She giggled, letting him off the hook. "I am feeling

better, and happier, and thanks for noticing. Let me know though any time you are willing to babysit, because I'm not proud enough to pass up a nap."

He turned to face her. "About that. I am a little confused. Am I babysitting Tuesday, or are you teaching me your secret yoga poses?"

She snickered then let out a hearty laugh like she had in the restaurant, and Brant's heart pitched in his chest. "Oh, definitely the yoga poses. Unless, of course, she decides to keep me awake again, then all bets are off." She tucked her lip between her teeth trying to stifle more giggles.

"Got it." He smiled, and she returned it. His phone chimed. She waved and crawled in her car. He waved as she started backing away.

"Hey Cody, what's up?"

"Did you get the e-mail?"

"What e-mail?"

"All of the fire stations are doing a bar-b-que and ride along for the firefighters and paramedics in training Friday. They divided all the trainees between stations. I got station three."

"Let me check." He pulled the phone away from his ear and clicked on his e-mail. Scrolling through the ads, he clicked on the invite. Bar-b-que, ride along, station three. "Looks like we are hanging out together. I got station three."

Chapter Four

Bekah leaned over Maizy. Her wavy brown locks fell over one shoulder. Multi-colored crystal combs held her hair back on both sides. She had checked herself in the mirror at least four times making sure her outfit was perfect. Her red top and printed skirt were new, and the fan-shaped dangling earrings pulled everything together. She felt pretty. The thought of having to cover everything up with a heavy coat annoyed her, but it was better than stepping out in the cold without one. The temperature had dropped considerably over the past week.

"Okay baby girl. We are going to go surprise Daddy. He will be so happy to see you." Her mind flashed on the phone call she got late last night. Bobby had called and they had stayed on the phone for two hours. She apologized for getting upset when he called with his good news and told him she was excited about their new adventure. And she was. Wasn't she? She hadn't said anything to her grandpa Dale though. When the time was right she would. Her thoughts returned to the first time she visited after her grandma passed. *He will be fine.*

Things felt like they were on a much better footing now. Bobby had told her he missed her and Maizy and said he wished he could be home with them to celebrate his birthday. She smiled. April and Jenna had pulled out all the stops to help her. She was going to be a moving birthday party. All she had to do was get everything to his apartment. Luckily, it was on the first floor and the parking spot was right in front. Everything was loaded, balloons, cupcakes, and party hats. There was even a tiny one for Maizy. The only thing left was the luggage and getting Maizy strapped in.

The weather report had ice and sleet coming in, but they should be there before it started.

After feeding Maizy and getting her tummy nice and full, she clicked the carrier in the base, climbed in, and started their adventure. Two and a half hours on the road and Maizy was still fast asleep. Pulling into Lancaster, a bedroom community north of Tulsa, Bekah noticed the sky had grown dark with the impending storm. She checked the clock on the dash. It was nearly six, so Bobby should be back at his apartment by now.

A smile filled her face when she saw his gray Toyota Avalon. And there was a parking space right next to it, so she pulled in. She quietly unloaded the car at his door and then went back to get the carrier. Smoothing her hair, she checked her clothes then knocked and was startled when the door pushed open. Slowly she stepped inside and called out. There was no answer.

Setting Maizy's carrier down, she moved the box of party supplies inside, then viewed her surroundings. The TV was on. Two wine glasses sat on the coffee table that was in the middle of a plush white rug. Her heart raced, and a lump formed in her throat. Scanning the rest of the area, she spotted a pair of black pumps beside the sofa, and a woman's jacket lying across the arm. Heat filled her face as she continued to see other signs that Bobby was not alone. Dishes were left on the counter along with a purse. Bekah's body shook as the truth set in. The balloons were blowing against the open door making a thudding noise similar to the way her heart was pounding in her chest.

Moving the box away from the door, she quietly closed it and stalked up the hallway to the bedroom, already knowing what she would find. Her hand reached for the knob. High pitched giggles came from the other side of the door. She paused, second guessing if she wanted to see what was on the other side. But knowing this was something that had probably been happening for a while, she decided she needed it for final confirmation.

Tears streamed down her cheeks as she pushed the door open. An audible gasp escaped before her throat clamped shut, as she realized she wasn't prepared for what she saw. She couldn't even speak. She simply closed the door and hurried back up the hallway. All she needed to see was the platinum blonde hair and she knew her suspicions were correct. A muffled voice came from up the hallway, but she didn't want to wait around to hear some lame excuse. She had no breath left to discuss anything.

A tornado had come through, and within a matter of minutes ripped everything from her life. Grabbing the carrier, she walked past the balloons and hats, then spied the box of cupcakes and stopped. Growling, she flipped the box and furiously ground each of the red velvet cupcakes into the fancy white rug where they landed, then, hearing the bedroom door open, she carefully stepped out of the mess and headed to the car.

A light mist was starting to fall as she clicked the

carrier into the base and shut the door. When she turned to pull open her door, Bobby appeared in front of her wearing only his boxer shorts.

"Bekah. Please wait. I—"

She put her hands up. "Don't say I can explain." She wiped her face then reached for the door handle, but Bobby stepped in between her and the door, trying to get his hands on her. She flailed her arms pushing them away in disgust.

"Don't you ever put your hands on me again," she shrieked.

"Come inside so we can talk." Her thoughts flew back through the last few months. It explained so much. The weekends away. His waning affection that he blamed on her pregnancy. *How could I be so stupid.* She couldn't decide if she was upset that she trusted him even though she knew she shouldn't, or that she wasn't good enough to keep him from cheating.

"Seriously? You want me to come into your house," she heaved; her face soaked in tears, "where I, I just saw"—she pointed— "—she's still in there, Bobby; probably still in your bed naked."

"Bekah." His hands reached for her again.

"No!" she roared and batted them away. "There are no words, Bobby," she seethed. "Nothing you say will fix this."

She pushed him away from her car and reached for the handle, but he bumped her out of the way. Rage rip through her and she growled, then lunged at him pushing him to the ground. She reached for the handle one more time. The door swung open, and she climbed in and locked the door. The car hummed and backed out. Bobby hopped up and pounded on the window.

"Bekah, don't leave." Her tires squealed as she pulled out onto the road keeping her focus straight ahead, not wanting to see what was in her review mirror. Visions flipped through her thoughts of the shoes, the glasses, the blonde hair. How long had they been together? It had been a while, and it was more than an occasional hook up, because there were other things she noticed. There was the white fuzzy rug in the living room and candles on the dining table. A painting hung above the fireplace. Marissa was living there.

She tried to remember the last time she had been to his apartment. It had to have been months. When she talked to him about coming to visit on a couple of occasions he'd always talked her out of it, saying he worked long hours and with the baby coming he didn't want her on the road. How could she have not known? It was so obvious. *I am such an idiot. He never wanted to commit.* When she became pregnant, he never spoke of marriage or settling down.

Memories came flooding back of when they met in the library. She had been doing research for one of her projects and he asked if he could share her table, then asked what she was studying. She was psychology. He was environmental engineering. She liked that about him. When she finished her research, he walked her to her apartment since it was dark, and they talked for hours watching the sun come up. After that night, they were inseparable. He planned romantic dates, sent her flowers, called her, and texted often. He was the perfect boyfriend in the beginning.

The closer it got to graduation the more Bekah was sure she wanted to move to Arkansas with her granddad. Bobby wanted her to move to Houston with him but said it would all work itself out. When she moved to Arkansas hoping to maintain a long-distance relationship, it had only taken a month before Bobby showed up saying he loved her. She believed him.

The visions and memories washed through her mind. She took deep breaths to calm herself down and stop sobbing so she could focus on the road. Trying to erase the thoughts, she turned on the radio. The sun had disappeared, and she stared at the glossy black strip in front of her. Tiny droplets of ice started pelting her windshield. Flipping the wipers on only proved what she already expected. The ice storm had hit. *Great.* Her heart raced. She turned on the defroster and slowed her speed. As darkness blanketed the landscape, her anxiety ramped up, and she tensed every time a car came near. Their bright lights blinded her. All she wanted to do was get home so she could break down.

As if on cue, Maizy whined. "It's all right, baby girl, we should be home in a few minutes. I know you are hungry." Bekah glanced at the clock. It had been nearly five hours since Maizy ate. She probably needed to be changed too. She hadn't made a peep the entire trip. Poor baby. Her whines turned into wails within moments, and Bekah pressed the gas a little more. They needed to be home. She could see the lights of Dalton.

Headlights approached, and a glare filled her windshield. In a split second she felt the steering give and instinctively she gripped it trying to keep the car on the road. Everything spun out of control like she was on some kind of crazy carnival ride. She screamed as she braced for impact, then darkness engulfed her.

****

Brant sat in a folding chair next to Cody and Steve,

another trainee, in the dining area of fire station three. Five other guys were there, with their plates full of brisket and potato salad, discussing the horrible roughing the passer call at the Superbowl. He took a long, slow look around at all the faces, recognizing some of the guys from working out at the gym. This would be his life. It reminded him of his time in the military. The guys he worked with were a tightknit family. They knew each other well, and would be there for each other, and their families, if anything should happen. Before dinner, the captain, Jeff Yeager, had taken him, Cody, and Steve on a tour of the station and the trucks, giving them a brief description of how their station operated and the average number of calls on any given day. Brant had hoped he would be able to get certified as a flight medic also, but he figured he would primarily be ground support.

He picked up his plate and rinsed it off in the sink in the kitchen before heading back to the dining room. Three loud tones sounded, then a voice echoed through the station over the intercom. "MVA, east bound highway fifty-one, mile marker thirty-six. Car off road. Repeating, MVA, east bound highway fifty-one, mile marker thirty-six. Car off road."

Jeff eyed the trainees. "Spencer, Ellington, you will ride with me and Phillip. Wagner, you ride with Patrick and Jerry."

Brant's pulse increased as the adrenaline set in. He nodded to Cody, and they headed through the door to the trucks. Climbing into the back of the ambulance, they were on the road within minutes with lights on and sirens blaring. Snow was now a steady strobe in the headlights. The smell of disinfectant filled his nose. He glanced at the shelves beside him carrying portable EKGs and equipment. An oxygen tank rested on a shelf across from him. Everything they needed was at their fingertips. There was nothing like this when he was a medic in the military. Red lights flickered through the windows on the doors from the firetruck behind them. The rig slowed. Brant took a deep breath.

He stepped out of the back of the ambulance and jogged to the front. An older couple was standing by a white sedan, lit up by the headlights of the ambulance. They were talking to Jeff and pointing to a yellow vehicle crushed against a tree. When he shined his large flashlight onto the car, Brant's body locked up and he struggled to pull air into his lungs. His head jerked to Cody who was standing a few feet from him. "Shit, Cody. It's doc."

"Who?"

"Doc! Doctor Adkins." The thought of Bekah and Maizy in the car had Brant running down the steep snow-covered embankment at full speed. Airbags were deployed in the front of the car that landed against the tree with such force the windshield was buckled and shattered, and the front passenger door was crushed in. Brant could see Maizy, red faced, wailing, with her tiny fists flying. He yanked open the rear door. Her little cries filled the car.

Visually checking Maizy for blood or trauma, he didn't see any signs of injuries, and he breathed a sigh of relief. His eyes caught sight of the other damaged passenger door and was thankful that Maizy hadn't been on the other side of the car. Turning his attention to the front seat, he hollered, "Doc," hoping she would stir. She was slumped forward and didn't move. He reached over trying to press his fingers against her neck for a pulse and yelled again. "Bekah!" His voice became more frantic when he couldn't get a good read on her pulse. Jeff pried opened the driver's side door. Brant wanted to be there for her, but he knew she would want him to make sure Maizy was okay. He turned back to the tiny girl screaming at the top of her lungs. "Maizy. Shhhhh, don't cry, baby girl." He looked back at her, then turned to Jeff who had carefully repositioned Bekah. Brant noticed blood on the deflated airbag, and his stomach dropped. *What was going to happen to Maizy if...* Pulled from his thoughts with the sound of Cody pulling at the rear passenger door, Brant pushed on it to help, but it was jammed. He turned to the captain. "Jeff, there's no noticeable injuries to the baby. I'm going to get her car seat out so the others can get in here."

"Go for it."

He lifted the carrier out of the base and backed away from the car then glanced up at Cody and nodded for him to take his spot. Cody climbed in to help Jeff. Brant eyed him, waiting for a sign Bekah was alive, but was unable to read his face. Phillip jogged down the embankment with his arms full of equipment, and Brant watched as Jeff put a collar on Bekah. It was the first indication to him that she was alive. Cody backed out of the back of the car, and Brant hollered to him. "Cody, can you get the base out for me?" Cody nodded.

Maizy fussed as Brant headed up the hill to the back of the ambulance to get her out of the cold and snow. She quieted when he stepped up into the back under the bright lights. Her eyes squinted and were locked on him. He wanted to take her out of the carrier but knew protocol was to transport her to the hospital to be examined. A noise outside pulled his attention from Maizy. Jeff, Cody, and Phillip were carrying Bekah on a backboard. They slid her onto the gurney and loaded her into the ambulance before stepping in. She still hadn't regained consciousness. Her right arm appeared to be broken and possibly her nose which was still dripping blood. She had a few cuts, including one at her hairline, probably from the broken windshield. Cody made eye contact with Brant and lifted the base of the carrier plus Bekah's purse and a diaper bag.

The ambulance roared to life, and the sound of the sirens startled Maizy and her brows furrowed. She stuck her lip out and wailed. Brant rocked the carrier on the seat, hoping to soothe her. It didn't. He rubbed his thumb against her cheek and let out a soft, "Shhhh." Her face turned toward him, and she began sucking on his finger. "That finger is probably really dirty little girl." He turned to Cody. "I probably already know the answer to this, but there wouldn't be any bottles in that bag, would there?"

Cody pawed through the bag. "Nope, but there is this." He held up a pacifier.

Brant took it and wiggled it in Maizy's mouth until she latched on. His eyes shifted to Jeff who was relaying information to the hospital and hooking up an IV to Bekah. Cody watched over his shoulder. Jeff pointed. "Spencer, grab the oxygen." Cody pulled a rubber tube from the wall and wrapped it around Bekah's head. Although she let out a soft moan, she didn't stir while they worked on her. Jeff's focus landed on Brant. "So, did I hear you right? Do you know her?"

"We both do. She's a..." Brant stumbled not

wanting to own up to the counseling yet, "friend."

The ambulance pulled into the hospital bay a short time later. When he stepped out from the back of the ambulance with Maizy, Brant was guided inside to a curtained cubicle by a nurse who was waiting for them. The doctor appeared and carefully lifted Maizy out of the carrier. Brant let her wrap her hand around his finger while the doctor examined her. Sucking on her pacifier, she gazed up at him and kicked her legs. After a few x-rays, the doctor released her to Brant who immediately requested a bottle of formula. He changed her diaper while he waited and was thankful it was just wet. Then he made his way to the curtained cubicle where they had taken Bekah. She was still out. He sat down next to the gurney and held Maizy in his arms while she sucked down the bottle. Cody pulled back the curtain.

"The doctor should be back by in a second. They gave her a sedative so they could set her arm. She should wake up soon."

"Everything else okay?"

"Concussion, whiplash, and a few cuts. Other than that, she's okay. Nose isn't broken." The doctor walked up behind Cody, and his focus landed squarely on Brant and Maizy. Cody stepped to the side.

"I'm Doctor Arnold. Are you her husband?" Brant's eyes grew wide, and he shook his head. "No. I'm one of the paramedics. I was taking care of her baby."

"Oh, sorry."

"I am a friend though. I know her."

"Well, do you know how we can get in contact with her family?"

Brant quickly searched the area and spied her purse. "Cody, hand me her purse. We can call her granddad. If we can't get him, we can try her boyfriend, although I think she said he was working out of town."

Cody picked up the purse and dug her phone out. He pressed the button, lighting up the screen, then swiped it. "No good. She has a passcode."

"Do you know her granddad's name?"

"She told me I think, but I can't remember."

"Well, if you remember, and can get in contact with him, I can go ahead and release her once she wakes up. She needs someone to keep an eye on her tonight and tomorrow. Otherwise, we will need to admit her. She has a mild concussion and a greenstick fracture of the right radius and ulna at the wrist. We will need to cast her arm once the swelling goes down."

"Can you release her to me? I can make sure she gets home and gets taken care of."

"That would be fine if she agrees to it. Let the nurses know when she wakes up, and I will sign off on it." The doctor pulled the curtain closed and stepped away.

"Could I get you to drive my car up here so I can stay with her and Maizy? I know it's a lot to ask, since it's already ten and it's snowing like crazy out there—"

"Sure." Cody brushed his hand through the air. "I will get Steve or one of the guys to follow me up." Cody looked at the baby lying in Brant's arms with her eyes almost closed. "I think you got the baby thing down."

"Wanna try your hand at it, to get a little experience?" Cody shook his head. "Come on, she won't bite." Brant lifted his arms slightly, raising Maizy off his lap. Cody carefully wrapped his arms around her and picked her up, then grabbed ahold of the bottle. She stretched and scrunched her face, then settled. He gazed down at her and swayed. Her eyes closed and Cody pulled the bottle away.

Brant set her bottle on the table next to him and watched Cody, suddenly feeling protective of the little girl.

Cody's voice pulled him from his thoughts. "She's so tiny."

"You better get ready for one that size. When is Jenna due?"

"May twenty-fourth. Thankfully, after classes are out. Although, I was hoping to take classes over the summer. Are you?"

"Nope. With my degree and military experience, I should be able to complete the program and get certified once I'm done with this semester. Let me know if you need any help or want to borrow books."

"Oh, trust me, I will take all the help I can get." He leaned down and handed Maizy back to Brant.

"Hey. I hear you are going to be playing at TopHops next week."

"Yeah. I found some guys wanting to put a band together, and we have been working on a few songs, mostly covers. I mentioned it to Gavin, the manager at TopHops, and he asked if we wanted to play."

"I will be sure to be there. Maybe I can manage not to get dragged out by the law this time."

Cody arched an eyebrow. "Just don't hit on my wife again."

Brant put up his hand. "I promise. At least she wasn't your wife back then."

Cody glanced at the ceiling. "I, for one, am glad all that drama is over." His eyes landed on Brant, and he reached out his hand. They slapped palms and then bumped fists.

"You're telling me."

Jeff pulled the curtain back. "Who's riding?"

"Just me." Cody piped up.

"I'm staying to keep an eye on our patients and make sure they get home safely."

"All right. Spencer, take the cart of supplies out. Phillip will help you load."

Cody grabbed the cart and saluted to Brant before walking away.

Jeff grabbed the curtain. "You did good out there Ellington. I know it's hard when they are friends. I'm glad they will be okay."

"Thanks." Without another word, Jeff pulled the curtain shut. He had no idea how true his words were and didn't know the half of it. This accident immediately made Brant question whether he could handle the job. The memories of his accident roared back when he saw the yellow car smashed against the tree. Flashes of Abbie slumped over next to him still caused his breath to catch. It was painful to remember, although, what he hadn't expected was the sheer panic he felt when he realized the car they rolled up on was Bekah's. He barely knew her, and yet she had already gotten under his skin. Was it just the accident? Was it Maizy? It hadn't even been a year since he lost Abbie. He shouldn't be even noticing another woman. It was too soon. She was off limits anyway. She had a boyfriend, and she was his counselor.

He glimpsed up at Bekah, still sleeping peacefully. *This can't happen.*

Chapter Five

A familiar whine pierced through the thick fog in Bekah's head. *Maizy.* She tried to call out to her, but something was wrong. Her head throbbed. Body hurt. *Why? What happened? Bobby. No!* Her chest heaved. Tears burned. *Car lights, spinning. Explosion. Silence. Maizy?* Panic engulfed her body. "Ma...." *Dammit, what is wrong? Wake up.* The fog slowly cleared. Something warm caressed her hand. *Bobby?* Her heart raced. *Car lights. Can't see. Oh God. Spinning.* "MAIZY!" She screamed. "MAIZY!" A low rumble echoed. "She's fine." Blinking against the bright lights and the tears, she tried to focus. Standing before her was a giant of a man grasping her hand with one hand, cradling her baby with the other, and balancing a bottle with his chin. A crease formed between her brows.

"What are you doing here?" Her voice rasped.

A smile crossed his face. "Isn't it obvious? I'm babysitting," Brant said, trying to talk while keeping the bottle pressed to Maizy's mouth with his chin.

The corner of her mouth raised, and she sniffled. "You are pretty talented."

"Oh, you have no idea." A wolfish grin appeared as he continued to hold the bottle under his chin. She tucked her lips between her teeth and slid her hand away from his to wipe her tears. "Oh, sorry, I was just trying...you were screaming—"

"It's fine. I was having a hard time waking up." She lifted her head slightly, winced, and dropped it back to the pillow.

"They had to set your arm, so they gave you something to sleep."

Tears continued to stream down her face. "And Maizy's okay?"

"Yes. They ran x-rays and checked her out. She's fine."

Bekah pursed her lips and let out a long breath. "What time is it?"

He pulled his arm from beneath Maizy and checked his watch. "Twelve forty-five."

She squeezed her eyes shut trying to wrap her brain around what happened. "Okay, so I know I had an accident. I'm confused though, why you are here. Where's my granddad?"

"I told you, I'm babysi—" he said playfully.

"I heard you the first time. However, I don't understand how you found out—"

"I was riding with the paramedics. I'm training. And to answer your other question, we would have contacted your granddad or your boyfriend, except your phone is locked, and I couldn't remember your granddad's first name."

At the mention of her boyfriend, Bekah flashed on the revelation and fresh tears spilled down her cheeks. "Ah. Well, thank God you didn't call Bobby. He doesn't need to know anything regarding Maizy or me."

"Okay?" Brant responded. "I'm not going to ask."

"Thanks." A knot formed in her throat as her brain chose to replay the day. She was so excited to surprise Bobby then mortified to find him with Marissa. He was with Marissa. And not just today. How long had it been going on? Noticing Brant's concerned expression, she turned away and closed her eyes, failing to keep the sobs at bay.

After a moment she heard his voice. "Is there anything I can do?" She couldn't speak. The knot in her throat wouldn't allow it, so she shook her head. "Since we couldn't get in touch with your granddad I asked if they would release you to me. They said that would be fine as long as you are okay with it."

His voice was soft and soothing, and she could tell by his tone he was uncertain how she would respond. Trying to compose herself, she grabbed some tissues from the table and dabbed her cheeks. "You don't have to do that. I can call my grandpa Dale."

"Dale? Okay, maybe you didn't tell me. Anyway, it's no trouble, I already have the car seat base in my car."

"I feel terrible," she said hiccupping through her words. "I already have asked way too much of you."

"I don't mind. I want to make sure you get home okay. It's not like I have anything to go home to anyway."

"Are you sure?"

"I told you I don't mind. Geez, woman, you don't listen very well. Do you?"

His obvious need to make her smile finally worked and even had her laughing.

"I'm going to go let the nurses know you are awake so we can get out of here."

Bekah stared at the now sleeping baby in his arms. "I think she will be fine if you lay her beside me."

She scooted over, and he tenderly laid Maizy

against her. "I'll be right back."

****

Snow covered the road and continued to pelt the windshield as they turned up the driveway and made their way to the small rock cottage.

After giving Brant directions to her house, she dozed most of the way home. The sound of Brant opening the door stirred her from her dream, and she reached for her seatbelt.

"Stay here while I unload everything, and I will come get you."

"I can walk."

"Again, with the not listening. Stay here"—he motioned with his hands— "I am going to unload Maizy and the bags, and then I will come get you."

She lowered her head. "Yes, sir." Her mouth pinched together.

"Keys?"

"In my purse, I'm guessing?" She had never had anyone want to take care of her, and he was just one step up from being a stranger. She hated that she was so needy, but she was in no shape to decline his offer. Truth be told, her whole body hurt. It took everything within her not to cry out in pain just stepping from the wheelchair to the car.

"Found them." She heard the rear door shut and watched this hulk of a man make his way to her door like it was a normal day, with a baby carrier in one hand, two bags thrown over his shoulder, and big fat snowflakes pelting him from every direction. The security light came on and shined down on the top of his beanie, giving him a well-deserved halo.

He pushed open the door and disappeared for a

moment then returned to the car. Bekah opened the door and started to get out. She froze and hissed with the pain shooting down her back. Brant reached in and gently lifted her, then wrapped his arm around her waist pulling her close to him and walked her to the house. The smell of his cologne hit her nose, and she suddenly had the desire to bury her nose in his shirt. They stepped inside, and he ushered her to the sofa and carefully lowered her onto the cushion. With every movement, it seemed the pain was getting worse. More parts of her body hurt.

She let out a harsh moan, and Brant's eyes met hers. "I will get you something for that in a minute."

Her mind reeled. The pain surged through her body to the point she felt like she was shaking all over. Was it the pain or was she in shock? Possibly both. Tears threatened as the memories of the day flooded her thoughts again. She thanked God she and Maizy were okay, but the pain...there was no way she could take care of Maizy. Her gaze fixed on Brant as he gently returned a pacifier to Maizy's mouth, waiting until she latched onto it. How much exactly was she willing to let him do? She already felt horribly guilty for what she had put him through.

"Brant. You don't know how much I appreciate this but let me call my grandpa to come over and take care of me. You don't need to stay."

He kneeled and started unbuckling her shoe. "First off, it's one thirty in the morning. We do not need to be waking him up with the news that you have been in a car accident and need to be taken care of." He pulled her shoe off, set it on the floor, and started on the other. "That is not what a parent or grandparent wants to hear at one thirty in the morning. Second, I am already awake. Third, I am trained to take care of people." He pulled the other shoe off, set it on the floor, and grabbed a blanket from the end of the sofa and draped it across her legs. "And I am pretty damn good at it." He stood, and his hands hit his hips. She stared up at him. "Now, where is Maizy's room?"

"Second door on the left." He picked up the carrier and headed up the hall. She closed her eyes and leaned her head against the sofa cushion. How could this have happened? Tears formed as anger filled her chest and crawled up her throat threatening an audible growl. Visions of the platinum blonde hovering over her boyfriend...ex-boyfriend, captured her thoughts. Marissa was living with him. Bekah had suggested Bobby move in with her right after he showed up in Dalton, saying he didn't need to waste money on a place. Then she made the suggestion again after Maizy was born. He declined both times saying he wouldn't get any work done. He needed his quiet space. Obviously, he was lying, or didn't need that anymore.

Brant returned. "Your turn."

"Brant I—"

"You are not going to win this argument."

"I wasn't going to argue, I promise. I..." *Geez, this is embarrassing*, "I need to use the bathroom."

She saw the slightest flinch in his expression, then he let out a long sigh. "Okay." He leaned forward and helped her stand. "Which way?"

"First door on the left."

She could feel her cheeks burning like red coals as they entered the bathroom. How was this even possible? Could she even allow him to do this? *He's*

trained in this. It's just like if I were in the hospital.
Tears again streamed down her cheeks, not so much
from pain but from…all of it. It was getting to be too
much. The rumble of his voice pulled her from her
thoughts.

"Okay, we are going to do this together. You are
going to lift your skirt up, and I will do the rest. If you
need any help, say the word."

She nodded, completely giving up any dignity she
might have still had. At least she was wearing cute
panties not the granny panties she had to wear after
Maizy was born. She gathered her skirt up, and he used
his body to steady her while he pushed her panties
down averting his eyes along the way. Slowly he helped
her sit, then she let her skirt drop.

"Where are your pajamas?"

"Bottom right dresser drawer."

"I'll be right back."

He left, and she let out a long gush of air. Trying to
lean her elbow on her leg, she quickly realized it wasn't
going to happen when her back revolted against the
movement. Her whole body trembled from the pain,
both physically and mentally. Running her hand over
her forehead, trying to rub away the distress, she felt
something hard in her hairline and fished it out. Glass.
*When is this nightmare going to end? My life
disintegrated in one day.* She heard a knock on the
adjoining door to her bedroom.

"You done?"

"Yes."

The door pushed open, and Brant entered, still
obviously uncomfortable. "I was thinking. Do you want
to try to get a shower before bed? You have some dried

blood in a few spots."

She had to chuckle. "And apparently some glass too." She laid the granule on the counter. Yes, a shower would probably feel fantastic. However, she had basically surpassed her humiliation level for the year. It wasn't so much him seeing her naked. She was usually very comfortable with her body even though having a baby did make her a little self-conscious. It was more the constant feeling of utter helplessness. She let out a chuckle at the whole ordeal she couldn't seem to get past. "You are wanting to see me naked. Aren't you?"

Her glance captured something flash in Brant's expression. *What was that? Oh my gosh. What the hell is wrong with me? Not even twenty-four hours after I end a relationship and I'm imagining a guy I barely know hitting on me. He's here to help you, you moron.*

"God. I'm sorry. I shouldn't have…I didn't mean—"

Brant's face tightened. "Look, I know this is extremely uncomfortable for you. I get it. It is for me too. In all honesty though, whether I help you in the shower or help you put on your pajamas you are going to have to get undressed either way. I thought you might feel better rinsing off."

His sincerity surprised her. "I'm sorry for the remark. I am just so overwhelmed and thought laughing about it was better than crying." She let out a breath. "You're right. It's awkward because you are also my patient. Well, maybe." She tried to stand and winced. Brant quickly grabbed her arm. "It's just hard for me to wrap my head around all of this." Her eyes landed on his and the closeness had her sucking in a gasp to steady her heart that had suddenly decided to take off like a bullet. The more she spoke, the more unsteady her voice became. "Honestly, it's more about feeling helpless than you seeing me in all my naked glory." She grabbed her skirt while he pulled up her panties. "Why don't we do this. I am so exhausted I just want to go to bed and forget this day ever happened. But maybe washing off with a warm washcloth would feel good."

"Sounds like a plan. Let's get you to the bed, and we will go from there." Slowly he walked her into her room and got her settled on the bed. After removing the sling on her arm, he gathered her skirt and slid it down and helped her out of it, then grasped the hem of her shirt and lifted it gently over her head. *There it was again. That look. Almost like a spark flicker. Then with a twitch, it was gone. I didn't imagine it, though he is fighting like hell to conceal it.* Most wouldn't have caught it. But she was trained to read even the slightest twitch and knew exactly what it meant. However, she suddenly was second guessing her instincts wondering if her own attraction was coloring her thoughts. Heck, he rendered her speechless when they met, and she stared at him for a good five minutes when he was napping with Maizy on his chest. He was massive, well above six foot tall, and had a quiet composure about him that continually captured her attention. He turned and walked into the bathroom and returned quickly with a washcloth. The heat felt good against her skin. His touch was gentle as he ran the rag over her back and down the back of her legs then handed it to her to wash off areas she could reach without pain, which weren't many. She rubbed it over her face then handed it back to him. He leaned forward closing the distance between them and brushed the rag up into her hairline. She flinched when he hit a sensitive spot.

"Oh, sorry. Looks like the glass got you." He dabbed at it, and then set the rag down and picked up an oversized, pale blue T-shirt with 'Donut Disturb' and a photo of a glittery sprinkled donut on the front. His gaze centered on her eyes, but she noticed it drop to her chest for a split second as he wadded the side and slid the T-shirt over her splint. She pinched her lips together so she wouldn't smile. She could tell how hard he was trying to keep it professional, and it was kind of cute. He gently stretched the shirt over her head then retrieved the cotton shorts and slid them on. Once he was done, she shoved her legs under the covers and lay back.

"Okay, are you good?" She chewed her bottom lip. *Dear lord, this poor guy will be so glad to get away from me.* "What do you need?"

"I uh—"

He rolled his eyes. "It's okay," he said, almost sounding exasperated. "I'm here to help."

"I need to pump. Maizy hasn't nursed in eight hours. I'm dying."

"Okay. Where is it?"

"On the counter in the kitchen."

He disappeared up the hall and returned with his hands full of equipment and set it on the bed. "Did I get everything?"

"Yeah. Looks like it." She started trying to assemble it, although with one hand it was almost impossible. He grabbed up pieces and helped.

"You probably should dump that one after you pump since they gave you a sedative to set your arm."

"Oh, good point. I wonder when it will be safe for

her to nurse."

"I think you would be fine tomorrow, and the doctor said he prescribed you painkillers that were safe to take while you are nursing as long as you follow the prescribed dose."

"Wow, I'm glad he mentioned that."

"I asked," he stated continuing to assemble the pump.

"You did?"

He glanced up, meeting her eyes. "I figured you would want to know." After everything was put together, he stood.

"Thanks for everything, Brant. I don't know what I would have done without you."

"Oh, I'm not leaving. I'm going to get you some meds, then I'm sacking out on the sofa. I've got the baby monitor set up so I will hear if Maizy or you need anything."

"I—"

"Don't even start."

****

Light filtered through the gauzy curtains of the bedroom. Bekah shifted, and pain swiftly swept through her body. She groaned and tried to sit up but found it impossible.

Maizy hadn't been interested in sleeping in her bed after sleeping in the car, and then in Brant's arms. Bekah woke to her fussing several times only to see Brant, barefoot and shirtless, standing over her crib, or kicked back in the rocker, with Maizy sprawled across his chest. She pretended to sleep but kept peeking just to take in the scene. The streetlamp outside the bedroom window cast enough light to enhance the ripples of his muscular build. Maizy seemed so content sleeping in the center of his huge chest, and it almost seemed like he kind of enjoyed it, especially when she heard him whisper to Maizy while stroking her back.

Her nose caught a whiff of something. Was that coffee? *Oh my gosh that smells like heaven.* "Brant?" she called out tentatively. A clank came from the kitchen, then she heard the floor creak, and Brant appeared at the door.

"You okay?"

"Yeah. I just smelled something delicious."

"I'm making French toast. Want some?"

"Sure."

He stepped into the room. Although his feet were still bare, his shirt was back on, hanging loosely over his jeans. "Do you feel like getting up, or would you like me to bring you a plate?"

She laughed at the thought of him serving her breakfast in bed, though the edge to his tone made her think this whole attentive thing was a bit out of his wheelhouse. She tried to push herself up again and winced. "No, that's sweet of you to offer," she said through gritted teeth, "but I need to get up."

He reached down and threw the covers back, moved the pillow from under her arm out of the way, and grabbed her other arm lifting her up. She stood slowly.

"You good?" he asked, still supporting her.

"Yeah." With his arm still wrapped around her, she walked over to Maizy's crib and stared down at the tiny baby sleeping peacefully, with a fuzzy, pale pink blanket pulled halfway up. It was still surreal for her. Every time she saw Maizy, she couldn't believe that she was her baby; hers and Bobby's. A knot formed in her stomach as the memories of the previous day came crashing back. They would, now, forever be connected by Maizy. For months, that thought made her happy. Now, it made her sick.

She caught Brant out of the corner of her eye. His dark brown eyes held a softness to them, and his attention was solely on the sleeping baby. The warmth of his arm left her when he reached down and ran his fingers over Maizy's head. *This is what life is supposed to be like. Dammit, I can't. He's a client.*

"Thank you," she whispered without glimpsing back at him, because if she did, she would cry. The floor creaked, and she knew he had walked back up the hall. How in the hell did this man, this angel, get dropped into her life? She was supposed to be helping him get through a tough time in his life. Instead, he was thrust head-first into the shitstorm of hers. After this weekend, she doubted very seriously she would be comfortable with him as her client.

She gingerly made her way up the hall and caught him in the kitchen yawning into the back of his hand. Four bottles sat on the counter beside the sink. "She kept you up." He raised a brow and glanced at her from the corner of his eye. His hand reached for a cup and poured some coffee and set it on the counter. "I am so sorry."

"No need to apologize. I offered…actually, I didn't even offer. I told you I was staying and didn't give you a choice."

"I know, and you have no idea how much I appreciate it. I honestly don't know what I would have done if you hadn't been here."

"You wouldn't have been able to handle it. Heck, after last night, I have no idea how you are able to function when she doesn't sleep."

"You witnessed it. Sometimes there are days I am there only in body."

Brant served up two pieces of French toast and set the plate on the small table before returning to the kitchen.

"I assume you are either a vegetarian, or heaven forbid, an all-out carnivore, since I found eggs and butter and cheese in your fridge. I have to admit, I was a bit surprised."

Bekah put her finger to her mouth. "Shhh…someone might hear you."

"So, what is it?" She shook her head then braced herself on the table, and Brant quickly moved around the island to help her as she slowly sat down, then put some syrup and butter in front of her. "Let me know if you need me to cut it up."

Not wanting him to think she was completely helpless she glared at him then chuckled. "I'm not five."

He snickered, and she quickly realized eating with her left hand wasn't going to be easy. He sat down in the only other chair at the table and focused on her.

"I'm fine. It's soft enough that I can manage." She picked up a piece and slid it into her mouth. Setting the fork on her plate, she covered her mouth and spoke around the food. "It's delicious by the way."

"Thanks. I don't cook much, but I make do when I have to."

"You did pretty good for not being in your own home."

"I hope you don't mind."

"Seriously? After all you have done, I'm considering hiring you as my nanny."

"What's the pay?" Brant asked as he dredged his bite in the syrup.

"Unfortunately, I currently have no money in the coffers due to an ill-timed car accident." Her heart stumbled. "Oh shit. I have no car. I can't get to the office." She let out a sigh. "This just gets better and better."

"Does your granddad have a car?"

"Yeah. He still works part-time at the university though, and volunteers at the food bank, so he needs it."

"Do you think he could drive you until you can get your insurance settlement?"

"How much do you think it will take to fix it?"

Brant glanced at her and lifted his cup. "It's totaled. There is no fixing it." His expression turned solemn. "You and Maizy are really lucky."

Her gut clenched. "How bad was it?"

"The whole front fender well and passenger area were caved in so bad the windshield popped out. I can take you by to see it if you want."

"No. I don't think I could stomach it right now." She took a bite of her French toast. "I need to figure out what I'm going to do to get to work."

"I can take you to get a rental."

She tipped her head and gazed up at him. "You must think I am the most pathetic human being on the planet, because you keep riding up on your white horse to save me."

"Actually," he said with a chuckle, "the word Cody used was unconventional when he recommended you."

"I think I probably get that moniker quite a bit."

"Not gonna lie. When I first laid eyes on you, I kind of wanted to turn tail and run."

"I noticed. You paced like a caged wild animal."

"I wasn't sure if you were going to counsel me or perform some witchcraft voodoo shit on me." She wasn't sure if she should laugh or be offended by his comment. "But April and Joe and Cody and Jenna all said you were good at your job, and you came recommended from rehab, so I stayed, and I'm glad I did. You really are smart and have good insight." He shoved a piece of French toast in his mouth. "Anyway, everyone goes through tough times where they need help."

"I guess I'm really not used to it." She stared down at her plate feeling a pang of embarrassment. "I truly appreciate it though. You have been a godsend this past week. It feels like my life is out of control, and I'm normally a fairly independent and laid-back person. You have just walked in on a particularly messy time in my life."

"Yeah, you are going through some stuff. We all do though. Listening to my troubles, I guess, is what you are good at. Helping you get through yours is what I'm good at. And it is helping me along the way."

"How so?"

"When I was in the military, I always got a rush when we were called out. I had a chance to save lives, to help, maybe give someone a second chance, prevent another family from the shock of seeing the military on their doorstep."

"And you said you are in training to be a paramedic right now?"

"Yeah, I am taking a few final courses, and then I should be able to take the test and get certified in May. I'm hoping to go on and get my certification as a flight medic."

"What made you get into that field?"

"I think it was a combination of things. One, my family has always been in the spotlight, and I was never comfortable with all the focus on me and my life. I enjoyed helping others. When I was in high school, I played baseball, and initially I had planned on being a coach. That's what I went to college for, but when I took my first anatomy and physiology class, it fascinated me, and I wound up getting my degree in Athletic Training.

"While I was still in college, a crazy story broke out about our family, and I started getting hounded by the tabloids. It was all a bunch of lies, which was par for the course, and I tried to ignore the reporters, but at least once a day they chased me down. I was walking through the student union to try to get away, after noticing a photographer following me, and saw a recruiter from the air force. I figured it would take me off-grid for a while, and I enlisted."

"That's a pretty drastic move."

"I had thought about it before, and at the time I felt like I had no choice."

"Were you married then?"

"No. I met Abbie after I finished college and OTS. She worked at the BX at the base I was stationed at. I had seen her working up there off and on, and finally got the nerve up to talk to her. She had no idea who I was, or who my parents were, so that was a huge plus. Things clicked, and before I left for my tour in the middle east, we ran off and got married."

"You eloped?"

"Sure did. No tabloids, no paparazzi, just Abbie and me and the justice of the peace."

"So, how long were you married?"

"About a year and a half." He paused. "We barely got to see each other though. I knew her for about six months before I asked her out, then we dated for about four months before we eloped. We were together for about two months before I left, and then I was gone for almost a year." He peered up at her. "I was honorably discharged, and we moved to California. It didn't take long to realize that was not going to work. The minute we got settled, the paparazzi started hounding her. We had decided to move right before the accident." He leaned back in his chair. "So, how about you?"

She suddenly realized what she had put him through, having to see her and Maizy in the mangled car. His continual act of selflessness baffled her. "What?"

"You said you lived in California? Somehow I believe you were far removed from the Hollywood hype."

"Yeah, I was actually raised—"

"Let me guess. In a commune."

She laughed. "No. You aren't far off though, actually. My mom was."

He raised one brow. "Are you serious? I was kidding when I said that."

"Totally serious. So, mom was a dyed in the wool hippie. My dad came to California to go to UCLA and met her at a Farmer's Market. He said she was the most beautiful woman he had ever seen, and she converted him, to my grandparents' dismay. He dropped out of school, where he was studying biochemistry, to become a farmer. We lived on a plot of land with goats and chickens and other animals. Dad basically used his education to grow organic crops. Now, they are living off the grid and growing hemp."

Brant chuckled. "Sounds so cliché. I am surprised you aren't named Moon or Star or something." Bekah lifted her brows and pulled her mouth to one side, letting out a sigh. "Oh?"

"They didn't go quite that far, but my middle name is Lake, after the place they met."

He chuckled again and nodded. "Good thing it wasn't at the gas station."

"Yeah. Dad and his buddies had gone to the lake for the weekend, and there was a big Farmer's Market set up nearby. Needless to say, Grandpa and Grandma were not happy with the arrangement. Grandma was a middle school teacher and Grandpa a professor in technical design at the college. They had much higher hopes for their son than farming. So, since they figured they weren't going to get their way with him, they would shoot for the grandkids. They told me and my brother they would pay our way through college if we would go.

"In all honesty, I appreciated the fact that they pushed me to think independently. Don't get me wrong. I love my hippie heritage too. There are many qualities that have molded me into who I am. People tend to think hippies go through life flying by the seat of their pants, and I guess some do. For me though, I wanted more."

"Okay. So how in the world did you get into

forensic psychology?"

"I was a reader. We didn't have a TV when I was growing up, and my mom would take us to the library pretty much on a weekly basis. When I got to be, oh, maybe thirteen, I got my hands on my first murder mystery, and I was hooked. By that time, Mom really didn't pay attention to what I was reading, so I was checking out all kinds of psychological thrillers and mysteries. I always tried to solve the crime before I got to the end of the book and kept a journal of who I thought had done it. I had a pretty good track record. I loved trying to get into the mind of the criminal."

"So, are you getting to do much crime work living here?"

"Not too terribly much. I love what I am doing though. It all kind of fits together. I have my own practice. I can set my own hours, and I have a decent clientele. That is if I can get little girl on a schedule that doesn't cause my clients to have to become babysitters."

"Eh, I was happy to help."

"Truth be told, you looked way out of your element when I put her in your arms. But I was so exhausted I was too tired to care.

He sat for a second and twisted his lips. "Can I ask you something?"

"Sure."

"Why did you say you were glad I didn't call your boyfriend when we were in the ER?"

Her heart thudded in her chest. Why was he asking? Did she really want to delve into her private life with him? She had probably already bored him to tears with her life history. However, her girlfriends who are also his friends, were bound to find out, so he was going to find out anyway eventually. Letting out a deep breath, she contemplated where she should start. "Well, long story short, I was going to surprise him at his apartment in Oklahoma because today is his birthday. I got balloons and cupcakes and party hats, and piled everything in the car yesterday, and drove all the way over to Lancaster, only to find him with one of the women he works with in a very non-platonic situation."

Voicing it felt like fingers closing on her throat. "What's worse is, I am pretty sure this isn't the first time. There were signs in the apartment that led me to believe she has made it her home." Her throat closed a little more, and she could feel tears coming. "I actually brought up moving in together a few times especially when I found out we were having a baby, and he always said he needed his space so he could work." She bit the corner of her mouth. "I guess now I know what he was working on."

Chapter Six

Brant knew he didn't like the guy from the first time Bekah mentioned him. Seeing her try to fight back tears made him want to find the bastard and level him. Who, in their right mind, would leave their wife or girlfriend with a week-old baby to go back to work in a different state? Bekah looked so hurt, telling him about finding the dipshit hooking up with another woman. It made Brant feel guilty for asking. Curiosity got the best of him. He knew she was angry at him for some reason but didn't quite expect that. A tiny cry came over the monitor. Brant perked up. "Someone's awake." He picked up their plates and set them in the sink then turned to head up the hall.

"When did you feed her last?" Bekah called to him still sitting at the dining table.

"She had a bottle at about six, so she's probably getting hungry," he responded as he made his way to the bedroom. Maizy stared up at him when he peeked into her crib. His chest tightened, and a smile crossed his face. "Did you sleep well, baby girl?" She opened her eyes wide. "Did you? Did you have good dreams?" He propped her up on his shoulder and felt her tiny fingers wrap around the collar of his shirt.

He walked back out to the living area and saw Bekah staring at the monitor on the table and smiling with tears streaming down her cheeks. Heat flooded his face. He hadn't realized his voice was carrying through the monitor when he talked to Maizy. She glanced back at him wiping tears away. "I bet she had great dreams."

The doorbell rang.

Saved by the bell. "I'll get it."

"It's probably my grandpa wondering whose car is in the driveway."

Brant pulled open the door. The frigid air caught him by surprise, and he quickly wrapped his arms around Maizy to shield her. He was fully expecting a gray-haired man to be waiting on the other side. Instead, a slender guy with thick plastic-rimmed glasses stood, wearing a wrinkled gray suit-jacket over a T-shirt. *Must be Bobby.*

Confusion filled the man's face, then irritation, as his eyes scanned Brant.

"Uh…is…Bekah here?"

Brant held back a smirk at the weakness in his voice. If he weren't holding the baby his hands would already be wrapped around the weasel's throat. He quickly glanced back at Bekah wondering if it was a good idea for her to deal with him right now, then turned back to Bobby. "She is not available right now." He growled.

Bobby took a step back and crossed his arms. "Where is she, and why in the hell are you holding my daughter?" His voice increased in volume as he spoke.

"Let him in," came an exasperated voice over Brant's shoulder.

"Are you sure?" He responded still glaring at Bobby. "This is your house. You don't have to talk to him if you aren't up to it." He turned slowly to face her.

"Now is as good a time as any. I want to get this

over with."

Brant stepped away from the door not even pulling it open fully. Bobby pushed his way in, then stared at Bekah, who was slowly pushing herself up from the table. Brant quickly moved to her side to help her to the sofa.

"Do you want to try to feed Maizy, or do you want me to give her a bottle?" Brant asked ignoring Bobby.

"I want to feed her. Can you get me the nursing pillow under the crib?" Brant nodded, and she smiled up at him. He was proud of how she was handling the situation. Not letting Bobby take control.

Bobby stood in the middle of the living room with his mouth open. His eyes bounced between Brant and Bekah. "What happened to you, and who is this asshole holding our baby?"

Brant turned and walked out of the room with thoughts of laying out Bobby's whiney ass with a fist to his face. He didn't like him when Bekah was talking about him. Now, after seeing him, he couldn't stand to be in the same room with him. But for Bekah's sake, he also didn't want to leave her alone with him. He grabbed the pillow and returned moments later to see Bekah trying to get comfortable on the sofa and Bobby standing there watching as she winced in pain, not lifting a damn finger to help her. Handing her the pillow, Brant made sure she was comfortable by adding a couple of pillows behind her, then lowered Maizy into her good arm and draped the blanket over her shoulder.

His phone buzzed in his pocket, so he walked into the kitchen although he kept Bekah in his line of sight. She still hadn't uttered a word to Bobby. Dragging his phone from his pocket, he noticed a message on his screen.

—Soon we will be together—

The messages were creeping him out, and he hadn't wanted to respond, but it was the same one that had sent the two previous texts and figured the person hadn't realized they had the wrong number. He texted back "wrong number," and dropped his phone back in his pocket then let his attention settle back on Bekah.

After getting Maizy settled, she slowly met Bobby's glare, and that was all he needed.

"What the hell is going on? Who is he?" He pointed toward the kitchen.

"Why do you care?" She kept her voice even.

"He is carting around my baby."

"*Our* baby. He's helping me take care of her. And again, I ask, why do you care? You have made it perfectly clear that you don't want to have anything to do with her or me for that matter."

Bobby glanced at Brant before returning his attention to Bekah, and his shoulders lowered. "Can we discuss this in private?"

Bekah fixed her gaze on Brant, and he wondered if she was going to ask him to leave. He already knew he would argue with her to stay. There was something about Bobby, beyond what he did to her, that he didn't trust. "No. I need him here to help me."

"I can help you."

"No. He's trained. I want him to stay."

"Fine." His fingers pulled at his hair as he paced. "I know I messed up, Bekah," he mumbled, lowering his voice, obviously trying to keep Brant from hearing his comment. "That's why I'm here. I came to apologize and tell you I'm sorry. I have tons of work that I need to be doing this weekend, but here I am." He started pacing again and turned away from her.

"Then maybe you should have been doing that instead of having a joy ride with Marissa last night."

"It was a moment of weakness." He wrapped his hand around the back of his neck.

"It was?" Bekah said in a patronizing tone.

He turned to face her. "Shit, Bekah. What do you expect? We haven't had…" His eyes cut to Brant and his voice quieted even more. "We haven't been together in months."

Brant moved out of the kitchen and pulled out the chair at the dining room table. "She expected you to keep it zipped up. That's what a man would do."

Bobby glared at Brant.

Bekah's eyes bored into Bobby. "That was on you, not me. I told you the doctor said it was fine."

"Seriously, Bekah? You were huge."

Brant stood. He couldn't stand to let this moron take one more minute of Bekah's time. "And now you need to leave," he said opening the door.

"I'm not going anywhere until I get some answers."

Brant looked at Bekah and pinched his lips. She smirked and waved him off. He shut the door, although he stood by, ready to grab Bobby and throw him out if necessary.

"You were always great with compliments," she said sarcastically shaking her head. Bobby set his hands on his hips and rolled his eyes.

"You know what I meant."

"No. No, I don't," she said as she adjusted the pillow Maizy lay on. "Anyway, not that I really should waste my breath on you, what's your question?"

"Questions," he immediately shot back. His head jerked to Brant. "Who is he, and why is he here?"

"And I told you, he is taking care of me and Maizy because I can't right now."

"What happened?"

"Car accident on the way home yesterday."

"Why didn't you call me?"

"You aren't seriously asking that question, are you?"

"Yes, I am."

"Uh…could it be because you were busy planting your seed in Marissa?"

"Bekah, you don't have to be disgusting."

"Well, it's kind of hard not to be disgusting when that's all I feel for you right now. You knew how much I wanted to spend your birthday with you. I made that very clear. And to know that you out and out lied to me, saying that you had to work, then to find you with her—"

"Dammit, Bekah, I said I was sorry. It was one time. It won't happen again. I just made a mistake."

"Oh, are you sure that's the story you want to stick with?"

Bobby's face blanched. Brant tucked his lips between his teeth trying not to laugh. His eyes met Bekah's. She smirked as she hammered the nail into Bobby's coffin.

"Wha…what are you talking about?"

"What? You didn't think I would notice she had moved in when I was too busy running away? Did you forget that part of my job is to notice things? Seems like you and Miss Marissa have made yourself a happy little home in Oklahoma."

"Why do you think that?"

"Oh, there were plenty of clues. I don't think you bought that shaggy rug in the living room on your own, or the candles that were nicely placed on the tables for that matter. And I'm certain the pictures of flowers on the walls were not something you purchased for yourself just to dress the place up. However, Marissa could have just helped you make the place homier, I guess. Although I don't really believe it's even close to your style. No. The one glaring clue that stood out to me was probably the makeup and mirror on the vanity in the bedroom that gave me such a great view of her from both sides as she—"

"—that's enough."

"Is it? Are you sure? I could go on." Bobby hung his head obviously realizing she had him, and Brant couldn't have been happier.

"Bekah, I can ex—"

"Explain? How's this. You never wanted us to be a family. I asked you several times about moving in together, and you always said you needed your space to work. It became quite clear to me yesterday what you needed to work on."

"Come on, Bekah."

"No, Bobby. It's okay. You made your decision, so I've made mine. This—" She motioned between them. "—is over. You are free to go about your merry way and spread your seed wherever you please." Bobby threw his arms in the air then turned to leave. "Before you leave," he rolled his eyes as he glanced back at her, "I think I will answer your question." Her head slowly turned, and her gaze landed on Brant. "That man there."

She tried to point with her splinted arm. "He is more of a man than you will ever be. He is the medic who took care of Maizy at the accident and afterward at the hospital. He offered to help me because he realized I had no one, and I wouldn't be able to take care of her by myself. He has held her, rocked her, fed her, and changed her diapers more in one night than you have since she was born."

Bobby's face paled as he glanced at Brant, and silence fell, before he turned back to Bekah. "Did you do it on purpose?"

Bekah's brows dipped. "Do what?"

"The accident. You know, because—"

Her face filled with color as anger washed over it. A growl filled her voice. "Hell no. You seriously think I would do anything to hurt this little girl because you cheated? You are a true piece of shit to even think that. You aren't worth it." Tears streamed down her face. Brant stepped closer to the door. Thoughts of grabbing Bobby and tossing him out in the snow brought a smirk to his face.

Bobby's face softened, and he stared at the blanket on Bekah's shoulder. "Is she okay?"

"Finally," she barked, with a sarcastic chuckle.

"Finally, what?"

She tipped her head and sucked her bottom lip in. "How long have you been here?" Sitting up, she winced as she checked the clock on the TV console. "Looks like about twenty minutes." Her eyes met his again. "In all that time, you haven't once asked about Maizy, other than treating her like she is nothing more than a piece of your damn property that someone had taken. It took you this long to ask if she was all right. That tells me everything I need to know. You haven't asked to see her or hold her. Hell, you barely even looked at her. Since you asked though, and only because you are her father, I think you deserve to know. She is fine." She lifted the blanket and stared down at Maizy. "Now, I am getting kind of tired, and I'm in quite a bit of pain, so I would like you to leave." Brant opened the door. "I think I have answered all the questions I care to."

Bobby's eyes stayed fixed on her; shame now evident on his face. "Bekah, I—"

"She asked you to leave. I suggest you do it," Brant rasped, "because you don't want me to get involved. Trust me."

Bobby's head jerked to Brant then back to Bekah. She opened her eyes wide and tipped her head. He turned and walked out the door. Brant slammed it behind him and then spun around to Bekah. "You okay?"

She sighed. "Yeah. I think so."

"You know, it's none of my business, but he never asked if you were okay either."

She shrugged. "I really don't care anymore. He's not worth my time."

A smirk crossed his face, and he shook his finger in her direction. "You are a badass, young lady. You had him shaking in his shoes."

"It helped to have a brick wall on my side."

Brant crossed his arms. "My size comes in handy sometimes."

The doorbell rang again. He huffed preparing to pummel the bespectacled ass. However, when he yanked open the door, he found a distinguished older gentleman with white hair and eyes the same translucent green as Bekah's.

Brant glanced back at Bekah.

"Hey, Grandpa." The gray-haired man glanced at Bekah, then Brant, then back to Bekah with concern. "I'm okay. I had an accident last night coming back from Oklahoma."

"I think she hit some black ice," Brant added shutting the door.

"Are you okay? Is Maizy okay? I came by because I saw Bobby leaving in a hurry, and he seemed a bit miffed. I figured something was up." He quickly closed the distance between them. "Why didn't you call me, kiddo?" His hand caressed her hair before he pulled out a chair from the dining room table. Positioning it facing her, he sat down.

"You see this, Brant. This is why I love my grandpa so much. He loves us. He would do anything to protect and take care of me and Maizy."

She let her eyes settle on Dale. "I would have called, but it was already past one when they discharged me from the ER. I didn't want to bother you so late." Her attention traveled to Brant. "Brant was the medic taking care of Maizy, and he is also a friend and offered to stay and take care of us."

Dale turned to Brant. "Thank you, son."

"Oh, I guess I should introduce you. Grandpa, this is Brant Ellington." She glanced at Brant. "Brant, Dr. Dale Adkins. Otherwise known as Grandpa Dale."

Brant reached out and shook his hand. "Pleasure to meet you, sir. Bekah speaks highly of you."

"She and that little girl right there are pretty special people to me."

"Apparently, it's mutual." Brant smiled, paused,

then clapped his hands together. "Well, let me give you a run down on what is going on." He pulled out the other chair from the dining room and sat down. "Bekah hit some black ice and spun into a tree out on highway 51. The car was totaled. I will let Bekah know where it was towed in case something was left that she needs to retrieve. As far as injuries, Maizy is fine. She was checked out thoroughly, had a few x-rays, and they found nothing. Other than deciding she would rather stay up all night than sleep, I haven't seen anything to indicate otherwise.

"Bekah has greenstick fractures of her radius and ulna just above the wrist. They set the arm and splinted it, and she has an appointment to get it casted once the swelling has gone down. The card is over there on the table. The doctor said she has a level two whiplash which will heal on its own although she probably shouldn't be lifting anything other than Maizy for the next week or so. She is moving pretty slow. The doctor prescribed something for the pain for the next couple of days. She also has a mild concussion. When we arrived at the scene, she was unconscious and remained unconscious until we got her to the hospital."

"So are you an EMT or—"

"Paramedic in training. I'll get my certification this summer. I was a PJ medic in the Air Force for about five years."

"Well, thank you for your service, and thank you for taking care of these two." He paused. "So, was Bobby here too? I'm a little confused."

Bekah let out a sigh. "We broke up."

Grandpa Dale leaned forward on his chair, and Brant saw a slight twitch of his mouth. "Can't say that

I'm not relieved. He wasn't good enough for you, kiddo. Never thought he treated you right."

"Well, he sure didn't yesterday."

"Do I need to have a talk with the boy?"

Brant chuckled. "I think she handled it pretty well. Your granddaughter is kind of a badass." Bekah's mouth dropped open.

Dale joined Brant, chuckling. "I know. She takes after her grandma."

Shaking her head at the two of them, her gaze then turned to the sleeping baby.

Brant stood. "Would you like me to take her and put her down?"

"Sure."

He leaned over and gently gathered Maizy in his arms and walked away."

"I like him."

"Grandpa. He can hear you."

Brant chuckled as he headed up the hall. "No, I can't." He slowly lowered Maizy in her crib and got her tucked in before strolling back down the hall.

"So, Grandpa, do you want to help me with Maizy the next couple of days? I am still getting used to this." She motioned to the splint wrapped around her arm. A flash of worry spread across Dale's face. Brant raised a brow to Bekah then rubbed the stubble on his jaw.

"If it's all right, I thought I would hang out a little while longer, maybe give your granddad some pointers."

"I would appreciate that. I haven't changed a diaper or fed a baby in a long, long time. I guess since she was a baby." Dale's head bobbed to Bekah.

"Well, you probably won't have to do much

feeding. Those diapers though—" Brant made a sour face. "—they can be pretty potent."

"Well," Dale stood. "I was actually leaving to go pick up some papers from the college when I saw Bobby." He patted Bekah on the shoulder. "Let me go grab them so I can get my grading done, and then I'm all yours."

"That sounds great."

He grabbed his chair and returned it to the table then placed a soft kiss on the top of Bekah's head.

"Is there anything I can get while I'm out?"

"Wanna grab some burgers for lunch?" Bekah responded quickly.

"Ha! You are a full-blown carnivore," Brant said with a satisfied grin.

"I love meat. Nothing against those who are vegan, I'm just not one of 'em."

"She gets that from me," Dale said proudly.

A bright smile lit up her face. "He took me on secret hunting trips."

Dale winked at Bekah then pulled the door open and disappeared.

Brant grabbed the rest of the dishes from the table and walked into the kitchen. "I like him."

"Funny, I think he said the same of you."

He came back into the living room. "So, you wanna try to get a bath while Maizy is asleep and your granddad is out?"

A flash of concern pierced her face. Then she answered, "Sure."

"You can wait. I figured you wouldn't be able to do it on your own and unless you wanted to call one of your girlfriends, it was either me or Grandpa Dale."

Her expression turned to horror. "We're good. Actually, a shower does sound really nice." She scooted to the edge of the sofa, and Brant grabbed her hand and helped her stand. "What am I going to do without you?"

"Well, you did say you needed a nanny."

"I also said all my funds will be going toward finding me a new ride."

He walked with her into the bathroom. "I don't need money. If you need help, I have some time before I have to be on set. That would at least give you time to get up and around better."

"Watch out, or I might take you up on that."

"I'm serious." He turned on the shower and adjusted the temperature.

"That's sweet—"

"You said your granddad had to work, so his help is going to be limited. My schedule is fairly open other than my classes, and they are more or less a review so—"

"You're serious?"

"Geez. Pay attention, would you. I just said I was serious."

"Then you're hired."

"Okay then. We can work out the schedule later. Right now, let's focus on getting you cleaned up."

Grabbing the towel and washcloth, he set them on the side of the tub then gathered the bottom of her T-shirt. The back of his fingers brushed against her skin, and his entire body tightened. *Oh crap.* Turning his head away, he sucked in a deep breath and lifted her shirt over her head, then gingerly slid the sleeve over the splint. He glanced back at her face as her arm draped over her breast and eyes stared at the ceiling.

She turned away, and he pushed the elastic of her shorts down, letting her step out of them along with her panties before grabbing her hand to help her into the tub.

She reached up and pulled the bright pink band from her hair, letting her caramel and honey-colored waves loose. Biting into his lip, he tried to calm the fire that had ignited in his gut. Taking another deep breath, he soaped up the washcloth and let the soap travel down her back and legs, before he rubbed it against her bronze skin, all while trying to keep his body from having a complete meltdown. *What the hell was I thinking?* He swallowed hard and tried to keep his eyes averted, but there was no way not to see her standing in front of him. Even with the little baby belly, she was a goddess. Every part of her was toned. She dipped her head under the stream of water, and an inferno swirled through him as he watched the water cascade down her face to her neck and over her breast. Quickly turning away, he handed off the washcloth and grabbed the shampoo. The rich sandalwood scent filled his nose. A smell that had become familiar after being around her. He poured some in his hands and rubbed it into her hair and suddenly was facing the inferno head on as the suds somehow moved in slow motion over every portion of her body.

"I think I'm good."

Her words jerked him from his trance. "What?"

"I'm good to rinse."

"Oh. Right."

He guided her under the water hoping to bring this bad idea to an end. The water running over her body just increased the desire that had flared up like a strike of lightning. After squeezing the last of the suds out of her hair, he turned the water off and handed her a towel before helping her out of the tub, thanking God that it didn't take a second longer. But, as she stepped out, her foot hooked on the edge of the tub, and her wet naked body crashed into him. Letting out a pained grunt, and not from her collapsing on him, he grabbed the towel that was threatening to fall to the floor, if they moved, and held it up long enough for her to gain her balance, then wrapped it around her.

Helping her into some flannel pajama pants and another tank top that said "I come in peace" with a peace sign, he finally let out a breath, glad that the whole ordeal was over. Brant figured she could tell he was struggling. His eyes met hers, and she smirked, before he led her back into the living room and helped her curl up on the sofa. *Mental note. Call her girlfriends to help with showers.*

Chapter Seven

This can't be happening. Bekah's head was spinning and not from the concussion she currently was nursing. The afternoon was spent on the sofa, listening to her grandpa and Brant talk like they were old friends. Grandpa Dale was telling Brant some stories about when Bekah was young, and although she feared her cheeks were going to be permanently flushed, her heart was on fire. It was probably because she was coming off a very traumatic accident and he helped her. Or it could be that she had been thoroughly humiliated by her ex, and Brant was paying attention to her. Whatever it was, something in her brain had kicked into high gear when he put his hands on her, helping her bathe. He was lucky she didn't throw her cold, wet body against his when she got out of the shower. Oh. Wait. She kind of did. It was strictly an accident because she lost her balance. Sort of.

Even worse, she could swear she saw that fire in his eyes too. *Holy cow, what am I going to do?* Against her better judgement, *because let's be real, that seemed to be way overpowered by her other desires at the moment,* she worked out a deal with Brant to stay at her house for the next few days, to help her with Maizy and take care of daily chores that she wouldn't be able to handle. Grandpa Dale would fill in when he was available which would allow Brant to take care of his business. The weird thing was, with all the excitement of the accident yesterday, she felt peaceful today. Even with the confrontation with Bobby, she couldn't explain the quiet calm she felt. It was something she hadn't felt since Maizy was born, and possibly before. Brant had been a godsend.

When he ran home to grab some clothes after lunch, he stopped by the grocery store to stock up for the week and then cooked dinner for them. She watched her grandpa and him laughing like it was something they normally did after dinner. That would have never happened with Bobby. He had barely spoken to her grandpa the entire time he'd been living in Dalton.

There was one thing on her mind she hoped to talk to Brant about after her grandpa left for the evening. When he finally said goodbye and the door shut behind him, Bekah's heart took off like a racehorse at the sound of the starter pistol. Brant turned to her. She could tell from the heaviness of his eyes, he was beat. Maizy hadn't slept well after the accident, and he had been up with her most of the night. This last detail needed to be addressed though. Might as well get it taken care of now, so they could move forward.

"So, how do you want to do this tonight? Do you want me to bring her to you, or do you want me to bottle feed her?"

"I don't mind feeding her if you will deal with the diapers."

"Sure, make me deal with the smelly end."

"Well…I don't know if I can—"

"I'm just picking on you. I'm good with whatever."

"Okay. I just don't want you feeling like I am taking advantage of you."

"Isn't that what I'm supposed to do to you?"

Bekah's mouth dropped open at Brant's question. That was the second time he had out and out flirted. His face filled with color.

"I'm sorry. I didn't mean…I was joking. And, from the expression on your face, it was a bad, bad joke."

Bekah couldn't hold back a laugh from the sheer embarrassment on his face. Probably similar to the expression she had after her comment earlier about him wanting to get her naked. Seems they both had their thoughts taking them to places they shouldn't be visiting. Thoughts she wasn't sure she could even act upon if she wanted to. "Gotcha!" Brant smirked and let out a nervous chuckle then stood.

"What time did she go down?"

"I think I fed her about an hour and a half ago. I'm betting she will be up in the next half hour. She's only been sleeping at max a couple of hours."

"Do you want to go ahead and get comfortable in bed?"

"Yeah. I need to talk to you about something first, if you don't mind." Her voice filled with a serious tone.

Brant slowly sat back down on the end of the sofa opposite her. A pained expression filled his face.

"I really appreciate all you have done for me and Maizy this past week. There is no way I'll ever be able to repay you—"

"No need—"

"I say it because it has led me to a realization about your counseling." Brant's head tipped, questioning. "I can't take you on as a client."

"Okay," he said slowly. "Wh—"

She put her hand up halting his question. "I have guidelines that I follow when I accept patients. One is, that they are complete strangers to me. Or I am only at an acquaintance level with them. I try to keep my personal life and business life separate. Once I have crossed the line into a friendship, I can't be objective in my counseling. I become vested in that person. Feelings can get in the way of giving the best advice. With all we have been through in the past twenty-four hours, I would say we are more than acquaintances."

Brant twisted his mouth. "Well damn. Okay, I understand. I was kind of looking forward to learning some of those yoga moves though."

"Oh, I can still teach you that, if you really want me to. Although, it will be off the books so you can't sue me if you pull a muscle. It's friends helping friends."

"Got it." He nodded. "Yeah, I can see where trying to counsel a friend on a professional basis would be difficult."

"I have plenty of former clients who are now my friends. There is a tendency for that to happen in such a small town and especially if they are in my age range. April and Joe, and Cody, and Jenna were all my clients at one time. Unfortunately, our friendship happened before I got the opportunity to counsel you, and I wanted you to know why I have to turn you down as a client."

"I would still like your advice and insight if you are willing to give it."

"Oh, trust me, I am always willing to offer up advice. Sometimes even when you aren't asking for it."

A rustling sound came through the baby monitor followed by several grunts and whimpers. "Sounds like someone is up. Let me help you get settled in bed, and then I will bring her to you."

Brant grabbed her hand and pulled her up off the

sofa and escorted her to the bed. Once she was settled, he brought Maizy to her. "Where are your extra blankets and pillows?"

"Oh, the linen cabinet is at the end of the hallway." He disappeared, and she could hear him rustling in the cabinet. A few minutes later he returned. "Did you find what you needed?" she asked without lifting her head.

"Yeah, I made me a bed on the sofa." His hands were perched on the footboard of the bed. "Is she asleep?"

"Yeah. She just hasn't eaten well today, and she has been so fussy." She passed Maizy off to him and smiled as his face softened when he focused on the sleeping baby.

"Probably a phase she is going through." He laid her in her bed then turned back to Bekah. "I'll get up with her. You feed her."

"Sounds like a plan."

****

Bekah sucked in a long breath when she saw Brant leaning over the crib for the second time. The clock glowed twelve fifteen in the morning. She flipped on the bedside lamp then slowly scooted up. Pain shot through her. She just wanted to get some sleep, and she felt bad having Brant do all the legwork even though he never once complained. The last time they got up, Maizy rutted around for a few minutes but wouldn't eat. He changed her diaper, then sat and rocked her for half an hour before she went back to sleep. And now, she was up again. Bekah had to admit though, she didn't mind peeking at Brant shirtless while he rocked her.

"Are you ready for miss fussypants?" he asked while staring at Maizy.

"Sure. I'm hoping she will eat this time."

He gently placed her in Bekah's arms. "Let me know when you are ready for me to come get her." The floor creaked as he made his way back to the living room.

Bekah closed her eyes and napped while Maizy nursed. Finally, she seemed to be eating. A cough pulled Bekah from dozing. She sat Maizy up and patted her on her back. Maizy coughed again then spit up. Pink milk spilled onto the burp cloth. At first Bekah was confused. *What in the world? Why is it pink?* Maizy hiccupped and spit up again, this time a deeper shade of red. "Oh crap! Brant!" She heard the thuds of his footsteps as he came up the hallway.

"What's wrong?"

"Maizy." Her voice caught. "She threw up blood."

"Let me see." He flipped on the overhead light and checked the burp cloth. "Oh, yeah. That's blood." He slowly sat on the side of the bed. "Okay. Could you have blood in your breast milk?"

"I mean, I could. I think I would be in pain though."

Maizy hiccupped again and more pink-tinged milk poured out. Bekah's heart raced. Terror filled her as she lifted her eyes to Brant.

"Okay, let me get my clothes on, and I will be right back. Sit tight."

She watched the light go on in the living room and heard him banging around. He came back into the bedroom carrying the car seat. "Let's get her bundled up and strapped in, and then I will get your coat and shoes on."

Within five minutes they were out the door. Light

snow was now falling. There was a new untouched layer on the road. The highway was desolate. Bekah rolled the scenarios through her brain. What if Maizy was hurt in the accident? What if they didn't catch it when she was examined? What if it's serious? She fixed her eyes on Brant, whose sober stare out the windshield tore her to pieces. She could tell he was worried too. Trying to see how Maizy was doing, she turned, but her back locked up on her. She let out a pained groan and tipped her head against the seat trying to fight the tears. She was crumbling inside.

The warmth of his hand wrapped around hers. "She is going to be okay, Bekah," he said softly. She wasn't used to hearing her name on his lips, and somehow it gave her comfort. His eyes twinkled from the passing streetlights as he glanced at her. They were filled with reassurance, though she could still see the worry behind them, and she broke.

Turning away, she stared out the window as tears streamed down her cheeks. "It's all my fault. I shouldn't have gone to Oklahoma. I knew the weather was going to turn bad."

"It's not your fault, Bekah. This may not have anything to do with the wreck."

"What if it does? What if she's hurt? What if something wasn't caught? I should have been more careful."

"If there is something wrong, we will deal with it. She will be fine."

"God. I should have known something was wrong. She wasn't eating."

"Bekah. Stop. She is going to be okay." His voice was stern yet caring. He rubbed his thumb across the back of her hand, and she brought her gaze to his.

Silence took over. Mile marker after mile marker passed. She felt like they were moving so slow. Finally, they pulled up under the awning of the emergency entrance. Brant hopped out and grabbed Maizy and then helped Bekah. The emergency room was almost empty, and they were able to take Maizy back immediately.

"I'm Dr. Coleman," a bearded man with curly black hair stated, when he pulled the curtain back on the cubicle. His badge let them know he was a pediatrician. "What is going on with this pretty little girl?"

Bekah swallowed hard. "She wasn't nursing well today, and about thirty minutes ago she started spitting up blood."

Dr. Coleman's lips pinched together. "Have you eaten anything spicy that might have upset her stomach?"

"No." She shook her head emphatically.

"She was in a car accident last night. We brought her here, and they checked her out. Said she was fine," Brant offered.

The doctor tilted his head. "Well, let me take a look at her, and then I'm going to order a few more tests just to be on the safe side."

Brant pulled the sleeping baby from the carrier and laid her on the gurney. The doctor unsnapped her sleeper, grabbed his stethoscope, and warmed it in his hands before laying it on her bare belly. He gently lifted her and listened to her back, managing not to wake her. "Okay, we are going to get a couple of x-rays and then an ultrasound."

Brant grabbed the carrier and baby bag, put his arm

around Bekah, and followed the doctor, who was carrying Maizy into another room. As the technician placed Maizy in a black pouch, Bekah and Brant stepped behind a glass partition. Bekah's fingers covered her mouth. Her chest heaved as she tried to stifle her tears. Brant wrapped his arm around her and leaned into her ear.

"She's fine. This doesn't hurt her. They are just getting some x-rays."

She buried her face in his chest. "I can't watch."

The technician pulled Maizy from the pouch. Maizy's eyes were blinking rapidly but she wasn't making a sound. The doctor moved them into another room and laid Maizy on a gurney then left the room. A technician stood beside the bed and dropped some jelly on a tiny wand and placed it on Maizy's belly. She squirmed and kicked her legs then let out a whimper. Bekah put her hand on Maizy's head to try to calm her. After several passes with the wand, the technician tore off several photos from the machine that she had taken. Within a short time, the doctor returned with the x-rays in hand and studied the photos the technician provided. He looked up at Brant, then Bekah.

"I don't see anything to be alarmed about. Everything appears absolutely normal."

Bekah put her hand to her chest and let out a sigh of relief. Brant wrapped his arms around her.

"She's strictly breast fed?"

Brant's eyes widened. "When we brought her in after the car accident, Bekah was still unconscious, so I got a couple of bottles of formula to feed her."

"Ah. That might have been the culprit. She may have been sensitive to that formula. The formula might have caused her to have reflux, and it irritated her esophagus. I'm going to get you some liquid antacid to give her. A nipple full before she eats for a while will coat and heal that esophagus. Stay right here. I'll be right back."

Brant snapped her back into her sleeper and locked her back into the car seat. "See, she is fine. It had nothing to do with the accident."

Bekah let the tears flow now that they were alone. "I kept picturing all the bl—"

"Bekah." Brant grabbed her shoulders and lowered his body where he was face to face with her. "She's fine. She just needs a little antacid, and she'll be good as new."

"God, I don't know what I would have done without you here. If there was something seriously wrong with her," she said, hiccupping through her words and tears, "I wouldn't have been able to handle it."

Brant pulled her into his arms. "Nothing is wrong with her." Her arm wrapped around him. She felt his lips press against the top of her head. The warmth of his body against hers felt safe, like as long as he held her everything would fade away. She didn't want to move and was disappointed when his arms released her at the sound of the door opening. "Here is the antacid." The doctor put the bottle on the table. "Give it a good shake, then fill a nipple, and give it to her before she eats, maybe once in the morning, once in the evening, and once before she goes to bed. Do that for about six weeks. If she continues to spit up blood after three days, bring her back in." He picked up the bottle. "Dad, you want to take this?"

Brant's brows raised. "Oh, I'm—"

The doctor shoved the bottle and papers in his hand. Bekah's eyes widened as she glanced at Brant and pinched her lips between her teeth. They all walked out of the exam room, and the doctor pushed the button to the heavy metal doors, escorting them through it into the empty waiting room. Brant pulled the cover over the carrier and held out his arm for Bekah to grab as they exited the emergency center for the second time in two days. By the time they made it back to the house it was three in the morning. Maizy was wailing. Brant got Bekah settled, grabbed a nipple from the counter, and let Maizy suck the antacid out, before handing her over to Bekah. He turned to head to the living room. "Will you stay?"

Putting his hand on the doorframe, he stared back at her. Without saying a word, he walked to the end of the bed, sat down, and toed off his boots. Then he scooted up to the pillow, dragging a yellow quilt from the end of the bed with him. Fluffing the pillow, he rolled over on his side and faced Bekah.

"Thanks for taking care of Maizy and me." Her words came out nearly slurred, and her eyes felt heavy.

****

She awoke with a jerk, not knowing how long she had been asleep. There was a heaviness on her belly, and she blinked trying to focus. The last thing she remembered was nursing Maizy. "Maizy?" she said softly.

"In her crib." A growly voice responded in her neck. Her hand slowly reached down to feel a huge warm arm wrapped around her. Somewhere in the night he had removed his clothes except his boxers and crawled under the covers. The feel of his body molded to her sent flames dancing throughout her. She knew it should be the last thing she should be thinking of. Her relationship with Bobby wasn't even cold, and she still really didn't know Brant. Although he had been so selfless to come to her aid more than once, she still didn't know if he was someone she should consider dating. After all, he came to her for help. But lord, what she would do to have his lips against hers just once. She could feel his breath against her neck. Her body trembled, and she snuggled down. The massive hand pressed against her belly, and his arm tightened around her.

Chapter Eight

He felt her body jerk next to his, and he thought about pulling away, then she settled back into his arms and her warmth and the feel of her soft skin on his made him want to lie there with her for the rest of the day.

He quickly realized the old house was a bit drafty, and the light quilt wasn't cutting through the chill in the air. When he moved Maizy to her crib, he stripped down and climbed under all the covers to get warm. Waking up with Bekah cuddled up to him felt so good it was almost instinctual to drag her in close. His mind still managed to torment him with thoughts of Abbie though. Bekah was nothing like her. He couldn't figure out what exactly was drawing him to her. She had such a pure beauty about her that every time she smiled it was like she was piercing the dark wall he was hiding behind. Could it be that he was just wanting to protect her and Maizy, to help them? Heck, there had been one problem after another since he met Bekah. Or maybe he just wanted the happiness back that he felt when he was with Abbie. But he didn't want a relationship. Did he? It was too soon. Wasn't it? He had too much baggage to work through. Except he couldn't deny he liked being with Bekah. It felt so natural, so easy. She was such a paradox. Extremely intelligent and yet free spirited in so many ways.

The bed gave, and he watched her slowly stand. She wandered over to the crib and reached in. He raised up on his elbow. "Is she okay?" he asked, his voice sounding a bit hoarse.

Bekah turned and ran her fingers against her neck. "I think so. When did you put her in the crib?"

"About three thirty."

"She's been asleep for four hours. We've been asleep for four hours." She grinned.

He moved his arm and laid his head back on the pillow. "Get back in, and we can sleep for a little while longer."

She turned her head and gave him a coy look, then slowly climbed back in and lay down facing him.

"How's your back feeling?"

"Better actually."

He grabbed hold of her and slowly slid her into him again, pulling the covers up and shutting his eyes.

Maizy's whimpers dragged him from his sleep-induced haze. The clock read almost nine.

He made his way across the room to her crib. Her eyes were bright as he stared down at her. A smile spread across her face when she saw him, and her arms shot up above her head in a stretch. His heart twinged at the sight. "You slept for a long time, baby girl." Tucking his hands beneath her, he lifted her out of the crib and cradled her in his arms. Propping Maizy up on his shoulder, his large hand tucked snugly under her diaper and the other against her back. Her head rested on his shoulder. He rhythmically patted her diaper and felt her little hand grab at his bare chest. Her little fingers kneading into his skin sent an immediate warmth across his chest. It was quickly becoming one of his favorite things. He glanced over at the bed and realized Bekah wasn't there.

Making his way into the living room, he found Bekah in front of the big picture window, staring out at the snow-covered yard. Brant was stopped dead in his tracks. She was in some kind of yoga pose with her uninjured arm extended above her head and one leg raised with her foot gently placed below the opposite knee. Her brown wavy hair cascaded over one shoulder. A red headband held it back from her face. Her full red lips parted. Brant walked closer. The light shining through the window reflected on her face and in her eyes. Were they gray? Green? Whatever color they were, they shimmered with the sun and made sparks crawl up the back of his neck when she let them rest on him with a look of desire. Combined that with the rosy tone of her cheeks that added a splash of color to her sun kissed skin, it made her damn near irresistible.

He cleared his throat. "Someone decided to finally wake up."

"I heard. I was headed in to get her, but you were too quick." She moved slowly, dropping her foot to the ground. Spreading her feet apart, she lowered her arm directly in front of her.

"Be careful doing that stuff until your back feels better."

"Oh, don't worry, my back is guiding me on what I can and cannot do. I actually think it's helping. The splint is throwing my balance off though."

"Do you do this every morning?" Brant grabbed a cup from the cabinet and poured him some coffee then poured some antacid into a nipple and gave it to Maizy.

"Yeah, I try to. I usually do mindful meditation

then yoga. It helps me get my day started.

"How?" Walking back into the living room, he sat down on the sofa and propped his leg over his knee, then lowered Maizy down so she could see him.

"The mindful meditation and grounding help me clear my head, and the yoga gives me energy. It's a fantastic way to start the day. That's why I use it with my clients." Moving out of her pose, she peered over at him. "I haven't been practicing what I preach though. Since Maizy was born, I kind of got out of the routine. I had been so stressed with the new baby, I pushed it aside, doing what I could, just to keep my head above water, not realizing that it was probably the one thing that would help me focus. This morning I woke up so rested that I decided it was time to get back into it." Bekah walked over and settled on the sofa, picked up the nursing pillow, then Brant passed Maizy to her.

"How long have you been up?"

"About an hour," she said glancing down at Maizy.

Brant noticed a sadness in her tone. "Everything okay?"

A sigh escaped as her fingers stroked Maizy's hair. "Yeah. Bobby texted me. Maizy's on his insurance and he said he got a notification from the hospital about the accident. He started apologizing again and told me I shouldn't have left. Maybe I should have called him."

Brant broke in. "You weren't conscious."

"I know. It's just...so complicated."

It felt like a rope tightening around Brant's chest. He didn't like the guy. There was something about him that didn't sit right. He didn't deserve Bekah. "Are you having second thoughts about breaking up?"

"No. Honestly, it should have happened a long

time ago. I've been thinking about it since I got his message. We weren't balanced. We were always going and doing things, but it was things *he* enjoyed. He controlled every aspect of our relationship. I'm a psychologist. I have a doctorate for Pete's sake. What's that say about me that I got sucked into his web. I think the only reason he came to Dalton was because in college he knew he had control of me. I was his toy, and when I left, he didn't have anything to play with anymore. I can't believe I let it happen. I've always been kind of a free spirit. That's the hippie in me. I led my life by my intuition. Then he came along, and it was like he hypnotized me. I always did what he told me to do. I never questioned it, until I got pregnant."

"What made you question it then? I would figure he would feel like he had more control of you then."

"He didn't want kids. At least not now. He never came right out and said it, but he didn't want me to have her. He said we weren't ready. There was no doubt in my mind though. I wanted her. And from that point on, he resented me for standing up to his desires."

"So, now that you have seen his true colors, what's the problem?"

"I know this sounds harsh but it's the thought of him being her daddy. He is going to be in her life forever. I don't want her being controlled by him the way I was."

"Well, if he didn't want kids then maybe—"

"It's like I told him when he was here. She's a possession to him. He doesn't love her, he just doesn't want anyone else to have her, because that would mean he had lost his control. I'm honestly worried he's going to make this breakup hard. I want him to move to

Houston and leave me and Maizy alone. I know it won't be that easy though."

"Wait, he's moving?"

"Yes. Got a big promotion and transfer to Houston. He and the little lover. It will work out perfect for him because his family lives in the area and so does hers. Well, they have a summer home."

"Wow. That does kind of complicate things." He could see the hurt in her expression. Something within him wanted to grab her and Maizy up in his arms, and never let go. He had to remind himself, he was only there to help. A glorified babysitter. He needed to get a grip on his emotions. "I'm sure it will all work out fine. No need to worry about something that may never happen," was all he could think of to say, though he suspected she was right. Her ex had no intentions of leaving things be.

"You're right. Maybe things will turn out fine," she said, but didn't sound convinced.

The sadness that still enveloped her face had him moving the conversation on. "Would you like me to make you some breakfast?"

"I was going to have some oatmeal."

"Okay. Do you need me to make it for you?"

"Nah. It's those little packets that you add water to. I can manage. Do you have plans for today?"

"Actually, I thought about hitting the gym and then running by and checking on Grams. That's if your granddad is available. I should be back by late afternoon if that works for you."

"Oh yeah. You haven't been able to do much on your own the past couple of days. I know you are probably needing to get away."

He rubbed the back of his neck. "No. It's not that. I haven't minded helping. On Sundays I like to spend time with my grandma. We have kind of made this our day. She and my granddad have always been a big part of my life. I still feel guilty that Grams wasn't there when I got married. When Abbie died, she was the first one to reach out to me, and suggested I come to Dalton." As he thought about it, his throat closed, and the words stuck. "Every Sunday she drove down to the facility while I was in rehab. She has helped me get my life back."

"Well, you take all the time you need. I will be fine. We need to spend some time with Grandpa anyway."

"Are you sure?"

"Positive."

****

It felt good to lift weights and release the pent-up stress. Bekah had her yoga. He had his weights. It gave him time to think. Even when he was drinking himself blind, lifting gave him some semblance of normalcy. He chuckled thinking how his life had flipped upside down in a matter of a couple of days. He was a nanny and for whatever reason, he really didn't mind it. In fact, he kind of enjoyed it, especially waking up this morning. What he didn't like was seeing the worry in Bekah's eyes when she talked about her ex. He knew, deep down in his gut, the guy wasn't going to leave her alone. He would make trouble, and that was the last thing she needed, and Brant had no idea how to help her. And with filming about to begin, he would be just a ghost, in her and Maizy's memories.

It didn't feel right, although there was nothing he

could do. He'd already signed the contract and committed to the project. *God, what is wrong with me? It is too soon. I don't need to be in a relationship, and neither does she. Her breakup was literally hours ago.* But all he could think about was the way her skin felt against his this morning, and the way the sunlight lit up her eyes. She almost appeared ethereal. *Why is she invading all my thoughts?* And Maizy. The expression on her face when he picked her up. That smile. *Damn.*

As much as he wanted to deny it, they had burrowed their way into his heart. Even now, driving to his grandma's he thought about stopping by and picking them up so he could introduce them. That would have to be another time. Pulling into the driveway, he let out a growl at the sight of the wispy older lady, with her hair in a braid that was draped over one shoulder, outside sweeping the porch off. "What do you think you are doing, Grams? Where is your coat?" he scolded as he stepped out of his car.

"I knew you were coming, so I figured I needed to clear the snow away."

"Geez, let me do it." He tried to take the broom then realized there was nothing left to sweep. "Never mind, it's done."

"I'm old, not helpless."

"Oh, trust me, I know. No one in their right mind would ever say you were helpless. They would be too scared you would kick their ass." He knew his language didn't faze her, and if truth be told, she probably used more four-letter words than he did. But she had a heart of gold.

She chuckled at his comment as he pulled open the storm door and they went inside.

"You're a little late today." He followed her into the kitchen where she started pulling out sandwich meat, condiments, lettuce, and tomatoes from the refrigerator.

"I'm sorry. I kind of got thrown off my schedule a little bit." He brought out a couple of glasses from the cabinet then retrieved a pitcher of iced tea. Their weekly routine had almost turned into a dance. "How was your week?" he asked as he assembled his sandwich. It wasn't a benign question that he asked every week. He meant it every time. He loved their visits. She always had a funny story to tell him.

"It was fine. Had coffee with my lady friends Monday and lunch with the usual group Friday. Ellen said she got together with her poker buddies and lost again. She's not any good. She should be glad it's not strip poker, cuz she'd been naked."

"Yeah, I don't need to have that visual, Grams." He chuckled and she put her hand on his and laughed out loud. "How were the roads? I can't believe you got out on the streets with the snow."

"They were fine. I was careful. Again, I'm old, not—"

"I know. I know." He set his knife in the sink. "I'm sorry I didn't get to talk to you much this week. I've—"

"—been busy." Her brow lifted, and she captured his attention from the corner of her eye. "Your mom sent me the article a couple of hours ago."

Brant's gut soured. "What article?"

"What? She didn't send it to you?"

Brant pulled his phone out and checked his text messages then his e-mails. He hadn't had time to go through them. Instant frustration penetrated every cell of his body when he saw his mom's e-mail, and he let out a long sigh. It didn't help that at the top of the e-mail she'd typed, "any publicity is good publicity." She wasn't bothered by the paparazzi. In fact she worried when things got quiet. For him though, he moved from California to get away from it. Clicking on the link, a tabloid article opened from one of the rag mags. The title was, "Recovering Nicely." A small grainy photo of him holding the carrier, with his arm around Bekah, opened. He scanned the article that talked about his stint in rehab after the tragic death of his wife, and his new relationship, and upcoming film.

"Shit! They're already starting," he said, continuing to scan the article. "How in the hell did they get this information?" Scrolling down the page, it felt like a bomb went off as he read the words. "Dammit. They named her." He chunked his phone on the small wooden table.

His grandma calmly set the two plates with sandwiches and chips on the table, then turned and grabbed the two glasses of tea and sat down adjacent to him. "Who is she?" she asked, still keeping her voice even.

"She's a girl I am helping. We aren't dating."

"It says she is a doctor," she said around a mouthful of sandwich.

Brant didn't want to get into the story. However, his grandma had a sixth sense about her, which made it hard to keep anything from her.

"She is a psychologist. I went to her for a consult. With the upcoming movie shoot, I wasn't sure if I was ready to handle everything. Rehab recommended her, and so did some of my friends who have been to her."

He shoved a chip in his mouth. "She got into a car accident Friday, and I offered to help her. I was walking her out of the hospital in the photo. What you don't see is that she broke her arm and injured her back."

"Did you see the accident happen?"

Brant took a bite of his sandwich, leaned back in his chair, and wiped his mouth. "No. I was shadowing at the fire station when they got the call. I helped rescue her."

"And she has a baby?"

"A six-week-old baby girl, named Maizy." His heart melted remembering her smile from this morning. "Luckily, she didn't get hurt. But, with Bekah's injuries, she needed help taking care of the baby, so I offered to help when her grandpa can't be there."

Brant's grandma kept her gaze fixed on him, listening to his story. "You…are helping take care of a baby?"

"Geez, Grams, have some faith. Turns out I'm pretty good at it."

She shook her head. "It's not that. I was just wondering if it was hard for you, with the memories."

"Not going to lie, when I realized it was Bekah and Maizy in the accident, I wasn't sure I was going to be able to handle it. But I pushed through it."

So…is this doctor lady from around here?"

He took a drink of his tea. "Not originally. She is like me. She's from California. She moved here a couple of years ago to be closer to her granddad."

"What's her name again?"

"Bekah Adkins."

"Adkins. What's her granddad's name?"

"Dale Adkins. He's a—"

"Oh, you gotta be kidding me. I know Dale. He is part of my lunch group." She smiled. "Lord, he and your granddad go way back. He works up at the college."

"Yeah, he's a professor."

"He used to bring his junker cars in, and he and your granddad would try to fix them up, then he'd go out and sell them, and they would split the profit. I think Dale paid for his education on the money he made from selling the cars he and your granddad fixed up." Taking another bite of her sandwich, she continued. "I could tell you some stories on those two."

"If it involves Grandpa, I bet you could."

"Yeah, I've known Dale for ages, and I remember Rebekah from when she was little. I haven't seen her in forever, and I wouldn't recognize her if I did. She and her brother came to visit a couple of times."

"I can't believe that you know each other. He seems like a good guy."

"Oh, he is, and I am sure his granddaughter is too."

"She is. Really sweet. Kind of a hippie. In a way, she kind of reminds me of you. She's very intuitive." His thoughts went back to the issue at hand. "God. I hope I haven't ruined her life."

"Why would you say that?"

"The way this article is written, it sounds like she is dating one of her clients, and that's basically against the rules. It pisses me off because I went in for a consult, so I'm not a client and I won't be, and I'm not dating her, I'm just helping. I don't want to get her involved with all the tabloid trash."

"Well, I will contact the magazine and tell them to write a retraction."

Brant smirked with the thought of his grandma giving the editors at the tabloid a piece of her mind. "It won't do any good, Grams, it's already out there. People have seen it. Regardless of a retraction, many will still believe it." He paused. "I need to let her know it's out there." He grabbed the phone from where he threw it on the table. Staring at the screen, he chewed on his cheek. "I think this is something I need to tell her face to face. Would you be mad if I skipped out a little early?"

"Not at all. You go take care of your business."

He stood, shoved the rest of his sandwich in his mouth, and picked up his plate and glass. After setting his dishes in the sink and throwing away his napkin, he leaned over and gave his grandma a backward hug and a kiss on the cheek. "Love you, Grams."

She turned around, patted one cheek, and kissed the other. "Love you too Leo."

He rolled his eyes and shook his head at her nickname for him. He had been obsessed with the Ninja Turtles as a child and for a while would not leave home without his blue mask and sword. After spending the summer with his grandparents, his grandma started calling him Leo after his favorite Ninja Turtle, Leonardo, and she had never quit. It was their own private little joke.

As he drove down the driveway, he played the words of the article in his head. It was written to sound like he was getting his life back together which would normally be great publicity for him if the article were true. Unfortunately, it wasn't, and it could do some real damage to Bekah's practice. He checked his rearview mirror. Something he hadn't had to do since moving to

Arkansas. The road was empty. His phone buzzed in the cup-holder, and the sudden noise made him jump. It was all starting again. Maybe doing the film was a mistake. He had gotten comfortable with being just another resident of Dalton and enjoyed it. He wasn't ready for the nosey news to be after him again. Turning up the driveway, he pulled up next to the cottage and turned the car off. When he lifted the phone, the screen lit up with the message, and his heart stuttered as he read it. Another message from the unknown number, only this time, he knew it was meant for him.

—Brant, how could you? Who is she? —

He knew it couldn't be Abbie. She was dead. He watched her die in his arms. Still, there was an inkling of wonder. Inhaling deeply, he tried to steady his pulse, curious as to who would play such a sick joke on him. He was so stunned he didn't know how to feel. He wanted to text back and ask who it was, though he was a little scared at what might come back. His thumb hovered over the number, finally deciding it would be best to block it, then something stopped him. Staring at the now black screen, he bit down on his lip, let out a sigh, and simply stowed the phone in his pocket before exiting the car. Lifting his hand to knock on the door, he stopped when he heard Bekah's voice. She was upset. The text message was a mist in his thoughts now as he pressed the lever, testing to see if the door was locked. Finding it wasn't, he pushed it open. Bekah was standing in the middle of the living room with the phone pressed to her ear. She turned quickly and shot Brant an angry glance.

"It's. Not. True. And besides, you can't dictate what I do with my life. It is no longer your damn business. That was your choice, not mine," she said through clenched teeth into the phone. "I'm done. I have told you the truth whether you choose to believe it or not." She growled and hit the disconnect button then tapped her forehead with the edge of the phone. "God, why in the world did I ever think he was the one?"

Brant stood quietly in the doorway not quite knowing where to start. He could tell her how pretty she looked, to try to soften the blow of what he already suspected had exploded or take his lumps as they came. Though the mess wasn't his fault, it came with the territory, and she didn't deserve to be dragged into it. He lifted his eyes expecting to be pummeled with a stream of angry words. Instead, her expression was filled with concern. "Are you okay?"

What? She's worried about me? How could she not be mad? Pressing on, still feeling the need to apologize, he lifted his hand to his chest and closed the space between them. "I'm so sorry."

She carefully slid herself against him, catching him completely off guard, and gently wrapped her arm around him and squeezed. "What are you sorry for? You've done nothing wrong. Crap, I don't know what I would have done if you hadn't been here this past week. You have been a godsend."

The feel of her body against his had his arms instinctively encircling her. "I didn't mean for you to get pulled into my mess. I never should have taken that part. Living here has made me forget how my life was in California. I should have known the rag mags would be sniffing around." He slowly let his arms release her, and he stepped back. "We haven't even started production. The paparazzi usually doesn't show up until everything has started."

Bekah walked to the sofa and sat down. "Don't worry about it. It's just tabloid rumors. I gotta admit, I was kind of excited that I made it into the tabloids."

"Oh God, don't be. Those people are evil incarnate. They will lie about their mother if they think it will make them money. The way they wrote the story sounded like you were dating me. Your client. I know that can't be good."

"It's not true. You aren't my client. I never received any payments from you. I'm not worried." Brant sat opposite of her on the sofa. "So, what is the movie called? What's it about?"

"It's called Rest for the Wicked. It's about a secret underground gambling ring in Hot Springs, Arkansas. Back in the day it was the vacation spot for notorious gangsters like Al Capone and Frank Costello. One of the hotels even had an underground passage to some casinos. Hot Springs was a hotbed for illegal gambling and bootlegging. Gangsters could hide out there and not worry about the law coming after them because basically the local government found it to be great for the economy. It was Vegas before there was a Vegas."

"Wow. And this story is true? Who do you play?"

Brant cracked a smile. "Well, yes, the history of Hot Springs and the gangsters is true. The movie has true elements, but it's pure fiction. I play John Dillinger. It's a supporting role, so larger than what I've played before. It should be fun."

Bekah eyed him. "Can I ask you a question?"

"Sure."

"If you hate the Hollywood life so much, why *did* you take the part?" She tucked her feet under her and grabbed the fuzzy blanket that was folded between them.

"My mom sent it to me and said she and my dad were involved. The character seemed interesting, and the story was good, so I thought it would be fun."

"Uh uh. I don't buy it. You have another reason. Have you taken any other parts in movies other than ones your mom is in?"

"No. I've never been offered anything."

"You never went to casting calls or anything?"

"No. I never really was that interested. My mom just asked me from time to time. Apparently, with this part, it wasn't her per se. It was one of her buddies who wanted me on the film. Still, this film is a pet project of hers. She wanted to do something in her hometown. It is a good revenue maker. So, she is in control of quite a bit."

Bekah nodded her head and stared off.

"You think I am doing this because of my mom?"

"Are you?" Brant shrugged. "You've done this since you were a child. Haven't you?"

His lips pursed, and he thought for a moment before shaking his finger at her. "You, you are really good at what you do."

"It's not that hard. You said you got shipped off to school and to your grandparents a bunch, so what's a kid to do who never sees his parents. Figure out a way to see them." Brant sat speechless with a smirk and continued to shake his head.

"Yeah. Maybe. I'm not a kid anymore though. I'm about to turn twenty-eight."

"Does it matter?" She sat back. "If it makes you feel better, I think your mom was putting you in her films because of the same reason."

Brant tipped his head and shrugged, then smiled with the thought that his mom missed him as much as he missed her. When it got down to it, he really didn't get to spend much time with his parents, and neither of them knew him very well. They loved their jobs, and unfortunately it meant he and his brother often took a backseat to their careers. The smile slowly faded, and he suddenly was tired of the subject. "So, what was Bobby calling about? I am guessing that was who was on the phone."

"Yes. He called to tell me he didn't want you around our daughter since you are a recovering addict. He said he saw the article on his social media."

"Well, you know that part is true."

"Technically yes—"

"There is no technically. I am. I went to rehab."

"Yes. However, the way you explained it to me the other day, I suspect you don't have an addiction problem. You drank occasionally before, not excessively. Then after your wife died, self-medicating was your way of dealing or not dealing with the pain. That sounds more like you had a problem coping. You never had anyone around you as a kid to teach you how to cope. So, you had to figure it out on your own. When your wife died, you didn't have the skills to deal with it, and it was exacerbated by the fact that you didn't have anyone around you at that point to help. Your military training didn't help because it taught you to take emotion out of the equation. You couldn't with this."

"How do you do that?"

She tapped her ear. "I listen, and I pick up on things. You said you haven't had a drink since rehab and haven't had a problem being around people who are drinking. That told me a lot. If you didn't have a problem with alcohol before, and don't now, then it's not an addiction problem. It's a coping problem. From what I've seen, you are not the classic definition of an addict. I have no problem with you being around Maizy. I'm her mother, and I should have a say in the matter. Bobby is no angel. He can put away the liquor."

Just hearing Maizy's name brought up thoughts of her cuddled under his chin. "Is she napping?"

"Yeah. I'm thinking the tummy issues were the problem all along. She has been so happy today. Grandpa came by before he went to church and watched her while I got dressed."

His eyes skimmed her body. She had on a pair of wide-legged flowy pants and a printed shirt with fairy sleeves. "Good job on getting dressed. Very pretty."

"Aw, thanks."

A crooked smile spread across his face. "I was wondering where your grandpa was. I was hoping he would be here. I have a really funny story." He chuckled. "So, I guess your grandpa and my grandpa were buddies back in the day. My grandma knows your grandpa very well. She told me the story of how he would bring my grandpa junker cars, and they would fix them up in his shop, then your grandpa would sell them and split the profit."

"That would be him. He still has an old Chevelle under a tarp in the barn out back. Bought it several years ago before my grandma died and started fixing it up. He got it nearly done and then quit working on it when Grandma died. It doesn't run."

"I would love to see it sometime. When I was here during the summer, I used to help my granddad some in his shop. I probably worked on some of your granddad's cars."

Chapter Nine

Bekah sat on the sofa with her eyes closed and legs crisscrossed in front of her. Her long cotton shirt puddled on the sides over her multicolored leggings, and her hands rested in her lap. She caught sight of her tie-dyed cast that covered her arm from below her elbow to her hand and breathed in deep. It was day five of the most glorious sleep she had had since Maizy was born. There was only one thing that could have made it better. Brant. She replayed the night he slept in her bed over and over in her head. The way his body felt curled around her made her feel safe and protected. Sunday night he slept on the sofa and after he took her to get her cast on and rent a car, he deemed her fully capable and decided it would be best to part ways so she wouldn't get caught up in the tabloid news. He was probably right. Two of her patients had seen the article and asked about it. It didn't make it any easier though. She had grown attached to him being around, and she knew Maizy had too. She watched Maizy's face around him. She smiled for him so easily.

When he slung his duffle bag over his shoulder, she felt a knife drive straight into her heart. And when he kissed her on the cheek, and Maizy on the top of her head, it was everything she could do not to grab his shirt, pull him to her, and kiss the life out of him. She missed him the minute the door shut. There was just something about him that she felt connected to, beyond the fact that he had basically rescued her. He had texted to check on them a few times, and they had planned to meet up at TopHops with everybody to watch Cody's band make their debut. Cody's brother-in-law, Jack, agreed to watch Maizy. He wasn't big on crowds, and he was used to kids since he was a part-time stay at home dad.

Her phone buzzed. *Ugh, Bobby. He really needs to get a clue.* He had texted her several times throughout the week, wanting her to forgive him.

—*I'm coming into town today to get some stuff from the apartment. We need to talk. I will be by around six*—

"Shit." *He's not going to screw up my night out.*

—*I can meet with you this afternoon. Not this evening. I have plans*—

—*I won't be there until four and I have to turn around and head back first thing in the morning. Can't you change your plans?* —

She let out a growl then closed her eyes and took a deep breath.

—*No. I can't. If you want to see me, then I suggest you change yours, and come in earlier*—

—*What is so damn important that you can't reschedule?* —

—*You know, it's really none of your business. If you want to meet, come by around three, I will be here*—

—*Fine*—

Well, my afternoon just decided to suck.

Three thirty the doorbell rang. Bekah let out a sigh and pulled the door open. Bobby stood with a smirk on his face and a fistful of flowers in his hand. His camel-colored bomber jacket topped his pressed navy chinos. He looked good. Bekah scowled and took the flowers. "Thanks," she said unenthusiastically. Walking into the kitchen, she found a vase under the sink, leaving Bobby standing at the opened door. She half hoped he would turn around and walk away. Instead, he stepped inside and closed the door.

Trying her best to be a good host, she asked, "Do you want some water or tea?"

"Water would be great."

Maizy was on the floor playing with a baby gym, batting at the toys hanging above her. Bekah motioned for Bobby to have a seat and handed him a glass of water. He strolled to the sofa, but then pulled up one of the dining room chairs and sat down without giving Maizy another glance. Bekah wondered if he had even noticed her there. She sat down and stared at the happy baby.

"So, what did you want to talk about?" she asked, continuing to stare at Maizy.

Bobby sighed. "Bekah, I know I screwed up, and I am really sorry. I love you, and I want you back. I told Marissa and had her move out."

"Oh, so you are finally owning up to it?"

"Yes," he confessed, adding a long breath. "We were living together, and I'm so sorry I lied and cheated on you. She meant nothing to me. I know it was wrong. And saying sorry is not enough." He paused. "I want you to come to Oklahoma with me. We can go to Houston together and hunt for a place to live. I love you, Bekah, and I really want us to be together."

Bekah leaned back on the sofa and brought her

hands together like a prayer. She wasn't mad at him anymore. She was resolved. It was like he was someone she used to know. "Bobby." she said softly. "You really sound sincere, and I appreciate that. I do accept your apology. I know the pregnancy was not planned and not easy for either of us." Bobby's brows shifted up his forehead, and hope spread across his face. "I've had a lot to think about these past few days, and I realized something. We aren't good for each other. We want different things. Our lives are going in two different directions. I am willing to forgive you, but that's it. I don't want a relationship with you anymore. You don't love me, otherwise you wouldn't have cheated, and you would have wanted a commitment with me. What we had was not healthy. I didn't have control of my life, and I realize that now. I'm happy here. This is where my life is now, and I want to stay."

"But what about Maizy? It's a nine-hour trip to Houston. I won't ever get to see her."

She knew he was using Maizy as a pawn in his quest to gain control once again. Now that she was onto him though, his manipulation tactics were blatant, and he wasn't going to win. "That's your choice. Believe me, I have thought about it, and it's something we will have to work out."

"So, what? Are you expecting me to give up the promotion and stay in Oklahoma?"

"No. Absolutely not. I am very proud of you for getting that promotion, and I think you will be happy living near your family. I honestly think you and Marissa make a cute couple. She seems nice. We will just have to work out the trips."

"Bekah." The sound of her name on his lips now

made her hair stand on end and not in a good way. Not the way it did with Brant.

"I'm serious, Bobby. I'm not what you need in your life. And you aren't what I need in mine. I know I said I wanted to move back to the coast when we were in school, but that was a long time ago. I love it here."

"God, Bekah. You are willing to throw away a five-year relationship?"

She stood and walked into the kitchen for some more tea. "Um…I think I was the one who tried to make it work if you recall. I was the one who wanted you to move in so we could be a family. You were the one who decided to walk away from the relationship. That was your call." She felt the irritation building and took a deep breath trying to continue to stay calm. "Do you want some more water?"

He stood, walked to the bar, and handed her his glass.

"I. Was. Wrong. Okay. I want to commit now. I realized how much you mean to me. I want us to be a family."

"Oh. So, you are saying you want to get married?"

Bekah could see the color drain from Bobby's face. "Well, not right off the bat. But at some point."

She pinched her lips together to stifle a chuckle. "That doesn't sound like a commitment at all. It doesn't matter anyway because I don't want to be in a relationship with you anymore."

"Only because you are in a relationship with the actor. Or are you are still wanting me to believe nothing is going on?"

"No. Again, he is a paramedic. He was strictly here to help care for me and Maizy after the accident. The tabloids were hunting for a story since he is about to do a movie here."

She refilled the glass and handed it to him. He sat in one of the chairs at the bar. "So, he wasn't in rehab?"

"He was for a short time, after his wife and baby were killed in a car accident."

"I'm sorry that happened. I still don't want him around Maizy though."

She took a deep breath. "Look around. He's not here." A burning pain singed the inside of her chest the minute she spoke the words, and the memory of his arms around her immediately filled her thoughts. "Even if we were together, you can't tell me who I date or not. And I can't tell you either."

He stood. "He's an addict, Bekah."

Maizy started to whimper, and Bekah walked out of the kitchen.

"You know what? This conversation will get us nowhere. You believe what you want from the tabloids. I know the truth and as you can see, he isn't here. We aren't dating. He was just helping."

Bobby set his glass on the table and grabbed Bekah's wrist. Pulling her to him, he wrapped his arms around her waist.

A sharp pain shot through her injured arm, and she shrieked. "My arm." He released his grip but only slightly. "What do you think you're doing?"

"I want to show you that I still love you." She pushed against his chest with her good arm, but he pulled his arms tighter, then leaned in to kiss her. She turned away quickly, and his lips only caught her cheek.

The thought of his lips touching hers now sent a

sick feeling to her stomach. "Let me go."

He held tight, his brows dipped, and his eyes bore into her. For a moment she thought he would push further but she wasn't going to let him bully her, and she accepted his challenge locking their gaze. When he realized he wasn't going to win, he loosened his arms. "Fine," he huffed and donned a defeated expression. "You have to believe me Bekah. I love you. I want you in my life. We are good together."

"No, Bobby, we're not." Bekah walked over to Maizy who started kicking her legs and whimpering. Reaching down, she carefully rolled Maizy over so she could balance her and pick her up one handed, something she quickly had to learn to do since Brant left. "Hey, sweet girl. Did you get tired of playing?"

"Can I hold her?" Bekah was unsure she heard him correctly. Did he really asked to hold her?

"You wanna go see your daddy?" Bekah stood and carefully passed Maizy to Bobby who pulled her in close.

"Is she sleeping better?" he asked in a low soft voice as Maizy snuggled down against him for a moment but then started whimpering again and he started to sway.

"Yeah. She had the little issue with her tummy, but we got it figured out. I think that had a lot to do with her not sleeping."

"That's good to hear...I mean, that she is sleeping better...not that she has tummy troubles."

Bekah nodded then took a deep breath. "She's probably getting hungry." Bobby patted her on her diaper trying to get her to settle down. She couldn't help but appreciate how hard he was trying. "Do you want to try to feed her?"

"Do you have her on formula now?"

"No, but I pump, so I have some bottles in case I have someone watch her."

Bekah pulled her lips between her teeth trying not to react to Bobby wrinkling his nose.

"No. That's okay, it's probably better if you feed her."

Somehow, she knew that would be his answer. "Well, listen, I know you have stuff to do, and I need to get her fed…"

"Yeah. I guess I need to get going." He pulled Maizy away from his shoulder and passed her back to Bekah, rubbing her back when she was snuggled up to Bekah's shoulder. He swallowed hard, and his lips pursed. His gaze cut through Bekah, and her whole body shook when his eyes began to glisten. He stared off for a moment.

"Bekah…I'm so sorry."

She could see how much he was hurting. Still there was a glint of something else, making her wonder if he was being sincere or playing her? He was an expert at manipulation, and now she questioned everything he did. It wasn't worth dwelling on though. There was no need to question it. She'd made her decision. "I know, Bobby. But this is for the best." She walked to the door and pulled it open. He leaned over and kissed her on the cheek, then rubbed his hand over Maizy's head.

His eyes met hers one last time. "I really do love you."

Lifting her hand, she waved goodbye, then let out a long breath once the door closed.

****

She'd checked her outfit in the mirror three times, then again in the reflection of the glass door when she tugged it open at TopHops. Her wide V-necked cotton top hit her mid-thigh over her tanned leggings that disappeared down her knee-high fringed moccasins. Over the outfit, she had a multicolored, floor length, flowy sleeved shawl, pulled together with a wide belt. Her hair was left down framing her face in thick caramel waves. She thought she looked okay, and the minute Brant laid eyes on her, she smirked, knowing she had hit the mark.

April bounced up to her first, followed close behind by Jenna, who grabbed her arm and dragged her to a dimly lit area on the side of the dance floor, close to the stage, where a couple of tables had been pushed together, next to a red vinyl booth. She waved at Joe, who was deeply engrossed in a plate of wings, then shyly glanced at Brant who was standing next to the booth. He hadn't taken his eyes off her since she walked through the door. She couldn't fault him though; she hadn't really been able to peel hers off him much either. His dark washed jeans and baby blue cabled sweater fit him in all the right places. Her heart felt like a herd of mustangs were running through her body.

"Bekah." She heard her name and managed to shift her attention. "This is my brother Ben Corbett," Jenna said pointing to a guy with shaggy strawberry blond hair and a heavy beard. Then she continued around the booth. "And my dad, Will, and Hillary, Cody's sister."

Without letting Bekah respond, April continued the introductions. "And this is Kaysi and Kaleb Grayeagle. They are Joe's sister and brother." Kaleb stood, gently grabbed her hand, and winked, then grabbed another wing from the plate before sitting back down. Somehow she figured that was his norm, and she gave him a smirk. "Guys, this is Dr. Bekah Adkins."

Bekah rolled her eyes. "Call me Bekah, please. Joe and April have told me all about you. I have to agree with April. Joe, you and Kaleb really do resemble each other."

"Yeah, but I'm better looking," Joe quickly responded.

Kaleb punched him in the arm. "You wish."

"I *love* your outfit, Bekah," Kaysi cut in, trying to ignore her brothers just as Joe turned and hit her glass of water, splashing it all over her. Ben grabbed a napkin and immediately started patting her down, obviously not realizing where his hands were going, until Kaysi grabbed the napkin out of his hand.

His face turned a deep scarlet. "Oh, sorry." He grabbed another napkin and wiped the droplets that had managed to hit him.

Kaysi slugged Joe.

"Ow!" He flinched and rubbed his arm. "I'm sorry. Geez. You hit harder than Kaleb."

Kaysi side-eyed Kaleb with a smirk, then lifted her gaze to Bekah. "Sorry. I apparently can't have a nice conversation with anyone with these two children near me."

Bekah laughed knowing Kaysi wasn't serious. It had only been a few months since Joe had found out he was Kaysi's brother. April had shared the story of an illness that put Joe in the hospital, and through a chain of crazy events dealing with his rare blood type, Joe found out that not only was he adopted, but he had been stolen as a baby from the Grayeagles and thought to have died. "Oh. No. That's okay. I was just going to say thanks. I haven't been out for fun in a while, and I had no clue what to wear."

"I have to agree," came a voice in her ear. "That outfit looks great on you." She turned. Brant had slipped up behind her.

"Hi," was all she managed.

Brant pointed to one end of the table. "I'm sitting over there, if you want to join me."

"Sure. You look really nice yourself." She sat down next to him and fought to keep from breaking into a smile as he continued to stare at her. Scanning the surroundings, she tried to compose herself, and commented, "This place is so nice now," and slowly turned back to him.

"Yeah it is. I've been here a couple of times since they remodeled it." They both sat quietly dropping glances at each other. The side of her mouth slowly curved up, and so did his. "I'm sorry. I know I'm staring. It's just…you look amazing."

Flames roared up her body and filled her cheeks. She tucked her chin, suddenly feeling very shy. She couldn't remember the last time she had gotten a compliment from Bobby. Since she got pregnant, he always managed to make her feel self-conscious. Her eyes finally made contact with his. "Thank you," she said softly. "It's a good thing I like stuff with big sleeves." She held her pink and white cast up that appropriately was tie-dyed. Brant laughed.

"Do you want something to drink?" She noticed a high ball glass on the table with ice and a blond-colored liquid, and she was mad at herself when Bobby's voice suddenly crept in and gave her a twinge of worry.

"What are you having?"

"Ginger ale. Nonalcoholic." He shrugged. "I can still pretend."

Bekah grinned, remembering their first encounter and her ginger spritzer. "That sounds delicious."

She scanned the room again while Brant disappeared into the darkness. Jenna quickly took his seat and gave her a knowing smile. "So, tell me about this."

"About what?" Bekah tried to appear confused then realized Jenna wasn't buying it.

"Cody told me Brant took you home from the hospital. I thought about calling, but I didn't want to bother you. So? Is there any truth to the rumor?"

Bekah decided to string her along. "What rumor?"

"Give up the goods, lady."

"Fine." She put her finger to her lips. "Well, I drove to Oklahoma to surprise Bobby for his birthday, as you know. Instead, he had a surprise for me. Another woman. By the time I was heading back to Arkansas, the ice storm had rolled in, and I hit a slick spot and wound up smashed into a tree. Cody and Brant were doing their shadowing at the station that got the call. Brant took care of Maizy at the scene and at the hospital and offered to drive me home, since it was already after midnight when they discharged me. Once we got back to the house, he decided to stay, since I was in no shape to take care of Maizy."

"So, rumor is not true?"

"Rumor is not true. I mean, we are friends now. But nothing happened."

"Doesn't mean it won't."

"Well, he was pretty pissed when the tabloids took the photo. He was worried it would affect my business. So, he took off pretty quick because he doesn't want me and Maizy caught up in it."

"Tell the truth. Was it completely adorable when he was taking care of Maizy?"

Bekah looked around to see if he was approaching. "My heart barely could stand it. He's so big she almost fits in one of his hands, and he would talk to her so sweetly. One time, I swear to you, I heard him singing to her."

"God, I hope Cody is like that."

"Oh, he will be. I know he is excited." She leaned back in her chair. "A little scared maybe. That's expected." Her eyes focused over Jenna's shoulder to see Cody on stage setting his guitar in a stand. "So, what made him put together a band?"

Jenna followed Bekah's focus. "Oh, that was kind of a funny story. Cody wrote a song a while back. I really liked it, so I recorded it on my phone and showed it to April. She loved it and posted it on her blog and talked about it. A band from Fayetteville, who happened to have their lead singer bail on them recently, saw April's post and liked the song. They reached out to April who told Cody. The rest is history."

"So, how long have they been playing together?"

"About three months off and on."

"What's the name of the band?"

"They are going with NewStory. Cody came up with it. Kind of represents our lives together.

"I like that."

Brant appeared with two new glasses of ginger ale

and set them on the table. "What are you ladies discussing?" He pulled out the chair next to Bekah and sat down.

"Cody's band."

"So, what kind of music do they play?"

"A little of everything actually: rock, country, alternative. They even have a couple of originals."

Brant nodded. "I heard him once when he did the karaoke night. He has a good voice."

"I know, someone spilled their drink on me." Jenna stared Brant down and giggled.

"Oh, right. That was you. Cody was not happy with me for talking to you either."

"He still believed you were the one who attacked me at that time."

"Yeah, he might have mentioned that. Nearly got me arrested."

"He actually did get Joe arrested accidentally. Well, I don't know that they actually arrested him, but they took him to the station in handcuffs for questioning."

Brant's eyes widened. "Seriously? I can't believe I haven't heard about this."

"I'm surprised. Joe kids him about it all the time. It was kind of an unfortunate coincidence."

"I will have to ask them about that one."

The speakers crackled, and a voice came over the system. "All right, my favorite people, let's have some fun tonight. We are going to kick off our premier night of live music with a brand new band. Welcome to the stage for the first time at TopHops, NewStory!" A roar from the crowd came with the first thump of the bass drum playing "My Hero" from the Foo Fighters. People rushed the stage and joined in singing the song. Brant grabbed Bekah's hand and pulled her into the crowd. Cody smiled from the raised platform. He stared into the crowd, and a huge grin spread across his face. Bekah turned to see Sergeant Mitch Gallagher sitting in his uniform on a stool at one of the raised tables. The group swayed and cheered as the band played through Shawn Mendes' "Mercy," and a classic from Kansas, "Dust in the Wind."

"Thank you, guys," Cody said with his guitar slung low on his hip. "We've got an original song we would like to do for you now, called "24 to Life." Hope you like it."

A deep rumble came from the bass and the drums rolled behind it. The piano joined along with Cody's twelve string guitar. His voice was smooth and soft with a slight echo that gave it an ominous resonance.

Staring at myself in the rearview mirror
I didn't know the man looking back at me
I lived a life that was not my own, too busy putting others on a throne.
And now a ghost's reflection is all I see.

The storms of life left me battered and bruised.
I didn't know if I would survive.
Until that fateful day when her green eyes looked my way
And at that moment I was glad to be alive.

You can live to survive, or you can die living, living, living
With pain cutting deeper than a knife
But take a chance, speak your heart, don't let the

pain tear you apart
Live every second every minute every hour, 24 to
life

Sunlight paints the sky with its brilliant colors
breaking through the deepest darkest night
let go of the past because the hard times won't last.
if you choose to live and don't give up the fight

In life There's no guarantees. So, love like it's your
final day
Take faith's leap, there's no mountain too steep
It's about living every moment in the best way

You can live to survive, or you can die living,
living, living
pain cutting deeper than a knife
But take a chance, speak your heart, don't let the
pain tear you apart
Live every second every minute every hour, 24 to
life

As the last note played, the crowd surrounding the stage erupted into cheers. After a couple of other covers, Cody smiled at Jenna and started into Ed Sheeran's song "Perfect." Bekah knew the song well and started to quietly sing along.

Brant leaned close to Bekah. "Would you like to dance?" His eyes creased with his smile.

Bekah's heart skipped, and she nodded. He pulled her out of the crowd at the stage and brought her in close. His hand tenderly wrapped around her and warmed her back. Standing a foot taller than her, he towered over her, yet somehow she felt comfortable in his arms. Scents of vanilla and cedar filled her nose as she leaned her head against his chest and heard him humming to the song. The beat was easy and just as she melted into him, he grabbed her hand and pushed her away, twirling her around, then pulled her back into him, still careful of her injured arm. The feel of his arms around her gave her thoughts of wanting more. His fingers played in her hair, and her eyes closed as her fantasies took over.

The feel of his fingers wrapping around her cheek, lifting her face to his, pulled her from her daydreams. He was singing the lyrics to her. *Was this happening?* Her breaths stuttered with the feel of his thumb brushing her cheek. And then he leaned in. Fingers curling in her hair, his nose brushed against hers, and he paused. She stilled. Then his lips were on hers, and she was completely stranded from her breath as he gently sucked in her lower lip. The sweet taste of his ginger-ale was still on his lips. Tilting his head, he captured her mouth fully. His body was hard and strong, but he was gentle, and his lips were so soft. Her lips parted, and their tongues slowly brushed against each other as their bodies swayed.

The sound of the music disappeared along with everyone in the room. She had never been kissed so perfectly, feeling her soul being consumed by him. When he finally pulled away, she wasn't sure she would be able to stand on her own. He gave her one last soft kiss on her lips and one to her cheek. The song's ending was distant compared to her pulse ringing in her ears. Tilting her head, she caught him staring at her with fire in his eyes.

Chapter Ten

Nothing could have prepared Brant for what he saw walk through the door at TopHops. He had desperately tried to put his mind on other things when he left Bekah's, although nothing worked. He studied his class material, his script, even worked out. Still, his mind kept coming back to Bekah…and Maizy. He knew once the tabloids started, they probably wouldn't stop, and he needed to keep his distance from Bekah for her sake. But after day two of being miserable and not sleeping, he texted her to check on them. The thought of calling her was out of the question because hearing her voice would make things worse.

There was something so captivating about her. She wasn't afraid to be herself. At first it caught him off guard, and tonight, his whole body became a raging wildfire the minute she stepped through the door. Nope. Not prepared at all. He stared at her standing in front of him, and every cell in his body immediately craved her. His mouth had to taste her. His hands had to touch her. And when he did, all he wanted to do was pick her up and carry her to some dark place away from everyone and—

"Brant?"

Shit. Did she say my name? He leaned down. "Sorry. What?"

Bekah tipped up on her toes.

"I probably need to get out of here. I don't want to leave Maizy too long. Hillary's husband Jack is watching her, and he has two of his own to watch."

Cody's voice rang through the speakers. "Thank you for being here tonight. You have been tremendous. We are going to leave you with what has become my favorite song. The familiar melody of Bon Jovi's "It's My Life" caused the crowd to whoop. Bekah tapped Brant on the arm and motioned him to follow her. She walked over to the table and grabbed her bag. By the expression on her face, he could see she was thinking about something. He had taken a chance by kissing her, and now he wasn't sure he'd made the right move. He couldn't stop himself though. There was a charge, an almost palpable buzz between them every time they were in the same room, and to have her that close, within his arms, there was no way he could fight the desire that poured through him, even if he tried.

Every time he was with her, he was fascinated by her even more. He wanted to peel back another layer and find out more about her, and tonight, just touching her had him losing complete control. It wasn't enough. He thought she was feeling the same thing...but maybe not.

Bending down, he put his mouth to the shell of her ear. "Listen, about the—"

She turned her head just enough to where their noses brushed each other. "Would you like to come over and hang out for a little bit?"

It took a good two seconds for his thoughts to catch up with the words she'd spoken. It was completely opposite of what he thought was going to come out of her mouth. His mind suddenly raced remembering the rag mag tabloid story and what could happen if she got pulled into all the nonsense. It could destroy her life. He had seen it happen. And even though he didn't like Bobby, it could cause trouble for him too. Nothing else had been published about him since the initial story though. Could it have been a one-time fluke? He had to admit, he wasn't ready for her to go. He missed her and Maizy. "Are you sure?" She nodded. He dug for his phone in his pocket, and the screen lit up with a message. But it would have to wait. "Is nine thirty too late?"

"No. I doubt I will even have Maizy down by then, so you would be able to see her."

Dropping the phone back in his pocket, he lifted the corner of his mouth. "I would like that." He stared down at Bekah, and her mouth lifted into a shy smile. "Okay. I will stop by for a little bit."

The crowd erupted again with the final song. Brant and Bekah both clapped, then Brant followed Bekah through the crowd out to her car. He held her door open and gave her a quick peck on the lips before she left, then walked back into the building with his body and mind at odds with each other. He wondered if going over there was such a good idea. He could think of a thousand reasons he shouldn't, and only one why he should. He worried when he first met her that she was some kind of sorceress, and now he wasn't so sure she wasn't, the way he was drawn to her. It was like he was caught in an undertow that was pulling him to her.

After considering sticking around for a while longer, the thought of hanging out with Bekah and Maizy won out and had him wanting to make a quick exit. He waited for Cody and the band to join the group.

Everybody crowded around chatting with them.

Brant stepped up and slapped Cody on the back. "Bekah had to leave, but she wanted me to tell you that you were excellent. I don't know that I would go that far," he teased, and watched Cody's face pale, then he let out a chuckle. "You did a great job," he said shaking Cody's hand. "I think I'm going to bug out too." His eyes caught Jenna's. "Thanks for the invite. I had a great time."

Jenna reached around and gave him a one-armed hug. "I saw," she said with a quick wink. "Thanks for coming. I can't believe the turnout. Cody was really surprised. It meant a lot."

Brant waved to the group and walked out the door. Crawling into his car, he pulled his phone from his pocket, and it lit up again with another haunting message.

—I can't believe you've already forgotten about me—

His gut clenched. *What the hell?* He was tired of the sick game the person was playing. Debating whether to block the number or respond, he was now wondering if the person was stalking him. They already had his number. He responded.

—Who is this, and how did you get this number?—

Pulling out onto the road, he checked all around him to see if anyone might be following him. He hated feeling like he was always being watched and scrutinized. Now with the lunatic sending him messages, he wondered if his life was in danger. All because he wanted to spend time with his family. Bekah was right. He never realized it before. Being in the movies had worked as a kid because the tabloids avoided stories about kids for the most part. Now though, too much was at stake. He needed to get out of the film industry for good and figure out other ways to stay in contact with his parents and brother, without having people write fake stories about him and the people in his life.

His mind went back to Bekah, and again he played through the reasons he should stay away from her. He had rolled the same thoughts around in his head over and over the past few days. Still, something about her kept sucking him in. She made him lose every ounce of self-control. Even when she asked him to come over, he knew he shouldn't. But the sound of her voice was so sweet, and the thought of seeing her again, even for a little bit longer, had him checking in his rearview mirror one more time before pulling into her driveway.

Her car was there, so he knew she was home. Glimpsing at the clock on the dashboard, he realized he was early. Really early. His heart ticked up. *Maybe I should drive around a little bit. Or would she even mind if I showed up early?* Minutes went by as he debated with himself, and he finally unsnapped his seatbelt and exited the car. When he knocked on the door, Bekah quickly tugged it open with Maizy in her arms, still looking as heart stopping as she did at TopHops. He couldn't hold back the chuckle that erupted. It was the perfect sight. Maizy stared at him and gave him a gummy smile.

"Hi, baby girl." He rubbed his finger over her cheek. "Did you miss me?" He reached out and grabbed her right out of Bekah's arms and stepped inside. Bekah shut the door.

"I just got home. She will probably want to be fed in a little bit."

"I'll take care of her if you want to go get comfortable." A coy smile danced on her lips. "Although do me a favor, don't change your shirt."

"My shirt?" Confusion filled her face while her hands absentmindedly drifted over her form.

"I like that shirt on you."

Shyly dipping her chin, she hesitantly responded, "Okay," and did a cute little shoulder shimmy, then walked out of the room. He sat on the sofa, crossing his ankle over his knee, and laid Maizy in the bend. She gazed up at him pumping her legs up and down, giving him another toothless grin. He pulled her tiny hands over his fingers. She gurgled and cooed, and he suddenly felt like she needed to talk to him about something, so he picked her up.

"What did you say? Are you trying to tell me something?" He studied her as her mouth moved and she made little squeaks. His brows went up like she had said something important. "Is that right?"

"You better watch out, or I'm going to say something you aren't going to like."

Peeking back over his shoulder to see Bekah in her white shirt and nothing else, he sucked in a breath and coughed trying to clear his throat. "And what would that be?"

"That I think she has you wrapped around her tiny little finger."

"Can I be totally honest?"

"Of course."

"I think you might be right. Her manipulation game is strong. She's cute and wields it well."

"She's definitely adorable." Maizy cooed then scrunched her face, and a rumble filled her diaper.

Brant snickered. "Stinky. But adorable."

"Come on, Chickie, let me get you changed and fed." Bekah reached down and slowly gathered the baby in her arm.

"Need my help?"

"I think I got it, thanks. I'm getting pretty good at this one arm thing."

"Do you have any of your ginger spritzer stuff in your fridge?"

"Yes. Make yourself at home. You know where everything is."

Brant stood and walked into the kitchen, pulled open the refrigerator door, and retrieved a couple of cans.

When Bekah returned, Brant was a bit disappointed seeing a pair of purple leggings with tiny stars, under her loose white cotton shirt. She settled on the sofa with Maizy and started nursing her. Brant didn't even flinch. He set a highball glass next to her before kicking his shoes off and sitting down across from her on the other end of the sofa. It was funny how comfortable he had become around her, remembering what his first encounter was like.

"That was fun tonight. They did such a wonderful job. I really liked Cody's song," Bekah admitted after silence had taken hold.

"Yeah, I was pretty impressed. I hope they keep it up."

"You should get up there sometime. You have a great voice."

Brant wrinkled his face up. "Pssh. No, I don't. You

couldn't hear me well over the music."

"Ah, you forget that sometimes people play like they are asleep when they aren't."

Completely confused, he searched his memory for what she might be talking about, then realized she had caught him singing to Maizy late one night. "Oh." Heat crept up his neck. "Sorry, I didn't think I was that loud."

"Your rendition of Twinkle Twinkle Little Star was the best I've ever heard."

He kicked her foot that was sticking out across the sofa. "Be quiet."

She dropped her mouth open. "I mean it."

"You're too kind," he said sarcastically then paused. "I guess all the acting and dance and vocal classes my mother insisted we take paid off."

"You took dance classes too?"

"My mom had us in just about everything you can think of. I think it was to keep us out of trouble more than anything. If we weren't at our grandparents' during the summer, we were taking classes or going to camp."

"So?"

"So what?"

"Did it keep you out of trouble?"

His mouth tipped up to one side thinking of his childhood. "Not completely, no." Not really wanting to delve into his past he decided to change the subject. "How was your week?"

"Deflecting again, are we?" He nodded, and she giggled. "My week was pretty good. Maizy has been sleeping really well, so that was huge. How about you?"

He wondered if he should be honest with her and tell her about how he couldn't sleep because she wasn't there. Or how he couldn't concentrate on anything because he kept thinking about her. "Eh, not great."

"More tabloid issues?"

"No. At least not that I know of."

"Then what was the problem?"

He shifted his focus and played with the tassels on the blanket lying on the back of the sofa. "Do you really want to know?"

"Yeah, of course. Maybe I can help."

"I kind of missed you and Maizy." He moved his foot to touch hers.

A shy smile slowly crept over her lips. "I kind of missed my brick wall too."

"God, the minute you walked in tonight I couldn't take my eyes off you."

"I noticed," she said quietly, and she bit down on her lip as her attention shifted, and she rubbed her hand along Maizy's leg. "I liked it though. No one has undressed me with their eyes like that in a long time." Brant continued to tap her foot with his. "So, what do you have going on next week?"

"Mom and Dad are coming in Friday along with most of the rest of the cast and crew. We have a read through of the script Saturday and if everything goes well, shooting starts Sunday."

"How long has it been since you saw your dad?"

Brant took a deep breath and let it out thinking. "Four years?"

"Seriously?"

"He does quite a bit of stuff out of the country. He wasn't even able to make it in when Abbie died. He and

Mom never actually got to meet her. Her funeral was the only time I actually met her mom and dad. She wasn't very close to either of them."

"That's too bad. I only met Bobby's folks once. They didn't approve of me. Well, his mom didn't. His dad was indifferent."

"Why didn't she approve of you?"

"His family is rather wealthy, and they didn't like their son dating a hippie. I guess they didn't like the way I looked. They had all these preconceived notions that I was into drugs and didn't bathe on a regular basis. They didn't even take into consideration that I was completing a PhD at one of the top universities in the nation. On a fellowship to boot. I mean, yeah, my parents are somewhat unconventional, but I like to say I took from them their best qualities and then added my own twist."

Brant suddenly felt shamed for what his first impression was of her, even if it was partially due to his friends saying she was unconventional. He was no better than Bobby's family. He was just glad he decided not to walk away. "I'm sorry they didn't give you a chance. It's their loss." His thoughts went back to Abbie, and he wondered what his family would have thought if they had met her.

"What are you thinking about?" Bekah's voice pulled him from his thoughts. "Something's bothering you." Brant studied her as she stared him down. She was reading him, so there was no use in lying.

"I was wondering what my family would have thought of Abbie."

"Is that all?"

He again lifted his eyes to hers and let out a long

breath. "There's some weird stuff going on…" Bekah's brows furrowed, and Brant wrestled with the idea of telling her everything that had happened. "I've been getting these creepy texts." He paused wondering if he should have opened his mouth when he noticed Bekah's expression turn to concern. "I'm sure it's someone who knows me and is messing with me."

"What do they say?"

"One said, 'I miss you.' Another said, 'I can't wait to see you.'"

"Could they just be a wrong number?"

"I thought the same thing, but the next message, after the tabloid photo came out, called me by name. I had another on my phone tonight that said, 'I can't believe you've forgotten about me already.'" He paused. "I know it isn't Abbie, but I have to admit, it has rattled me."

"Totally understandable, and normal reaction."

"Really? I mean, I seriously thought—"

"Brant. What happened to your wife was tragic and unexpected. Of course, your rational mind knows what happened, can probably recall it moment by moment, but there will always be a part of you that will struggle to accept it, even if you saw it with your own two eyes." She lifted Maizy from under the blanket and put her up on her shoulder. "Now. Is there anyone that you can think of that would want to mess with you like this?" She patted Maizy on the back.

"Honestly, I can't think of anyone. I think it's kind of strange that it started with the heightened publicity of the movie."

"Do you get fan mail, or has anyone posted anything odd on your social media?"

"No. Not that I know of. I try to stay away from that stuff as much as possible."

"Have you reported it to the police?"

"Nah. I mean, it's a few text messages."

"You might check your social media though, just to see if there could be someone stalking you."

"I had someone a few years back kind of stalk me, but she's long gone, and I haven't noticed anyone following me or anything. It's creepy as hell, but I didn't think it was dangerous. I did think about blocking them, then I thought it would probably be better to keep it in case I do need to make it a police matter."

"I agree." She continued to rub her hand on Maizy's back. "Come on, baby girl. You need to burp."

"Want me to try?"

"Sure."

Brant stood and took Maizy in his arms. The sleepy baby's head drifted forward as Bekah draped the blanket over his shoulder, and he propped her against it. Having her snuggled against his shoulder, and the powdery smell of her skin, always made his chest tighten, but in a weird way it was comforting. He rubbed his hand up her back and within a couple of minutes came the sound he had hoped for.

After laying her in her crib, he covered her with a fuzzy mint green blanket with tiny blue flowers. Bekah walked up beside him. "You are really good with her."

"I think she likes me." He spoke quietly, his eyes never leaving Maizy.

"Funny. I kind of feel the same way."

His fingers rubbed up against the baby's head, and Bekah wrapped her hands around his bicep and leaned her head against him. He turned and brought his hand to her cheek. The light from the outside streetlamp shone through the window and lit up her face. Her light green eyes were a deeper shade now and spoke volumes into his soul. It was the connection between them that had been there from the very first day. One that was almost eerie how well they could already read each other. He knew she was trained in that area. This was different because it was mutual. Instinctual. He knew her thoughts, her needs. When she walked into the club, he knew it was her before he saw her. What he wasn't expecting was the way she looked, and how his body completely combusted at that moment. And when his lips met hers for the first time, he knew it wasn't going to be enough, no matter how hard he tried to fight it. And although he questioned it, he knew she felt the same way. And she confirmed it when she invited him over.

Leaning down, he brought his lips to hers and slowly feasted on her soft plump mouth. She tasted so sweet it was intoxicating. The more he kissed her the more he needed to kiss her, to claim every inch of her. He was struggling to hold himself back from completely devouring her. As her tongue met his, he tilted his head and continued to savor her as his hands moved down her body, stopping below her hips and lifting her up against him. Her legs wrapped around him, and he held her as he walked out to the living room without breaking their connection. She felt so light in his hands and so perfect pressed up against him.

His heart pounded. A thousand thoughts flashed through his mind, yet somehow, none of it mattered at the moment. What mattered was her, in his arms. Bekah straddled him as they sat on the sofa, and he reluctantly pulled his lips away. His eyes captured hers. "What are we doing?"

Her voice was low and raspy. "What I have wanted to do since you walked out that door." He chuckled and pulled her in again. Her fingers threaded through his short hair. She wrapped her hand around his neck and pressed her lips against his, letting her mouth plunder his. Her intensity and aggressiveness only added to the wildfire burning through him. His hands caressed her velvety skin beneath her cotton shirt, slowly skating up her ribs.

A low growl rumbled in the back of his throat before he spoke. "This shirt." He tugged on it causing it to drop off one shoulder. "Didn't leave much to the imagination. I was dying when you walked in tonight." Sliding higher, his fingers brushed against the sensitive skin of her breast. Her eyes fluttered and lips parted as she released a whimper and leaned in for another kiss. His kisses trailed down her neck to her ear. "Are you sure you're okay with this?"

She leaned her forehead against his. "Trust me, I know how to say no, and I know I don't want to."

He lifted the bottom of the shirt and pulled it over her head, being careful of her arm. Remnants of the accident were still visible in a couple of spots with cuts and scrapes. His breath caught taking in her bare skin. Closing his eyes, he leaned into her shoulder, then he began dropping kisses in the hollow of her neck. "You are so beautiful," he whispered as his lips dusted kisses up her neck, over her jaw, and to her mouth.

Prickles trailed up his stomach as her hands pulled on the bottom of his sweater. He quickly reached down and pulled it over his head. His eyes met her pleading expression, and he reached up and began unbuttoning the shirt while still kissing her. When he was free of both shirts her fingers dug into the light brown hair on his chest. The minute their bodies touched skin to skin, sparks pulsated through him. *God, she feels so good.* Her hand moved from his chest to his cheek, and her mouth met his with a kiss that was so gentle yet so intense he could barely breathe. What was it about her? How was it possible to feel like his body now required the connection? One glance from her could send him into an all-out meltdown. No one had ever had that kind of effect on him. Not even Abbie.

Her hips slowly began to roll against his, and he knew he was moments away from losing any control he had. Having her in his arms was better than any drink or drug he had ever had. She was his new drug, and he was helplessly addicted. His mind was telling him this was insane. He hadn't known her that long. There was too much at stake. Too many things could go wrong. But his body was winning the battle. His hands gripped her, pressing her into him and he let out a moan. She grabbed at his belt tugging it loose while her mouth continued its hungry assault.

His heart raced, and one last thought flitted through his mind suddenly making him back away. "Bekah." His words came out strained. "God, you feel so good, but you were just in a car accident and just had a baby. I'm scared I'll hurt you."

"Umm." A smile skirted across her mouth, and she giggled. "I've been cleared to resume *all* activity."

His body flinched. Every reservation, and every ounce of control he possessed vanished and was replaced with an insatiable craving. This beautiful, smart, unconventional woman was the only thing he saw. Capturing her mouth, ready to devour her, he scooted to the edge of the sofa. Tucking his hands beneath her perfect butt, he lifted her with him as he stood and carried her back to the bedroom. Gently lowering her to the bed, he laid her back, pushed her legs apart, and covered her body with his. She giggled as his lips met hers. He couldn't get enough of her and how she felt beneath him. His hands explored as his mouth continued to feast on her lips, then traveled over her neck to her breasts.

Breathlessly she whispered in his ear. "Brant." The sound of his name on her lips made his body shudder.

His kisses trailed back up her neck. "Hmm?"

"Make love to me." His head lifted, and he could see the desperation on her face. "Please."

"That was my plan." Pushing at the waistband of her pants, he moved down her body kissing her stomach as he pulled her pants off and left them in a puddle on the floor. He stood, gazing at her naked form, slowly tugging his belt from his pants and lowering his zipper. Reaching into his pocket, he retrieved his wallet and pulled out a small packet, then tossed the wallet on the nightstand next to the bed and removed his pants. The empty foil packet dropped next to his wallet before his eyes met hers again. She moved on her knees, to the edge of the bed, her hands skating up his stomach, wrapping around him, and pulling him into her.

His fingers threaded through her hair as she pressed her lips to his bare skin. With each feathery kiss, his muscles tensed, and a little more control disappeared. Finally, he pressed his body against hers and slowly pushed her back down on the bed. Her chest heaved, and she whimpered as his lips dropped soft kisses on her breast then traveled up her neck to the shell of her ear.

"Don't let me hurt you," he growled, moving slowly, pressing into her, and trying desperately to be gentle. But the desire in her eyes, and her velvety skin against his, made it nearly impossible not to grab her and have his way. He nestled his face in her hair, breathing deep the fresh scent. Bekah traced her fingers down his back as she wrapped her legs around him.

Brant leaned back and moved the hair away from her face and stared down at her. Long dark lashes brushed her golden cheeks. Everything about her was exquisite. She was so unique, and he was completely lost in her. His lips traveled from her mouth to the sensitive dip in her neck. A sigh escaped her, then a moan. Her breath swept over his neck making his body burn. He could feel his need growing, demanding more. Their hands explored as they moved in sync, and the feel of her fingers digging into his skin let him know she was getting close. He gazed at her partially shadowed face. Her rosebud lips parted, and her eyes opened and stared up at him. In that moment there was nothing else but them in the universe. Their connection was more than physical. His kisses trailed down her neck to her breasts, and he brought his mouth over the soft nipple. She gasped, and he could feel her body trembling. Their movement increased with the building need. He lightly kissed her jaw as she let out a cry. Her body tensed and shuddered and gave way to the pleasure. With each cry, each whimper, each moan, it drew him closer and finally set off an explosion in him.

Wave after wave drowned him in a release so intense he wasn't sure he was going to survive.

Finally, with their breaths ragged, Brant moved hair from Bekah's face and stared into her eyes. His breath stilled when he noticed a tear spill from her lashes.

His hands rested on each side of her head. "Bekah? You okay? Did I hurt you?" He placed a light kiss on her neck.

Her hand reached up and swiped the tear away. She chuckled. "No. You were…I have never felt anything like…" She coughed, and more tears spilled.

Brant brushed his thumb over her wet cheeks. "Me neither." He leaned his forehead against hers then tenderly kissed her lips and rolled off her. His arm reached around her and pulled her in close. She pulled the covers up around them and laid her head on his chest.

"I was kind of worried we would wake Maizy, but I guess she is catching up on all the sleep she's been missing."

He chuckled, and his hand dug into her hair combing through it and separating the tangles. His thoughts flashed on Abbie, and a knot lodged in his throat. He loved her, but his mind was trying to reconcile the fact that there was something about Bekah, something he couldn't put his finger on, that absolutely consumed him. Something that, if he was honest with himself, he didn't have with Abbie.

Her lips pressed against his chest. "Thank you." He tilted his head and dropped his focus to her. Moisture still covered her cheeks, and his heart sank.

He leaned up on his elbow and swiped at the tears.

"What is going on?" She raised up on her elbow too, and he tucked her hair behind her ear so he could see her face fully.

"It's nothing," she said waving her hand in dismissal.

"No, it's not nothing. Something is making you upset and I want to know, especially if that something is me."

"Oh, believe me, it's not you…well it is, but that's a good thing."

"Well, if I'm involved at all, good or bad, I need to know."

Her expression begged him not to pry, but he needed to know. "I don't—"

"Try me."

She remained silent and shifted her focus away. After a moment, her gaze slowly returned to his, and she studied him then let out a sigh. "I always had this idea in my head of what sex was supposed to be like. It was never just about satisfying an itch for me. It was more."

She collapsed on the pillow and draped her arm across her forehead. "Let's just say that wasn't the case for Bobby." Brant's chest burned as her tone weakened and she turned away. "When we first met, he always complimented me and seemed like he couldn't get enough of me, but it was always…just sex. And when he found out I was pregnant, I felt like he was repulsed by me, because of the things he would say, and the way he acted. He barely touched me." She let out a frustrated breath. "I was always okay with my body and how I looked, until I got pregnant. The one time I should be excited to show off my baby bump, I felt the need to cover myself up with as many layers of clothes as I could." Her eyes lifted to his. "But tonight, you made me feel beautiful and desired and the way you touched me and kissed me, it felt like more than just sex. It was everything I had imagined it was supposed to be." He opened his mouth to speak but she continued. "I'm sorry. I'm sure the last thing you wanted to hear was that I was thinking about my ex."

He pulled her to him, tightening his hold on her. "Actually, I felt the same way. And if I'm being honest, I was thinking about Abbie too. You are my first since her."

Her thumb rubbed against the scruff of his beard. "She was a lucky lady."

Chapter Eleven

Bekah sat back on her feet then folded forward and stretched her one good arm out in front of her, letting her breath escape from the back of her throat. Her body felt loose. Satisfied. Moments flashed through her mind of the previous night causing a smile to spread across her face. She didn't get much sleep, but this time it had nothing to do with Maizy. When she woke up tangled in Brant's arms, her thoughts got the best of her, and she finally decided to get up.

Tucking her feet beneath her, she slowly stood lifting her arms above her head, breathing in a deep breath. Her fingers touched and she lowered her hands releasing her breath bringing her hands together over her heart. The floor creaked pulling at her attention. Brant appeared from the kitchen in his boxers and nothing else except a cup of coffee in his hand. His hair was beautifully messy, and his body was rippled with muscles. The V at his hips had her body twitching causing her to bite down on her lip. He had a long scar on his left thigh, and she noticed occasionally he had a slight limp. She remembered his story about being shot in Afghanistan. He was a true hero. Trying to continue with her yoga, she acted like she didn't see him, though her eyes seemed to have a mind of their own, especially when he headed straight for her. His lips touched her cheek while she tried to hold warrior pose, and a giggle snuck up her throat. "You broke my concentration."

"Couldn't help it. You are a bit irresistible in that shirt. You did that on purpose, didn't you?"

She shook her head no, but her smile betrayed her.

Brant's eyes narrowed, and she finally nodded.

He took a drink of his coffee and set it on the side table. "How long do you have left?"

"I just got started. Wanna try it?"

He lifted a brow and grimaced. She gave him a wide smile, and his face softened. He let out a heavy sigh. "Okay, sure, on one condition."

She batted her lashes. "And that would be?"

"That you come work out with me at the gym sometime."

"Deal." She shimmied her shoulders slightly then continued. "I actually wanted to check it out anyway. I have been thinking about asking what it would take to do a yoga class there for a little extra money."

"Good idea." He rubbed his hands together, let out a long breath, and squatted with his toes pointed out like a ballet dancer, then tossed his head from shoulder to shoulder. Bekah snickered and rolled her eyes. "What? I'm loosening up."

She moved her feet and squared her shoulders. "It's all about keeping your core tight and breathing. Right now, I am working with flow yoga. It's a type of yoga that moves slower and holds poses longer. It is supposed to help with circulation. Move slowly and hold each pose until I tell you."

Brant put his hands on his hips. "Okay."

"I still can't do some of the poses, so I will talk you through those." She could see the doubt written all over Brant's face.

"I probably won't be able to do most of the poses, so—"

"Don't worry. You will do fine." She was giddy with the thought of him trying yoga just for her. "Okay, stand with your feet slightly apart and your hands by your side." Brant got into position. "Take a deep breath in. Point your chin to the sky. Lift your hands up over your head and touch your fingers together. Release your breath and bring your head forward and hands down. Drop forward at your hips and relax your arms. Let them dangle. Deep breath in. Come all the way up lifting your chin and bringing your hands above your head. Touch your fingers. Release your breath and let your arms come down and bring your palms together in front of your heart." Brant followed her lead. "That is sun salute."

He winked at her.

"Stop it." She narrowed her eyes and unsuccessfully tried not to smile. "Okay, do that again…" They moved through the poses together. "…now when you bend down walk your hands out in front of you and pike your hips." Brant did as she said.

"Hold that pose."

"This is probably not the best thing to be doing first thing in the morning."

"Why?"

"Blood is rushing to my head. I'm getting dizzy."

"Take a deep breath and walk your hands back, lifting your hands above your head. Touch your fingers. Release your breath and bring your hands together over your heart." She waited for him to return to the resting pose. "That is downward dog."

"So, was this something you learned as a child?"

"No, and I know what you are thinking. This was not a part of my hippie upbringing. I got into this when I was in college. They had open sessions at the student union during finals along with the mindful meditation and massages."

"So where do the crystals come in?"

"Crystals?"

He pointed to some hanging in her window.

"Oh! Ha! I saw some in a store once. They were glittery, and they reflected these pretty prisms across the ceiling. So, I bought one. Then another and another."

"So, you just think their pretty? They aren't part of your practice?"

She giggled for real this time. "No. I honestly don't know any of the healing powers of crystals. I don't discount anything if it helps the patient resolve whatever it is they are dealing with though. By the way, I like chimes too. For the same reason."

"Noted. For the record, I do too. Especially the big ones."

"Yes," she said enthusiastically.

She continued to take him through several other poses and could tell Brant was getting a good workout by how out of breath he was and the amount of sweat he had worked up. Her heart about exploded because she knew he was wanting to quit a couple of times and kept going just to show off. He had been a good sport about it all though, only making a few snide remarks.

"Okay, this is our last pose. Lie down on your back.

"Oh yeah, I like this one already."

"Let your arms and legs rest comfortably. Close

your eyes. Take a deep breath. Notice how it feels against the back of your throat and how your lungs feel expanding in your chest. Notice how your head feels against the floor. Now relax your shoulders…your arms…your hands. Touch the floor beneath you, feel its coolness. Now relax your back. Sink into the floor. Let all the tightness go. Relax your legs…your toes." Each word she spoke slowly and softly. "Breathe. Now focus on your thoughts. Let them roll in like waves. Picture them coming to shore and dissipating. They have no power. They are just thoughts." She paused, letting the quiet take over. "Now take a deep breath and sit up."

Bekah slowly sat up and opened her eyes to see Brant sitting upright with his legs crossed. "How do you feel?"

"Relaxed." He slowly tipped his head from shoulder to shoulder. "Damn, I didn't realize yoga was so tough."

"It sneaks up on you."

"Now I know why you are in such good shape."

"There is a lot more to it than people think." She dug her fingers into her hair and noticed Brant staring at her.

"What?"

"I was just wondering if your tattoos had any meaning."

She glanced down at her right hand that was partially covered with the cast. "Yeah they do." Her finger traced over the lacy scrolling with a leaf pattern that swirled over the part of her hand peeking out from the cast. "I don't know if you are familiar with the henna tattooing in some of the Indian and Middle Eastern cultures." Brant nodded his head slightly, so she pushed on. "It's usually done in association with a celebration. Anyway, one of the girls I was friends with in college would do henna tattoos on me occasionally. I always thought it looked pretty. When my grandma died, I wanted some way to remember her, to celebrate her. She was such a huge influence in my life, and her advice was always so wise. One thing she taught me was to never settle and to always seek what is just out of my reach." She pointed to the words hidden in the scrolling tattoo on her hand. Then she pointed to her left. "Something else she taught me was to always believe I can achieve my heart's desire."

"And what's this?" Brant pointed to her ring finger.

"My grandma and grandpa had a special love. My grandma told me 'Only marry a man who adores you.' I saw the love between my grandma and grandpa. They adored each other, and I saw how devastated my grandpa was when she passed away. It took him a long time to start living again. I want that kind of love. So, I remind myself. It says adore." Brant gave her a raised eyebrow. "I know. I kind of lost my way…" A whimper came through the monitor. "Right on time." Bekah started to get up.

"I'll get her and bring her to you." She loved when Brant got Maizy because he never remembered about the monitor and always talked so sweetly to her. She sat down on the sofa and waited. And a smile formed on her lips when she heard him.

"Hey, baby girl. Did you sleep good?"

Bekah's lips tucked between her teeth.

"Your momma was trying to kill me this morning with her yoga stuff. I'm thinking of suggesting it to the military as a new torture technique. It was worth it though because I was only doing it to sneak peeks down her shirt."

Her mouth dropped open. "Brant, don't be telling her that." She yelled down the hallway and heard him snicker through the monitor. He came out of the bedroom with a big grin on his face.

"Hey, don't get all high and mighty on me, missy. I saw you sneaking peeks too."

"Oh. Well, I wonder why since you were doing yoga in your skimpy boxers. I'm not complaining though. Do that as often as you like."

He kissed Maizy on the cheek and handed her off to Bekah. "Do you want me to make some breakfast?"

"Will you make me your famous French toast?"

"Sure." He wandered into the kitchen, and Bekah heard a few clanks of pans. He came back into the living room and grabbed his coffee and held it up. "Would you like a cup?"

"I think I'll wait until I eat."

"Okay. I had a thought," he said, as he headed back into the kitchen.

"What's that?" Bekah called over her shoulder.

"Do you think your grandpa would let me take a peek at his car?"

"Probably."

"I mean, to maybe work on it."

"I don't know. Why?"

"Well, if we can get it running then it would give you a car to drive, at least until you could buy one. I worked on a few of the cars that came through my granddad's shop, so I do know my way around an engine."

"I don't know. He might. I mean it would be better

than letting it rust in the barn."

Her phone buzzed. A text from Bobby.

—I'm heading back. I can't stop thinking about our conversation Bekah. I don't know how to make you understand how sorry I am. I want you back in my life. I love you. You need to come with me to Houston so we can be a family. You, me, and Maizy —

She threw the phone down and let out a growl.

"What was that for?" Brant's voice echoed above the noise of the French toast in the pan.

"Bobby texted me." She paused, wondering if she should tell Brant about him coming over and the conversation they had. "He came by yesterday."

Brant came out of the kitchen with two plates. He set one next to her and carried his with him and sat down on the end of the sofa.

"Is it okay if I eat here? I can't see you if I'm over there." His nose tipped in the direction of the dining room.

"I normally eat sitting on the sofa, actually."

"So, what happened? What did he say?"

"He apologized, of course. Then he said he kicked the girlfriend out and wanted me and Maizy to come to Houston with him."

She stared at Brant whose face turn solemn as he dredged his French toast in syrup. "So, what did you say?" he asked slowly.

"I told him no. After seeing him with Marissa, I took a long hard look at our relationship. We were not right for each other for so many reasons. I see it clear as day now. He doesn't love me, although he said he did, and tried to kiss me." Brant's eyes darted up without saying a word. "I said *tried*. He didn't succeed." She glanced over her shoulder. "The only reason he wants me is because I told him he can't have me. Now, it's a game to him. He doesn't like losing. He has to have control."

"So, what are you going to do about Maizy though?"

"We are going to have to work that out. I won't keep her from her father if he wants to see her. Until yesterday though, he showed no interest in her whatsoever."

"What happened yesterday?"

"I think I actually saw him break for like a split second. He asked to hold her, which, that surprised me in and of itself. And then when he had her in his arms I think I saw a slight crack in his armor."

Brant sat silent. Bekah studied him wondering. His jaw ticked. "What are you thinking?"

"Honestly?" His hand gripped the back of his neck. "What it would be like to have to share my kid. Especially with someone nine hours away."

"Trust me, I have no idea what I'm going to do. I mean, the job he is taking is a wonderful opportunity and, as I told him, I think he should take it. It's what he's always wanted. Still, the thought of trying to work out the logistics of shuttling Maizy back and forth makes my head hurt. There is no good solution." She shifted Maizy up to her shoulder. "I'm glad, for right now, he is too busy with the move and new position to have time for any of that."

"What did he say in the text?"

"He is still telling me he loves me and wants us to move down there. I know in some ways he probably thinks he does. The problem is, he wants a puppet, and I don't want his strings attached to me anymore."

Brant looked at Bekah then Maizy. "Do you want me to take her so you can eat?"

"Sure." He stood up and grabbed the sleeping baby and sat back down. Propping his feet up on the sofa, he laid her on his bare chest and rubbed her back. Bekah sat and watched him, wondering what it would be like to have him there every day. It was obvious how much he cared for her little girl. Why couldn't he be her daddy?

After she finished her French toast and dressed, Bekah was cleaning up the kitchen when someone knocked. She pulled open the door to see her granddad standing there.

"I got your message. You wanted to see me?"

"Yes, I did. Well, actually Brant did."

"I noticed his car was here."

"He's putting Maizy down, he'll be out in a second."

Brant walked up the hallway in his button-down and jeans from the night before. Dale glimpsed at him with a bit of a side eye, and Bekah knew he suspected something.

"So, you are Rex Gerard's grandson?"

"That I am. I'm guessing you and Grams had lunch Friday."

"Yes. She was telling me all about you."

"Oh boy." Brant's cheeks pinked up. "I'm sure she had a lot to say. She and Grandpa had their hands full with me and my brother. She took the willow switch after us many a time."

"Sounds like you were no ornerier than she is."

"If you wanna know the truth, I think she has me

beat."

"You're probably right. But let me tell you what, she wouldn't trade you for the world."

"The feeling is mutual."

Dale turned back to Bekah. "What did you need me for?" Bekah's eyes shifted to Brant, who donned a confused expression, then realized why Dale came over.

"Oh! I was telling Bekah that you and my granddad used to work on cars together. She said you had an old Chevelle that you had been working on out in the barn. My granddad taught me a few things about cars over the summers I stayed with him and Grams, so I was wondering if I could take a look at it."

"I worked on that car for I don't know how long. It was in bad shape when I got it, but I had always loved the 1971 Chevelle and when I found this one, the price was right, and I had to have it. I got the body and interior all done and started working on the engine when my wife got sick. After she passed I lost interest."

"I wasn't sure what your plans were for it, but I thought maybe if we can get it up and running, Bekah could use it for a while until she can get another car."

"Well, if we get it running I'll use it and she can have my car." Dale eyed Brant. "You want to go take a look?"

"Absolutely." Brant turned to Bekah. "Be back in a little bit."

She grabbed the monitor. "I'm coming too."

****

Bekah had to laugh. She stood at the window two days later watching Grandpa Dale steal her new boyfriend again. He had spent most of his time at her

187

place, though it wasn't with her. He and Dale had gotten up early Sunday and spent the entire day out in the barn, only taking lunch to spend it with his grams. When she walked out with them the first time Dale showed Brant the car, the expression on his face when it was revealed was priceless. He looked like a kid surprised with his first bike at Christmas. And that evening, when he returned, he was covered in mud and oil and had a huge grin plastered across his face as he talked about the old car. She had never seen him so animated. Today, Dale had knocked on her door at seven fifteen to talk to Brant before he headed to the university. He wanted to show him one more thing before he left. Brant didn't seem to mind. In fact, he seemed like he was excited about it. Her phone buzzed. Another text from Bobby.

—*I may have found a place. I set up an appointment with the realtor for Wednesday. I will send you a link in your e-mail—*

She took a deep breath and let it out trying to calm herself as her fingers tapped her reply.

—*Great. Glad to hear it—*

—*Do you and Maizy want to come and look at it with me? —*

—*No, Bobby. There's no reason. We aren't getting back together. I'm sorry—*

—*Bekah, please. This is killing me. You're the only woman I want. I love you—*

Closing her eyes, she rubbed her fingers across her forehead wondering if her words would ever sink in.

—*No! It wouldn't work—*

Her phone buzzed again. She tilted her head back and rolled her eyes. This time though, when she glanced back at the screen, a smile filled her face. The text was from Brant, and her whole body warmed.

—*Do you need me for anything for a little while? I need to run to Fayetteville for a part*—

—*Well...Depends on what you mean by need*—

Her teeth bit into her lip as the dots kept rolling across the screen. She couldn't imagine what he might come back with. She didn't have to wait long because the door flew open, and Brant stalked her like a lion on his prey as he ripped his grimy T-shirt over his head. His faded jeans were slung low on his hips and with each step he took toward her, heat pulsated through her body. Smudged grease and dirt dotted his face, and the look in his eyes told her he was there for one thing and one thing only. Closing the distance between them, his arm wrapped around her waist, and he pushed her up against the wall.

With his mouth to her ear, he growled, "How long do we have?" His chest heaved trying to catch his breath while he gathered her shirt and gently tugged it over her head, being careful of her arm.

"I think you put her down around six, so not long." His mouth was on hers in a hungry kiss, and her core stirred when a moan rumbled in his chest. Bekah closed her eyes letting the desire wash over her. God she loved the way he acted like his life centered around making her happy. Even when he was trying to keep his distance, he texted her just to make sure she was okay. His hand slowly caressed her breast. And good lord did he know how to make her happy. She could see the fire in his eyes and feel the charge between them. Her hands traveled down his chest to his jeans and unsnapped them. Brant suddenly backed up, threw her over his shoulder, carted her off to the bedroom, and dumped her on the bed. "I guess I should have asked what you needed instead of assuming—

"Oh, your assumption was pretty spot on and even more so looking the way you do right now."

He ran his fingers through his hair, and dust particles floated in the air. "I'll go wash up."

"Don't you dare." His eyes opened wide at her comment, then a smirk formed on his face. He kicked his boots off, yanked his pants off and then, tucking his hand behind her, dusted kisses up her bare stomach to her breast as he positioned himself over her. His hand caressed her cheek, as his mouth consumed hers in another desperate kiss, then moved down gently brushing against her breast. She let out a moan and dug her fingers in his hair, and another puff of dust flitted through the air.

She giggled when he waved dust out of the air then propped himself up with a smile on his face. "Sorry. I'm pretty dirty."

She raised her brows at his comment. "I know."

A wolfish grin spread across his face.

Her eyes darted back to the crib. "She is probably going to be waking up hungry pretty soon."

"Well, she will just have to wait." His mouth pressed against hers while his hands skimmed her body. She closed her eyes and drank it in. The way he kissed her and touched her, caressing her tenderly, yet almost ravenous, had her wading hip deep in a pool she didn't know if she was ready to swim in. But God, was he making her dreams come true. Over and over. His kisses stole her breath away every time his lips met her mouth and skin. His hands knew exactly where to touch, and each touch completely destroyed her control. Within moments he had her begging him for more, and only he knew how to provide it. He moved off her long enough to remove her pants then their legs entwined, and their bodies joined together in a dance so intense they both struggled to breathe. Her body craved his every move and responded pushing her closer and closer to her release. Slowly opening her eyes, she could see the intensity in his, and the hunger. Her fingers dug into him as his movements became more frenzied and the sensation intensified. His teeth scraped against her sensitive skin, and white heat shot through her body. Her back arched, and a scream crawled up her throat. "Brant." His hand quickly reached up and gently covered her mouth, then he replaced his hand with his lips, kissing her hard. His body tightened, and he let out a low growl. Holding her against him, his hot breath grazed her neck as he struggled to breathe, and they continued to ride out the waves of pleasure until their bodies relaxed.

Bekah lay in Brant's arms quietly for a few minutes waiting for Maizy to whimper. When the cry didn't come, she asked, "So where do you have to go?"

"There is a salvage yard in Fayetteville that has a part I need. I called them, and they have it on hold for me. I'm nowhere close to being the mechanic my granddad was, but I think, once I get this part installed, I might be able to get the car running."

"That's fantastic. It will be fun to drive."

"Well, I spoke to your granddad about that. He's going to drive the Chevelle, and you will take his Chevy SUV. The Chevelle only has a lap belt and no airbags. It's not safe for you and Maizy." Bekah was a smidge disappointed that she wouldn't be able to drive the classic car but smiled at how protective Brant was. "Do you want to go with me?"

"To the salvage yard?" They hadn't been out in public together since the night of Cody's concert. Brant was concerned. With the movie shoot looming, he figured the paparazzi had already set up camp somewhere, waiting for the stars to hit town. He had already warned her, once the shoot started, they were probably not going to be able to see much of each other. He didn't want any other stories coming out that might hurt her or her practice.

"Yeah. I mean it's nothing romantic, but I figure we would be safe going to a salvage yard. I doubt there would be any photographers there, and I think there is a little hole in the wall deli, right around the corner we can go to and grab some lunch."

"Sure. That sounds like fun."

After feeding Maizy and replenishing the baby supplies in the diaper bag, they headed to the salvage yard. Bekah marveled at the acres of old cars that surrounded the metal building. She wondered how they kept track of them. Brant purchased the part he wanted along with a couple of hoses the guy said he might need, and then they headed to the deli, but it had closed. Bekah checked her phone trying to find a place that might be safe. They settled on a seafood restaurant on the edge of town. The place was larger than what they expected. It was stark white, with rectangular tables butted up against each other, offering communal style seating. Several smaller tables sat along the perimeter of the dining area against the large windows. Fresh fish and seafood sat in a display case with the menu on the wall above.

A tall, dark-haired man stood behind the cash register. He nodded to Bekah. "What can I get you?"

"I'll take the fish k-bob with green beans and coleslaw." He tapped the information into his computer.

"And to drink?"

"Water."

"And for you?" He lifted his focus to Brant who had Maizy in her carrier.

"I think I will take the grilled seabass with a baked potato and the vegetable medley. Oh, and water to drink."

He entered the information into the computer. "That will be thirty-two ninety-six."

Brant handed him his card. "Do we sit anywhere?" The guy nodded and handed his card back with the receipt after swiping it.

They found a booth away from the window, and within moments a server brought their waters.

Bekah put her elbows on the table and leaned in. "When do you move into the hotel?"

"Friday. My mom and dad should be in around noon. I will probably head up there after breakfast. Since this is a bigger part, I want to sit down with my mom and kind of go over everything."

"You said the movie was about the gangsters in Hot Springs. What exactly is the story?"

"The history of Hot Springs talks about underground casinos and how all the gangsters and outlaws kind of had this agreement that they would respect each other while they were in Hot Springs. Even though they might have been enemies any other time, they knew Hot Springs was off limits. It was their vacation spot. They knew they had it good there. The city turned a blind eye.

The movie story is fiction. It's about a wanna-be Irish gangster named Lou O'Hanlon. He gets word about the underground gambling in Hot Springs. He doesn't, however, know about the unwritten rules. Figuring there could be oodles and oodles of money to be had, he devises a plan to rob the casinos. Trouble is, it's vacation time for a lot of the usual gangsters and when he trespasses on their happy vacation territory, they decide to gang up on him."

"That sounds really cool."

"It's action packed and has a comedic edge because each of the gangsters thinks they should be the designated leader of this would be gang."

"Oh yeah. That would be hilarious."

"It really is a great script. I hope it transitions onto film well."

The server arrived with their food. She smiled politely and refilled their glasses then left.

"Okay. Here's a question." Brant picked up his utensils. "How did they know where we were sitting? We had no number on the table, and we were able to sit anywhere." He picked up the receipt. "Our receipt only had our food order on it."

"That's a good question. I have no idea."

"It's a mystery."

They sat and ate, chatting more about the movie and how delicious the food was. After finishing their meal, they headed out to the car. Brant loaded Maizy's car seat, gave Bekah a quick kiss before shutting her door, and hopped into the driver's seat to head back to Dalton. Bekah took a deep breath. *What a perfect day.*

Chapter Twelve

The musty smell of the old hotel mixed with disinfectant burned Brant's nose as he stepped through the door. The lobby had a charm of the bygone era with an ornate arched ceiling that curved into columns along the walls where sconces hung. At the edge of the lobby was a grand marbled staircase. The hotel at one time had been a getaway for the rich, but in recent years, other, newer hotels had stolen its livelihood, and it had been bought and sold several times.

With his duffle slung over his shoulder and a coffee tumbler in his hand, he took in the view, still unsure if he should be there. He couldn't decide if he was excited for the opportunity or apprehensive. He felt prepared to play the part, although something had him on edge. His chest ached having to leave Bekah and Maizy this morning.

He had spent most of the week at Bekah's trying to get the Chevelle running. As of yesterday, it was. He and Dale had taken it out for its first run. And boy did it run. Out on the highway they opened it up. The growl of the engine made him want to see how fast it could go. Dale couldn't contain his giddiness. He laughed the whole time they were pushing the pedal to the floor. He happily handed over the keys to his SUV to Bekah and told her she could have it. All they needed to do was the paperwork.

As Brant approached the reception desk, he smiled at the older blonde woman behind the counter.

"Name?" She smiled back at him.

"Brant Ellington?"

"Well, well, well, look what the cat dragged in." The voice behind him made the hair on his neck stand on end. It couldn't be. His jaw clenched, and his stomach dropped. Why was she here? He hadn't seen her in almost eight years, and he could still recognize the voice. The receptionist gave him his room key. He thanked her and slowly turned. Out of his peripheral he saw her. She was tall, with board straight brown hair, parted in the middle. She'd obviously had work done. Her full lips and chest, bought and paid for, and courtesy of one of the many plastic surgeons in California, he was sure. What he wasn't sure about was why. When he met her years ago, there was no denying how beautiful she was. Unfortunately, he found out quickly, there was a very good reason she was single. Her arms crossed over her lemon-yellow button-down sweater that didn't quite make it to her skintight black leggings.

Ignoring her, he started to walk away, hoping she would get the hint. After joining the military, he thought he was rid of her. At one time he thought he might have to have her arrested after she broke into his apartment in Los Angeles. Now he was forced to deal with her again.

"What? Are you seriously going to completely ignore me?"

He let out a sigh, stopped, and turned just short of completely facing her. "Hello, Natalie." His voice was devoid of emotion.

"It's good to see you, Brant. I guess we get to work together again."

He couldn't bring himself to say anything and started walking away. She had made his life hell for at least a year after working with her.

"I'm sorry to hear about your loss." Her voice echoed in the lobby, and he could tell by her tone she was anything but sorry.

He sighed and stopped, "Thank you," and again tried to walk away.

"It appears you've moved on though." The thought of the tabloid story filled him with anger, and her remark stung. Had he moved on? He had to admit he hadn't stopped thinking about Bekah since he left. Exactly what he felt about her though, he still wasn't sure. It was more than a casual hook-up. Was it too soon to move on? It hadn't even been a year. Was he moving too fast? She had barely gotten out of her relationship. He didn't turn. Didn't want to engage.

"Why won't you talk to me? It's been years, you know."

The memories of their brief relationship, if it even constituted being called that, peppered his thoughts. Yes, it had been years, though it seemed like yesterday that it all happened, and he worried that if he gave even an inch, she would take a mile. "It's not a good idea, Natalie."

"Fine. Although, you know, we are going to have to work together so might as well call a truce," she hollered. He continued walking, wondering exactly how much she was going to be involved. The thought crossed his mind to drive back to his or Bekah's house, but he didn't want to give Natalie, or any of the paparazzi, the chance to find out where either lived, if they hadn't figured it out already. It made it much easier for the production team anyway, having everyone in the same location.

He unlocked his door, hoping like hell registration didn't put Natalie anywhere near him.

The room was nice. It contained all the necessities for an extended stay, including a kitchenette. This would be his home for the next six weeks or so, unless Natalie decided to make his life a living hell like she did before. The decision to go out with the woman was still undoubtedly the worst decision he had ever made. The mistakes of being young. She was eighteen and he was nineteen and even though they were older now, she still made him uncomfortable.

He set his stuff on the bench across from his bed and grabbed his phone. He'd told Bekah he would text her when he got to his room.

—I'm in room 408. Nice room but things have already started out bad—

—I guess you saw the article—

—???—

Bekah sent him a photo of them kissing outside the restaurant with a link beneath it. Brant sat on his bed. He thought when Natalie mentioned "moving on," she had seen the other article. He clicked on the link titled "It's Official." Although the article wasn't blatantly wrong, he wanted to keep the relationship quiet for Bekah's sake, not his. He wasn't so much worried about her practice, as much as he knew Bobby didn't want them together, and if he saw this article, he could make things very hard for Bekah. He took a deep breath as he responded to her text. There was nothing he could do now. It was out there for all the world to see.

—*Has Bobby called yet?* —

—*No. He's been in Houston so I'm hoping that he is too busy to see it*—

—*Well, since we have been outed, wanna come see my place for the next six weeks?* —

—*Can I?* —

—*Yeah. It will be a closed set starting tomorrow so this may be your only chance*—

—*Okay. I will come by later when Maizy wakes up*—

—*Text me when you are on your way*—

He debated momentarily whether to stay in his room, to avoid Natalie, or explore. After scanning the room, his desire to see what secrets the historic hotel held got the best of him, and he headed back down to the lobby. Noticing a plate of cookies at the reception desk, he grabbed one and started wandering around. Behind one door, he found the pool area and was hit with the pungent smell of chlorine. The water was warm to his touch and seemed decently clean. The large hot tub at the opposite end of the pool also caught his eye. A sign on the wall above it said, "Natural hot spring fed." He knew of several areas that had natural hot springs but didn't know there was one right in his town. It might be a good way to relax after the long hours he figured he would be putting in. Strolling up the hallway he peeked into the exercise center. *What a joke.* With only one treadmill and one stationary bike and a small rack of free weights, he knew he would have to sneak out when he could to hit the gym. Maybe he could talk his dad and some of the other guys into going with him. It would be good publicity for Cody.

Down a couple of stairs was a large informal dining area. It was still a few hours before they served cocktails. Everyone was supposed to meet at that time. Off to one side was a more formal dining area that they had already converted to a 1920s era hotel dining hall. Velvet red ropes were strung across the entire area to block it off. His stomach fluttered with the thought of filming in the next couple of days.

"Brant?"

He turned to see his mom and dad standing at the top of the stairs. A smile spread across his mom's face as he turned and headed toward them. He gave his mom a hug and then turned to his dad. A lump formed in his throat when his dad pulled him in for a tight hug. He looked older. His hair and beard were grayer than Brant remembered. He was still fit, but his face had more lines.

"God, it is good to see you, son." His dad pulled away and put his hands on both sides of Brant's face. "You look great. Look at you. You're a man." He hugged him again.

Brant couldn't hide his excitement to see his father. A broad smile filled his face. Although he had been absent for most of his life, when he was home, Brant always felt close to his dad. "I can't believe you are here. How long has it been?"

"I think you were on leave. Four, maybe five years?" He paused. "Far too long."

"Have you gotten checked in?"

"Yeah, they put us in 404."

"Great. I'm two doors down in 408."

"I think they are trying to put as many of the cast and crew as possible on the fourth floor." His mom's voice chimed in over his shoulder, and he turned. "There is a conference room up there that we are going to use as a base. We will do our first read in there, and then Natalie should have our schedules ready. I wonder if she has shown up yet."

"Oh yes. She is here. And if I find out who hired her, I will beat them within an inch of their life."

His mom's eyes opened wide, and she sheepishly raised her hand. "I gave them her name."

"Why the hell would you do that?" he barked, and immediately regretted it from the reaction his mom had. "Don't you remember the trouble I had with her?"

"Well, I remember she had a cute little crush on you."

The realization set in, that he had never really confided everything that had happened with Natalie to his mom. He had mentioned to her that Natalie wouldn't leave him alone, but he never went into detail. That was how most of his life was with his parents. Just scraping the surface with the necessary information. Even his life with Abbie and her death. They knew when he started dating her. And he called and told them when they'd eloped, and then called them when she died in the car accident. They had no idea she was even pregnant, or that he did chest compressions until his arms gave out, trying to save her. "It was cute, if you call stalking me for nearly a year, cute."

"Seriously?"

"Yes. I nearly had her arrested because I came home one evening to her in my bed. How the hell she got in, I have no clue. I had to change my locks and phone number because she wouldn't leave me alone."

"Well, Calvin Turner bailed on us at the last

minute, and I knew Natalie had been a second AD recently on a few other projects I had my fingers in, so I suggested her. I had no clue she had stalked you, or I would have steered clear."

With that information, Brant knew he would have to work closely with Natalie, and wondered if she had applied for those jobs, just to stay close to his mom, and ultimately to him. He hoped that she had gotten past her infatuation, and he was just blowing things out of proportion, but something told him he wasn't. "It's not your fault, Mom. I should have told you what happened."

They started up the stairs and found some comfortable seats in the lobby. "I see you and your doctor friend have made quite the splash in the tabloids. They have taken an interest in you."

"Yeah. I can't quite understand why. And I'm not happy about it."

"Why not? You're an up and comer. You're famous. You have an interesting story. Everyone wants to hear about the tragedy turned triumph."

"Well first off, I'm not famous, my parents are. And I wish they would mind their own damn business. Bekah has a baby, and her ex is not too keen on us dating. And the last thing I want to do is stir up trouble for her."

"Well, she should have taken that into consideration when she decided to date you."

"She got pulled in before we ever started seeing each other, Mom. And she, like Abbie, had no clue who I was, and didn't care. I came into Bekah's life trying to get help. Instead, she needed help. I was merely trying to be a good Samaritan."

"Well, it will all blow over eventually. For now, it's good publicity for you."

"I just don't want it to hurt Bekah. She is a really good person."

"Sandra? Oh my gosh. It's so good to see you again."

That voice. He seriously doubted he was going to make it the entire six weeks without stuffing a sock in her mouth. She always used it when she wanted to kiss up to someone or wanted to get her way. It was as fake as her lips that moved with the voice. And how anyone could fall for it was beyond him, even though he knew he had at one time. *What was I thinking?*

He glimpsed up at her. She had a surprised expression on her face. Was it real or did someone get carried away with the plastic surgery? He was unsure, but he now knew why it was called plastic surgery. Something inside him felt sorry for her. Why anyone her age would want to alter their appearance that much, was beyond him. He had nothing against plastic surgery. There were times that it was needed, and it helped. But the media had created an obsession with a false perfection, and nowhere was it sought after more than Hollywood. And unfortunately, Natalie got sucked in. But his mom was against having anything done. She said her face was what got her the parts, so altering it seemed counterproductive. Even when she got older and the parts were becoming fewer, and someone suggested a little nip and tuck, she said she earned every wrinkle and was going to wear them proudly. And it wasn't long before the studios started calling again. This time for older parts. And she graciously took them.

"Hi, Natalie." Sandra stood and wrapped her arms around her.

Natalie reached out and grabbed Brant's dad's hand. "Hello, George. How are you?" She turned to Brant. "Hello again," she said softly. He couldn't bring himself to speak, so he nodded.

She scowled, then turned back to Sandra. "Everyone is scheduled to be here by five. We are going to have a mix and mingle to get everyone acquainted. Tomorrow morning, we have our first read scheduled at eight. I will be handing out our schedules then. After that, we will be touring the area, getting the lay of the land, and figuring out wardrobe. We have a few sets we still have to finish. Otherwise, we are hoping to start shooting tomorrow night."

"Sounds perfect. Looks like you have this all under control, Natalie," Sandra said politely.

"I hope so. Getting the script and information so last minute made it a challenge. Hopefully, it all goes smoothly." Something caught her attention. "Oh, there are some others I need to talk to. Toodles." She wiggled her fingers to Brant's folks. "Bye, Brant." Her voice lowered a couple of octaves, and Brant's skin crawled.

Turning his focus to his mom, he saw her staring up at him through her long lashes with a look of shame. It was unfair to be mad at her because she didn't know what had happened. But it didn't make the situation any less unnerving. His phone buzzed. Bekah.

—*Are you busy?* —

—*No. Just hanging out with my parents*—

—*Oh, would you like me to wait?* —

—*No. You can meet my dad*—

—*Okay. I will be there in a few minutes*—

The volcano, threatening to erupt inside Brant, suddenly was extinguished and replaced with a million butterflies in his stomach. He had never formally introduced his parents to a girl before, and he wondered how he would introduce her. Was she his girlfriend? His mom had met Bekah before anything had happened, and they had seen the tabloid article, so they knew there was something going on between them. But being in a relationship was never discussed. It just happened, and he didn't exactly know where it was going. All he knew was, he hadn't been this happy since he found out he and Abbie were having a baby.

Brant sat in the lobby and chatted with a few of the cast and crew, but his attention kept returning to the windows and doors, waiting for her to arrive. When he spotted her, his heart stopped. She had on a peach printed skirt with tassels on the bottom and a peach T-shirt on the top, covered by a powder blue shawl that matched the tiny blue flowers on her skirt. A wide striped scarf was wrapped around her hair that was pulled into a messy knot at her neck. Dangling earrings hung to her shoulders. Her face was fresh with a natural tinge to her cheeks, and she had added a little mascara, and lip gloss.

Brant jumped up when he saw her. Her face lit up. She turned and saw his mom and waved.

"Bekah, you've already—" He stopped when he realized he was outshined by his mom. Seeing the smile on his mom's face told him that Bekah had already won her over.

She set the carrier down and uncovered Maizy, then reached up and hugged Sandra tight. They rocked back and forth a couple of times, and Sandra backed away. "I knew I liked you the first time I met you." Bekah wrinkled her nose then grinned.

Brant interrupted their girl time. "This is my dad, George Ellington." He held out his hand, but Bekah released Sandra's hand and stepped around her to give him a hug.

"It's so nice to meet you. Brant has told me so much about you." She backed up and stared at him then Sandra then glimpsed at Brant. "Wow, I can see your resemblance to both your mom and dad."

Sandra gazed down at Maizy. "And this is the star of the show." Maizy cooed back at Sandra and kicked her legs.

Brant reached down, unbuckled her, picked her up, and turned to his dad. "This is Maizy."

George reached up and rubbed his finger along her cheek. "She looks like her momma."

Sandra caught Maizy's attention by patting her hands together. Maizy cooed again. Sandra lifted her eyes to Brant who glanced at Bekah then back at his mom and chuckled. "Do you want to hold her?" he asked with an exaggerated sigh.

"Too obvious?" Sandra held her arms out. Brant passed the baby off and draped the burp cloth over his mom's shoulder, then stood back watching his mom sway with the baby in her arms grinning from ear to ear.

George eyed Brant. "She hasn't gotten to do that since you were little."

Bekah smiled and laced her fingers through Brant's.

George shifted his attention to Bekah. "I don't think you will be getting her back any time soon." They

DeDe Ramey

all sat back down in the chairs in the lobby, and Brant put his arm around Bekah.

A hand suddenly brushed the back of his head, and he flinched. "We've had a change to the schedule already." There was that annoying voice again.

Brant leaned forward to get her hand off him. Natalie came into view. "We will be meeting tomorrow at 7:30 not 8." She walked around to face Bekah. "I don't believe I have had the pleasure." She held out her hand. "I'm Natalie Holcomb."

Bekah gave her a kind smile and took her hand. "Bekah Adkins." Brant swallowed hard and tightened his hold on her.

Natalie tilted her head and smiled. "It's a pleasure to meet you. Any friend of Brant's is a friend of mine." Her eyes cut to Brant, and she wrinkled her nose and smiled, before turning to his mom who was making faces at the baby on her lap. "And who is this lovely little lady?"

Sandra continued to stare at the cherub-faced child. "This is Maizy."

Natalie brushed her hand over Maizy's dark hair. "She's precious." Brant didn't know exactly what Natalie was up to, but a queasiness had settled in his stomach, and he wished she would leave.

Bekah smiled. "Thank you."

"You're welcome." Natalie straightened her shoulders. "Well, I need to go spread the word, so I had better continue on my mission. Hopefully, I will have everyone's phone number programmed in my production phone by tomorrow. Then I can send out a group text."

Brant cringed at the thought of her having his

208

phone number. But like it or not, he was going to have to work with her. It was a long time ago. Maybe she had changed. He doubted it though. The way she looked at him and touched him already told him this was going to be a long six weeks.

"I'm going to take Bekah on a little tour. You are welcome to join us."

Sandra glanced at Bekah. "Would you mind if I sat here with Maizy?"

"Not at all. If she gets fussy, her pacifier is in the side pocket. If she has a dirty diaper, the diapers and wipes are in the zipper pocket."

Brant turned to his mom. "Just hope and pray that doesn't happen."

Bekah giggled and swatted his arm.

"What? Those things could be used for biological warfare."

Sandra's eyes widened. "You've changed diapers?"

"Unfortunately." Bekah giggled again and swatted at him a second time, but he jumped out of her way and made a face.

Brant turned to Sandra. "We shouldn't be too long."

"Take all the time you want. I'm having fun with this little doll."

Brant's attention turned to his dad who waved them off.

"I will go exploring on my own later."

"Suit yourself." Brant grabbed Bekah's hand, and they stepped down the stairs into the dining area. "This is where we will be getting fed. And over there"—he pointed—"they will be using that area in the film."

"So, who is Natalie to you, and why don't you like her?"

He peeked at her from the corner of his eye. "Was it that obvious?"

"Oh, yes. Your body was as tight as a drum the minute she spoke. You pulled me into you when she introduced herself."

"Natalie and I have a history, and it's not a good one. I worked with her on another movie, and she hounded me to go out. When I finally relented and went out with her, I quickly realized we were not compatible and told her so, but she refused to leave me alone. She broke into my house at one point."

"Oh my gosh, did you call the police?"

Brant let out a long sigh. "No. I should have. She begged me not to, so I finally told her I wouldn't if she would leave me alone."

"Did she?"

"For the most part. It was right before I joined the Air Force, so once I got stationed away from California, it became a nonissue. I haven't seen her in like seven or eight years. Still, there is something that unnerves me about her."

"I can imagine. What is she doing here?"

"She is the second Assistant Director for the film. The first guy bailed, and since she does have some credentials, they brought her on at the last minute."

"I don't know what that means. It sounds like you are going to be working pretty closely with her though."

"I am."

Chapter Thirteen

A loud pounding woke Bekah up from a deep sleep and scared Maizy who immediately began to squall. Bekah quickly checked the clock. It was seven thirty in the morning. She threw on a robe, grabbed Maizy, and rushed to the living room. After peeking through the peephole, she leaned her back up against the door and growled.

Flipping the lock, she jerked open the door. Maizy was screaming, and Bekah felt like doing the same. "What the hell is your problem, Bobby? You scared Maizy half to death with your banging."

"My problem is this." Shoving the paper tabloid magazine at her, he didn't wait for her to invite him in. Front and center was Bekah in a tender kiss with Brant. "Tell me again how you aren't seeing him; that he is simply helping you with Maizy. Tell me Bekah. Because that"—he pointed to the picture—"doesn't look like he is just helping."

Bekah took the paper, examined it, and threw it on the side table by the sofa. She knew Bobby would have a fit when he saw it, but she thought she would get a nasty text, not have him practically breaking down her door at the crack of dawn. Maizy continued to wail like she was in pain, and Bobby stood and stared at her as if she was interrupting him.

Bekah sat down, pulled the nursing pillow onto her

lap, and laid Maizy down carefully. "Okay. So, he kissed me. Big deal."

Bobby glared at Bekah as she threw a blanket over her shoulder and pulled Maizy close. She adjusted her, trying to get her to nurse, but the baby was crying so hard she was having trouble. "Christ, Bekah, do you have to do that right now?"

A deep rage filled her. "Why yes, Bobby, I do. You scared the life out of her. I am trying to calm her down, and your screaming isn't helping the matter."

Bobby closed his mouth, stood in the center of the living room with his hands on his hips, and stared at Bekah. When she was finally able to get Maizy calmed down enough to nurse, he stepped closer and growled, "I told you, I want you to stay away from him."

She returned his tone. "And I told you, you have no control over what I do now."

His voice rose and he paced. "I don't want him around my daughter. He's dangerous."

"He is not dangerous." Maizy pulled away and wailed again. "Shhhhh, baby girl." Tightening her hold, the baby again began to nurse.

"He is an addict."

"Bobby, his wife and unborn child died in a car accident a year ago. He was self-medicating, trying to cope with the horrible loss. Before that, he didn't have a problem. He had coping issues, not an addiction."

"I don't give a damn what he was doing or why he was doing it. I want him to stay away from my daughter."

"Well, that's too damn bad. I should have a say so in who I want in my life, and he takes much better care of me and Maizy than you ever did."

His eyes narrowed at Bekah, and his jaw clenched. "I have tried every way in the world to make you see that you and Maizy are the most important things in my life."

"Well, you sure have a funny way of showing it. Tell me, Bobby, how would sleeping with another woman show me that I am the most important thing in your life?"

Bobby threw his arms in the air dramatically. "I apologized. It was a momentary lapse of judgement."

"Momentary? She. Was. Living. With. You."

"And she's not now."

"That doesn't wash away the fact that she did." Bekah took a deep breath trying to calm down. "Bobby, we have already been over this a thousand times. I'm done."

"Bekah, sweetheart," his voice softened, "hear me out." Bekah tipped her head back and rubbed her forehead. "I found a house in Houston. The owners have agreed to let me rent it until I can close on it, which should be in a few weeks. It's perfect. Four bedrooms, three baths. Big back yard. I am moving my stuff out of the apartment this weekend and heading down. Why don't you at least come with me and see it? I know you will love it."

"No. I don't know how to say it more clearly. I don't want to be in a relationship with you anymore."

His body stiffened, and he growled. "Why are you being so stubborn? We need to think of what is best for Maizy. She needs both her parents, and it would be too hard on her to be shuttling her back and forth such a long distance."

"Well, if I remember correctly, I didn't cause the

issue."

"But you aren't willing to fix it."

"Why should I cave in because of something you did wrong?"

"Because it is best for Maizy."

"Oh, like you care. You know good and well you are using her wellbeing to manipulate me to go down there, and it's not going to work this time. I'm done with your manipulation tactics; done with your control. You know what would happen if I went down there? Nothing would change. You would be *working* morning, noon, and night, and I would be left to take care of her all by myself, because you want nothing to do with her. You. Don't. Love. Me. The only reason you want me down there is because you can't stand the idea of anyone else having me. You would have me and Marissa, just like before. It's all a game to you, and you hate losing. You can't stand to be told no. Well, no. I don't want to be in a relationship with you. No. I don't want to move to Houston. *If* you want to see Maizy, we will have to work something out. But my bet is, you will get down there and forget all about her."

His expression turned cold and hard as his eyes landed on Bekah. "You're wrong, Bekah. I do love you and Maizy, and if you choose not to come with me to Houston then I will be forced to file for custody of Maizy."

With his words, the air in the room vanished. "You wouldn't."

"Oh, don't bet on that. I have a respectable job. I will have a house with a nice back yard and family close, and you have an addict for a boyfriend. I think the judge will see that I would be a better option for the care and wellbeing of our child."

A knot formed in Bekah's stomach, and her teeth clenched. "How dare you threaten me."

"Oh, it's not a threat Bekah. I'm not going to let some drug addict raise my child. You are making this harder than it should be. It's a simple solution. Come to Houston."

Tears spilled down Bekah's cheeks. "That is blackmail, Bobby."

"No, Bekah. I'm trying to keep Maizy safe."

"No, you aren't. You just don't want anyone else to have me. That's all you ever wanted was to be in complete control of my life. And silly me, I let you."

"You can think what you want, however it's not going to change my decision. If you don't come with me to Houston, then I will file for custody of Maizy, and I will win." He walked toward the door. "I don't want that man to ever touch my daughter again. I will get a protective order if I have to."

"You are a monster. I can't believe you would do this to me."

Bobby opened the door and left without saying another word.

Bekah picked up her phone.

—*Bobby saw the story. It's front-page news in PrimeScene Magazine. He just left. Gave me an ultimatum. Move down to Houston with him or he would file for custody*—

—*He can't win*—

—*I don't know. He is buying a four-bedroom house with a big backyard. His folks live nearby, and they have money for the best lawyers in the area. I'm living in my grandpa's garage apartment and splashed all over the tabloids in a lip lock with a recovering addict—*

—I'm sorry—

****

The week passed slowly. Bekah barely held it together during her appointments. How was she expected to solve others' problems when she had a truckload herself? She kept expecting someone to show up on her doorstep to serve her custody papers. Brant texted her almost every night and called when he got a break from the hectic schedule. He said they were on set at least twelve hours every day. Every time he spoke, she could hear the pain in his voice. He kept apologizing for what the magazine had printed. She knew it wasn't his fault. He didn't have any control over it. Still, she didn't know how to dig herself out of the hole she had fallen into. He told her how much he missed her and Maizy, but for Maizy's sake, they needed to stay away from each other until they could figure out how to resolve the issue. His mother's lawyer wasn't even able to help.

Bekah was determined not to give in to Bobby's threats, no matter how credible they might be. She couldn't live her life that way, and she didn't want to subject Maizy to it. However, seeing what Brant was having to put up with, could she subject Maizy to a life in the limelight either?

Her phone chimed.

"Hey, Grandpa what's up?"

"I'm going to lunch. Wondered if you wanted to come with me."

"What time?"

"How about I come by in about thirty minutes and

pick you and Maizy up."

"Okay. I'm at the office. I should be done by the time you get here."

Bekah finished up with her client and some paperwork and stored away the files. She skimmed her schedule and realized she had the rest of her afternoon off, which was nice. It had been a long week. She needed a break. The chime of the door made her jump, but the sound of her grandpa's voice caused the corner of her mouth to curve into a smile. He looked like a professor with his black turtleneck and suede jacket. She stood from her desk and kissed him on the cheek.

"Thanks for the invite. I really needed this."

"Are you okay?"

"Yeah. Just stressed."

"About Bobby?"

"Yeah."

"I am so sorry he's putting you and Maizy in such a tough situation."

"Me too. I'm hoping it all works out though."

She settled Maizy in her carrier and got her locked into the backseat of her grandpa's car. He smiled when he started it up and the muffler of the old car let out a low rumble. Bekah remembered Brant, in his dirty T-shirt and blue jeans, throwing her over his shoulder. Her chest heaved with a sigh. "So, where are we going?"

"It's a surprise."

Bekah tried to be excited. She knew her grandpa wanted her to be happy, although even he didn't have any idea how she could get out of the mess Bobby had put her in. They drove a few miles to the outskirts of town and pulled down a dirt road. A small white house with a steep pitched roof came into view. Pulling up, Bekah could see the large tan metal building behind it. "Where are we?"

Dale unbuckled his seatbelt and opened the door. "You'll see." A twinkle sparkled in his eyes, and Bekah had a feeling he was up to something.

She crawled out and hauled Maizy's carrier and diaper bag out of the car. They made their way up the steps to the front door and rang the doorbell. An older lady with long gray hair pulled into a braid, dressed in blue jeans and an oversized long-sleeved gauzy white shirt, answered. Her smile when she saw Dale warmed Bekah's heart. *Does Grandpa have a girlfriend?* "You made it. Come in. Come in." They stepped into the foyer, and she closed the door then turned, and her eyes landed on Bekah. "You must be Bekah."

Confused, Bekah glanced at her grandpa then back at the lady. "I am."

The woman's attention drifted to the carrier covered with a blanket that was moving. "And this must be Maizy." Bekah pulled the blanket off Maizy's face. "Oh, she is adorable." The lady glimpsed back up at Bekah. "Your grandpa has told me so much about you and Maizy. He loves you so much." Bekah's eyes landed back on her grandpa hoping he would give her a clue as to who the lady was, and why they were invading her house. Although, whatever she was cooking smelled delicious.

The sound of shattering glass coming from the kitchen pulled her attention up the hallway. "Dammit." Bekah froze. "No one come in here." She knew that voice. Her coat and scarf flew through the air, and she took off running toward the voice. Rounding the corner, she saw Brant crouched down with a dustpan and broom. He peered up, and a smile spread across his face. "Hi."

Breathlessly she replied, "Hi." Tears filled her eyes, and her whole body shook.

He dumped the dustpan, set it and the broom back in the closet, dusted his hands, and turned, just in time to catch Bekah as she launched herself at him. Her heart thumped against her chest so hard it felt like someone was banging to get out. She wrapped her arms around his neck, legs around his waist, and peppered him with kisses. "I know our grandparents are probably watching, but I don't care. I can't believe you are here. Oh my God, I needed this so bad."

Brant laughed at her trying to kiss and talk at the same time. "Yep. They are watching. But they can't say anything, because those two came up with the idea."

Bekah unhooked her feet and dropped to the ground after several minutes, then turned around. Dale and Betty stood in the doorway of the kitchen, smiling. Betty stepped forward. "I'm Betty by the way. I think you have met my grandson."

Bekah laughed. "Yeah, we are well acquainted."

"Obviously."

Bekah's eyes widened with the wisecrack. "Oh my gosh, I love you already." She reached over and hugged her neck.

"I got a call from Grams saying she and Dale had coffee a couple of mornings ago. I had been telling her about what was going on, and that we hadn't seen each other because of the photographers, and I guess you had been telling Dale something similar. They figured if they picked us up, we would be safe from the paparazzi.

Pretty smart, huh? Grams said she would be willing to make this a weekly thing. It can be our little secret."

Bekah turned to Betty and Dale. "I could kiss both of you right now." Maizy let out a yelp.

Brant knelt. "Someone is being ignored." He glanced up at Bekah.

Her heart broke immediately. She had told him what Bobby had said, and she knew what he was thinking, but she was determined to not let Bobby take control of her life ever again. No matter what he threatened. "You can hold her, Brant."

He unsnapped her harness and pulled her from the carrier. Throwing the blanket over his shoulder, he snuggled her close. His eyes met Bekah's, and she could see the tears shimmering, as she watched him swallow back the pain. "We are going to figure this out." His voice cracked with each word.

****

Another week passed and then two. The texts and phone calls were less frequent, but luckily they were still able to sneak away for lunch. Brant said production was going well and ahead of schedule. The long days, though, were killing him. Bekah took photos to send to him of her and Maizy, and he snuck a few from the scenes they were shooting. Things quieted down. She hadn't heard from Bobby or gotten any papers, and she was hoping everything would blow over.

By the middle of the fourth week, Bekah was getting worried. She hadn't heard from Brant in three days, and in his last text he sounded upset, saying he was having a hard time, so she was looking forward to their secret meeting at Betty's. Thursday the custody papers came. She sat on her sofa holding Maizy in her arms and bawled. Her heart was torn to shreds. She couldn't believe Bobby actually went through with it. The court date was pushed out almost three months. She figured it was so he could close on the house and get settled in his new job. She knew in that time, there would be nothing else on her mind. She had to figure out a way to keep Maizy. There was no way she was going to allow him to take her away. Her phone chimed.

Bobby spoke before she even had time to say hello. "Did you get the papers?"

She stared out the window. How could he be that callous? "Yes. I cannot believe you are going through with this. This is unconscionable."

"I am doing it for your own good. You know we should be together, and I am trying to open your eyes and make you see that moving down here with me would be the best for you. The best for Maizy."

"No, it wouldn't, Bobby. How many times do I have to tell you, you don't love me, and I don't love you? We shouldn't be together. You said you didn't want Maizy. If it's a fight you want, it's a fight you are going to get, because I am not going to let you take her away from me."

"I do love you and Maizy. I know what I said early in the pregnancy. I was scared. I wasn't ready for a kid, and you have admitted that it has been hard having her around. No sleep, constantly having to work your schedule around her."

"She is the best thing that has ever happened to me."

"Fine. You must admit though, it would be easier if you and Maizy were down here where she has both of her parents taking care of her."

"Not if we don't love each other."

"Look, I know I screwed up and for the hundredth time, I'm sorry. But don't throw five years down the toilet for one lousy mistake. What we had was good. I know you love me; you are just mad, and that's fair. I screwed up. At some point though, I'm hoping you will realize how much I really do love you and see that what I am offering is a good thing."

"I'm not in love with you anymore, Bobby, and I'm not going to sacrifice my happiness, or my daughter's, to move to Houston just so you can have control of the situation. I would rather see you in court."

"Fine. Be prepared. The court is going to see things my way."

"Don't bet on it."

Bekah had no idea what she would do, but she would be damned if Bobby was going to get custody of Maizy. Her head was spinning with thoughts, but none brought her to a solution. She needed to get out of the house and clear her head. There had to be a solution.

Ten minutes later she found herself parked outside of the hotel where they were filming. A fence wrapped around the perimeter with signs covering the fence emblazoned with "Rest for the Wicked. Closed Set." Through the openings in the tarp covering the fence, she could see a couple of cameras and chairs off to one side. Faint voices came from inside the fence, then she saw a group walking into her line of sight. There he was. With his hair slicked back and dressed in a form fitting suit, he looked like a movie star from bygone days. He had a pile of papers in his hand and was talking to a heavy-set guy in black chinos and a sloppy bright orange sweater. Two other men stood with them. More than anything, she wanted to talk to him face to face. Every day away from him made the situation she was in harder. She started having doubts, questions would arise.

The tabloids had printed two other stories about him following in his mom's footsteps and overshadowing her in this production. They never said a word about Sandra basically heading up the whole project. A twinge of worry hit her. What if he did decide to follow in his mom's footsteps? Would she be willing to live with him constantly on the road like his mom and dad? He disappeared, so she got back in the car and drove over to a nearby sandwich shop. When she walked in, she saw Natalie standing at the counter. Bekah took a deep breath when Natalie turned and noticed her, then made her way over to the booth she was in.

"Hey," Natalie cooed. "Bekah, right?" Her singsong voice set Bekah on high alert. She could tell already, by Natalie's body language, something was off.

Bekah reached up and played with her earring. "Yes. How are you, Natalie?"

"Great. Mind if I sit?" Not waiting for her answer, Natalie made herself at home. "I am picking up an order for the crew, and they don't have it ready yet. Go figure, right?"

"Yeah. I'm sure—"

"So, I'm sorry to hear about you and Brant."

"Excuse me. What?"

Natalie batted her eyelashes innocently. "He told

me you guys weren't seeing each other anymore."

Bekah's stomach clenched. She didn't know how to respond. They weren't officially in a relationship, but they had been basically living together before filming started. Why would he say something like that to Natalie? She figured Natalie would be the last person he would confide in. Then it dawned on her that he had been worried about the tabloids, and since they hadn't backed off, she wondered if Brant had said it to throw the paparazzi off. Should she deny it, or just roll with it? Her eyes leveled with Natalie's. "I'm sorry, Natalie. I don't know you well enough to discuss my personal matters. I hope you understand."

"Sure. He's just one of those guys who doesn't seem to stay with the same girl very long. You know?"

"No, actually I don't." Even though she knew to be wary of whatever Natalie said, it was still causing her to wonder. She really didn't know anything about Brant's past.

"Well, I guess I shouldn't say that. We were together for a while."

"Oh really?" Bekah was becoming increasingly interested. From her training, she knew Natalie's expressions suggested she was not being honest, and the only way she would be able to get a good read was to press her for more information.

"Yeah. We met on set, and it became hot and heavy pretty quickly and after that, we went out for quite a while. It was all over the tabloids."

"How long were you together?"

"Almost a year."

"What caused you to break up?"

"It was a silly misunderstanding."

"Oh, was it when you broke into his house?"

Natalie's eyes widened. Bekah noticed fear, not confusion. "Broke into his house?" Natalie questioned. "I don't know where you heard that. I never broke into his house. If I did, he would have called the cops." She chuckled.

"So, what was the misunderstanding?"

"Actually, it, it was so long ago I don't remember. It doesn't matter now. We have worked through our problems."

"Well, I'm glad you worked it out. I can't imagine how hard it would be on set if you were at each other's throats all the time."

"Oh, we are at each other all the time anyway. It's for totally different reasons though. If you know what I mean." Natalie winked.

Bekah's stomach turned. She couldn't avoid feeling the stabbing pain of jealousy even if she figured what Natalie was sharing was a lie. She needed to talk to Brant, to get his side of the story. Until then, Natalie's words would continue piercing her heart.

"I'm sorry, Natalie. I suddenly realized I forgot to put more diapers in Maizy's bag before leaving the house, so I'm going to have to run." She scooted out of the booth and grabbed the carrier. "It was nice chatting with you. Tell Brant I said hi."

When she got to her car, she sat for a moment just to calm the thoughts rushing through her head of Bobby and Brant and Natalie. Her stomach growled in protest of leaving the restaurant, but she couldn't sit and listen to Natalie one more minute. She put the car in drive and headed to the drive-thru of her favorite burger joint and ordered a burger with fries and a shake. It was one of those days.

When she got home, she sat down at the table with her laptop and typed in Brant's name in the search. She was stunned by what she found. Along with photos of him and Natalie in several lip locks, there were stories of his wild bad boy days. Granted they were all of him as a teen and in college. It seemed he quieted down once he went into the military, or the tabloids couldn't get to him. She read the story of him saving soldiers from an explosion in Afghanistan only to be shot himself. A little farther down was the story of the accident that killed his wife and unborn child. Tears welled in her eyes. She wanted to trust him. Everything he did for her pointed to him being a good man, but if Bobby found some of these stories, it would fan the flame of his hatred toward Brant.

Her phone buzzed. Brant!

—I can't make it tomorrow. We are filming off set at a remote location about forty miles away. I'm sorry—

—I understand. Saw Natalie at the deli by the set today. She said you told her we weren't seeing each other anymore—

—She said what? Bekah, listen to me, don't believe anything she says. She is up to her old tricks again and about to drive me absolutely nuts. I don't want to get into it right now. I will call you later. Please, don't listen to her—

—We do need to talk. I miss you—

Little dots popped up on her screen and she waited for his response. It never came.

Chapter Fourteen

Brant's phone buzzed. He quickly lifted it thinking it was another text from Bekah. Instead, it was another message from the unknown number.

—*Nothing can stand in the way of us being together*—

Everything suddenly became crystal clear. He knew exactly who was sending the messages, and she was about to feel his wrath. His scene was coming up, but he had to find Natalie. After trying to tamp down his fury, he told the assistant director he had an emergency and to film something else for a while. He was livid. The two production assistants he passed pointed him in the direction of the dining hall when he asked where she was. Racing down the steps, he found plenty of production people milling around, but not Natalie. Then she appeared carrying a tray of fresh fruit. She smiled, set the tray on the table, and he wrapped his hand around her arm and dragged her off in the corner. The music playing throughout the lobby was loud, so he leaned in. "I know what you are doing."

Her fake lashes batted as she gazed up into his. "What do you mean?"

"This sick game you are playing. The creepy text messages. Lying to Bekah."

"I don't know what you are talking about."

"Bullshit. Bekah told me you talked to her. What

did you say?" He continued with his tight grip on her arm.

"I told her you said you guys were no longer together."

He let go of her arm and took a step back. His hand brushed across his mouth. "You know I said that to the photographer sniffing around so he would leave us alone. She said I told you."

"Well, I was standing there. Same difference." She shrugged.

"No, it's not, and you know it. You are up to your old schemes again, and it needs to stop." His voice dropped to a low, menacing tone. He grabbed her arm and leaned in closer so she wouldn't miss a word. "Don't talk to her, and don't talk to me ever again. I don't want you to call me or text me. If you need to change my schedule, send someone to notify me. Don't come around me, don't even look at me. I want absolutely nothing to do with you. Are we clear?" She batted her lashes innocently. He scowled. "Let me have your phone." He wanted to confirm what he already knew he would find when he scanned her messages.

"Why?" she huffed but handed it over.

"I am going to make sure my contact information is removed."

"I have it on the call sheets, idiot."

"I'm still removing it from your phone and blocking your number on mine."

She put her hands on her hips. "I don't know what you are so pissed about. I didn't tell her anything that wasn't true."

He glared up at her. "You really don't think you did anything wrong?" She shook her head. "You're sick, Natalie. You need help," he said, then found his name in the phone. As he scrolled through the messages though, he found only work-related texts. Had she deleted the ones she had sent him? He sent himself a message to block the number, and then realized it wasn't the same number. It didn't make sense. He knew she was the one sending him the creepy texts.

She snatched the phone from his hand when he handed it back, then narrowed her eyes saying, "Everything I said was true."

"Whether it was true or not doesn't matter. You implied I had specifically told you, and you did it on purpose to make her question my feelings for her."

"And what would they be?"

Completely disgusted he responded, "None of your damn business. Now leave me the hell alone." His volume increased and people around them turned. "I want nothing to do with you, Natalie. Have I made myself clear?"

Natalie scanned the area, obviously embarrassed, then glared back at Brant before storming away. Brant glanced up at the people staring. His face filled with heat, but he didn't really care that he had made a scene. His gaze landed on the seedy photographer who had questioned him earlier. His hands wrapped around his camera, ready for a shot. Brant turned away and noticed the bartender wiping the bar down, then saw the array of bottles stacked on the shelves behind his head. He was stressed from the shooting schedule. Stressed from the tabloids. Stressed from Natalie's shit. Stressed from what Bekah was dealing with, and on top of it all he was facing the anniversary of Abbie's death the next day. It had been eating at him the past few days. Brant took a step forward, studying the labels. The bartender lifted his head. "See anything you need to take the edge off?" he asked, continuing to wipe at the counters.

Brant stopped and swallowed hard. He could feel his pulse increase. His mouth suddenly felt like it had been wiped down with cotton. "Nah, I'm good, man. Thanks." Turning away quickly, he noticed the photographer with his camera lifted to his eye. Brant took off up the stairs heading back to the set. His mind raced at what had just happened. He had come so close to throwing it all away, but his mind went back to Bekah and Maizy. He wouldn't do that to them. Thoughts swirled about what he would need to say to her to straighten things out. He needed to talk to her as soon as possible. He'd pushed his shooting time later than it already was because of Natalie, which meant he would have to get up early tomorrow and try to call Bekah before he had to be on set. If everything stayed on schedule, they had one more week and it would all be over, and then he could figure out how he and Bekah could be together.

****

Sleep was becoming foreign to him. The thought of what happened the day before had him tossing and turning all night. He didn't get much sleep anyway with the shooting schedule. If he wasn't having to get up early to shoot, he was having to stay up late to shoot night shots. He had completely forgotten that he needed to be up and ready to go by four, because they were shooting at a remote location, which meant he wouldn't be able to talk to Bekah until lunchtime. Crawling in the van to head to the location, he retrieved his phone from his pocket. March twenty-third lit up when he clicked the button, and his heart pinched. *It's been a year.* He let out a breath and forced himself to stop staring at the date. Checking his social media, his stomach lurched when he saw the headlines "Old Romance Brewing." There was a photo of him leaning into Natalie's neck like he was about to take a bite out of her, and her eyes were closed like she wanted it. "SHIT!" He continued to read the article where Natalie told the reporter that they had been lovers several years back after being in a movie together, and their relationship had rekindled since they had been thrust back together in this new movie.

Brant felt sick. Could the day get any worse? Luckily, Natalie wasn't supposed to be on the location with them today because they were filming a gunfight.

He went through the morning of hair and makeup and wardrobe preparing to get into character for the scene. With this new revelation, it wouldn't be hard for him to appear angry like the script required. He had been sitting in the trailer waiting for the call when his phone buzzed. Bekah.

—Did you see the photo in this morning's PrimeScene? I seem to be on their list now, so it greeted me bright and early this morning—

—It's not what you think. I will call you in a little bit—

— Natalie implied that you were together. I didn't want to believe her—

Her words just added to his pain. He wished he had never taken this part and swore he would never step foot on a set again. No matter how long it might be between opportunities to see his family, it wasn't worth it.

Natalie's question rang in his ears. What were his feelings for Bekah? His mind bounced between his memories of Abbie, and Bekah. He felt guilty in a way. He knew he wasn't looking for a relationship when he met Bekah, just searching for a way to live again after the tragedy. He found it in Bekah, and he knew the answer to Natalie's question. It was obvious. He loved her. He loved everything about her, including her unconventional ways. That's what made her so unique, so captivating. He was happier than he had ever been when he was with her and Maizy. She was the next step in his life.

—*We aren't. Please, Bekah, believe me. I will call you in a little bit*—

Shooting began and was nonstop. Scenes were shot over and over, from one angle then another. There would be close ups, and reshoots, and time wore on. Brant glanced at his phone when there was a pause, and lunchtime came and went, and they were still shooting. When they finally broke for a break, there was a text from Bekah.

—*Call me now. It's urgent*—

It had been sent ten minutes earlier. Brant wandered away from the set and hit the number.

"Brant?" His chest tightened. She sounded like she was crying.

"Bekah? What's wrong?"

"It's your grandma. Grandpa and I were eating lunch with her, and she passed out." Brant's heart stopped. "The ambulance just left. They are taking her to Mercy. Grandpa and I are headed there now. I've already spoken to your mom."

"I'll be there as soon as I can." Shoving his phone

back in his pocket, he ran to the set. And after some arguing about what could be shot without him, he was given the keys to someone's car, and took off. He would figure out whose later. His heart raced as he sped down the back roads hoping he didn't get lost along the way. Tears stung in his eyes as he finally made it to the highway. Apparently the day could get worse. He had lost so many important people in his life. He couldn't lose his grandmother. Not now. He needed her. She had saved him more than once from the bad decisions he had made in his life. He wanted desperately for her to be around to see him make his life right for once.

Pulling into the hospital parking lot, he bolted from the car. The emergency doors opened with a swoosh, and he jogged up to the counter. Bekah ran up to him from the waiting room. He saw the fear on her face, and it rocked him to his core. Brant blinked back tears thinking the news was grim.

"They think she had a heart attack, so they took her up to the Cath lab on the second floor. Your mom and dad are already up there."

He leaned over trying to catch his breath. His fist bounced in front of his mouth. "I don't want to go up there alone. Will you come with me?"

"Are you sure?"

His throat thickened. "Please."

"Let me tell Grandpa."

She walked over to the waiting area, and within a moment she was back. He put his hand in the small of her back, and they headed to the elevator. When the doors opened on the second floor, Brant found his mom and dad in the waiting room. His mom was dabbing her eyes with a tissue. She stood, and he gave her a hug.

When he let go, his dad put his arm around him and pulled him into a hug. After a minute they all sat on the black vinyl benches lining the walls.

Brant turned to Bekah and noticed the space she left on the bench. Feeling completely defeated, he took a deep breath and rubbed his forehead. "What happened?"

"Your grandma called Grandpa this morning. She said she had already been to the store, to get stuff for stew, when you called and canceled, and asked us to still come for lunch. We got there, and Grandpa noticed she wasn't herself. When he asked her if she was feeling okay, she said she hadn't slept well, and said her arm hurt, but said it was probably arthritis. We sat down to eat, and she said her chest hurt, and she felt dizzy and then collapsed. Grandpa was quick to call the ambulance, and he gave her some aspirin."

"I'm glad you were there with her," Sandra said quietly. She turned to Brant. "What are they doing at the shoot? Didn't you have a key role today?"

"They are going to shoot without me. It's more action than anything so whether they have me there or not, it's not going to ruin the scene. I told them they could write me out of whatever they need to. I'm not going back until I know she is going to be all right. Anyway, I'm done with all of this. Mom, I have no idea how you have done it all these years. This is exhausting, and frustrating, and boring, all at the same time."

Sandra laughed. "Yeah, that about sums it up pretty well. There are days you shoot, and you are moving until your legs won't move anymore, and then there are days you are on set waiting for hours to shoot for thirty minutes."

"Well, I can tell you beyond a shadow of a doubt, this is my last one. It has had its fun moments, but for me there aren't enough."

A noise in the hall pulled their attention to a woman in green scrubs with a dark complexion. She entered the small waiting room. "Are you the family of Ms. Gerard?"

Sandra stood, followed by the others. "Yes, I'm her daughter."

"I'm Dr. Kapurali. Your mom did have a heart attack. However, because of the timeliness of the paramedics and the steps that were taken at the scene, she should be fine. We didn't see any damage in the initial tests. We did find a blockage in one of her veins and placed a stent to open it up. She should be able to go home tomorrow, barring any setback."

Brant grabbed Bekah, wrapped his arms around her, and gave her a squeeze.

Sandra shook the doctor's hand. "That is great news."

"You can go back and see her. She is in nineteen. We will be moving her to a room on the third floor for this evening."

They all followed the doctor through the double doors, and around the nurses' station, to the room. Betty was sitting up with a canula of oxygen in her nose. She turned and smiled at them as they filed in.

"Well, don't look so glum. I'm still here. Unless of course you were hoping I had kicked the bucket. If so, trust me, I've spent the inheritance." Everyone chuckled. She turned to Bekah. "Did you and Dale get to eat?"

Bekah laughed at her question and wondered how to answer. "Well, not exactly."

"Oh. Well. Make sure you go by and get some. It's too good to waste." Her eyes darted. "Where is Dale?"

"He is downstairs with Maizy. I'll go down in a minute and have him come up. He's really worried about you, Grams."

Brant about lost it when Bekah called her Grams. That was his special nickname for her. She had already bonded with his grandma over the few weeks they had been able to spend together. His grandma had told him on more than one occasion that Bekah was special.

Sandra leaned over and gave her mom a peck on the cheek. Betty patted her. "I'm fine. Just hungry. They said I can probably go home tomorrow."

"You scared us to death, Mom."

"You think you were scared. I thought I died. My head started spinning, then everything went black. I heard voices, and when I opened my eyes, there were these two good looking guys staring down at me. I thought they were angels, and I had gone to heaven. And it really kind of surprised me," she said with a chuckle.

Everyone busted out laughing. Brant always loved her sense of humor.

Bekah stepped forward. "I think I'm going to leave you and send Grandpa up. Maizy probably is going to be getting hungry pretty soon." She moved to the side of the bed and leaned over and gave Betty a hug. "I am so glad you are okay." She pulled back, and Betty grabbed her face with both hands. "If it weren't for you and your grandpa, I wouldn't be." She pulled her in and hugged her again. When Bekah backed away, her eyes met everyone in the room, and stopped on Brant. "Would you mind going down with me?"

"He nodded and stepped to the side of the bed and gave his grandma a hug. When he backed away, she grabbed onto him.

"I know that look, Leo, and I know this is hard for you, especially today. I'm going to be fine. Don't you worry." She closed her arms around him again, and he held on for a moment trying to compose himself. She knew how close he was to breaking. He backed away, and she patted his cheek and gave him a wink. "Now, go on."

His eyes darted to Bekah, and he grabbed for her hand, but she was already halfway out the door. When they got outside the double doors, she motioned for him to follow her into the empty waiting room and shut the door behind them.

Brant stared up at the ceiling feeling the burn taking hold in his nose. He closed his eyes trying to keep the tears from coming, but they couldn't be contained. His hand rubbed over his mouth, and he felt Bekah's arms circling his waist. Her hand rubbed up and down his back. "She's going to be fine."

"I don't know what I would have done if I lost her. Especially not today," he mumbled, his words feeling as thick as pancake batter.

Bekah looked at him, and then her mouth dropped open. "It's the anniversary. Isn't it?" Brant nodded. Her arms pulled him in tighter, and silence fell between them. The only thing that was heard in the room was an occasional sniffle. Bekah finally broke the silence. "I am so sorry, Brant."

"No, Bekah, I'm sorry. God, I don't think this

week could have gotten any worse. I missed you so much. They worked me until my ass was dragging. Then Natalie—"

"Wait. Before you start, I need to make something clear. We have never talked about what we have between us. So, regardless of what did or didn't happen, I shouldn't be upset. I'm going to be honest though, it hurt. My head has been spinning, and I want to believe you…" Brant's lips parted like he was going to speak, and then he clamped them shut as she continued. "From the first day we met, you have treated me and Maizy with the utmost care and respect, and I don't think that was an act. I don't know what I would have done without you. However, with everything that has happened, it made me wonder about your motives."

"What do you mean?"

"Are you sure you aren't with us because of what we've given you?"

"I'm not following." A lump crawled up in his throat, and he wondered what she was saying.

"I appreciate what you have done for us, but I have to wonder if you were simply trying to fill the void of what you lost."

It felt like a bullet pierced his chest, and his hands dropped to his side. His eyes stung as tears threatened again. "Bekah. No. I—"

"I want to trust that what you say right now is the absolute truth because honestly," she chuckled, "I don't have the strength or the time to be lied to. My life right now can't take much more."

"Trust me. I understand. I had no intentions of getting into a relationship with you. I've battled with the idea that this was happening too fast. It was too soon. You had too much going on in your life, and you had just gotten out of an unhealthy relationship. But I simply couldn't keep myself away from you."

She backed away from him. "Then I need you to help me understand. I realized after talking to Natalie that I really didn't know your past, so I did a search of your name online. There were so many stories of you being a wild child and having one woman after another. She said you dated her for about a year and that she didn't break into your house. She alluded to the fact that you were back together, and then this story came out." Tears streamed down her face. "Brant, I…I—"

"Bekah, I know what it seems like. Some of the stories you saw online probably were true. I got into a little trouble here and there, mainly because I really didn't have anyone telling me I shouldn't, and it was a way to get attention. But quite a bit of the stuff you read was fake stories like you have seen the past few weeks. You see how they manipulate a situation.

"Quite a few of the tabloid stories about my love life were lies. They took photos of me with any girl and tried to tie us together. I was pretty shy around girls honestly, even in college, and my grandma and grandpa got ahold of me and basically put the fear of God in me about what could happen if I wasn't careful. I settled into college life, and then a movie came along that I had a bit part in with Natalie.

"We played a couple on screen, and she was always flirting with me off screen, so I asked her out a couple of times. I realized she was crazy and broke it off, but she didn't want to accept that. She kept after me. Yes, no matter what she says, she absolutely broke into my apartment. She was naked in my bed when I got home one night. I told her I was going to call the cops, and she begged me not to. She left, and nothing happened. That is the truth. I never slept with her."

"She said you told her that we stopped seeing each other."

"The truth is, I did say that to a photographer. He has been hanging around the set trying to get incriminating photos that he could sell to the tabloids. He asked me about you a few days ago, and I thought if I told him we weren't seeing each other, the tabloids might stop trying to come after us when we tried to get together. Natalie had been talking to him before he asked me the question, so she was there."

"What about the photos of you guys kissing that are all over the internet?"

Brant's brows furrowed. "What photos?"

Bekah grabbed her phone and put his name in the search and pulled up the information.

"Those are from the movie. See"—he pointed— "our clothes are the same in all these photos. These are all from the movie shoot. You can even see a camera in this one."

"And these?" She scrolled to other photos.

"Also, from the movie on another day."

"What about today's photo?"

"Yesterday after you texted me about talking to Natalie, I got another weird text, and it suddenly hit me. Natalie was probably behind all the creepy text messages I have been getting. They started after I was asked to do the movie, and I figure she got my information from my mom. It made me furious, so I hunted her down. She was in the dining hall, and there were a bunch of people eating, along with music playing in the lobby. It was horribly loud. I was pissed as hell, and I got in her ear to make sure she heard me tell her to back off. She had been trying to flirt with me, and get me to react to her, and it was driving me crazy. When you told me what she did, I was so pissed I didn't think about the fact that there might be photographers nearby. When I left, I noticed the same guy I spoke to earlier sitting off in a corner. I wouldn't put it past her to have paid him off. If you want proof though, there are plenty of people, who were in there, who could corroborate my story." Brant took a deep breath. "And there's something else." Bekah peered up at him through her lashes. "I wanted to drink. There was a bar right there, and the bartender asked if I needed anything to take the edge off. With everything that was going on, I did."

"Did you?"

"No. I couldn't do that to you, knowing what Bobby said about me."

Bekah looked away and chewed on her lip. She took a deep breath and scratched her head not saying a word. Brant's heart felt like it was shattering within him. The last thing he wanted was to hurt Bekah, and right now she seemed lost, trying to sort through the information. She finally turned to him. "Honestly, I knew she wasn't being truthful when she sat down to talk to me. She was pretty easy to read. It was more the fact that I didn't know what exactly she was lying about. When I pulled all the stuff up on the internet, and saw the photo today, it seemed like the story she told me was true."

"I'm going to be honest. Some of the stuff I did as a kid I'm not proud of. Joining the military was probably the best thing that could have happened to me. My grandpa had said something about it one time. I blew him off at the time, then I saw the recruiter up at college and decided it would probably be for the best. And it was."

"You got shot though."

"Yes, I did. But I also saved lives, so it was worth it." He stepped closer to her. "Now, can I kiss you, before I absolutely die right here?"

Her eyes still appeared wary, but she nodded. He pulled her in. His hand swept her hair from her face, and he tilted his head gently brushing his lips to hers and then waited, hoping her lips would part, and they did. A fire swept through him, and he captured her mouth completely, savoring the way she tasted, wanting to devour her right there. He finally pulled away licking his bottom lip, still wanting more. He studied her, searching for a glimmer of hope, then leaned his forehead to hers. "God, I have missed you so much."

"Where did you learn to do that?"

"Do what?" He smirked.

"Kiss me into submission."

He let out a light laugh. "I told you a long time ago I was talented." He put his hands on either side of her face and gazed into her eyes. "Are we good?" He still saw hesitation, but he didn't blame her.

"Can I ask you one more thing?"

"Sure."

"Are you really done with acting? I mean, what you said to your mom earlier. Is that really how you feel?"

"Hell yes. This shit is hard. There are days when we get up at four in the morning, like today, and we may not be done until eight at night, only to get up at four again, and then we may shoot until the next day."

"You're kidding me."

"I'm dead serious. Maizy's sleep issues had nothing on shooting a movie." She snickered, and his brows raised. "You think it's funny. I'm serious. This is my last rodeo. I would be much happier doing something important like what those guys did today for my grams."

"I would be too."

"So?"

"We're good." She tipped up on her toes and pulled him in for another kiss. "Let's go see how Grandpa and Maizy are doing."

Brant pulled open the door, and Bekah's phone buzzed.

"Bobby," she growled. "Here we go again. I'm sure he saw the article." He let the door shut and Bekah sat back down on the bench next to the door.

—How are you doing? I saw the article. I'm so glad you came to your senses Bekah. The guy was bad news. I could tell from the first time I saw him—

—Bobby, the article is completely fake—

—What do you mean fake? Didn't you see the photo?—

—Yes. He was trying to talk to the girl in a noisy room. That's all—

—Oh Bekah, you can't be that naïve. The guy is scum—

—You have no room to talk. He has treated me with the utmost respect, unlike you—

—What are you saying? Are you still with him, after I told you I don't want him around Maizy? —

—*I'm saying, it's still none of your business who I am with, and I also have a say so, as to who our daughter is around—*

—*Wake up Bekah. He is playing you—*

—*Like you did—*

—*Let me say this, when it all blows up in your face, I will be here—*

—*Don't worry about me. I can take care of myself—*

—*Well, in any case, I wanted to tell you, I'm all moved in. The house is great. You will love it. If you decide to come check it out, let me know. I'm leaving this weekend for a business trip, but I sent you a key—*

—*Bobby you shouldn't have done that. I am not coming to Houston—*

—*I'm not arguing with you. If you need it, you have it. I love you—*

Brant pulled open the door to the waiting room. "God. He just won't let it go."

"You don't think he would do anything stupid. Do you?"

"Oh, no. He wouldn't do anything to jeopardize his job. It's way too important to him."

They headed down to the first floor where Dale was rocking a crying Maizy. Brant had to pick on the old man. "What did you do to that sweet baby?"

Dale chuckled. "I don't have her food."

Brant let out a laugh, and Bekah rolled her eyes but snickered at the comment. "I will relieve you of your duties, sir. Ms. Betty is asking for you anyway. She is on the second floor, cardiac wing, room nineteen."

Dale rose from his seat and headed to the elevator. Bekah threw a blanket over her shoulder and prepared to nurse Maizy.

"You want to go out to the car so you can have a little more privacy?"

"What? Did you meet me yesterday or something? I've gotten used to people seeing my boobs. It kind of comes with the territory of having a kid."

Brant thought back to their first meeting when she nursed Maizy in front of him. It seemed like so long ago, but it had only been a few weeks.

"So, I gotta ask you."

Brant was pulled from his thoughts. He wondered what else she had left to ask him.

"What's that?"

"Do you think my grandpa has the hots for Grams?"

Brant chuckled and shrugged. "Probably."

Chapter Fifteen

Bekah sat back in the cream leather seats and listened to the roar of the Chevelle engine. Dale had given Brant the keys and let him drive it to the gym, to avoid possible photographers, since Bekah was along. Grandma Betty had gotten out of the hospital earlier in the day. Brant said the staff was probably happy she was going home after she'd given them an earful about the food they served her. Sandra, George, and Dale were at Betty's house taking care of her and Maizy.

Bekah and Dale had agreed to take care of her the rest of the week so the others could finish production of the film. Betty really was doing fine. It was more about supervising her to make sure she was following doctor's orders to take it easy, which was definitely a harder job than expected. The woman never stopped from what Brant said.

She peeked over at Brant behind the wheel. The conversation they had the day before had played over and over in her head. Her trust had been tested, but the more she was around him, the more she believed his side of the story. She knew Natalie was putting off some warning signs from the beginning. Bekah had plenty of training in reading body language, micro expressions, and behavior patterns. Because of her degree, she had it ingrained in her to listen to inflections in the voice, watch movements of the body, and track facial expressions, and she pretty much read everyone she talked to automatically. Although there were no true one hundred percent tells when a person was lying, there were several indicators that would make them highly suspect, and Natalie had run the gamut.

Though Natalie smiled when she met her, she noticed she tipped her nose up slightly, which was an indication of dislike. And when Natalie slid into the booth across from her at the restaurant, she took an intimidating posture by crossing her arms and leaning in. She wanted Bekah to believe her. Bekah listened carefully and watched her mannerisms. She noticed small twitches in her eyes, and a nervous habit of pinching her lips, which led her to suspect Natalie was lying, or at least not being totally honest.

Something in the back of her mind, though, kept nagging at her. Were her feelings for Brant affecting how she approached the whole situation? She knew there was no way she went into the conversation with Natalie without some emotion. And listening to Brant's side of the story, she knew what she wanted the outcome to be. Could she trust her instincts? Beyond that, seeing Brant so emotional about the anniversary of Abbie's death had her again wondering if his feelings for her were genuine.

"You are being awfully quiet. What's wrong?" Brant's voice pulled her from her thoughts. She turned to look at him and it was like, in that one glance, their souls connected. She reached up and stroked his whiskers with the back of her fingers, and hoped her instincts were right, because she knew she had fallen hard and fast for him. If she were wrong, it would be devastating.

"I was thinking about yesterday." Brant's brows pinched together. "There was so much that happened. It's hard not to dwell on it. Sometimes I get in my own head and second guess myself."

"Well, if you have any more questions for me, shoot. I'm an open book."

"No. It's not that, as much as letting my emotions cloud my judgement. I know I told you yesterday that I thought Natalie was being deceitful when I spoke to her. My issue is, I already had a bad image of her from what you told me, and so I went into our conversation with a negative thought process."

"So, what—"

"Again, it's me second guessing myself. It's why I couldn't have you as a client. I was already getting close to you and when that happens, my emotions get involved. It is hard not to want to read the situation a certain way."

Brant turned to her with a solemn expression. "You do believe me. Don't you?"

"Yes. I do," she said quietly, but she knew her trust had taken a beating. Why couldn't she simply believe him and be done with it. It wasn't like he could control what was going on in the tabloids. She thought back to what Natalie said about their relationship and then Brant. He said he had gone out with her a couple of times. "Did you kiss her?"

He glanced at her. "Who? Natalie?"

"Yeah."

"You know I did. You saw the photos."

"No. I don't mean on the set. You said you went out with her a couple of times." Her voice went quiet.

"Did you kiss her then?"

"Probably. I don't remember really. I tried to block all of that out of my mind." She stared out the windshield and saw him glance at her. "We only went on a couple of dates. It was during production, like after we were done shooting for the day. I remember taking her to eat pizza. I was in college, so pizza was a good date. She didn't live too far away from the university, and I remember driving her home. I kissed her that night I think, but it was a goodnight kiss, so, more like a peck. Again, I was shy. I wasn't much of a player."

"You looked like you had plenty of game in those photos."

"Oh, trust me, those on set kisses were completely staged and we had probably, at the least six people standing around us filming us and giving us directions. There was nothing romantic about them.

"Anyway, she seemed pretty normal on the first date. I remember we had a half day of shooting and there was some kind of art festival going on, so I asked if she wanted to go. It wasn't so much a date as just someone to hang out with.

"We spent the afternoon at the festival, and then went to a restaurant to eat, and that is where things went off the rails. She started talking about marriage and kids like she had already planned our future together. I was nowhere close to wanting anything long term with anyone, so I told her that, flat out, and suddenly she started showing me how crazy she really was. She said she knew I was the one the first time she saw me, and I was the perfect match for her, and started giving me this long list of why. She told me she wasn't going to let me get away, and she wasn't kidding. From that point forward, she was leaving notes on the set for me, calling me, and texting me at all odd hours of the night.

"When production was over, I changed my number and thought everything was over, because I never showed her where I lived. Then somehow, she got my address, and started sending me letters asking why I wouldn't respond to her texts and calls.

"A few months went by, and I got invited to the viewing of the film. She was there, of course. She asked why I never called or texted her back. I told her I had to change my number. When she asked for my new one, I told her I had to keep it private. She didn't like that. Then, I started running into her at various places. She would act like it was a coincidence. I tried to be polite at first, but after about the third time in a week, I wasn't so polite. I told her to leave me alone.

"Things settled down for a while, then I was out with some friends from the university, and she showed up. I was sitting next to a girl, and Natalie blew a fuse. She started ranting about me cheating on her. That's when I knew she had serious issues. And it wasn't long after that, maybe a week or so, that I came home one night from a party and found her in my bed. It scared the shit out of me to find her there, not to mention she was naked. I was done with her crazy antics and started calling the police. But she started crying and begged me not to. She said she would leave me alone and never try to contact me again. I gave her five minutes to find her clothes and get out. And she did. She pretty much stuck to her word, until my mom had to dip her fingers in and stir the pot."

"What happened?"

"Well, evidently, Natalie started working as a

second assistant director. That is someone who kind of corrals all the actors and gets them where they need to be when they need to be there. She had worked on a few films with my mom when I was in the military, and when the guy they hired for this film had to bow out, my mom suggested Natalie."

"Why would she do that though, with all you went through?"

"To be fair, I really didn't talk a lot about what went on. Mom thought Natalie simply had a crush on me."

"So, you didn't tell her about Natalie coming to your apartment?"

"No. You have to understand, there wasn't a whole lot of chit chat that went on in our house. I was not living at home anymore and although we didn't live too far away from each other, we didn't see much of each other. Honestly, I don't think my parents know me very well."

"That has to be hard to come to terms with."

"It's the nature of the beast."

"Dealing with a situation like that all by yourself must have been scary."

"More frustrating than anything." They pulled into the gym parking lot. "It was nothing like what you are having to deal with right now though. I can't imagine the frustration."

"Yeah. Let's not go there. It makes me extremely angry. I honestly don't get it. He has shown little to no interest in Maizy. I mean let's face it, he doesn't even want to hold her. And now he wants us to be a family?"

"Well, this is the place to go if you want to get rid of some anger." He pointed to the gym doors.

"Yeah. Maybe I can use their punching bags and just picture Bobby's face on them."

"Well, just because you got the cast off doesn't mean you can go nuts. I told you I was going to help you build your strength back up in your arm, so we have to start light." She nodded and pushed her door open.

A chilly wind caused goosebumps to pepper Bekah's skin. The door dinged when they entered the gym. Cody, Joe, Kaleb, and Ben were huddled around the counter. Cody's gaze tipped up. "Now there's the man with the answers."

Brant's eyes widened. "What's that?"

"We are at a stalemate, and we need the voice of reason."

Brant and Bekah walked up to the counter. "Oh, I can't wait to hear what you are discussing now. Is it X-rated? Should I ask Bekah to leave?"

"Oh, no, she's fine. Heck, who knows, she might have an opinion."

"Okay, so what's the question?"

"So, Ben here was at a cattle auction last weekend and wandered over to a gun and knife show. They had an AK 47 on display as the best weapon for a Zombie Apocalypse. I say no way, too heavy. What do you think?"

Bekah started to giggle. She looked at Brant whose brows had pulled together, considering the information.

He placed his hands on the counter. "Civilian legal, or no?"

"I'm guessing all bets are off, if it's an Apocalypse."

Brant stood for a moment and twisted his lips.

"Can't go wrong with Heckler and Koch MP5. It's lightweight, rapid fire, low recoil, and the bullets are compatible with a 9MM pistol."

Ben looked at him. "What about the CZ-85 combat? It's available with carbon fiber which would make it lightweight. It's reliable, and it can be fired from both hands."

"For a pistol. Yes. That would be an excellent choice." He nodded. "I would probably carry both since they have compatible bullets."

Joe chimed in. "See. I told you."

Cody looked back at him with a raised brow. "You told me nothing, my man. I told you Heckler and Koch."

Brant looked at Kaleb. "What do you think?"

Kaleb's eyes widened, then a cocky smirk filled his face. "I don't need guns. My devastating good looks and charm, not to mention my huge brain, are my weapons of choice."

Joe's head swayed. "Oh, good God."

"And what will you do when they eat your face?"

Kaleb smirked and brushed his hand through the air. "Pssh. Not happening."

Brant chuckled, shook his head, and turned back to Cody. "Yeah, I definitely say Heckler and Koch is the way to go. Either an MP5 or even an HK416 for its versatility and add a 9MM handgun and you would be pretty set." Bekah laughed and Brant gave her a sidelong glance. "What? Everyone should be prepared for a Zombie Apocalypse." He turned back to the guys. "Any other questions, gentlemen?" He saw Mitch walk by with his headphones on. "You should get Mitch to weigh in on it. I bet he will say the same thing."

Cody nodded, "Probably," then tipped his chin to Bekah. "And what do you think?"

"Oh, I'm totally a Heller and Kohl fan. Have been for years."

They all laughed, and Brant leaned into her and loudly whispered, "It's Heckler and Koch."

"My thought is, if I am fixing to be eaten by zombies I want whatever will kill them the quickest, whether it be a gun, a stake to the heart, or a cannon. Bring it on."

Cody laughed. "Speaking of bringing it on, I need you to bring on your signature for this liability waiver."

"Sure." She leaned over the counter. Cody pushed a piece of paper to her, and she signed. "Hey, I have a question for you."

"Is it about zombies?"

"No. It's nothing quite that entertaining."

"Too bad."

"How much does your classroom rent for, and do you have someone doing yoga classes?"

"Actually, the lady that was our yoga instructor left a few weeks back. Are you certified?"

A big smile spread across her face. "I am."

"We do a flat rate of fifteen percent on your take, and we ask that you do at least two classes per week."

"I was thinking three classes of different styles. It might take me a little bit to build up the classes though."

"Our previous instructor had a good group that attended. I could give you her roster."

"That would be great."

"I know Jenna would come once the baby is born, and I'm sure Joe could talk April into coming."

"You guys are welcome to join too."

Brant stood behind her motioning with his finger across his neck and shaking his head. Joe's eyes lifted to his. "Don't do it. I'm still sore," he said in a strained whisper.

Bekah turned to Brant wide-eyed. "You do realize, they both have been subject to my 'torture' before. Right?"

Brant's eyes darted to Cody. "You made it through the entire thirty minutes?"

"Thirty minutes? She went easy on you, Bud. We had to endure an hour." Joe nodded in agreement.

Brant's face grimaced. "Never mind then."

Cody turned back to Bekah. "Yeah, that would be great. I can't believe I didn't think of you when Shelly left. Get with me before you leave. I'll make you a good deal."

"Great."

Brant grabbed her hand and ushered her around the corner to the lockers.

"Do you always discuss such entertaining subject matters?"

"You mean like zombies? That's tame compared to some. Good thing most people have earbuds."

He pulled off his hoodie to reveal a Captain America tank top.

"Where did that come from?"

He followed her gaze to his shirt. "It's kind of a running joke in my family. When the first movie came out, I was eighteen or nineteen, and someone said I looked like Captain America. That Christmas I got a bunch of Captain America T-shirts and memorabilia. I figured since I had the shirts, I might as well put them to good use. Then everyone started buying me everything Captain America. I have all kinds of tanks and T-shirts, so I wear them all the time to the gym."

"I'm going to start calling you captain."

"You wouldn't be the first." He glanced up as Mitch approached. Brant motioned for him to remove his earbuds. "Hey, Sarge."

"Hey, Cap."

Brant turned back to Bekah. "See." He tipped his head. "I was a captain in the Air Force, so it really isn't a lie."

He turned back to Mitch. "Did Cody get your opinion?"

"Geez. What now?" Mitch said on a sigh.

"He and the guys were discussing which gun would be the best for a Zombie Apocalypse."

Mitch snickered. "What'd you say?"

"Heckler and Koch of course."

"MP5?"

"Yeah. That or 416."

"Why Heckler and Koch?"

"Several reasons. Low recoil, light weight, but mainly because they are compatible with the 9MM bullets."

"Agreed."

"I'll let them know."

Mitch shook his head and chuckled, then turned his attention to Bekah. "Did you have a chance to review the file?"

"I did, although I haven't made it all the way through, because Brant's grandma got sick. Can you give me a couple more days?"

"Oh, yeah. Take your time. It's not urgent. I just

wanted to get your input."

"No. I will have it back to you this week."

"Great. I appreciate it." He turned back to Brant. "Yeah, HK MP5 would be my pick." He paused. "I still say you are wrong on the candlestick though."

Brant laughed.

Mitch put his earbuds back in and headed off to another piece of equipment. Bekah's brow raised in confusion. "Another discussion. He and his kids were playing Clue and got into a heated discussion as to which item was the best murder weapon. I said that if it were a crime of passion it would need to be something readily available like the candlestick. He said no because you would have to get too close to the victim. Too easy for them to fight back."

"Oh my gosh. You are weird." They both laughed.

"So, are you working with Mitch on something?"

"Yeah. He calls me from time to time on different cases. I love working on stuff like that. That's when I feel like I can really use what I've been trained for."

"So, what does he have you working on?"

"Sorry, can't share that information."

"Oh, of course. It's classified."

"Something like that."

"Very cool."

His eyes remained focused on her, and she wondered what he was thinking. "What?"

"You seriously impress me."

She snickered. "Oh yeah?"

"Yeah, you do."

Tingles shot through her at the sincerity of his tone.

After putting away their stuff Brant walked Bekah around to the equipment and showed her the classroom.

He helped her with some of the weightlifting exercises, and they ended their workout with some light cardio.

Heading back to the locker, she scanned the gym again before retrieving her stuff. "Weightlifting is definitely different then yoga, but I like it."

"It kind of gets addicting after a while."

"I can see how it would be."

Cody lifted his eyes to meet Bekah's as they approached the counter. "So, what did you think?"

"I like it. This place is great. I can't believe I haven't been in here yet. I peeked in the classroom, and it is absolutely perfect."

"Awesome. So, e-mail me what times you have available, and I will see if there are any conflicts. Once we have the time slots in place, I will e-mail you the roster, and you can figure out when you want to start. You also have free membership to the gym if you are an instructor. So, you can utilize all the facilities except for the other classes that are available."

"I will definitely be in contact."

They headed out the door, and once they were on the road, Bekah let her excitement take hold. "I'm going to teach yoga." She clapped her hands quickly. "I'm so excited." Brant's eyes twinkled when she glimpsed at him.

Her phone buzzed. There was an unknown number listed when she pulled it from her bag.

—*Is this Bekah?* —

"Oh, this is creepy. Someone I don't know texted me asking if it was me."

"Crap. You're getting creepy calls now? It could be some tabloid that got your number somehow."

"Should I answer?"

"I wouldn't. Once they find out they have you, they won't leave you alone."

She took a deep breath. "Geez, is this what you always have to put up with?"

"Not always. It comes in waves. If someone does a story on anyone from our family, it seems like we are suddenly in the spotlight, and all the magazines want a piece of us."

"You've had to deal with this all your life?"

"Most of it. When I was in the military, I was able to avoid it. I mean, there were still people who recognized me, but I didn't have the magazines hounding me."

Bekah's phone buzzed again.

—*Bekah, this is Marissa. I need to talk to you*—

"Oh great! Not unknown anymore. Now Bobby's lover is trying to talk to me."

Brant let out a huff. "Ignore her."

Chapter Sixteen

"And cut." Brant relaxed but didn't move from his spot. He was exhausted, and his body ached after a grueling shooting schedule the past couple of days. He barely had four hours of sleep in the last forty-eight hours. He and the other actors waited, while the first AD and the director discussed what they had shot. The words "that's a wrap for Rest for the Wicked" never sounded so damn sweet. He was ready to kiss the Assistant Director on the mouth for uttering them. Claps rang throughout the set. Checking his phone, he realized he had only a few hours to go back to his room and grab a nap before the wrap party. A party he really didn't want to go to, since they wouldn't let anyone outside the production attend. His mom made it clear that he was expected to be there, since she had such a large stake in the film. He figured he better make an appearance, although he was so tired he was about ready to fall asleep on his feet.

Stepping into his room, he toed off his shoes and collapsed on his bed. His phone chimed, and a number popped up on the display. A number he was all too familiar with. "Who is this?" he rasped, wanting to get to the bottom of whoever was leaving him the creepy messages.

"It's Natalie. You left your wallet on the set. I wanted to tell you I was bringing it by."

"Leave it with the Production Assistant. I will get it from the PA later."

"Too late," she sang. He heard a knock. *Shit.* He wondered if she would leave it if he refused to answer the door. "I'm not leaving, so you might as well open the damn door."

Does the woman read minds? He opened the door a crack. Natalie stood in the corridor wearing a deep V-neck red sweater with black leggings and black spiked heels. She held the wallet in her hand and peeked into his room.

"What are you up to now?"

"What do you mean? I told you, I'm bringing you your wallet."

"Where exactly did you find it? I kept it in my computer bag, and I never opened it today." He picked up the bag next to the door and showed it to her with the clasps closed.

Her eyes shifted quickly. "On the ground by one of the chairs. Must have fallen out. Can I come in?"

"That's awfully strange since, again, I never opened the bag today."

"Whatever. Can I come in for a minute?"

"No, Natalie. I'm not letting you in my room."

"Geez, Brant. It's not like I bite or anything."

"No. You're worse, and I want nothing to do with you."

"You treat me like I have the plague. What the hell happened?" She stepped closer, but Brant immediately stepped back and held up his hand to keep her away. "At one time you thought I was quite the catch. Why the hell are you so mean to me now?"

"Because, Natalie, every time I'm around you, my

261

life goes to hell. I don't know why you have this, this infatuation with me, why you refuse to leave me alone, but it needs to stop."

"I have no idea what you are talking about."

"Oh, you don't?" He opened the door a little wider and stood in the doorway with his arms crossed. "Explain to me then, what exactly did you mean when you told the reporter that our relationship had been rekindled?"

Natalie's face paled, and she let out a puff of air. "I, I—"

"Oh, and just so you know, I know it was you sending the messages."

"What messages?"

Brant chuckled but from complete frustration. "The creepy messages I kept getting when I was offered the part for the movie. You know, every one of those messages brought back the memory of my *dead* wife. What the hell were you thinking? I know. You weren't."

"What? I didn't—"

"Cut the crap Natalie." Brant held up his phone. "You just called me from the same phone you sent the messages from. Not the production phone."

"Brant, I never—"

"Stop. Lying. I'm done. Stop texting me. Stop following me. Just leave me the hell alone." Brant cast his eyes over her shoulder and searched the area. "Where is he?"

"Who?"

"Your buddy the photographer? I am sure the reason you have my wallet, and you were wanting to get into my room so badly, was so he could take photos of it and plaster it all over the front-page tomorrow. How much are you paying him?"

She took a step forward again sweeping her hair over her shoulder and scanning Brant's body with a sultry expression. Brant put his hand up again stopping her in her tracks. "Why are you being so mean?"

"Because you're crazy if you think I want anything to do with you. You're sick in the head. You need psychiatric help."

Natalie's eyes narrowed but before she could say another word, Brant grabbed the wallet from her hand and slammed the door. A low rumble came from the back of his throat. *Damn, that woman makes my blood boil.*

He was so tired and angry and needed something to calm his nerves. A glint of sunlight from his hotel window bounced off the screen of his phone in his hand. Bekah's face filled the screen when he swiped it. Her. His fingers quickly moved across the screen.

"Hello?"

Just the sound of her voice caused his body to relax. "Hey. Just needed to hear your voice."

Sinking onto the bed, he leaned back against the pillow.

"So, how did it go?" Every time she talked it was like the vibrations of her deep raspy voice set something right inside him.

"We are officially done. I need to make an appearance at the party tonight, and then I am leaving this place first thing in the morning."

"Yay. That is awesome news. I am going to Grams' tomorrow for lunch so when you get settled, come by."

"Okay. I will let you know when I am on my way. I don't know what Mom and Dad's plans are. I know they were supposed to have a flight out tomorrow although their plans might have changed since Grams got sick."

Bekah giggled. "Well, she definitely doesn't act sick."

"Is she being a pain?"

"Oh no, not really. She does like her independence though and gets frustrated when we try to help her. It's sweet to watch her and Grandpa when they get together though."

"Thanks for taking care of her."

"Oh, yeah. I'm glad to do it. Between Grandpa and me, I think we have done an okay job."

"I'm sure." Glancing at the clock by the bed, he realized he only had a half hour to shower and get ready before the wrap party. He let out a sigh. "Hey, I'm going to have to get ready for the party."

"Okay. Well, have fun. I will see you tomorrow."

"I can't wait to see you and Maizy." It took everything within him not to tell her about his revelation before he hung up, but that was something he wanted to do in person. Natalie had done one thing right. She helped him realize that he had fallen in love with Bekah. He had gone through every question of it being too soon, every hesitation of causing problems in her life. He knew there would probably be consequences. But the idea of not having Bekah and Maizy in his life was simply unfathomable. He had no doubt about what he was feeling, and he was in it for the long haul. Things simply had to work out. Her reckless abandon attitude hit him like a lightning storm inside his chest. The day she threw herself at him at his grams, he felt it.

Opening the closet, he pushed his clothes to one side, withdrew his tux, laid it on the bed, and started undressing. Turning on the shower, he stepped in and stood in the steaming water, hoping it would soothe his aching body. It didn't. He was bone tired.

After dressing, he stood in the mirror and finger combed his hair, then pulled on his jacket. His mind drifted to Bekah, imagining how beautiful she would have been all dressed up. If only she could have come. His fingers ran through his hair one last time trying to get it to lay right. Adjusting the collar and sleeves, he buttoned his jacket, and walked out the door.

Outside of the ballroom, velvet ropes and a red carpet had been set up. Several photographers and reporters already stood outside the ropes waiting to interview those associated with the movie.

Brant searched the area to see if he could find his mom or dad. He didn't see them, so he figured he would wait for a little bit. While he waited, he grabbed a ginger spritzer from the bar. A tap on his shoulder made him jump. His mom stared at him with concern.

He knew what she was thinking. "Ginger ale spritzer. Want some?"

She smiled. "That actually sounds delicious."

He ordered her one and passed it to her. "Where's Dad?" he asked, letting his attention drift past her.

"He already found a place to sit."

"Oh. So, you have done the red carpet?"

"Yes. It really wasn't too bad."

"Well, you haven't been embroiled in a fabricated love triangle."

"True. I'm sorry the tabloids have been so hard on you and Bekah. How's she doing?"

"Okay. I guess. I just don't want her hurt. She is having to deal with her ex who hates my guts and has threatened her with a custody battle if we stay together."

"Is that why you needed Skip?"

"Yeah. He wasn't much help though. He said that it wasn't his forte. The tabloids have made things worse." His eyes caught Natalie approaching. "Along with that one there." He pointed with his drink.

Sandra turned. Natalie gave her a smile that Brant could tell was far from genuine. Her eyes moved to him and narrowed then returned to Sandra.

"Hey, Sandra. What do you think? Did it turn out like you had hoped?"

Sandra smiled back at Natalie, but Brant noticed her stiffen. "Oh, I guess we will have to see what it looks like once the editors and special effects get their hands on it."

Natalie turned to Brant. "Can I speak to you?"

Brant glanced at his mom then back at Natalie. He lifted his drink to his lips. "I am visiting with my mom right now. I'll find you later."

She gave him a sour expression, tipped her nose up, and headed for the red carpet.

Sandra turned back to Brant. "What was that all about?"

Brant's eyes followed Natalie. "I am pretty sure she has been the instigator of some of the tabloid stories, including the one saying we are in a relationship. I saw her talking with that greasy photographer. What's his name?"

"Are you talking about Lonny?"

"Yeah. I think that's him. I've seen them with their heads together."

"Honey don't let them get to you. It's all publicity."

"I understand that. I just don't want that publicity. Not for me, and especially not for Bekah. She didn't do anything to deserve them preying on her."

"Well, you know if you want to be in a relationship with her, it comes with the territory, especially since you are back into acting."

"Not anymore. I told you. This is it. I don't know how you do it. It's horrible, and I don't need people spreading rumors about me for the rest of my life. I am going to finish my training as a paramedic and hopefully enjoy a normal life as a flight medic."

"Do you think Bekah will be a part of it?"

"It's up to her. I would like her to." He paused. "She is a very special lady."

"I agree. She is exactly what you need in your life."

A smile crossed Brant's face, and he looked up through his lashes. "So, you approve?"

"Oh absolutely. I liked her from the first time I met her, and I could tell she was special to you. She is extremely bright, and a bit of a free spirit, and everybody needs a little bit of that in their lives, especially you. You have always been a bit too serious. She doesn't seem like she would take any crap from anyone, which is good for you. You need someone who will keep you in check."

He smirked. "Oh well, gee thanks."

Sandra bumped his elbow as they headed for the

red carpet. "You're welcome. It helps that she has an adorable little daughter too, and you know how much I want to be a grandma."

"Oh no. I have no idea. It's not like you bring it up every time I talk to you." Cameras began to flash. They paused staring in different directions letting the photographers have their fill. A young blonde woman jabbed a microphone through the crowd.

"Mr. Ellington. This is the first large roll you have had in the movie industry. Did you enjoy the shoot?"

He leaned forward so he could be closer to the mic. "I have never worked so hard in my life. I respect my mom for being in the industry for so long. Making movies is not a walk in the park, like many think. It's very long hours, and I'm exhausted, but it was fun to get a real feel of what it is like."

Another reporter pointed their mic at him. "Do you think you will continue in this industry and follow in your mom's footsteps?"

"I don't know. The first thing I'm going to do is get some sleep, then I will think about it."

Another mic pushed forward, and he noticed Lonny was behind it. The arrogant expression on his face told Brant where the question was going. "What's your current status with your love life? Rumor has it you broke up a relationship between a local doctor and her fiancé, and then dumped her for someone on set."

He cleared his throat. "I really don't like discussing my personal life and would rather keep it private. However, I would like to clear these rumors up. The doctor in question was not engaged, and I didn't break up her relationship. I helped her and her child after they were involved in a car accident, and our relationship developed from there, after her other relationship had ended. As for the story of the relationship on set, there wasn't one. That was completely fabricated."

He was satisfied with his answer, but Lonny refused to step back, even though he tried to move down the red carpet. "Is it true the child's dad is seeking custody of the child, because of your recent stint in rehab and your relationship with the doctor?"

Shit! Where the hell did he get that information?

The question devastated him knowing that Bekah's personal life was going to be put on display, and the last thing he wanted to do was give Lonny any more information, but if he didn't answer, he figured the tabloid would just make up another lie. "I am not ashamed of my treatment in rehab. I was struggling to deal with my wife and child's death, and I checked myself in to get help. Anyone who is struggling with grief, as I was, should not be ashamed to seek help. As for your question, that is between the doctor and the child's father. For the record, she is an amazing mother, and my rehab treatment should not have any bearing on her keeping her child." He zeroed in on Lonny, nodded, and smirked. *Check Mate.* Lonny opened his mouth like he was going to ask another question, but Brant stopped him. "Thank you. No more questions."

He walked into the ballroom that was adorned with gold and white balloons grouped in bunches around the room. Gold chargers sat in the center of several standard sized tables, as well as bar top tables, with tea lights surrounding short white vases of white roses. A bar sat at the back of the room, and tables of stainless food warmers lined two walls. At the front of the room was a stage, flanked with black velvet curtains. A podium was positioned center stage, awaiting the director and producers. Brant pulled out the white chair next to his dad who had already dug into a salad. He couldn't shake the agitation he felt from the invasive reporter.

George peered up as Brant sat down. "How did the red carpet go?"

Brant let out a groan. "Well, I'm glad it's over if that tells you anything. They're a bunch of piranhas."

"That's why I work behind the scenes. No one really cares what is going on with me. Hell, the only time I've ever been photographed is when I'm with your mom."

"You're lucky."

"It will blow over. Give it a couple of weeks."

"I hope so because I am tired of this shit."

His dad patted him on his back. "What are your plans now since the movie shoot is over?"

"I was telling Mom I want to finish my classes and training and hopefully get hired on with one of the fire departments and work as a paramedic. Then maybe sit for certification as a flight medic. Even though I was wounded, I really did enjoy working as a medic in the Air Force. It made me feel like my life was worth something."

George remained silent for a moment. "I'm really proud of you, you know. You haven't had it easy, and you figured out what you wanted and went after it."

"Thanks. That means a lot." He jiggled his glass to break up the ice and tossed a piece of it in his mouth. "I think I'm going to get me another drink. Do you want anything?"

"What are you having?"

He chuckled knowing why his dad was asking. "Ginger spritzer. It's pretty good."

"I think I'm good for now."

"Okay, I'll be right back." He headed to the bar and placed his order. Looking around at the people, he realized he had made some great friends while making the movie, and there were some fun times. But there were far too many days that were spent continually redoing scenes until late into the night. And there were people he would be glad to say goodbye to and never see again after this evening. One, Natalie, was staring directly at him. He grabbed his drink, took a sip, and turned to head back to his table. With no reserved seating, he hoped that his table would fill up before she decided to sit next to him. When he reached the table, he realized at least one of his wishes had come true.

The first speaker approached the podium as he took his seat. The older balding gentleman, with gold-rimmed glasses, gave a rundown of the different events of the night, then announced it was time to eat. During the dinner, different speakers including the director and the producers, which included his mom, spoke briefly about their hopes for the film. Finally, a DJ took the stage and announced the party was starting. People filled the dance floor as the music started playing, and lines formed at the bar.

Brant polished off the last of his chocolate marbled cheesecake and headed to the bar to get another drink. Milling around talking to a few people, he spied Natalie making a beeline to him. His eyes scanned the room for a path to escape, but too many people were crowded around him, and he felt her hand tap his shoulder. It was time to play nice. He flipped around, trying

271

desperately to plaster a smile on his face, although he felt as if his smile was more of a grimace, and before he could make an excuse for needing to walk away, she spoke.

"You know you really should slow down on those." Natalie stated pointing at his drink.

"It's non—"

"Hey, I wanted to tell you I'm sorry about earlier, and I hope there's no hard feelings. I know how you feel about me, and unfortunately, you and I both know nothing is going to happen, regardless how one of us might want it to. I would rather we part as friends." She tipped her head and smiled. "So, friends?"

He knew she was up to something, but he didn't want to make a scene and come off like an ogre, giving the tabloids yet another flaw to point to in their articles. She held her hand out, so he set his drink down, and shook her hand. A voice called to them, and Brant turned to see Lonny. "Let me get some photos." Lonny motioned to him. "Can you stand with your arms crossed?" Brant took a deep breath but obliged. After a couple of photos of them individually, he said, "Now let me get a few of you both." Natalie turned and smiled putting her arm around Brant. A shiver crawled up his spine. *Probably her plan all along. Shit. Oh well, it's too late now. Can't wait to see what the tabloids say tomorrow.* She returned her focus to him once Lonny disappeared.

"Well, it was good working with you again, Brant. Take care." She started to walk away, then turned back. "Don't forget your drink." He picked it up and headed back through the crowd to find his parents and tell them goodnight. He had about all the partying he could stand.

All he wanted to do was crawl into bed, get some sleep, and leave first thing in the morning.

Strolling back to the table, he was stopped by the director who praised him for the work he had done. Brant thanked him for the opportunity, and when he turned, a guy backed into him, spilling some of his drink on his shirt. He had really had enough now and was ready to leave. He was tired, and his eyes were starting to feel heavy.

When he got back to his table, his parents were nowhere in sight. He didn't want to leave without saying goodbye, because he didn't know when their flights were scheduled for tomorrow. Everyone was supposed to be out of the hotel by ten. He had neglected to ask if they had delayed going home, to make sure Grams was okay.

Across the room, he thought he spotted his mom, so he headed in that direction. Suddenly, a wave of heat hit him. His fingers fumbled with loosening the bow tie, and he pulled his jacket off and laid it over his arm. Realizing his mom had disappeared, he scanned the crowd again. His eyes felt so heavy that his vision was blurring, and he shook his head. *Shit, I need to get out of here and go to bed.* Finally, he found his mom and dad on the other side of the dance floor. As he threaded through the crowd in their direction, his head started swimming. A hand grabbed his arm, and as he turned, he saw Natalie.

"Are you okay? How many of those drinks did you have?"

Squinting his eyes, trying to focus, he stared at her, wanting to answer, but his head felt foggy.

"Brant?" Natalie's voice sounded strange.

He waved her off and tried to walk away but his legs felt weak, and his stomach was getting queasy. She stayed in step with him. "I'm not feeling well. I need to find my parents, then I'm leaving." He could hear his words slurring as he spoke. *What the hell is going on.*

"Okay. Let me help you. I just saw them."

Sliding her hand in his, she started to pull him along. He tried to pull away, but a wave of dizziness hit, and he struggled to stay upright as they walked toward his parents. By the time he got to them, the room was spinning, and he could barely stand. Natalie put her arm around him to stabilize him.

"What's wrong, Brant?" His mom seemed alarmed.

"I don't know. I'm dizzy. I think sleep deprivation is catching up with me. I'm going to call it a night and head to my room." He fell into his mom and nearly knocked her down. His dad caught him, giving him a glare, but then hugged him.

"I'll make sure he gets back to his room. He probably had too much to drink." Natalie reassured. She put her arm around him, and he reluctantly draped his arm over her shoulder.

With a roaring noise building in his ears, he stumbled into the elevator, and then up the hall to his room. He could hear voices, though he couldn't make out what was being said. He felt his head hit the pillow and everything went black.

Chapter Seventeen

The sky was filled with a white sheet of clouds that felt like a chilly wet coat wrapped around Bekah. A scent of smoke hung heavy in the air. Even though the temperature still kept her in her winter coat, she could see signs of spring peeking up through the wet ground as she bounded up the front steps of the little white house. She knocked a couple of times, then pushed open the door. "Grams? I'm here." Betty had asked her to call her that, after she and Maizy had joined her for lunch a couple of times.

"Come on in. Did you have lunch?" The silver haired woman appeared from the hallway.

"No, I brought us some. I stopped and got us soup and sandwiches. How are you feeling?"

"I'm fine for an old lady."

"Grandpa Dale will be coming by later. He had to make a stop at his office this morning, and Brant said he would be by once he got checked out of the hotel."

"Oh, are they done?" Betty's face brightened.

"Yes. He called last night before he went to the party."

"I'm so glad. I'm sure he is too."

Bekah's phone buzzed. "Speak of the devil."

—Leaving now. Stopping by my house to drop off my stuff. Are you at Grams? —

—Yes. Can't wait to see you—

A smile crossed Bekah's face. She hadn't seen him in nearly a week and had come to find more comfort in having him around than being alone. He was so good to her and Maizy.

The sound of the front door opening made her jump up. She and Betty headed up the hall and saw George and Sandra coming in. Sandra hugged Bekah before hugging Betty. George nodded.

"I'm so glad you are here. Brant wasn't sure he would be able to see you before you headed out."

"We pushed our flight back a day. We leave tomorrow around noon." Sandra glanced around. "Where's Maizy?"

"Oh, she is in the kitchen napping in her carrier. Have you had lunch?"

They strolled back to the kitchen. "Yes, they had some food set up for us at the hotel." Her face turned sober. "Have you heard from Brant this morning?" Sandra asked pulling the blanket off the sleeping baby.

"Yes. He just texted me. He said he was dropping his stuff off and then coming over."

"Good. I was worried about him last night, and I didn't see him at breakfast this morning."

Bekah's throat tightened. "Oh. What was wrong?" She noticed Sandra glance at George. A surge of concern pulsed through her body.

"I think he might have been drinking last night."

Her heart plummeted. *Why would he do that? Why would he risk being photographed and give Bobby ammunition for the custody battle? He said he fought against it because of us. Unless he decided he didn't want to be in a relationship. Unless the tabloids got it right.* Nothing in his words or actions hinted that he was not being honest with her though. And during their first encounter his main concern was remaining sober. Had she steered him wrong when he asked if he should take the part? Was he not strong enough? Her mind was reeling with the thoughts swirling like smoke in the wind.

Sandra's phone buzzed, and she answered it. Her brows furrowed, and she quickly walked into the living room, out of earshot. Bekah set the sandwiches and paper bowls of soup out on the table and tried to listen to Sandra's conversation, but she kept her voice low. When she walked back into the kitchen, her face told Bekah something was wrong.

"Who was that?" Betty asked as she took a bite of her sandwich and then wiped her mouth.

"It was Jerry, one of the producers. He said the police showed up to the hotel hunting for Brant."

Bekah turned to her. "Why?"

"I have no idea. Something happened last night, and they want to talk to him."

"You said you thought he was drinking last night. What made you think that?"

"He came up to us at the party and said he was tired and was heading to his room. He was swaying and slurring his speech. Natalie said she was going to help him get to his room."

"Natalie? I thought he told her to stay away from him after the fake story in the tabloid came out."

"Oh, I don't know. He didn't say anything to me about that."

Bekah was becoming more and more confused. *Why was Natalie with him last night? Why were the police looking for him?*

The sound of the door, and voices, caused her to hop up from the table and traipse out to the hallway. Brant and her grandpa were chatting about the movie. Brant had on a gray hoodie and navy warm-ups. She smiled when she saw him, but her heart felt conflicted with the latest information she had been given.

He walked up, wrapped his arms around her, and gave her a chaste kiss, then looked in her eyes. His brows drew together. "You okay?"

"Well, the question is, are you?"

He took a step back releasing his grip on her. "Yeah, other than a massive headache. Why?"

"Your mom was worried about you last night." They started walking back toward the kitchen.

"Why?"

"She said you appeared to be drunk."

Brant stopped in his tracks. "When?"

Sandra, George, and Betty sat around the table as they entered the kitchen. Dale was pouring himself some tea. Sandra had Maizy up on her shoulder.

"I hope you don't mind. She woke up."

Bekah smiled. "No. Of course not."

"Mom, why did you think I was drunk last night?"

"Well, you were staggering when you walked up with Natalie. She said she was going to help you get to your room."

"When was that? I don't remember…" Brant stopped and put his hand to his mouth.

Bekah's phone buzzed. She knew who it was without even looking.

—*I sent you an e-mail. You need to open it now. I hate to say I told you so. But I told you so. Now there is no doubt—*

Her eyes shifted to Brant, and her breath caught in her throat. The last thing she wanted was for Bobby to be right. She wondered what he had found that had him sending her an e-mail. Walking into the living room, she slowly lowered herself to the sofa. Brant followed. Her finger hovered over her e-mail icon, and she clicked it. Bobby's e-mail simply said, "come to Houston" and had an attachment. She clicked on it and several photos popped up. There was a photo of Brant with Natalie. He had a drink up to his lips. It seemed innocent enough. Another looked like he was talking to her. One was him facing the camera with his arms crossed with Natalie turned away. Still another, Natalie had her arm around Brant, both smiling for the camera. Again, somewhat innocent. But the following photos showed Brant obviously drunk. Several were of him with his arm around Natalie. The last was of him with Natalie standing outside of a hotel room. Bekah stood, feeling like the air had been sucked out of the room.

She blinked back tears and glanced at Brant who had no idea what she had seen. His eyes narrowed in concern, and he grabbed her phone. She watched as his thumb pushed up the screen. His Adam's apple bobbed in his throat and a look of horror took over his face. He stared up at her.

"I…" Bekah felt like her legs were going to give way and she sat back down on the sofa. "I don't remember. I swear Bekah, I didn't drink. I had ginger ale with tonic. That's it."

A knock came at the door. Bekah quickly wiped her eyes and answered it. Mitch stood in uniform with a grim expression on his face. When he saw Bekah, he appeared confused. "Is Brant here?"

She stood aside and motioned for him to come in. Brant stood from the sofa and stared at Mitch.

"What's up, Sarge?" Any other time Mitch probably would have smiled at the nickname. This time his face remained sober.

"Do you want to tell me what happened with you and Ms. Holcomb last night? You don't have to. I'm basically on a fact-finding mission." Dale, Betty, George, and Sandra appeared from the hallway.

Brant scanned the room. He still had the phone in his hand, and he glanced down at it. "I…I don't know." Panic filled his voice as his focus returned to Mitch. "I can't remember. What happened?"

"What do you remember about last night?"

Brant sat back down on the sofa. He rubbed his hands down his face. "Where do you want me to start?"

Mitch slowly sat in a chair across from Brant. "What do you remember from yesterday?"

His hands moved through his hair then rubbed against his sweats. Bekah could see the confusion on Brant's face. It matched her own.

"We started shooting at five yesterday morning. Between yesterday and the day before, I had about four hours of sleep, so by the time we were done yesterday I was exhausted. I got back to the room at around four. I had planned to take a nap before getting ready, but Natalie texted me saying she had my wallet and showed up at my room. She kept asking if she could come in for a minute, but I said no. I don't trust her."

Mitch sat forward. "Why don't you trust her?"

"She is notorious for lying, or let's say, telling half-truths."

Mitch's brows went up. "Okay?" He sat back in the

chair. "We will revisit that later. Continue."

"She said I was being mean to her because I didn't want to talk to her. I told her that I couldn't trust anything she said or did, then I grabbed my wallet and slammed the door." He paused. "After that, I called Bekah, got ready, and left for the party."

"Okay. And at the party, who did you visit with?"

"When I got there, I went to the bar and got a ginger ale with tonic water. Mom came up and we talked, then I spoke to some reporters on the red carpet. I chatted with the people at our table and then a few others I worked with."

"Your drinks had no alcohol?"

"No."

"Did you talk to Natalie?"

"Yes. Before the dinner she asked if we could talk, and I told her I would catch her later. Then after the dinner she found me at the bar. Honestly, I tried to avoid her, but she grabbed me, and I didn't want to make a scene. She said she wanted to end on a good note and set aside our issues. I agreed. She shook my hand and then a photographer wanted to take some photos." He took a deep breath.

"Did you talk to her after that?"

Brant sat on the edge of the sofa staring at the floor. "I remember going back to the table to find Mom and Dad. I was ready to leave, so I wanted to make sure I found them before I left, because I wasn't sure when their flight was leaving today. They weren't there." Brant's eyes darted like he was trying to remember, but he was silent.

"What happened next?"

"I got hot and took my coat off." He wiped his

fingers across his brow. "I, I looked across the room and…" He slowly lifted his head to Mitch, "I was so tired."

Mitch leaned with his elbows on his knees. "Anything else? Specifically, anything with Ms. Holcomb?"

"No, nothing. I woke up this morning. My head was killing me. I slept until nine, which was weird because I'm usually up by six. I thought it was because I was sleep deprived."

"Did you have clothes on?"

"My boxers. Why? What the hell is this about?"

"We'll get to that. Back to Ms. Holcomb. You said you don't trust her?"

"We have a history, Mitch. We worked on another movie together. I went out with her a couple of times and realized she was a little too crazy for me and I tried to break it off. She didn't want to break up and broke into my apartment. She begged me not to call the police so against my better judgement, I didn't. I thought everything was over, and it was, until she showed up at this movie. I tried to stay as far from her as possible, but since she was second AD, we had to work together."

Bekah's phone buzzed. Bobby had sent her a link. She debated opening it because she knew it couldn't be good, figuring it had to do with why Mitch was asking Brant about Natalie. Her finger tapped the link, and her body shook when she read, "he fell off the wagon and is now accused of rape." Tears rolled down her cheeks as she glanced at Brant sitting on the sofa. She studied his face. Brant lifted his head, obviously confused.

"What's—"

Mitch's expression was stern. His tone was even. "Any other reason?"

Brant turned back to Mitch. "She cornered Bekah at a restaurant. She said I told her that Bekah and I had broken up and insinuated that I had rekindled our relationship. Then, I think it was the next day, a big story was plastered all over the tabloids with a photo of Natalie and me. The photo looked like I was going to kiss her. In reality I was yelling at her." Mitch wrote something on his notepad. "Mitch, for Christ's sake, would you tell me what is going on?"

"She says you raped her, Brant."

"I what?" Brant leaped from his seat. Horror filled his face. His eyes went to Bekah then his mom and dad and grandma. "I swear Mitch, I didn't touch her."

"Evidence says you did."

"What do you mean?" Panic laced every word.

"She showed up at the hospital around two this morning, saying you were drunk, and when she helped you to your room, you grabbed her and forced her to have sex with you. They did a rape kit on her. Your DNA showed up."

"I didn't do it."

"How can you say that, if you don't remember?" Mitch responded. "The evidence is there, Brant. And there are witnesses."

"Witnesses?"

"Several people said you were drunk at the party. There were also several who stated they heard Natalie tell you to slow down on your drinking.

"I was drinking ginger spritzers. No alcohol. I swear."

"They also said they heard her tell you that she just

wanted to be friends."

"Shit. She set me up, Mitch. She said she knew we had had our differences, but she wanted to leave as friends."

"That could be true. For right now though, you are going to have to come with me until we can figure it out."

"Seriously? You are going to arrest me?"

"I have to. Your side of the story is you can't remember. She had a pretty clear story of what happened, and with all of the witnesses and evidence, it's a whole lot more believable than 'I don't remember.'"

Brant backed away. "No. I didn't do anything wrong." His teeth clenched. "I wasn't drunk."

Mitch stood. "That may be true, Brant, but you have to prove it, and that takes time. Right now, the evidence says you did. So, I'm afraid I have to take you in. Don't make this harder than it has to be. Don't add resisting to the charges."

Maizy started whimpering. Brant let his focus rest on her in his mother's arms. Tears pooled in his eyes, and Bekah had to avert hers to keep from falling apart. She could see it all flash before her. Brant would go to jail. She would go to court. Bobby would get custody.

Brant's attention went back to Mitch. He rubbed his hand over the back of his neck then cleared his throat. "Can I talk to Bekah before we leave?" His words came out broken.

Mitch's gaze shifted to Bekah then returning to Brant. "Go ahead."

Brant tipped his head in the direction of the kitchen. Bekah followed. He turned to her once they were out of earshot.

She crossed her arms and stared at the floor to avoid his pleading look. All of Brant's words rattled through her head. Every photo she saw. Everything Natalie and Mitch said was spinning, quickly becoming the perfect storm. She was so confused. All her misgivings, and all her insecurities, were wreaking havoc on her. She didn't want the story to be true, or for him to be anything like Bobby, who was a liar and cheater. But, if everything turned out to be true, Brant was even worse.

"Bekah, look at me." She slowly shifted her eyes to his, unable to hold back her emotions. Tears streaked her face. Her arms encircled her body, but she was unable to stop shaking. He studied her, and she wondered if he was thinking what she was thinking. Would this be the last time they saw each other? "I don't know what you believe, and I don't blame you if you take everything at face value. It's obvious something happened, and I am truly sorry. I hope you believe what I'm telling you is the truth though." He turned away from her and dragged his fingers through his hair. "I didn't drink anything. I promise. The only photos I remember taking were when Natalie was calling a truce. I can't explain why I can't remember, other than I was so exhausted. I seriously haven't slept in I don't know when."

"I'm glad you understand. It's hard for me because no matter what you say, whether it's true or not, it doesn't take the pain away. The pictures Brant—"

"I know. I know, and I'm sorry. I can't explain it, Bekah. But if you give me a chance—"

"You have to know how it seems and what is going

through my head. I told you in the hospital, with everything I've been through, the lies and manipulation, I just can't—"

"I know." He sighed as his hands landed on top of his head. Bekah noticed a tear slide down his cheek. He walked over to the sink and stared outside. "I don't want to lose you, Bekah. You are the best thing that has ever happened to me. Still, you need to do what is best for you and Maizy, and I'm not naïve. Right now, that isn't me." He took a deep shaky breath and chewed on his lip. "Regardless of what happened, Sarge is right, it's going to take time to fix." Turning back to Bekah, tears stained his cheeks. "I will fix it. I will prove I'm innocent." His hands reached out and rubbed her arms. "I just don't know how long it will take. But, Bekah, I need you to know…" His chin quivered as he tried to talk. "I love you, and I love Maizy."

His words completely broke her, knowing she loved him too. There was nothing about him she didn't love, although she couldn't reconcile what had happened. She wanted to believe him, wanted to see it in his eyes. More than anything, she wanted to give him that chance.

However, she knew if she did, if she took his side, she would more than likely lose Maizy, and that just wasn't an option. He was right. Regardless, if he was guilty or innocent, it didn't matter if she wanted to keep Maizy. Bobby had won. Her hand covered her mouth. Tears spilled down her cheeks, and she backed away.

Brant swallowed hard. "Bekah, I—"

She put her hands up halting his words and quickly left the room. Gently taking Maizy from Sandra, she placed her in the carrier and strapped her in, then grabbed her coat.

"I'm ready to go." At the sound of Brant's words, she turned, and watched Mitch pat him down, then take out his handcuffs. Brant hugged his mom and dad and grandma then reached down and stroked Maizy's face.

Mitch set the steel cuffs against Brant's wrists.

"You don't have to do that. Do you?" Bekah choked out.

Brant glanced back at her. "It will be okay." The complete brokenness in his voice wrecked her, and she lunged at him. Wrapping her arms around his neck, she pressed her lips to his. When she backed away, she could see Brant fighting back tears. Sergeant Gallagher finished cuffing him and escorted him out the door while Bekah hugged everyone and quickly left. Her heart shattered. She seriously doubted she would ever be able to breathe again.

When she arrived back at her house, she pulled Maizy from her carrier and sat on the sofa, hugged her close, and sobbed for what felt like hours. When Maizy was sleeping peacefully, she put her down for a nap. Her head felt like it was going to explode, trying to process what had happened. Nothing made sense. She sat on the sofa, opened her laptop, and went to her e-mail. Pulling open the e-mail from Bobby, she thumbed through the photos again. Her finger clicked through each photo, each one more damning than the last. Could he have been playing her this whole time the way Bobby had? Was she that blind? Was she crazy for still wanting to believe him? His words rang in her head. "Do what you need to do for you and Maizy." She couldn't get past the thought of standing before a judge, begging to keep Maizy. She couldn't live if she had to give her up.

Maybe Bobby really did love her. Maybe he learned his lesson. Could she trust him again? She was so tired of trusting people only to be taken advantage of. She felt she was constantly trying to decide if people were being truthful with her. All she wanted was to believe someone had her best interest at heart, for once. She thought Brant did. He treated her and Maizy so special, and now she was back to square one, wondering if she was being played.

Her phone buzzed. A number popped up. Bekah rolled her eyes. *I don't think I can take much more of this.*

—Bekah, it's Marissa. I really need to talk to you—

—How did you get my number? —

—Bobby gave me your information—

—This is not a good time—

—Bobby told me you had broken up. I would have never dated him if I knew—

Bobby lied to her too? Of course he did. Her initial impression of Marissa was good. She seemed very genuine.

—It's okay—

The next text came quickly.

—There's more Bekah. I really need to talk to you—

She wondered what Marissa was talking about. Why was she so desperate to talk to her? Part of her was curious as to what she wanted to tell her. But she really didn't think she could take one more problem.

—I'm sorry I can't right now. Too much has happened—

Chapter Eighteen

Bekah woke to the sound of Maizy's coos. She had fallen asleep with Maizy in her arms about four. Until then sleep had eluded her. Countless hours had been spent with her in tears, completely devastated by what had transpired. The day played over and over in her head, and she knew exactly what it meant. There were only two options. Move to Houston or lose Maizy. She knew what she needed to do. It was for Maizy's sake because that is what you do when you love someone that much. She gazed down at the little girl staring up at her. Her little eyes were bright. Her lips the perfect shade of red, and she was the only one who truly had her heart, she kept telling herself.

Yesterday was easily the worst day of her life. She had completely fallen for Brant and was ready to allow him into her and Maizy's life for good. The court battle scared her, but she felt like she had enough knowledge about what Brant had gone through to convince the judge his past was not a problem, and she was still the best parent to have custody over the parent who didn't want her in the first place. All of that changed in a matter of hours.

Although she wanted to believe Brant, there was so much evidence stacked against him, and being part of a family of actors, she didn't know if she could trust her intuitions with him. Could he be that good of an actor?

And if he were somehow innocent, it was going to take time, and some hard evidence, to get his name cleared. Time she didn't have. Even though there was a tabloid story that said they had ended their relationship, she would still be connected to him and still run the risk of losing Maizy.

Sitting up on the edge of the bed, she noticed the sun was already streaming through the window. She lifted Maizy into her arms and fed her, then returned the sleeping baby to her crib before heading up the hallway to the kitchen. After getting her coffee started, she checked the time.

Eight thirty is not too early. Scrolling down her list of recent calls, she came to Bobby's number and stopped. She hesitated. Seconds ticked by as she tried to come up with a better option, but thinking of Maizy, she knew there were none. She needed to contact him, cancel her appointments for the week, then make flight reservations. *How old do babies have to be to fly?*

Her thumb punched the number, and it rang. Her heart pounded replaying the conversation she was about to have. After several rings, his voicemail picked up. Oh crap, I bet he has already headed out for his business trip. She had gotten the key he had sent in the mail; however, he had neglected to give her the address to the house. Scrolling through her contacts again, she pulled up Bobby's mom. The one time she had met her didn't go so well, and the only reason she had her phone number now was because Bobby had given Bekah her number when she was wanting to make his favorite dish, and Bobby said she had the recipe.

The phone rang. Bekah's nerves had ramped up to the point she was physically shaking.

"Hello?"

"M-Mrs. Leonard?" Her voice wavered from her nerves.

"Yes."

"This is Bekah Adkins. I was trying to contact Bobby to get his new address, and I can't reach him."

"I'm sorry. Who is this again?" Bekah closed her eyes. The woman's nasally haughty tone irritated her last nerve.

"Bekah Adkins. I dated Bobby?" She paused, wondering why Mrs. Leonard didn't know her.

"Oh." Her voice still snippy. "You're the little hippie girl he dated a few years back?"

Bekah rolled her eyes, suddenly remembering how rude Mrs. Leonard had been when she met her, thinking she was one step above a street urchin.

"Yes ma'am. I was wondering if you could give me the address of his new house. Maizy and I are going to be coming in this week."

"And who is Maizy?"

Bekah froze. Surely, he had told his family about Maizy. She pulled the phone away from her ear. What if he hadn't? If she said something now, she might make things worse for herself, if they wanted to help him fight for custody. "Oh sorry. She is a friend."

"Did you run into each other recently? Why do you need his address?"

Bekah's nerves were replaced with anger. It was obvious his mom didn't know they were still dating, so there was no way she knew about Maizy. "Yes ma'am. He invited us to see his new house."

"He won't be back from vacation until next weekend."

What the hell. He said it was a business trip. "Oh, I must have gotten my weeks mixed up. I will try to contact him later."

"Do you want me to let him know you were asking about him if he calls?

"No, ma'am. That' not necessary. Thank you."

A growl erupted from her throat as she ended the call and pounded it against her forehead. *Why? Why do I let him do this to me?*

A knock came at the door causing her to jump. She peeked out the window to see the tall, buxom blonde on her doorstep. Marissa. "Dammit. Really not in the mood right now." She pulled the door open and didn't even try to smile. "Marissa."

"Bekah, I'm so sorry. I know I'm the last person you want to see. I really need to talk to you though."

Taking a deep breath, she motioned for Marissa to come in. Her thoughts went back to the message Marissa sent her, telling her she didn't know she and Bobby were still dating. Looking at her, she noticed a pained expression on her face. Suddenly, Bekah realized that Marissa was just as much of a victim as she was. "I'm sorry, Marissa. I shouldn't be mad at you. You didn't do anything wrong." Marissa shyly stepped into the living room. "Have a seat. I will be right back." She headed up the hallway to check on Maizy, then returned to the living room where Marissa was checking out the surroundings. Baby clothes filled a basket on the sofa. A baby swing sat next to it. "I'm sorry. The place is kind of a mess."

"Oh, no. I love your place. I'm sorry to barge in so early, but I couldn't sleep last night, and since you wouldn't talk to me yesterday, I decided to drive in."

Bekah moved the basket to the floor and sat down on the sofa, wondering why Marissa was so adamant to talk to her. "So, what is so important that you drove all this way to talk to me?"

"Oh, I didn't drive in from Houston, if that's what you are thinking. I'm still in Oklahoma." Bekah's brow creased.

"You didn't? Why?"

"Let's just say, I realized staying as far away from Bobby would probably be in my best interest, and definitely in yours too."

"Oh?"

"Listen, Bekah. I'm going to cut to the chase. I am so sorry for what happened. I really liked you when we met. And, at first when Bobby told me you broke up several months ago and asked me out, I was hesitant and turned him down. He persisted though, sent flowers, acted sweet, and I finally gave in. We dated for a couple of months, and then I moved in with him maybe three months ago. I had no clue he was still with you."

"Didn't you wonder where he was going when he would leave for a while?"

"Not really. He always said it was business, checking on equipment and stuff.

"Even after I found out, he never told me you had a baby. I had no idea until I saw the story in the tabloids. I felt terrible."

Bekah sat back on the sofa. "Don't feel bad, I just got off the phone with his mom. He didn't tell her either. I don't know what kind of game he is playing."

"I don't know either, and that's why I'm here. He is up to something, and it's not good."

Bekah tilted her head with her brow raised. A slight glimmer of hope sprouted in her chest, and she had a feeling Marissa was about to become her best friend. "I've got some ginger spritzers in the refrigerator." Her thumb hitched to the kitchen. "I have a feeling I might need a drink for this. Want one?"

"You drink?"

"Not right now, I'm nursing. I have rum though if you want me to add something to yours."

"No, I'm fine. It's a bit early," she said with a giggle. "I need to keep my head clear for this."

The comment didn't get past Bekah, and she wondered what bomb Marissa was about to drop. After retrieving the drinks, she handed Marissa hers, then curled her legs underneath her, and sat down facing her on the end of the sofa. "So, fill me in."

"When you came to the apartment and I found out he was still in a relationship with you, I broke up with him. He initially begged me not to, then got pissed when I insisted, and later said he was still in love with you anyway."

"Ha! He told me he broke up with you and kicked you out."

"No, I immediately moved out the weekend you came. But unfortunately, I still had to work with him, because I had to finish my project, and it was still a couple of weeks before the team was supposed to start transferring to Houston. The way he acted and talked about you didn't sit well with me."

"What do you mean?"

"He became obsessed. He kept talking about you moving with him to Houston, even though I overheard a couple of conversations he had with you, and it was obvious that you didn't want to. It started making me worried, and I thought about contacting you earlier, but I wondered if I was being too paranoid. I decided to talk to Marci, his assistant, about keeping an eye on him. She's a good friend of mine, although he doesn't know it. She already didn't like him since he tried to put the moves on her, even though she knew he was dating me."

"Oh, you gotta be kidding me."

"I'm serious. She tried to warn me, but by that time, Bobby had played with my head so much I just thought she was mistaken, and he was just picking on her."

"I gotta give it to him. He has the manipulation game down to an art."

"She actually tried to move to a different department, but when the opportunity to move to Houston came up, she had the chance to move closer to her family and make more money, so she accepted the transfer. And I'm glad she did. At first, she said he just talked about you moving down there with him, like you had already made plans to do so. Then she texted me a couple of weeks ago"—she squinted one eye, thinking—"maybe a little before, saying he had asked her if she knew of a private investigator."

Bekah's thoughts went back to the photos he sent her of Brant the day before. Must have been where the photos came from.

"After she told him she didn't, it was only a few days later that a seedy looking guy showed up asking for him. She said Bobby acted surprised when he saw him, so she knew something was up. She told him she was going to grab a bite to eat and once they were in his office, she hung around to listen. As soon as he shut his office door, she said Bobby started yelling at the guy about not meeting him in the designated location. Apparently, he had no idea how thin the walls were, because she said she heard almost the entire conversation. You were mentioned, and something about paying five thousand dollars to ruin some guy connected with you. From what was in the tabloids yesterday, I figured it might be Brant Ellington, and I knew I had to talk to you."

"Yeah. Bobby wanted me to break up with Brant and move to Houston with Maizy. Brant recently got out of rehab and Bobby said he didn't want his daughter around an addict. He told me if I didn't move to Houston, he would seek custody of Maizy. When I told him I wasn't moving, he filed, and sent me papers with a court date."

"Are you kidding me? That's extortion. Bekah, you can't move." She leaned forward. "Marci said last week she saw him kissing on some girl, while still talking about moving you down there."

"I don't know that I have much of a choice though. His P.I. got very incriminating photos of Brant at the wrap party Friday. He was arrested for rape. If I'm connected to him during the court case, Bobby will get custody of Maizy."

She leaned her head against the sofa, letting everything soak in. "The thing that I don't get is, why? Why is he so adamant about me being with him? I mean looking back, he manipulated the entire relationship. Like you, he sent me flowers and always said the right things. When I went out with him, he was the perfect gentleman. Before I knew it, he had complete control. I still can't believe I didn't see it. But when I got pregnant with Maizy, everything changed. She wasn't in his plan. He said she was a huge inconvenience to him. He didn't even attempt to bond with her. It's obvious he doesn't want her, otherwise he would have told his parents about her. It's almost creepy the way he dismisses her."

"That's what I'm trying to tell you. He's irrational. The guy has lost it." She scooted to the edge of the sofa and turned to Bekah. "From what Marci said, she didn't think the guy Bobby was talking to was a private investigator. The last thing she said Bobby told him was to do whatever it took to ruin his life. Then I saw the story about Mr. Ellington, and I knew I had to find a way to talk to you."

"So, you think Bobby had something to do with Brant's arrest?"

"I can't be sure. I think he may have though."

Bekah sat back on the sofa rolling the information over in her head. Could Bobby have somehow instigated what happened to Brant? Her thoughts went back to Brant's expression when Mitch told him the charges. There were no indicators that said he knew. Even though he accepted what Mitch said, he seemed genuinely shocked when Mitch informed him of the rape. And if Marissa was right, and Bobby had set Brant up, she would finally be free of Bobby. "Will you help me find out?"

"I'm all in, and so is Marci. I already talked to her."

"Right now, all it sounds like he did was hire a P.I., so we have to prove they set Brant up. That would mean Natalie Holcomb was in on it." Her mind searched for the scenario. "I need to make a phone call." She pulled her contacts up and hit call. Her teeth skimmed her bottom lip waiting for an answer.

"Mitch Gallagher."

"Hey Mitch. It's Bekah Adkins. I need to talk to you as soon as possible. It's about Brant."

"Brant posted bail about thirty minutes ago."

Her thoughts drifted, and she wondered if he would contact her. She had a feeling he would keep his distance so there would be less of a chance of her being connected with him through the tabloids. "Good to hear. I have some information that may be connected to the case. Would you have time this afternoon for me to come by?"

"Yeah. Give me about thirty minutes, and I'm all yours."

Bekah turned to Marissa pulling her phone away from her mouth. "Can you stick around for a little bit?"

"Sure."

"Great. We will see you then." Bekah put her phone on the end table.

"I'm going to run next door to see if my grandpa can watch Maizy for a little bit."

Marissa nodded, and Bekah headed out the door. After talking to her grandpa, she returned to find Marissa still sitting on the sofa. "Realized when my grandpa gave me a strange look that I am still in my pajamas. Let me get changed, and we can head out."

"Okay."

Bekah strolled up the hallway and changed into some leggings and a long shirt, then picked up the sleeping baby from the crib. As she stepped into the living room, Marissa sat up. Her face softened, and a smile appeared. It was the first smile she saw on Marissa's face since she arrived. "Wanna hold her?" Marissa's brows lifted, and her smile widened. Bekah passed Maizy carefully into Marissa's arms. Marissa stared down at the baby who was now starting to squirm.

"She is gorgeous. She has so much hair."

Bekah grabbed the baby bag and started stuffing items in it. Her eyes scanned the room then landed back on Marissa.

"God. Whatever happens, Bekah, you can't let him win."

She had felt so lost just hours before and had come a whisper away from making the biggest mistake of her life. "Thanks to you, I don't plan on it." She slung the bag over her shoulder. "Are you ready?"

Marissa stood gingerly trying not to wake Maizy. They strolled across the courtyard and rapped on the door. Dale answered quickly and after getting Maizy settled, they headed into town.

Bekah couldn't decide if she was nervous or anxious as they pulled into the parking lot at the Dalton Police Department and saw Mitch waiting for them at the door, holding a white bag.

"Were you waiting on us?" Bekah joked when she stepped out of the car.

Mitch chuckled. "No. Actually, you caught me."

"Oh no. What were you doing?"

He chuckled again. "Getting donuts." He pointed at the donut shop across the street. "Really bad idea to have a donut shop across from the police department."

"I would say genius," Bekah said stepping through the door and then letting Marissa in before continuing.

"Mitch, this is Marissa. I'm sorry, I don't remember your last name."

"It's Bellamy."

He moved the paper bag and shook her hand then escorted them through the security door to his office. Brown paneling lined the walls. A dozen boxes were piled up in the corner with a white plastic table pushed up against one wall. Mitch circled his desk and sat down in his chair. Bekah and Marissa pulled up two old wooden chairs with worn tan fabric on the seats.

"What do you have for me, Ms. Adkins." Bekah smiled knowing Mitch was using her last name to pick on her more than anything. He had called her in on several cases to get her take, and had even asked her to review one recently, that she had yet to get through completely.

"Well, like I said this pertains to Brant's case. I promise I will have some information back to you on the other one really soon."

Mitch waved his hand in the air. "Eh, you're fine."

"Okay." She took a deep breath. "Let me give you a little background first. I don't think you ever met my ex, Bobby Leonard. He is Maizy's dad and worked at Pepin Energy in Oklahoma until recently transferring to Houston. I broke up with him several weeks ago. I met Brant soon after, and things just kind of happened. Anyway, there were some tabloid photos that came out with me and Brant. Bobby was not happy that Brant came into my life so soon after we broke up, especially after he found out Brant had been through rehab. He told me to stay away from him or he would take me to court for custody of Maizy, which he has decided to do when I refused to reunite with him and move to

Houston."

"Okay, so far, not following how this all falls together."

Bekah glanced at Marissa wondering if she should give Mitch the sordid details of Marissa's involvement. "Marissa worked with Bobby. She noticed that he was becoming rather obsessed with me after I broke up with him and became concerned, so she decided to keep an eye on him and enlisted Bobby's assistant to help her. The assistant overheard Bobby pay someone five thousand dollars to ruin someone's life who was associated with me. So, what if that someone was Brant?"

Mitch leaned back in his chair, grabbed his wrist, stretched, then laid his wrists on his head. "So, let me get this straight. You have Mr. Leonard's assistant telling Ms. Bellamy here, that she overheard Mr. Leonard tell someone he would give them five thousand dollars to ruin someone's life."

Bekah put her hands up. "I know. It's flimsy."

Mitch chuckled and leaned forward. "Ya think?"

"Mitch. What if Brant was set up?" Mitch tapped a pen on his desk and Bekah stood up. "Here is my thought. Bobby basically was blackmailing me, telling me he would file for custody of Maizy if I didn't move down to Houston with him. He saw the tabloid stories of me with Brant, and it pissed him off. He called him an addict. Before you showed up yesterday, Bobby had sent me photos of Brant at the party." She picked up her phone and scrolled to the e-mail he had sent her. Flipping the phone around, she gave the phone to Mitch, who scrolled through the photos. "I'm betting those photos came from the same person who took the photo for the tabloid."

"Okay. Except all those are, are photos of him drunk. Yeah, it helps your ex's case against you, but those photos aren't the problem. Brant is doing nothing illegal in the photos. Brant's problem is the rape charge from Ms. Holcomb."

"What if Bobby and the photographer and Natalie are in cahoots? She wanted a relationship with Brant, and he didn't want anything to do with her. You heard him say she couldn't be trusted."

"That's not what we are getting from witnesses."

"What have you gotten?"

"Ms. Holcomb said she told him she thought they should just be friends, which was corroborated by one of the bartenders. She also said she told Brant he should slow down on the drinking. That was also corroborated by the bartender."

"Did you ask the bartender if he made any alcoholic drinks for Brant?"

"We asked all of them, and each said they didn't. Still, that doesn't mean he didn't add something later."

"Possibly. However, it could be true. Did you test his blood?"

"Too many hours between the party and when he was arrested."

"He could be telling the truth that he didn't drink though."

"Could be. Although there were several witnesses that said he acted very drunk. These photos don't lie."

"Couldn't he have been drugged?"

Mitch leaned back in his chair. "If that's the case, we need to prove it. He'll need to get tested, and some drugs don't stay in the system very long. He may have already passed the window."

"Mitch, listen to me. I have talked to Natalie, I have talked to Bobby, and I have talked to Brant. Out of the three, one lied to me outright, one I am pretty sure lied to me, and the other, in all the talks we have had, I have felt pretty certain they were being truthful."

"That one, you have a relationship with though."

"I'm just saying we need to hunt for evidence to prove his innocence. Or is the 'innocent until proven guilty' no longer practiced?"

"I understand, and you should know, the last thing I want is for this story to be true, and him to be guilty. I was not excited about arresting him. But the problem is, there is concrete evidence that he had sex with her. We have a positive match from the military database. It was definitely him."

"But if he was drugged—"

"You would have to prove it."

Bekah fixed her eyes on the floor and chewed on her lip. "Have you interviewed anyone else from the movie, about their relationship?"

"No. We haven't had time. The investigation has just started. Why?"

"I was thinking of one of the other tabloid stories. The photo is of him and Natalie, and the story said we broke up, and he and Natalie were together." She picked up her phone from the desk and tapped on it, then handed it to Mitch. "See? The whole story was fabricated. Brant said he was actually yelling at her for trying to convince me that she and Brant were back together."

"That is what he told you. How do you know that is what happened and not what is pictured here?"

"He said they were in the dining area and a bunch of people overheard him yelling at her. Should be easy enough to prove."

Mitch scribbled on his tablet then tipped his eyes up to Bekah. "Okay. Still doesn't discount that he could have been so drunk that he took advantage of her."

Bekah rolled her eyes. "Mitch, I'm telling you, the more I think about it the more I think he was set up. Especially with what Marissa has told me. Didn't you wonder why he was just hanging out at his grandma's house yesterday? And think about how he reacted to you."

Mitch let out a loud sigh and leaned forward on his desk. He picked up his pen and tapped it against the yellow legal pad. "Okay, let's go back over what you have said. The assistant overheard your ex paying off someone to ruin someone else's life, although no one heard Brant's name.

"Bobby's assistant said he asked her about a private investigator, but my money is on the tabloid photographer."

"Why is that?"

"Because one of Bobby's photos is very similar to the tabloid photo. I noticed it yesterday."

"Okay. Can you send me those photos he sent you?" He studied his yellow pad once more. "If he paid the photographer to take the photos, he might have paid Ms. Holcomb." His eyes lifted to Bekah's. "We would need to be able to follow the money, possibly check Ms. Holcomb's bank account and see if we can trace it back." Chunking his pencil down on the pad, he leaned back in his chair and put his clasped hands on his head. "We really need to figure out who this private investigator or photographer is." His eyes turned to Marissa. "Do you think this assistant could identify him if we brought someone in?"

"I'm sure she could. She had to talk to him a couple of times, I think. I know she said he had greasy hair and a moustache and goatee."

"We need to be able to connect the three of them." He scratched at his stubble and rubbed his hand across his mouth. "And we need to prove he was drugged, not drunk. If we can do that, it would definitely throw a wrench into the rape charge." He leaned forward in his chair, and his eyes landed squarely on Bekah. "Basically, we need all of that to come together before the rape charges can be dropped. That or a good confession."

Chapter Nineteen

Brant laid on his sofa, in just a pair of blue jeans, wondering what time it was, as his hands slowly descended his face. After being bailed out of jail, his dad drove him over to his grandma's house so he could pick up his car. He talked to his folks until they had to leave for the airport to catch their flight. There was no reason to talk about the case though. He didn't remember anything, so they couldn't help him. It had been turned over to the lawyer. Most of the night in the holding cell was spent playing back the previous two days. It was the worst nightmare he had ever had, except it was real. It seemed like his whole life, he had bounced from one nightmare to another, with very few moments of happiness. To see Mitch, someone he called a friend, look at him with such contempt, still shot an arrow of anger through him. How could Mitch believe he raped someone? Things seemed to happen so quickly. Thoughts played over in his head. The questions. The angry looks. The silence.

Tears streamed down his grandma's face as she kissed him on the cheek before he left. Even though she told him, over and over, she believed him, he had broken her heart. He had only seen his grandma cry once, and that was when his grandpa died. She had been his rock. She and Grandpa had done so much for him and now, under no fault of his own, he had let them down. It was everything he could do to not break down right there. The thought of the people he loved so hurt was almost too much. And finding some way to take the pain away crossed his mind more than once. The only thing keeping him grounded was something in Bekah's eyes when she kissed him. Maybe he was fooling himself, and it was a goodbye kiss. Maybe it would be the last time he saw her and Maizy. But something told him to hang on a little longer. Fight for their life together. Even though she made it clear she was unsure if she trusted him, when she kissed him, it gave him hope. It was his lifeline for the moment. All hell had broken loose in his life but having that one inkling of hope sustained him.

When Mitch had read Brant his Miranda rights, it was surreal. A sick feeling in the pit of his stomach set in. Sitting in the back of the cruiser, he had watched as Bekah headed down the stairs. For a brief second, her eyes met his, then she headed for her car.

At the station, Mitch took him to be processed, getting his fingerprints and mugshot, then asked if he wanted to give his statement or wait for his lawyer.

"I will tell you what I remember. I've got nothing to hide." Mitch escorted him into a stark empty room and sat him in a metal chair. For forty minutes Mitch peppered him with questions. Some he readily answered and some he could only say he didn't remember.

Brant's eyes shifted as he stared at his ceiling searching for more information. Why couldn't he remember? It was like he fell asleep at the party. One minute he was searching for his parents, then nothing. Even when he would get drunk, most of the time he remembered portions of his escapades. This was like the light shut off. Could that be just from sleep deprivation?

A tap at his back door broke through the quiet. He jerked, not expecting the noise. An emotional storm flooded through him when he saw Bekah's face in the window. She waved, and a shy smile spread across her face when their eyes connected, then he noticed she wasn't alone. He pulled open the door. "Hi," he said, trying to steady his nerves.

"Hi," she returned, then a stream of words came so fast, he was barely able to discern them before she leaped into his arms. "I've got so much to tell you, and you are not going to believe any of it, but first I wanted to tell you I love you too." His hands quickly wrapped around her as he tried to gain his balance, then pulled her in tight. Her kiss was deep and hungry. Then she slowly backed away.

"You do realize there is a woman who followed you here."

"Yeah." Her arm flew back. "Brant, this is Marissa. Marissa, this is Brant." After the introduction, she returned to peppering Brant's face with kisses. Brant managed a small wave with one hand still wrapped around Bekah. Marissa grinned and waved back. Brant backed away and smiled. His eyes went to Marissa. "She has a thing for public display of affection."

"I think it's more like a thing for *you*."

Bekah slowly released her legs and arms and slid down his body.

Brant reached his hand out to greet Marissa officially, and he suddenly made the connection.

"Are you *the* Marissa?"

Bekah nodded her head as Marissa shook Brant's hand and wrinkled her nose.

"Like I said, I have a lot to tell you. It's a long story. That's why we are here."

The thought of Bekah being at his house suddenly brought a sobering thought to mind. His brows raised. "Oh! But you, you can't be here right now."

Bekah's head tipped, and confusion filled her face. Her lips parted as she processed his words, then she scanned his shirtless torso, and her expression turned to sadness. "Shit. I should really learn not to drop in unannounced," she said before turning to walk out the door.

Marissa looked at Brant, confused, and shrugged.

Brant didn't understand at first, then remembered what happened with her visit to Bobby's. He grabbed Bekah's arm and spun her around. "I mean…there are photographers watching the house."

"Ohhh." Her head lolled with relief. "We came in Marissa's car. Parked a block away and snuck around back. I don't think anyone saw us."

"I just don't want you taking any chances." His hands cupped her cheeks. "But I'm really glad to see you." He took a deep breath, and a grin spread across his face. "Come on in." Backing away from the door, he asked, "Can I get you anything to drink? I got beer, wine, hard liquor." Bekah's eyes narrowed. He narrowed his back, mocking her, then winked and placed a kiss on her nose. "Or your favorite ginger spritzer."

She smiled. "That's better."

"That sounds good to me too," Marissa softly added.

"You got me addicted to these things." Brant grabbed three from the fridge, handed them out, and then headed into the living room picking up some dirty socks off the floor. "Be right back." He dumped the socks in the hamper in his bathroom and grabbed his T-shirt off his bed, pulling it on as he exited his bedroom.

Bekah popped the top of her drink as she took in her surroundings. "Your place is amazing. I can't believe I haven't been over here until now," she said looking around, still remaining in the kitchen area.

Brant followed her eyes. "Yeah. Sorry for the mess." He continued to try to straighten up. "For the most part, you were kind of homebound from your injuries, and then I moved into the hotel so there really wasn't an opportunity."

"Did you get hurt recently?"

"Oh, it was from the car accident." She looked at Marissa who was still obviously confused. "Let me guess, Bobby never told you about that either."

"No."

"The day I showed up at the apartment was when the snowstorm hit. I skidded on the ice coming home and hit a tree."

"No way." Marissa's mouth dropped open. "No. He never said a word about it."

"I broke my arm, got a concussion, and strained my back and neck." Bekah tipped her head to Brant. "Brant rescued me."

Watching the conversation unfold, he stilled, wondering how the two women got together. At some point he figured he would be filled in.

"So, you said you had something to tell me, and I am hoping beyond hope that it is good news."

"Oh, yeah. I guess we do need to get down to business. Grandpa has Maizy, so we are on borrowed time." Bekah glanced at Marissa. "You know Marissa has been trying to contact me, and the truth is, if I had answered her text in the beginning, I don't think any of this would have happened. She texted me again last night, and I still shot her down. Turns out she is a persistent little booger and came knocking on my door bright and early this morning, with some very interesting information, I might add. Bobby hired someone that we think set you up."

Brant's head jerked to Marissa. "You gotta be kidding me." She nodded. "Please tell me Natalie is a part of it."

"We'll get to that."

Bekah nodded to Marissa who sat down in the chair next to the sofa and leaned in. "Bobby told me he and Bekah had broken up like a year ago. I had no idea when I moved in with him that he was still with Bekah, or that she had a baby. When I realized he had lied, I broke up with him and moved out. Unfortunately, I still had to work with him. Over the following weeks he became obsessed with Bekah to the point I was getting worried. So, I had his assistant spy on him and report back to me. A couple of weeks ago, a sleazy looking guy came in and talked to Bobby. Marci, his assistant, overheard some of their conversation. Bobby paid the guy five thousand dollars to ruin someone's life. Whoever the person was, somehow was connected to Bekah."

Bekah turned to Brant. "It has to be you they were talking about."

Brant's pulse kicked up. "Did you talk to Mitch?"

"Already been there. I thought we would come by and talk to you. Maybe see if we could stir up some more memories."

"That's what I was doing when you knocked on my door. I was trying to remember what happened."

"I think you might have been drugged. That would explain the memory loss. You need to get tested. The problem is, Mitch said some drugs leave the system quickly, and you may be already outside that time window.

"So how would we prove it?"

"I don't know. For now, we need to focus on what we have, which are your memories and the photos. Can I borrow your laptop?"

"Yeah. Let me get it out of the office." Brant hopped up and jogged to the office. His heart was racing with the bomb Bekah dropped. He knew he was set up, because there was no way he would have knowingly slept with Natalie. Proving it, though, was more than he could hope for. Only hours ago, he felt completely helpless wondering how he could possibly beat the charges.

Retrieving his laptop from his desk, he hurriedly returned to the living room where the girls were continuing to chat about the case. Twitching his head, he motioned to them. "Let's go to the dining room table." They stood and followed him. Bekah pulled out a chair, and Brant set the laptop in front of her. She typed in her e-mail and pulled up Bobby's last e-mail to her. Several photos loaded onto the page.

"Okay. I forwarded these photos to Mitch, so he has them also. I have to believe the guy that Bobby hired is the same one who took the photo for the rape article. Bobby sent me a photo that is very similar." Brant looked over Bekah's shoulder as she pointed at the photos, and Marissa leaned in. "Same position. Same expression. I'm thinking the photographer is who Bobby paid." Brant stared at the photos trying to remember. "Whether Bobby and Natalie met and hatched the whole plan, or the photographer acted as a go between, I'm not sure."

"If it's the photographer, the same guy who took the photo of me and Natalie in the dining hall, took the photo at the wrap party. I definitely wouldn't put it past him."

"Can you describe him?"

"I may be able to do better than that. Hang on." He leaned over Bekah and clicked out of her e-mail then pulled up the website for PrimeScene magazine. Searching for the article of him and Natalie, he clicked on it, then found the photo and pointed at the name beneath it. "Lonny Ferrell. The photographers always want to be credited in case their photos become a hot commodity." He did another search and clicked on the photo of the article from the party. "Lonny Ferrell." His fingers moved over the keyboard, and he found a large photo of the man. That's him. I don't know how he managed to have access to the closed set, but I saw him a few times. I definitely saw Natalie talking to him."

Bekah turned to Marissa. "No moustache or goatee. Do you still think he could be our guy? He does have the slicked back greasy hair."

"Oh, he had a moustache and goatee when he was on set. This is an older photo of him."

Bekah turned back to Marissa. "This has got to be our guy. Do you have Marci's e-mail?"

"Yes."

Bekah turned back to Brant. "Can you share that to an e-mail address?"

"Yeah."

"Let me give you mine, and I will forward it to Marci. It's mbellamy@pepinenergy.eng."

Brant tapped it in. "Okay, you should have it in your e-mail."

Marissa's phone dinged, and she pulled it from her back pocket. "Great. I will send it on to Marci and see if this is the guy."

"So far so good. If it's him, we can connect him with Bobby and Natalie. That's a good thing. Now, let's get back to the photos. I want to go photo to photo, and you tell me what you remember." Brant sat down in the chair next to her. She clicked on the first photo. Brant was standing in front of the bar with his highball glass up to his lips. His eyes were squarely focused on Natalie.

Bekah zoomed in on the photo. "What do you remember about this moment?"

Brant leaned in and studied the scene. "Natalie had asked to talk to me before the dinner, and I told her to catch me later. I was trying to be cordial and not cause a scene. I went to get a drink from the bar, and she caught me there. She said she realized things weren't going to happen between us, so she wanted to be friends. I shook her hand, and then the photographer wanted to take our picture."

"Okay. The bartender said it sounded like she was telling you she didn't want a relationship and just wanted to be friends. Do you remember how she said it? Could it have been misconstrued?"

"Possibly. She said something like, one of us isn't going to get what they want."

Her eyes widened. "So, she may have been planting seeds."

"What do you mean?"

"Making guided statements knowing people around you were listening. She wanted them to hear what she was saying."

"Mitch said someone else heard her tell you that you should slow down on your drinking."

"Yes, she did say that. But when I tried to tell her that it was nonalcoholic, she interrupted me."

"Guided again."

Marissa tapped the table. "Marci texted me. She said that it's definitely the man that Bobby was talking to."

Brant leaned back in his chair. "Holy crap. Really?" His hand scraped through his hair. "How? How did Bobby find him?"

"Exactly the way you did. He found his name attached to the article of us and contacted him. It's probably not that hard."

Bekah smiled at Marissa. "He's our man. Mitch needs to talk to him."

She turned to Brant. "One box checked." A smile crossed her face. "Okay. Moving on." She clicked on another photo. "How about this picture?"

Brant and Natalie are standing in a posed position facing the photographer.

"That's when he actually asked for a photo. We were still at the bar. After that, we parted ways."

"Do you remember if you felt funny, or dizzy, or anything at that time?"

"No nothing, other than being tired. It was after that. I remember I walked back to the table because I was ready to leave, and I wanted to say goodbye to my mom and dad. I stopped and talked to the director for a little bit, and when I got back to the table my mom and dad weren't there." Bekah clicked through the photos. "Okay. Here is a photo with your parents. Do you remember this one?"

"Not really."

"You already seem really intoxicated here. So, you are saying, between the time you left Natalie and when you went in search of your parents, it hit." She pointed to the photo.

"I guess so."

"That couldn't have taken that long."

"I have no idea. Like I said, I talked to the director for a while, and I felt okay."

She pulled one photo up and zoomed in. "What is that on your shirt?" A large golden hue was visible on one side.

"Some guy bumped me when I was talking to the director. Spilled my drink all over my shirt." Brant commented nonchalantly. Bekah turned her head slowly and a sly grin spread across her face.

"Please tell me you haven't taken anything to the cleaners."

A crease formed between Brant's brows. "No. I think it's in a pile of clothes on my bed. Why?"

"Well, if you really weren't drinking and were drugged, then maybe it is detectible in the stain." Her finger pointed to the photo.

Brant jumped up from his seat and jogged to his bedroom. He dug through the clothes lying on his bed and found his suit and shirt. "Found it," he hollered as he returned to the dining area. He moved over to the kitchen and pulled out a bag. Dropping the clothes into the bag, he set it down beside Bekah.

"We need to take that to Mitch." Bekah continued to scan the photos. "Do you remember ever setting your drink down?"

"Only at the table, and I didn't leave the table, so I don't know how anyone would have spiked it. The only way I can think that it could have happened is if the bartender did it."

"Okay. So, how many bars were there at the party?"

"Two. One before entering the room and one inside."

"How many of them did you visit?"

"I got one when I got there at the bar outside the party room then two maybe three inside at the bar in the photos."

"Okay. Let's go back to the photos at the bar with Natalie. We'll zoom in on the bartender. Maybe we can catch something between him and Natalie."

Bekah opened one photo after another, zooming in on the bartender, and then Natalie. Then stopped. "Where is your drink in this photo?" Her finger pointed at the photo of him and Natalie staring into the camera. "Do you have it in your hand behind her back? The other one is in your pocket."

"I don't think so. I would normally hold it in my right hand. I guess it's up on the bar."

She clicked on the previous photo. Brant is posing for the camera and Natalie is turned. She zoomed in and shrieked, "This could be it," and pointed at the photo. "I thought this one was Natalie ordering a drink, but is that your drink in front of her?"

"Yeah, it looks like it."

"Look! Look where her hand is. It's right above your drink."

Brant's heart pounded in his chest. A chuckle curled up his throat as his fist pounded on his pinched lips trying to fight back tears stinging his eyes. Bekah turned to him. He grabbed her with one hand on each cheek. "Do you know how much I love you right now?" His lips met hers, and he stood, pulling her with him. His arms wrapped around her lifting her off the ground. Marissa sat smiling at the two of them.

She pulled away and whispered, "I love you too," she said smiling against his lips. He continued to kiss her. "Now who's into the PDA?" He chuckled as he lowered her back down until her feet touched the floor. "Okay," she said as she let out a gust of air. "I'm going to e-mail Mitch and let him know what we have." Her eyes quickly captured Marissa's. "Can you ask Marci if she remembers the exact date and approximate time Bobby had the meeting?"

"On it." Marissa's fingers flew over the keyboard of her phone.

Bekah checked her phone. "I'm going to need to relieve Grandpa pretty soon, but I will drop the suit and shirt by Mitch's office before we head back to the house." She dropped back into the chair and stared at the computer screen as she continued to speak. "How long do you think the crew will be sticking around?"

"Probably just a day or so. Why?"

"Well, if the shirt is positive for some kind of drug, I am sure they are going to want to bring Natalie in."

"She may be already gone. I don't think she was part of that crew."

"Crap. Okay. I will let Mitch worry with that."

"Marci said it was the morning of March twenty-eighth, like right before lunch."

"That was a couple of weeks ago." Brant's eyes bounced between Marissa then Bekah. "When did the article with our breakup come out?"

Bekah tapped on the computer and pulled up the article. "March twenty-first."

"I don't get it. Why would he hire someone if he thought that we broke up?"

Bekah took a deep breath. "Because I told him it was fake. Remember? At the hospital? He thought for sure he would get me back, and I shot him down. I'm thinking he realized he would only be able to get what he wanted if he took away the roadblock."

"Bobby and Natalie have been orchestrating all of this all along." Every text message, every encounter penetrated his thoughts. "I didn't even tell you that I confirmed it was Natalie sending me the messages that had me thinking my wife was texting me from the dead. She used the same phone to call me and tell me she found my wallet."

"You need to share all of the stuff she did with Mitch."

His hand wrapped around his mouth. The more he thought about it, the more he was certain it was true. "This is crazy." Pacing around the room, he rolled everything over in his head. "The bad thing is all we have on Bobby right now is Marci overhearing him with Lonny. It's her word against his about what exactly he said. I mean, yeah, he sent you the photos, but he could say he hired a P.I.. There is nothing illegal with what he did."

"Well, Mitch is going to see if he can find a money trail connecting him with Natalie."

"If not, maybe one of the others will turn on him."

"That might be what will have to happen, and something tells me one of them will." Bekah continued to type on the computer. "Okay. I sent Mitch the e-mail, and I will drop off the clothes to him." She reached over and picked up the bag.

Marissa stood, and Brant glanced at her. In that moment he realized what she had done. "Listen. I don't know how to thank you. None of this would have happened if you hadn't reached out to Bekah. I know it had to have been hard with everything that happened."

She gave him a shrug. "You know, it actually wasn't. Other than she wouldn't answer me." She giggled and raised her brows at Bekah. "I mean, she was really sweet the first time I met her, so knowing what Bobby did to her bothered me a lot. And the more I was around him, the more I knew something wasn't right and he needed to be stopped."

Chapter Twenty

A spring storm sent icy droplets pounding against the windows of the tiny cottage. Bekah puttered around in the kitchen, while Maizy played on the floor with her baby gym. Every now and then Bekah could hear the tinkling noise when Maizy would hit one of the toys dangling over her head. She couldn't believe how big Maizy was getting. Her thick black hair she had as a newborn was being replaced with caramel strands, and her dark eyes were now a light brown with flecks of green. Bekah continually glanced over at her from the kitchen as she chopped up pieces of asparagus to add to a bowtie salad. She would be glad when summer came so she could get fresh veggies from her garden. For now, though, the house smelled of roasted chicken and lemon, and fresh basil she'd picked from her herb garden she kept in pots on her porch. Brant was headed over for dinner.

With her hair pulled up in a loose bun, she wrapped one of her scarves around her head and tied it at the nape of her neck. Brant liked when she wore them. A long sweater with fairy sleeves covered her skinny jeans that she was finally able to fit back into. She felt pretty.

It had been over a week since Brant's arrest. Things had been quiet. Though they had chatted on the phone several times, Brant thought it would be best to not see each other until they had gotten word from Mitch. However, after giving Mitch the information, she had heard nothing. Neither had Brant, and she was up for taking chances. It would be stupid for the photographer, who had been the biggest culprit of the tabloid stories, to stick around since he had the most to lose. Her phone chimed. Brant.

"Hey," she cooed, leaning the phone on her shoulder, while she continued to cut up the asparagus and dumped it in a pan. "Are you on—"

"Bekah, listen to me," Brant rasped, cutting her off. "I'm almost to your house. Get Maizy and her stuff ready. When I get there, we need to leave immediately. I will explain when I have you in the car."

"Oh, okay." She swallowed, panic already starting to steal her breath. "Is everything okay? You are scaring me. What is going on?" The phone clicked. She laid the knife down and wiped her hands on the apron before loosening the strings and pulling it off. Her hands immediately began to shake, and her head swam, with scenarios of what could be going on. She trusted Brant completely, but why were they running? Grabbing the carrier, she fastened Maizy in it and then ran to the bedroom grabbing her shoes and the baby bag. A knock came at the door and then she heard it push open. Peeking around the corner, she saw Brant step inside. He wrapped one arm around her and planted a quick kiss.

"What is going on?"

"Get your coat. We need to get out of here now." He reached down and grabbed the carrier throwing a blanket over the top of it. Bekah grabbed her coat and the baby bag, and they ran out the door through the rain. After strapping Maizy in, Brant crawled in the car where Bekah waited.

"Mitch called," Brant stated, focusing over his shoulder to back the car out. "They brought Lonny in for questioning yesterday. He told Mitch, Bobby and Natalie had gotten together and cooked everything up. He claimed everything he did was on the up and up. Bobby paid him to take photos of me with Natalie and some of me drinking at the party. That was it. After he gave his statement, Mitch said they let Lonny go. He said he thinks Lonny went running to Natalie and Bobby, which is what they had hoped for, and means he probably was in on it as an accomplice. Bobby's work said he left on vacation and hasn't been heard from since. Mitch said it'd be best to get you some place safe since Lonny has probably tipped them off."

Bekah's mind raced. "Where are we going?"

"Grams. She has plenty of room. I think you will be safe there."

"I didn't pack any clothes or anything."

"We'll worry about that later. Right now, we need to get you and Maizy out of the house."

"What about you? Natalie is out there somewhere also."

A smile curled on his lips. "I'm staying with Grams too." Bekah's heart stuttered. "Only problem is, she has ears like a damn elephant. She hears everything."

Bekah backhanded Brant and snickered. "Then you will have to behave yourself."

"You too." Bekah tucked her lips trying not to smile. "She said she will have stew waiting for us."

Bekah's eyes widened as her hands flew to her

face. "SHIT!"

"What?" Brant swerved like he was about to hit something.

"I was cooking when you called. I don't think I turned everything off."

He took a deep breath then chewed on his lip. "Okay. We will drop Maizy off and run back by. You can pick up some clothes and check the kitchen. We just need to make it quick."

"Okay."

They pulled into the white farmhouse. Grandma Betty was standing at the door. Brant carried Maizy in, who was asleep from the car ride. Bekah dropped off the baby bag. She gave Grandma Betty a hug and Brant filled her in, then they returned to the car and headed up the gravel road.

"So, you didn't tell me, was that all Mitch said?"

"Labs came back on the shirt, positive for Rohypnol."

"The date rape drug?"

"I got roofied." Brant stared out at the road. "Mitch said the concentration they found on the shirt could have killed me."

"Oh God. Really?"

"He said, that is probably why it hit so fast." He turned and leveled his eyes at her. "He also said there was no alcohol found, only ginger spritzer." A smirk crossed his face and Bekah had to smile.

"So, what about the photos?"

"They are still working on those, but with the evidence of the drug, they have enough to bring Natalie in for questioning."

"So why is Mitch so adamant about us going

somewhere safe?"

Brant glimpsed at her then back at the road. "How much do you know about Bobby's past?"

"I don't know. Like I said, I didn't really spend any time with his parents, and he didn't go into details about his past. His family is wealthy. He grew up in Colorado. Moved to Kansas as a teen. I think his family moved to Houston his senior year. Played soccer. Was in the band. Made good grades. Got a scholarship to some prestigious college up north then transferred to Pepperdine."

"He must have left out the part of being arrested for assault."

Bekah sat up, horrified. "What? When?"

"Mitch said it happened in Kansas. He was seventeen. Had dated the girl. Beat her up pretty bad. Got off because the girl dropped the charges." He turned and looked at Bekah.

"How did Mitch find out, if the charges were dropped?"

"Apparently, just because the charges are dropped doesn't mean they aren't still in your records." Brant's eyes landed on her. "Did he ever lay a hand on you?"

"Not really." She knew that wasn't the complete truth but the thought of how much he manipulated her, now made her sick.

"What do you mean, not really?"

She let out a breath. "He grabbed me hard a couple of times."

Brant stared at her when she went silent, as she replayed the night of the argument she and Bobby had, when she told him she was pregnant. He said it was an accident when he nailed her with his elbow in the stomach. Now she wasn't sure.

"And?"

"The day I told him I was pregnant we had an argument and—"

"Stop. Just stop." Bekah could see the rage in his eyes. "I guess I will be going to jail after all, because I will kill him if I find him."

They pulled up into the driveway. Brant's phone chimed. Bekah whispered, "I'll run in and grab some stuff."

Brant pulled the phone down. "Be there in a minute."

Bekah hopped out and jogged to the door. She pushed it open and flipped on the light. A small puddle of water sat in the doorway. Confused, she looked around then remembered Brant came in from the rain earlier, so she made her way into the kitchen. Everything was off. A smile crossed her face. She was more clear-headed than she thought, with everything happening so fast. Grabbing the pans of food, she quickly put them in the fridge. *Maybe later I can finish the meal.* She prided herself on being a decent cook, although, up until now, she hadn't had the chance to show off for Brant.

After stowing her apron in the drawer, she traipsed down the hall to the bedroom and grabbed a bag from the top of the closet. Dropping it onto the bed she turned to grab some items out of the dresser. Her mind wandered trying to decide how much to pack.

"Going somewhere?" The menacing voice behind her caused her to jump. Cold chills scattered over her skin. She knew immediately by his tone he was dangerous. *How did he get in here? Why didn't I see his car?* She trembled as she slowly lifted her eyes to see Bobby blocking the doorway. His white button-down, wet from the rain, clung to him. She took in everything around her, but even if she tried to make a break for the adjoining bathroom, she wouldn't make it. There was no way out. In his hand, he held the butcher knife she had used earlier when she was cooking. "Good thing I stopped by. You left the stove on." He smirked. "I'm still having to clean up your messes." He took a step toward her, holding the butcher knife up, flipping it around in his hand. "It's obvious you still need me."

"How did you get in here?" Her voice quivered.

"A key, silly. Did you already forget we were in a relationship for five years?"

She stepped back. Her heart raced trying to figure out a way to escape. "So, tell me Bekah, what did you tell the police?" His lips pulled into a thin line, and he shook his head.

"What do you mean?" she said with the escape of a breath.

Bobby twirled the knife again and took another step toward her. "You know. You put ideas in the cops' heads. They froze my bank accounts. I had to cut my business trip short."

His words suddenly thickened her blood and dredged up the anger she had harbored against him. "Business trip my ass."

"They are searching for me. Aren't they?" he said, his voice low and threatening. He took another step forward and twisted the knife back and forth letting the light glint off the blade, obviously intimidating her.

Bekah took another step back but ran into Maizy's crib. She tried to remember whether the closet had a lock on it. Her throat went dry. Tears stung her eyes. Summoning the anger of what he did to Brant, she stared him down. "I told them the truth." The glare he returned only fanned the fury that was building. "You are the one who tried to frame Brant. You and Natalie." She scanned the room for anything hard enough to cause bodily harm.

"I didn't do anything wrong," he growled. "I merely had someone take pictures of what was inevitable. I had to prove to you he wasn't good enough for you." His eyes followed her. "You're mine, Bekah." His hand pounded his chest. "You should have done what I said and moved to Houston, but you wouldn't listen. You kept taking his side. He's an addict. The photos prove it."

Tears streamed down her face, anger continuing to build. "How exactly did you know that he would be drinking?" Bobby glanced away, and she knew he didn't have an answer. "The photos didn't prove anything other than you and Natalie drugged him and then accused him of rape." She wiped her face and took a breath to steady her pulse, then stood up straight, feeling her resolve take over. She wasn't going to let him intimidate her. "You wanted insurance that he would be drunk in those photos, so you made sure of it by drugging him. You paid the photographer to ruin Brant's life. Well, guess what? Your photographer proved Brant's innocence. His photos show Natalie drugging Brant's drink, and he told the cops you and Natalie planned the whole thing."

His shoulders stiffened, and his voice now carried a bit of a weakness. "No. The drugs and rape were her idea, I had nothing to do with that, Bekah. I promise."

"How were you going to get pictures of him drunk if he didn't drink. Huh? You had to make sure, so you drugged him."

Bobby took a deep breath and clenched his teeth. "Bekah, I am tired of playing your stupid game." He twirled the knife again. "You and Maizy need to be with me. I am what's best for you."

Bekah's blood boiled now with the mention of Maizy. "What's best? What's best?" Her voice suddenly turned soft and dangerous. "Let me ask you something, Bobby?" She emphasized his name. "Does your mom know about Maizy?"

Bobby's face sobered, and Bekah knew she had him. "What? Cat got your tongue? Maybe I should answer for you. She had no idea who Maizy was when I called her. And she thought we had broken up years ago. Oh, but don't worry. I didn't spill your little secret. Oh, and speaking of not knowing about Maizy, you neglected to tell Marissa about her also. Seems she too thought we had broken up a long time ago. She had no idea we were still together and had a baby. I wonder why that is?" The thought of the fight they had, played through her mind and spilled out of her in pure rage. "You never wanted Maizy. You would have rather me get an abortion. And seeing you like this; I have to wonder. Did you have plans to get rid of her once I got down to Houston?" Something flashed in his eyes, and Bekah's blood ran cold.

"I, I—"

Her teeth gritted together. "Don't you dare answer. I see it in your eyes. You're a monster. Did your family pay off the girl you nearly beat to death?"

Bobby's brows drew together in rage. His chest

rose as he let out a growl and took one long stride toward Bekah. She tried to jump out of the way but tripped, smacking the floor hard. She watched, in slow motion, as Brant lunged for him from behind and knocked Bobby to the ground with such force the knife flew from his hand across the room, landing with a clank on the floor under the baby bed. Bekah crawled over to pick it up.

"No. Don't touch it," Brant barked, while he kneeled on Bobby's back. Bobby gasped for air as Brant clasped his hands behind him like he was going to cuff him. "You don't want to smudge those fingerprints." He reached into his back pocket and tossed her his phone. "Call Mitch." Bekah grabbed the phone and watched Brant manhandle Bobby. He leaned down over Bobby's shoulder and spoke. His voice was low and menacing. "I could snap your neck right now, and no one would blame me," he growled. "You broke in and tried to kill us. It would all be self-defense."

"Get off me, you son of a bitch." Bobby's words came out slurred from his cheek being pressed to the floor.

"That's not happening, until they come to get your sorry ass and take you to jail." Brant sounded somewhat amused and tightened his grip on Bobby causing him to yelp in pain.

Bekah's eyes met his, after hanging up with Mitch. A satisfied smile crossed her face. "He said he will be here in five."

Brant leaned down again to where his face was inches from Bobby's. "Looks like you may have ruined your own life there, jackass."

Bobby let out a defeated sigh.

Mitch rapped on the door a few minutes later. Dressed in a black nylon jacket and khaki pants, he brushed his shoes against the welcome mat, and rubbed his hands down his sleeves to wipe away the rain before entering, after Bekah open the door. Brant still had Bobby pinned to the floor when Mitch retrieved the handcuffs from his hip pocket and tightened them around Bobby's wrists.

"There is a butcher knife over there." Bekah pointed, then crossed her arms and rubbed them like she was cold. Brant made his way to her and pulled her into his chest, and she realized she was shaking uncontrollably. How could she have not seen what a monster he was?

After Mitch had Bobby safely in the backseat of the patrol car, he walked back into the house to retrieve the knife. "Did you have time to tell her?" Mitch asked. Brant seemed puzzled, then his eyes rounded with the realization.

"Oh. No, I didn't." He turned to Bekah. "They picked up Natalie at the Houston airport. She was about to hop on a plane headed to Mexico."

Bekah's brow creased. "Getting out of the country. That sounds pretty guilty, if you ask me."

Mitch dropped the knife in the bag. "She is already blaming everything on Mr. Leonard. She said he paid her to do it."

Bekah became quiet. Her eyes darted back and forth between Mitch and Brant. "You know, I just realized she accused you of rape, and it's actually the other way around. She sexually assaulted you."

Brant smirked and jerked his head. "Can you blame her? Even when I'm unconscious I'm irresistible."

Mitch let out a bark of a laugh. Bekah rolled her eyes. "I'm being serious."

Brant smiled. "So am I."

Mitch grinned and shook his head, then his attention landed on Bekah. "In all honesty, with the concentration of drugs that were found in the shirt, she and Bobby could be held for attempted murder. If we can get a clear enough picture from the zoomed-in photo, that's all the evidence we need to show she did it." Mitch turned to Brant. "Once we figure out who paid whom to do what, I have a good feeling all charges will be dismissed against you."

"That would be great. This whole thing has been a nightmare and put the film and my future job in jeopardy."

Mitch turned back to Bekah. "But I will need you to come down to the station and give me your statement about tonight."

"No problem." He patted Brant on the shoulder and headed to the door. Bekah replayed the events of the night. "Who would have thought that the photos Bobby paid for, to ruin Brant's life, would have been the ones to prove his innocence."

"Criminals usually aren't the brightest crayons in the box."

Brant followed Mitch out the door. "We'll be there in a few minutes."

"Take your time." Mitch glimpsed back at his car. "It will take a bit to get him processed."

Bekah pushed the door shut, after Brant stepped back inside, and leaned against it. She tipped her head back only to feel Brant's hands wrap around her waist and his lips brush up against her neck. "Are you okay?"

His voice vibrated against the door.

She nodded, but the sound of his voice was all it took to cause the dam to break on her courage. The thoughts of Bobby lunging, with the knife ready to plunge into her, took hold, and the tears came. Brant pulled her in tight. His fingers laced in her hair, and he let out a soft shhhhh.

"Thank you." Her words were mingled with short breaths and sobs.

"I shouldn't have let you go without me. I'm so sorry."

"You saved me. He could have killed you."

"Eh. He was too focused on you to notice me, so I felt pretty safe." His thumb caught a wayward tear. "Are you ready to head to the station?"

"I guess so." Her eyes scanned the room. "I guess I don't need to pack anymore."

Brant pulled back. "Yeah. Go ahead." A sly smile crossed his face.

"Why?"

"I was thinking, after we grab a bite of stew at Grams, you and Maizy should come to my place."

She gazed at him through her lashes. "Seriously?"

"I mean, I know the charges aren't technically dropped, and I would understand if you didn't want to—"

"No, I would love to, if you are good with it."

Brant smirked and cupped his hands under her chin. "I wouldn't have asked if I wasn't."

Chapter Twenty-One

After hearing the backdoor open, Brant looked up from the computer and checked over his shoulder. Bekah had her arms full of groceries. He set his computer down on the table and hopped up from the sofa. Stepping over the baby gym and brushing past the highchair, he met her in the kitchen. "How many more?"

She set two canvas bags, covered in flowers and the store logo, on the counter. "Two." Brant headed out the door. "How did she do?"

"She slept the whole time. I've been working on my class," he called back while retrieving the other canvas bags from the back of her car. Bekah pushed the screen door open when she saw him with his arms full. He set the bags on the counter while Bekah continued to unpack.

It had been two weeks since Bobby and Natalie were arrested, and a week since the charges were officially dismissed against Brant in his case. The moment the words "dismissed of all charges" were uttered, it felt like a crushing weight had been lifted. Now he was free to be with Bekah and Maizy. He could finish his paramedic certification, and the movie could move forward in post-production.

The case was far from over, but at least he was on the victim side now. Mitch had informed him, the case against Natalie now consisted of tying up some loose ends. The enhanced photo came back from the lab with absolute proof that Natalie had drugged Brant. She would at least be facing sexual assault charges, if not attempted murder.

The case against Bobby was just as concrete, with charges of assault with a deadly weapon against Bekah, along with conspiracy charges, especially since Marci identified Natalie as the woman she saw Bobby kissing on the street.

Mitch was still unclear what Lonny would be brought up on. Brant wasn't worried about him though.

"I have something for you." Bekah smirked as she pulled open the refrigerator. Brant met her eyes. She nodded her head toward a small wooden café table with two chairs under the bay window off the kitchen. Resting on the table was a magazine.

He took a deep breath and kept unpacking the groceries. "What lies did they print this time?"

Bekah stood from the refrigerator and held the door open while she retrieved more vegetables from the bag. "Oh, you won't believe what they said this time."

He was so tired of the rag magazines having a field day with his life. He moved to Dalton thinking that living in a small town would save him from that. It didn't work. "What is it about? The movie? Or do they still think I'm guilty? Oh wait. No. I know. They have confirmed that you are my long-lost sister."

"Ewww. Not funny," she said even though she was giggling. "Just go look."

He pulled the box of baby wipes out of the sack and laid them on the counter before folding the canvas bag and tucking it into the drawer. "I'd rather not. I'm tired of their lies." He was hoping his decision to retire from making movies would finally cause the obsession the magazines had on his life to die.

"Seriously. You need to see this story." Another sigh escaped him, and his eyes darted back to Bekah who was now smiling.

"Okay, what's going on? What's that look for?"

She tipped her head motioning him to look. He took a step toward the table keeping his eyes on her. His hand rested on the back cover of the magazine, then flipped it over, to see a photo of him asleep on a sofa, with one hand gently holding Maizy, who was asleep on his stomach. The caption read, "Life in the Limelight-When the media gets it wrong."

Brant gaped at the photo. "Shit! Isn't this at your office? How did they—"

"I took it." His eyes darted to her. "The day we met." She paused. "I woke up and walked into the room, and there you were." Bekah closed the distance between them, wrapped her arms around him, and laid her cheek against his back. "I knew it was wrong. I barely knew you. But I couldn't help myself. It was so perfect." His fingers danced across the photo.

He pivoted and wrapped his arm around her, dropping a feather light kiss on her lips, then moved to her cheek, and then forehead. "But Bekah, you know how that maga—"

She put her hands up. "The editor of the magazine called me at my office. She said she would be printing a full retraction and asked if I would help to make sure the story was correct. I knew, from what you had told me, not to trust them even if she said it was a retraction. I told her that I would only help if they allowed me to read it before it went to print. Which she did."

"It still doesn't mean—"

"I read it in the parking lot at the grocery store." Brant's brows rose, and he glanced at her from the corner of his eye. "It's good. You need to read it." He strolled into the living room. The fireplace cast dancing shadows on his ceiling. Next to his sofa sat a small gray box on his end table, along with two pacifiers. A pink one with 'Future Princess' on it, and a clear glitter one with 'Glitter Diva.' The décor had changed a bit, since Bekah and Maizy had split the time between their house and his. His eyes scanned the room, and a smile crossed his face before he got comfortable on the sofa. Bekah sat down at the other end and entwined her legs with his. He felt something hard in his back and reached behind him to find a rainbow-colored jingle ball. He dropped it on his coffee table with a chuckle, and unfolded the magazine, staring at the cover once more. That was where it all started. Where both his girls had captured his heart. He peeked over the top of the magazine at Bekah. She had one foot pulled up close, and her head was leaning on her hands that rested on her knee, as she stared at the fire. He thought about what she said the day his grandma had the heart attack. That he didn't love her. He loved the idea of having the family he lost.

He loved Abbie and was excited to be starting a family. But that wasn't it at all. Staring at the photo, he knew he loved Maizy. There wasn't a doubt in his mind, and he loved taking care of her as well as Bekah. The day he walked into her office though, he wasn't seeking a relationship. In fact, that was the farthest thing from his mind when she slammed into his life like an avalanche.

He knew there was no way he could replace Abbie, and Bekah was nothing like her. Bekah was like opening a window on a snow chilled day and breathing in the fresh air to clear your head. She roared into his life and gave him a reason to live again, to take chances. She was vulnerable yet brave, carefree yet smart, and oh so beautiful inside and out. "I love you."

She smiled, still facing the fire. "I know." Turning her head, she propped her chin on her hands. Her eyes sparkled with the flickers from the flame. He patted the sofa, and she tipped forward, crawled up beside him, and snuggled in with her head on his chest. Her soft curls brushed against her cheeks. His arm rested around her. "Read the article."

"I can't quit staring at the cover. Did you know your man was going to be on the cover of a magazine?"

"No. But I wouldn't get all high and mighty. Remember, it is a rag mag. It's not like you are on the cover of TIME or anything. Although, I think you could be a prime contender for People's Sexiest Man Alive edition."

He puckered his lips and gave her his best smoldering expression.

She giggled. "Good lord, just read the article." Bekah pulled the magazine out of his hand and opened it up to the story. It was a center spread, across two pages. At the top of the page, below the title of the story, was a photo of Brant at about the age of six. His sandy blond hair was combed to the side, and tiny freckles sprinkled his nose. A slight smile was on his face, barely showing his missing front teeth. Photos from his childhood to the current photos peppered the pages. His eyes studied the photos one by one, remembering the moment of some, and not of others. He glanced at Bekah who was watching his every move.

What is it like to live in the shadows of famous parents? His eyes scanned the article. *It's not as easy or glamorous as some would think. That was the life of Brant Ellington, the son of Sandra Gerard and George Ellington. From the time he was little, Brant, and his older brother Greg, were sent to boarding schools, separating them from their families, thrusting them into the public eye, and constantly subjecting them to public scrutiny.* Brant stared at the photo of him and his brother standing with their parents in their school uniforms.

Photos of the princes of Hollywood's power couple, who between them have eight Academy Awards and six Golden Globes, have caused a media frenzy since they were born. Stories of their struggles through their teen years were constant tabloid fodder. Brant laughed and pointed at a photo of him about the age of twelve, with a police officer hanging off his arm. The caption read, "BUSTED." "Oh, I remember this one. There was a group of us who snuck out one night, and we got caught trying to pull up a stop sign."

"The police hauled you in?"

"Oh yeah. Scared the crap out of me. My parents were furious. I think that was the summer they decided that I would spend the rest of my summers in Arkansas."

In recent years Greg married and started a career of his own, in the film industry, writing several scripts that have made waves in Hollywood. Brant pointed to the photo of his brother and wife on the red carpet. "That must have been the premier of one of his shows." *Brant, on the other hand, joined the military, and until recently hadn't been heard from, until it was reported that he was injured while he was deployed in Afghanistan. When he returned to the states, it was discovered he had secretly married. Then, the tragic news came that his wife and unborn child were killed in a car accident.* Brant rubbed his finger over the photo of the wrecked gray car. His heart pinched, then he glanced at Bekah. The warmth of her body against his gave him the comfort he needed. *The slide into depression landed him a not so private stint in rehab.* Brant brought the magazine up close to his face and chuckled, as he stared at a grainy photo of a guy, wearing a beanie and a black T-shirt, with his hands tucked in his pockets, leaning against a building behind a tall fence. "That's not even me. Who is that?"

Bekah studied the photo. "Oh my gosh, it's not. That guy has a tattoo on his neck." She busted out laughing.

"Some girlfriend you are. You don't know your boyfriend's drugged-out photo."

"They didn't send me the photos they were going to be using. They just sent me the article, so I get a pass on that."

In January of this year, Ellington was pegged to join his parents on a movie project Gerard was producing and would possibly be taking on the largest role yet in his career. PrimeScene knew, with his recent stay in rehab, the story of his recovery would be of public interest, especially if he was making a move into serious acting. Reporters and photographers were clamoring to capture photos. What unfolded was something no one expected.

Photos began emerging of a new love. Ellington was seen carrying a baby carrier, and kissing a woman, who was later identified as his counselor. Sources stated that he had broken up a family. Brant gazed at the largest photo in the center of the page, of him and Bekah leaving the hospital, and then a smaller one below it at the restaurant. It seemed like such a long time ago. *As the movie production started, Ellington was spotted with an old flame, and rumors spread that they had rekindled their relationship.* His stomach churned, seeing the photo of him and Natalie. *The media was having a field day keeping up with the story. Then the news broke, at the end of the production, that Ellington had fallen off the wagon and was charged with rape. The story couldn't have been more salacious.* Photos of him drunk, then his mug shot, gave him a sobering realization of how close he was to losing everything.

The problem was…none of it was true…and PrimeScene Magazine would like to publicly apologize. We admit, we were the main media source spreading the false information and would like to set the record straight. Sometimes what is seen in photos is misconstrued, misinterpreted, and, in some circumstances, completely false.

Brant Ellington was the victim of a malicious attack. He did not break up a relationship, nor did he cheat on the woman he is now dating, who is, in fact, a counselor. However, she is not his counselor. More important is the fact that he did not get drunk or rape anyone. On the contrary, he was the victim. We apologize for getting it all wrong, and the part we inadvertently played in the attack. Setting the record straight though doesn't quite do enough. Who is Brant Ellington?

Brant Ellington is a military hero. Brant studied the photo of him, in his fatigues and helmet, standing inside the opening of the helicopter, ready to take off. *He's a captain in the United States Air Force and has saved countless numbers of lives as a PJ medic, and has even taken a bullet in the process, receiving the Medal of Honor for his actions. As a civilian, his plans are to become a flight medic in the near future. We at PrimeScene magazine offer our thanks for your service and best wishes for a bright future.*

Brant continued to stare at the pages then flipped it closed, studying the cover again. That day was burned into his memory. He'd questioned himself over and over as to why he offered to watch Maizy since he knew absolutely nothing about caring for babies. He hadn't even held one, that he could remember. But he knew the answer the minute he held her in his arms. Bekah's arm was wrapped around his chest, and her eyes were gazing at the fire. Tears stung, continuing to let the thought sink in, that things could have easily turned out so differently if Bekah hadn't fought for him.

Bekah's voice pulled him from his thoughts.

"So?"

"What?"

"What did you think of the article?"

"Well, the first word that comes to mind is, surprised."

"Yeah?"

"I've never seen them do a spread for a retraction.

Usually, it's a small column in the back section of the magazine no one reads."

"I'm guessing they are hoping you don't sue the pants off of them for slander."

"I hope that because of all this, they stay away from me for good."

"Well, Lonny won't be bothering you anymore. The editor I spoke with said he was fired."

"He will be lucky if he doesn't go to jail anyway."

His eyes went back to the magazine. "I still can't get over this photo." Brant held the magazine out so she could see it better. Bekah's hand moved up to his chest. "That was the craziest day. I have to be honest. I remember questioning my offer the minute it came out of my mouth."

"Oh, and you think I wasn't questioning taking you up on it? You were a total stranger, and I was trusting you to take care of my newborn. But the minute I gave her to you, and I saw the expression on your face, I knew she was in good hands." Brant lowered his eyes to Bekah and smiled. Bekah looked away. Her mouth pinched. "Can I tell you something?"

Brant sat up a little, feeling his breath stall in his chest. "Sure."

"When I took that picture, I remember being so mad at myself."

Brant sat up even more. "Why?"

"I stood there watching you. Maizy looked so content all sprawled out across your chest, and I remember thinking to myself that I wished you were her daddy."

Brant's chest tightened. He knew the same thought had crossed his mind a thousand times. He couldn't imagine not having Bekah and Maizy in his life forever.

"You know, you said something to me at the hospital the other day, that I haven't been able to get out of my head. You said you wondered if I was with you because I was trying to replace what I had lost."

Bekah sat up. "I am so sorry. I was so confused and—"

"No, actually it was a fair question, and you had every right to question my intentions."

"But I—"

"The last thing I intended to do, when I met you, was to get into a relationship. I didn't think I was ready. I thought I had a handle on the self-medicating issue, but I came to you in hopes that you would help me figure out how to get past the anger and sadness I constantly felt.

"I remember thinking the first time I saw you, with your bracelets, and hair pulled up with the headband wrapped around your head, I had never met anyone like you before. You were unique. You had this carefree confidence about you. You stared up at me, and there was this kindness in your eyes that pulled me in. Then when you started asking me questions, I have to admit, it bothered me. But something inside me was drawn to you. I was so conflicted. I didn't want you to know about my life, yet I needed to tell you everything. Before you, no one has ever had such a profound effect on me. Not even Abbie.

"And then when Maizy started crying and you brought her into the counseling session, I saw how much you were struggling." He could feel the lump forming in his throat and he paused. "I knew how hard it must have been for you to have me there. You were trying your damnedest to carry on, but I could see on your face, you were losing the battle, and it frustrated the hell out of you." He chuckled. "You don't know how much I wanted to leave; how uncomfortable I was. I couldn't leave you though. My feet wouldn't move.

"And then you laid Maizy in my arms, and I was done. The look in your beautiful green eyes at that moment, so full of fear and vulnerability, yet you still trusted me. And the feeling of her in my arms, it set my world on fire. I can't describe it. I felt something. Up to that point, I was dead inside. That car accident destroyed me. In that moment though, something told me we were there for each other. Every day I was with you, it was like we were feeding off each other's energy. I could feel myself coming to life, like I needed to be there for you and Maizy, to protect you, and you were there to help me remember how to live. When it was time for the movie production to start, it was hard as hell to leave you. And when Mitch hauled me off to jail, it shattered me inside, not because I knew I was being falsely accused, but because I was losing you and Maizy."

His fingers played in her hair. He couldn't imagine not having her and Maizy in his life, and just like she knew he was thinking about her, the little gray box blinked to life and a whine penetrated the quiet. Bekah's phone buzzed, and she sat up.

"I'll get Maizy," Brant said as he slid out from around her. He jogged into the bedroom and peered down into the crib. Maizy stared up at him and gave him a toothless grin. His heart pinched, and he smiled back at her. The magazine article was a complete surprise, especially seeing the cover of Maizy and him.

He reached in the crib and gently cuddled her close to him. She laid her head on his shoulder and cooed in his ear. His hand softly patted her back, then he reached back into the crib to retrieve her favorite blanket. It never got old. After changing her diaper and grabbing the nursing pillow, he strolled back into the living room. The look Bekah gave him had him confused. Her brow was raised, and her lips were pulled into a thin line. He had no idea who was on the phone and what her expression was supposed to mean.

"Yeah, that works for me. I can move my schedule around, don't worry. This is too important." She kept her eyes on Brant as he stood swaying with Maizy. "Thanks for asking me. I'd be honored." That was Brant's first indication of who she might be talking to. He was so sidetracked by the magazine he had completely forgotten about the earlier phone call. As she brought the phone to her lap, her expression changed slightly. "Do you have something to tell me, Mr. Ellington?"

"Um…I…I'm not sure. Wanna clue me in?"

"Did you get a phone call from my grandpa Dale?"

"Maybe. Was that Grams?"

"It was." A smile started to pull at Bekah's mouth. "She wants me to be her maid of honor at her and Grandpa's wedding." Her teeth dug into her lower lip. "They're getting married." The smile turned into a grin that completely took over her face. "Oh my gosh, I think I'm going to cry." Bekah put her hand to her chest.

"Yeah, Dale called me while you were at the grocery store. He asked if I would be okay with him asking Grams to marry him. He said after her heart attack, he knew he didn't want to spend a day without her, taking care of her. I honestly don't think he knows what he's getting into with her."

"Oh, trust me, he had plenty of practice after her health scare."

He handed the nursing pillow to Bekah and got Maizy comfortable. "I guess he didn't waste any time asking her after I gave him my blessing. Not quite sure why he didn't call my mom. Must have figured it would be much easier to get ahold of me."

"I think it's wonderful. They obviously love each other. Grams said they are going to have a small ceremony at the Lake Village Restaurant. She wants me to try to help her get it planned for next month." Brant's eyes widened.

"Wow. That's not much time."

"Yeah, I said the same thing. Grams said, 'Why wait when you know what you want.'"

The words played through Brant's head. "Well, if you don't need anything, I need to make a business call."

Bekah's brows pinched as she studied his face. "No. I'm good." Brant pulled his phone from his pocket and walked into his office.

Chapter Twenty-Two

Bekah felt like her head was going to spin right off her shoulders. Staring at the beautiful pergola, draped with white chiffon, greenery, and multicolored hydrangea flowers, with the crystal clear lake just beyond it, she couldn't imagine anything more breathtaking. White chairs lined the green grass with a white runner down the middle. Bundles of flowers were tied to each end chair, and white twinkling lights were strung from the back of the restaurant to the pergola. The early May weather couldn't have been more perfect.

When Betty had asked her to help plan the wedding, Bekah didn't realize exactly how much she would be doing. Every detail, from the cake to the flowers, to the food, even the bridal gown, Bekah had a say so. Betty had even asked her to try on dresses to see what styles she liked, saying she needed to see them modeled. That part was fun. It gave her a chance to dream about what she would like for her own wedding someday. At one shop, Bekah found a strapless lace dress, with a chiffon cinched waste, and sweetheart neckline, that took her breath away. It hugged her in all the right places and had just the right amount of sparkle. Betty said it was a bit young for her taste, although she loved the way it looked on her. Bekah was so caught up in her reflection, the lady attending them found a wide opalescent headband, with a glittery leaf pattern, that went perfect with the dress and placed it in her hair. Betty made her stand in front of the mirror while she took a photo.

After searching several shops, they found a satin and lace dress with a lace bolero jacket for Betty. Bekah knew the minute Betty saw it, the way her eyes lit up, it was the dress, and it fit her like it was made for her.

As she walked through the banquet room at the restaurant, she couldn't believe how beautiful everything was decorated. More hydrangeas were used for centerpieces on tables covered in different colored linens to match the colors of the flowers and decorated with strings of tiny lights. There was nothing extravagant. The beauty was in the simplicity.

After spying Betty entering the restaurant, she met her, and they strolled up the hallway to the room that was set up as their dressing room.

"The lady doing our hair should be here in a few minutes," Bekah said as Betty hung two garment bags up on the back of the bathroom door. Bekah wondered why there were two, but the thought quickly vanished when she realized, with Betty there, it meant the ceremony was fast approaching, and a panic filled her. She hoped everything would go off as planned. Things were organized so fast she kept wondering if they had forgotten something. She could hear voices in the hallway, and she peeked out to see Brant and Dale laughing about something as they strolled up the hallway with garment bags over their shoulders. Her eyes caught Brant's, and he smiled. Then it hit her. The baby!

"Where's Maizy?" she asked with a little fire behind her words.

Brant's expression went from confused to evasive, and she knew he was hiding something. "She, uh…" Bekah could tell he was trying to come up with some kind of funny story, although she wasn't in the mood for funny right now. She was too nervous.

"Brant. Just spit it out."

"Okay." He walked to the door and cupped his hands around her cheeks and dropped a sweet kiss on her lips. "We were going to surprise you." He paused. "Your family is here. Your mom has Maizy right now. They are back at Dale's getting ready."

"You're not serious. Are you? They drove in from California?"

"Yeah. They got here late last night."

"Mine are here too. You will get to meet my brother Greg and his wife Joanie."

"They're all here?" Bekah's heart raced with the thought of all the families gathered for the wedding. Now more than ever, she hoped everything would go off without a hitch.

"I know that look. Everything is going to be great, Bek. You did an amazing job."

"Do you think so?"

"It looks fantastic. Don't you like it?"

"Oh, I love it. It's all so organic, with all the flowers and greenery." Bekah's focus moved away from Brant to a slender girl with shoulder length peacock colored hair who was being escorted up the hallway by one of the restaurant staff. "Are you Summer?"

"Yes, ma'am." Bekah pulled the door wider and let

Summer in, then her attention went back to Brant. "I can't believe everyone is here."

Brant stepped forward and grabbed her hands. "Thanks for helping my grandma pull this all together."

"I hope she likes it. She kept asking me what I thought and what colors I liked, and then went with everything I suggested."

"Oh, I'm sure she would have told you if she didn't like something. You know her better than that. She kind of speaks her mind."

"True."

"Well, hey, I guess I better go help Dale get ready." Bekah nodded, and Brant headed up the hallway. The glint in his eyes caused an uneasy feeling within her. He wasn't telling her something. Was it the fact he had hidden that her parents were coming to the wedding? She hadn't seen them in…had it been that long? Over two years? How could that be possible? They hadn't even met Maizy. Well, they had now. She wondered how long it had been since she saw her brother, Justin, but doubted he was contacted about the wedding. He hadn't been with anyone from the family in several years. She was still in college the last time he made an appearance. Was he still living in Maine? The weight of the moment had her throat tightening. She needed to reconnect with him.

Turning back to Betty, she noticed Summer had already gotten her situated in a comfortable chair and had her makeup bag open. Bekah thought about her family and Brant's family meeting each other, and suddenly she was back to being nervous. What would his family think of her parents? That was why Justin had left. He couldn't deal with their crazy free spirit lifestyle. Brant's family seemed to genuinely like her, but she was an extremely toned-down version of her parents. Bekah shut the door and plastered on a bright smile. There was nothing she could do about it. It wasn't her wedding. Dale and Betty had obviously invited them, and she was excited to see them after so long.

Summer chatted with Betty as she pulled her hair half up in a sophisticated style that left silver curls down her back. A sparkly clip, holding her hair in place, was the only thing that adorned her head. Betty turned to Bekah.

"What do you think?" Bekah loved Betty's natural beauty, and Summer had simply enhanced it.

"You look absolutely beautiful, Grams. Grandpa Dale is a lucky man."

"You got that right," Betty shot back, and Bekah and Summer burst into laughter. Summer motioned for Bekah to sit. It was her turn. "I already know exactly what I want to do with you, sister," Summer announced. Bekah loved Summer's sassy personality. It matched perfectly with her crazy style. But beneath her purple hair and brightly colored fairy shirt, Summer was stunning. Her big brown eyes were played up with a shimmery dark purple shadow, and she had coated her lips with a pale pink.

"I like what you did with Betty. I don't do heavy makeup either."

"You sit back and let me work my magic. I have the perfect look for you." Summer went to work tapping concealer under her eyes, brushing blush on her cheeks, eyeshadow on her lids, and swiping mascara over her lashes. After she finished the makeup, Summer put her fingers under Bekah's chin, lifting her head and staring at her work, then she smiled and nodded.

"Can I see?" Bekah asked after a minute.

"Nope. Not until I'm done." Summer moved behind her and threaded her fingers through Bekah's wavy hair, tugging and pinning as she moved around her. After several minutes, she again stood in front of Bekah with a puzzled expression on her face. "It needs something." Betty stepped up beside her and tilted her head studying her. Bekah's eyes darted back and forth between the two.

"Oh, I know," Betty said. "I bought a couple of things for my hair because I didn't know what you were going to do." She reached for her bag and dug out a headband and handed it to Summer.

"That will be perfect." She fastened it in place then stepped in front of Bekah again. "Yes! That's exactly what it needed."

"Can I see now?"

Summer rolled her eyes. "I guess. So impatient." She reached around Bekah and produced a mirror and held it up. Bekah gazed into it, surprised at the reflection.

"Betty? Is this the headband from that store where you took the photo of me?" Betty turned back and glimpsed at her.

"Which headband?"

"The one I tried on? This looks like it."

"Maybe. I was trying to find something to put in my hair that might go with my dress."

Bekah stood and grasped the mirror from Summer. "Well?" Summer questioned.

"Oh, I love it." Summer had pulled Bekah's hair

into a messy bun at the nape of her neck, with wisps brushing her face. Her makeup was not too heavy with a light shadow on her eyes and a little shimmer on her lips. Put together, it was exactly what she had hoped for. Natural but enhanced.

After helping Betty into her gown, Bekah slid into her knee length, soft pink, one shouldered dress and donned her silver sandals with iridescent crystals that matched perfectly with her dress.

A rap on the door let them know the photographer was ready, so they hurried up the hall. Bekah stopped in her tracks when she spotted Brant dressed in his silver tux. His eyes landed on her, and a big bright grin spread across his face. "Wow. You look gorgeous."

"You do too." He grabbed her hand, placed a gentle kiss to her knuckles, then wrapped her hand around his arm as they strolled out to the location of the photos. People were starting to gather so Bekah scanned the faces hoping to spot her parents, but she didn't see them. *Maybe they are back with Dale since Grams didn't want him to see her until the wedding.*

The music began, and guests took their seats. Bekah and Betty finished with the photos and headed back to the room to wait. Through the French doors, Bekah could see the area filling up. She watched as Dale took his place at the front. Brant headed up the aisle and stood by the door. That was her cue. She grabbed Betty's hand and the flowers on the stand next to the door, and they made their way to the doors. When the music changed, Bekah headed up the aisle and took her place. Her eyes locked on Brant who had a huge grin on his face and somehow it calmed her, but she still couldn't get the thought out of her head that he was hiding something. He escorted Betty up the aisle and then took his place behind Dale. Bekah's eyes again did a quick scan and found her parents, dressed very conservatively to her surprise. Her mom was sitting next to Brant's mom, who was holding Maizy, and they were both smiling as they quietly entertained the baby who was wearing a frilly dress in a pale pink that nearly matched hers.

As Betty took her place next to Dale, Bekah saw his chin wobble. He really did love her. Her focus moved to find Brant staring at her, and then he gave her a quick wink. She silently scolded him with a look, but her lips betrayed her as they curved into a smile.

The minister started with a welcome to everyone then offered a prayer before the vows were exchanged. Betty and Dale spoke from their hearts. Tears puddled at Bekah's lashes. She lifted her finger wiping them away and then caught Brant doing the same. He loved his grandma so much.

The rings were exchanged. Simple gold bands. And when he was given the directions to kiss the bride, Dale was the consummate gentleman. He cupped her face with his hands and dropped a chaste kiss on her lips. Everyone clapped as the couple slowly made their way up the aisle and through the French doors. Bekah moved forward ready to take Brant's arm to make their exit. However, as Brant moved toward her, the minister handed him the mic.

Bekah's heart skipped. This wasn't how they rehearsed it. What was he doing?

He turned to the audience and chuckled before he spoke. "I want to thank everyone for coming to these two crazy kids' wedding. They truly are perfect for each other." He cleared his throat and continued. "Before we all dismiss to head to the reception, I would like to take the opportunity to do something. My grams made a comment not too long ago that kind of stuck with me. She said, 'Why wait if you know what you want.' There is something that I want, and I'm not waiting any longer."

He smiled at Bekah and reached out his hand taking hers and pulling her to him. A gasp spread through the crowd as Brant dropped to one knee. "Bekah." Seeing him on one knee and hearing her name cross his lips sent a rush of goosebumps throughout her body, and her breathing completely stopped to the point she had to put her hand to her chest to remember how. In and out. Her hand moved to her mouth, and her fingers trembled so bad it tickled her lips.

"You and Maizy roared into my life in the craziest way. It was what I needed to open my eyes to how wonderful my life could be. You are the sweetest most intelligent person I have ever met, and God I am so glad I didn't turn that knob and walk away." Bekah laughed at his comment knowing exactly what he was talking about. He reached in his pocket and pulled out a beautiful diamond ring set in platinum with a rose gold wrap. "I love you, Bekah. No, I adore you"—a smile filled his face, and he winked at her letting her know he remembered what she said about her tattoo— "and I can't imagine my life without you and Maizy in it. Would you please do me the honor of becoming my wife?"

Bekah wasn't sure if she had enough breath to even whisper the words she wanted to say. She nodded then opened her mouth to speak but Brant immediately scooped her up and pressed his lips to hers. When he pulled away, she breathed out, "Yes. Yes. I would love to marry you."

Everybody clapped as he placed the ring on her finger. Brant turned to the minister. "Can you give us five minutes?"

The minister shrugged his shoulders. "Sure. My hunting trip doesn't start until tomorrow."

Brant turned and held up a hand to the crowd then turned back to Bekah. "Go get changed. I'll meet you right here in five."

Bekah jerked her head at his comment. "What?"

"Go get ready." Brant shooed her away. Bekah still didn't understand. She turned to see Grams standing by the French doors motioning to her. Brant shooed her again, and she hesitantly walked up the aisle toward Grams. She studied all the smiling faces and wondered what was going on. *Is this a weird dream I'm going to wake up from just before I get to the really good part?* Betty grabbed her by the arm and tugged her back into the dressing room. The second garment bag was hanging on the door with the zipper already unzipped, and Bekah could see a small swatch of white material. She moved the fabric of the bag and saw the dress she had tried on at the store in front of her. Her dress. She turned back to Betty. "How did…"

"We kind of kept a little secret from you."

"I would say so."

She stepped out of her pink dress and gently lifted the gown from the bag. Betty helped her into it and zipped it up, then Summer did a quick touch up of her hair and makeup. She turned to Betty. "How do I look?"

Betty clapped her hands once. "Absolutely stunning. I think I'm more excited for Brant to see you than I was for Dale to see me."

"Oh my gosh, I'm so nervous. I can't believe you planned all this."

"Why do you think I was asking you all those questions? Dale and I were planning on having a nice dinner with you, then going out on the balcony with the minister and doing a quiet ceremony."

Bekah burst out laughing, realizing that all the plans were for her benefit, not Betty's. It was perfect in every way...because she basically chose everything she wanted. "Let's go get me married."

At the French doors Bekah met her grandpa. The song "Marry Me" began to play, and Bekah looked up to see Brant standing at the front with his hand fisted at his mouth. As she walked slowly up the aisle with her grandpa, she watched as Brant lost his battle with his tears. "I can't believe you did this," Bekah said quietly with a chuckle under her words. Brant took her hand, winked, and a big grin spread across his face.

The minister cleared his throat, and the music faded. "Round two," he said, and the audience laughed. Bekah's eyes darted and caught sight of a guy with a beard, standing in back with Dale and Betty. "Justin?" she said breathlessly. Her eyes returned to Brant, and he smiled again. She reached up and grabbed him and pressed her lips to his.

The minister snickered when she pulled away. "Hold on. We aren't to that part yet."

She mouthed to Brant, "I love you."

He mouthed back, "I know."

The minister looked out at the crowd. "I think we

better make this a quick one."

Bekah and Brant laughed and nodded.

He asked them to bow their heads, and he said a prayer over them. "Now, since this is on the fly, do you want to repeat vows I give you, or say your own?"

"I want to say mine," Brant responded.

"All right. Have at it."

Brant turned to Bekah, grabbed her hands, and took a deep breath. Bekah laughed. "I love you. And I love Maizy. You both are the most important people in my life. I want you to know, I will always be there for you. I will always guard and protect you. I will wipe away your tears when you are sad and laugh with you when you are happy. I know I will mess up sometimes, but I will always try to be the best husband and daddy I can be and do everything I can to never let you down. You and Maizy have been the best thing that has ever happened to me, and I am so thankful that you didn't give up on me."

Bekah couldn't quit staring at the man in front of her. His eyes glistened as he spoke from his heart, and she bit down on her lip trying to keep the tears at bay. "Well, shoot, you didn't give me time to write anything down." Her comment had the crowd erupting in laughter, and she hoped it would give her enough time to at least string something together, but no luck, her brain resembled the inside of a tornado at the moment. With a deep breath, she studied her groom, and let her heart speak. "Brant. I know you will always be there for me and Maizy, and you will protect us because you already have so many times. I can't imagine my life without you. I have to catch my breath every time you are with me because I can't believe how lucky I am, and I want you to know, I will be there for you. I will stand by your side through all the good times and bad. I can't wait to share in the adventures of our life together. I will try to be the best wife and mommy to our kids I can be. I know I will mess up sometimes, but I will try to never let you down. I will even laugh at your dumb jokes even when I don't understand them. You are the best thing that has ever happened to me and Maizy, and I love you so much."

Bekah turned back to the minister letting him know she was done. The minister turned to Brant. "Do you have the rings?"

Bekah's eyes grew wide. "I don't have a ring for you." Brant smiled and pulled his hand from his pocket and held out a diamond band for her and a silver band with rose gold roping around the edge for him.

Bekah held back a smile as she shook her head.

The minister shared the meaning of the rings and symbol in marriage and then turned to Brant. "Take her left hand with your right and hold it against your heart." Brant followed the directions. "Now repeat after me. With this ring…"

Bekah gazed into Brant's eyes, feeling his rapid heartbeat beneath her hand, and still wondering when she would wake up from the dream. "With this ring…

"I choose you as my forever."

The corner of Brant's mouth tipped up. "I choose you as my forever."

"My heart will beat only for you."

"My heart will beat only for you."

"This ring is my vow to you…"

"This ring is my vow to you."

"That, whatever we go through,"

"That, whatever we go through,"

"I will always love you, honor you and cherish you today, tomorrow, and throughout eternity."

"I will always love you, honor you and cherish you today, tomorrow, and throughout eternity."

The minister held out the ring, and Brant placed it on Bekah's finger. Bekah was breathing so fast she was getting lightheaded as she turned to look at the minister.

"Okay, Bekah, take Brant's left hand with your right and place it over your heart then repeat after me." She lifted Brant's hand and held it against her heart. Brant winked and gave her a sexy smile. The crowd laughed, and Bekah pinched her lips and shook her head.

She heard the minister's words as he began reciting the vows, and she could hear herself repeating them, but everything around her disappeared once she stared into Brant's eyes. She could see the love he had for her and feel it in his touch. She knew every word he spoke, he meant, and she did too. He was her forever. It all felt so right, so perfect. "I will always love you, honor you, and cherish you, today, tomorrow, and throughout eternity." She took the ring from the minister and slid it onto Brant's finger.

"By the powers vested in me by the state of Arkansas, I now pronounce you husband and wife." The minister smiled as both Brant and Bekah looked back at him and waited. "What? Did I miss something?" the minister teased. The audience laughed when Brant jerked his head at Bekah then hitched his thumb. "Ohhh, you may now kiss your bride."

Brant pulled Bekah to him and tipped her back, capturing her mouth with a passionate kiss that forever stole her heart and sealed their love. When he tipped her back up, Bekah whispered, "Please tell me this isn't a dream."

"Well, if it is, then I don't want to wake up."

"I love you."

"I love you too, Mrs. Ellington."

A word about the author…

DeDe Ramey is a Texas girl transplanted in the heart of Oklahoma. Her vivid imagination and love for people watching gave her a passion to write romance novels filled with swoon worthy heroes, smart, sassy heroines, unexpected nail biting suspense, and a good helping of steamy, heart melting romance.

She grew up in the beautiful historic town of Georgetown, Texas. Her crazy life experiences with family and friends helped develop her rich, colorful imagination. In elementary school she started writing pages of poetry which transformed as a teen into writing and performing her own original songs. As an adult she wrote skits and plays, some short stories, and even a script for a TV series.

Before deciding to write full time, DeDe received a degree in sound engineering and broadcast telecommunication but soon realized those jobs were hard to come by. She took a job as an apartment manager then later settled into the job of domestic affairs manager, raising two amazing kids. Once the kids left home to start their own lives, she revisited her passion for writing.

When she is not reading or writing she enjoys lifting weights at the gym, finding breathtaking waterfalls while exploring the national forests and parks, or searching for adventures in new cities, visiting thirty-one of the fifty states so far, and going to concerts of old rock bands with her husband Keith, her very own devastatingly handsome hero of over 35 years.

Thank you for purchasing
this publication of The Wild Rose Press, Inc.

For questions or more information
contact us at
info@thewildrosepress.com.

The Wild Rose Press, Inc.
www.thewildrosepress.com

www.ingramcontent.com/pod-product-compliance
Lightning Source LLC
Chambersburg PA
CBHW051128030726
47504CB00004B/769